DUE FOR DISCARD

DUE FOR DISCARD

SHARON ST. GEORGE

This book is dedicated with much love to John Higley, who understands full well the agony and ecstasy of writing and the irresistible call of yet another story.

Recycling programs
for this product may
not exist in your area.

Due for Discard

A Worldwide Mystery/April 2018

First published by Camel Press, an imprint of Coffeetown Enterprises, Inc.

ISBN-13: 978-1-335-50653-5

Acknowledgments

Special thanks to my dear friend and exceptional critique partner Chloe Winston for her constructive suggestions and her steadfast belief in my characters and their world. To my brother, George Souza, for his scrupulous attention to police procedure and investigative details, and to his wife, Mary, for her patience with all of the phone calls. Thanks to Michael Cuming, a proofreader with an eagle eye. A special nod to Forensic Librarian Jeff Teitelbaum of the Washington State Patrol's Forensic Laboratory Services Bureau for generously sharing his expertise. My deep appreciation goes to Jennifer McCord and Catherine Treadgold at Camel Press for their consummate editing skills and for believing in *Due for Discard* and the Machado mysteries.

ONE

I DIDN'T BLAME old Doolittle for spitting green slime in my face when I tripped over him in the dark. He was asleep at the bottom of the stairs outside my apartment, and spitting is what llamas do when they're startled. I blamed Nick Alexander. It was his fault I was living in a llama pasture. After we broke up eight weeks ago, I moved out of his apartment and into the converted bunkhouse above my grandparents' barn. It was the only option I could afford since I was struggling to pay off my graduate school loans.

The llama incident happened on the first day of my new dream job and forced me to skip my good luck breakfast with Amah and Grandpa Jack in the main house. Instead, I raced back upstairs to repair the damage Doolittle had done. I took another shower, chose another outfit, redid my hair and makeup and still drove the eight miles from Coyote Creek to Timbergate by seven o'clock.

I pulled into the Timbergate Medical Center lot with five minutes to spare and headed toward the employee entrance on foot. The Dumpster in the alley between the parking lot and the Happy Ox Café gave off a foul stench as I approached, so I held my breath and broke into a trot.

When I reached the employee entrance, a paunchy,

middle-aged security guard with thinning gray hair held his palm to my face.

"Hold it, Missy. What's your hurry?"

"Had to run…smelly Dumpster." I panted, trying to catch my breath. "Should I report it to someone?"

"It's not our Dumpster." He glanced toward the alley. "Belongs to the Happy Ox." The hot August morning already had stained the armpits of his khaki shirt. He pulled a crumpled red bandanna from his back pocket and mopped his brow.

I reached for the door, but he side-stepped and blocked my entry. "Not so fast. What are you doing here?"

"I work here." I should have offered my hand, but he didn't smell much better than the Dumpster. "I'm Aimee Machado, TMC's new librarian. Today's my first day."

The guard stuffed his kerchief into his pocket and hoisted his olive drab pants. As soon as he let go, they slid below his belly again. "Where's your ID?"

"It's right here." I reached in my purse for the name tag that Human Resources had given me on the day of my orientation tour.

"You gotta wear it." He tapped the badge on his shirt identifying him as Orrie Mercer.

I pinned mine to my red silk blouse, hoping it wouldn't snag.

Mercer squinted at my name. "Mikado? That what you said?"

"No. It's pronounced *Ma-SHAW-doe*."

He studied my face with an appraising look. "You're not from around here, are you?"

I understood the subtext of his question. *You're not*

exactly white, so what are you? My Portuguese/Chinese genes do cause people to wonder. With black hair and dark brown eyes that show a hint of my mother's Asian blood, I've been mistaken for everything from Latino to Hawaiian. I didn't want to start off on the wrong foot before I got into the building, so I let it pass.

"Actually, I *am* from around here. I've lived in Timbergate most of my life." I waited a beat, and he finally pushed the door open and waved me inside.

The encounter with the guard was disappointing, but it didn't dampen my excitement. After college I had worked for four years at the Sawyer County Library and moonlighted as a medical transcriptionist while I saved up for graduate school. Finally, with the help of some hefty loans, I spent two years back east in New Haven, Connecticut, earning my master's degree in Library and Information Science. It had taken another year to land this job, and I desperately needed the salary and benefits that came with it. The position of Health Sciences Librarian in a rural northern California hospital might not be a dream come true to most people, but it was tailor-made for me.

It was my good luck that the governing board of Timbergate Medical Center had decided to add a forensic component to its library collection. I had chosen forensic resources as a special interest in library school, and that gave me an edge. I just hoped the TMC board understood the difference between a librarian and a crime scene investigator. The only crimes I was qualified to deal with involved overdue fines.

After checking in with Human Resources, I started walking across the TMC complex to the library building where Dr. Vane Beardsley was waiting to show me around. Beardsley was the hospital's current chief of staff and principal supporter of the library's upgrades. Adding a component of forensic resources and sharing them with the money-strapped hospitals and law enforcement agencies in far northern California counties had been his brainchild.

In our initial interview, he had explained that he donated the necessary start-up funding, but it would be up to me to implement the project. If I failed, he would not be inclined to throw good money after bad, but if the consortium he envisioned took off and appeared to be successful, he would continue to advocate for it and for my full-time salary and benefits.

Beardsley knew his pet project would add something unique to Timbergate Medical Center's image as a cutting-edge innovator in health care and community service. Rumor had it he was a major shareholder in the corporation that owned TMC, so what was good for the hospital was good for his portfolio. He had assured me that his designation as my supervisor was only a formality. Development of the forensic component was to be a priority, but he encouraged me to come up with other projects or ideas for the library and submit them for his approval.

When I arrived at the library, Beardsley greeted me, looking every inch the successful physician. He stood close to six feet, wore a light gray suit tailored to perfection, and like many bald men, he sported facial hair. His red Van Dyke beard was salted with a hint of gray. If he caught a whiff of the Dumpster smell, he didn't let on.

"Congratulations again on your hire, Miss Machado. I hope your first day goes well."

"Thank you," I said. "I'm very glad to be here."

I was about to ask a few questions when he reached for his pager. He glanced at it, promised to be "back in a jiffy," and hurried away. I assumed he was needed at his busy plastic surgery practice across town.

Left alone, I looked around the deserted library. Housed in the medical center's oldest building, it seemed larger than I remembered from the brief tour of the hospital on the day of my orientation. Grimy rectangular windows high on one wall shed feeble light on the scuffed floor tiles and pale green paint. Hanging fluorescent bars blinked intermittently, and rows of metal shelves held a jumble of medical texts and journals. A dozen state-of-the-art computers along the back wall seemed out of place in their bleak surroundings. The smell of book dust filled the room, and several large boxes filled with outdated books and periodicals bore the stamp: DUE FOR DISCARD.

The dismal condition of the space made it evident that the position I was hired for had gone vacant far too long. I had a lot to do to make the library relevant and welcoming to patrons, but I looked forward to the challenge.

Fifteen minutes later, Dr. Beardsley still hadn't returned, so I sat down at an aging oak desk in the middle of the room. It held a name plate reading *Library Director*. I figured they'd put my name on it at the end of my probationary period. Six months should pass in a flash.

I had just used my newly assigned password to boot up the computer when a heady fragrance wafted my way followed by a wiry middle-aged woman no taller than my own five feet, four inches. She wore the peach-colored jacket of the auxiliary volunteers, and her hair color matched her jacket perfectly. Behind thick-lensed glasses, her eyes protruded in a classic presentation of overactive thyroid. *Exophthalmos.* Like many of the words I learned in my medical terminology course, it's hard to spell, but fun to pronounce.

"Hello, young lady, I'm Maybelline Black, auxiliary. You must be Miss Machado."

"Yes, I am." As I offered my hand, I couldn't help thinking of the mascara wand in my makeup case. "I'm pleased to meet you, Ms. Black."

"Same here. Call me Maybelline." The strength in her bony grip surprised me.

"And you can call me Aimee. Dr. Beardsley was called away, so I thought I'd have a look through the library's online databases while I wait for him to return."

"Good idea," she said, "but I'm afraid he's been detained."

"I see." I didn't, but I wanted to sound polite since this woman was one of my volunteers, and it's never a good idea to get on their bad side. "How long will he be?"

"Hard to say."

"Really? Why?"

"I shouldn't say anything more." Maybelline's orbs held the gleam of an incorrigible gossip bursting with juicy news.

"I'm sure it's okay," I said. "I signed a confidentiality clause when I was hired." If there was sensitive business that involved my new boss, I wanted to know sooner rather than later.

"Well then, I suppose I can tell you." She leaned

close and whispered, "His wife is missing. Since Friday night. He's talking to the police."

His wife was missing? I'd been on the job for twenty minutes, and my supervisor was being questioned by the police? A spitting llama, a smelly Dumpster, and now this? My dream job was getting off to a rocky start.

"That's awful," I said. "He must be terribly worried."

"I don't know why he should be. She's a flighty sort. His second wife, not the first. They always want someone younger when they...well, she was young. She set her cap for him right from the start. Didn't care that he was married. Poor Lorraine—his ex—didn't have a chance."

The staccato delivery made her story hard to follow, but I picked up the important thread. "You mentioned the police. Do they think she's been abducted or something?"

"It seems far-fetched to me, but there's talk about foul play. Bonnie Belle didn't show up for her tennis lesson or her acrylic nail appointment."

"Bonnie Belle? Not Beardsley?"

"Bonnie Belle is her professional name." Maybelline glanced around, looking apprehensive. "I'd best not say more."

She left, assuring me she'd find a stand-in for Dr. Beardsley, but who could that be when Beardsley was the reason I had been hired?

While I waited alone again, I put my favorite family photo on a corner of my desk. It had been taken a few months earlier when my younger brother, Harry, and I visited our parents in the Azores where they had just retired. Harry had charmed the young Portuguese women with his handsome Eurasian face and a body toned to perfection from years of martial arts. He got one of the few tall genes in the family, passing me when he was twelve and finally topping out at just over six feet. He loved reminding me that his big sister had to look up to him.

With my family photo in place, I felt more at home in my new surroundings and ready to get to work. I needed this job and wanted to prove what I could do for Timbergate Medical Center.

I didn't know much about Dr. Beardsley, except that his seed money had covered the cost of the library's new computers and a first year budget for the anticipated collection of forensic resources. In return, the medical center's governing board agreed to spring for a library director with an MLIS. Beardsley's backing had made my plum job possible, but excitement about my first day of work couldn't keep me from wondering what happened to his wife and hoping it was nothing serious. Maybelline had mentioned foul play, and our area did have its share of serious crime, partly due to our location on the I-5 corridor. Overcrowded jails and strained law enforcement budgets compounded the problem.

With a population of a hundred thousand, Timbergate wasn't a metropolis, but it was the largest city between Sacramento and the Oregon border. For decades, med school graduates had drawn to our nearby lakes and spectacular mountains. The economy was driven by outdoor recreation and medicine, the same two subjects that drove me.

My thoughts drifted back to Dr. Beardsley's missing wife. Surely there was some innocent explanation.

I was wondering what it might be when Maybelline returned alone.

"I couldn't find anyone else to meet with you just now, Miss Machado. Our administrator is out of town, and the assistant administrator is in a meeting." Apparently, she wasn't comfortable using my first name, so I didn't insist.

"Thanks for trying, Maybelline. I'm sure Dr. Beardsley will be back soon. I have enough work to keep me busy in the meantime."

"I'd be happy to help," she said. "I'm assigned to work with you every Monday and Wednesday morning. When I get back from my rounds, I'll show you the ropes."

Maybelline explained that her primary duty was the in-house bookmobile. Before I could raise the Bonnie Beardsley topic again, she had wrestled her book cart out the door.

I made good progress shelving new books and journals, but there had been no sign of Dr. Beardsley by the time Maybelline returned at noon. I asked her to join me for lunch, thinking I might benefit from her perspective on the hospital and its employees.

My self-appointed mentor led me through a maze of corridors to the cafeteria where we both chose the lasagna. We found a table to ourselves near an east-facing window with a view of the Cascade Range. In spite of our scorching August heat, random patches of snow still clung to the jutting gray slopes of Lassen Peak and Brokeoff Mountain.

Around a mouthful of pasta, Maybelline said, "Bonnie's run off with some man."

I waited a beat while a tremor of anticipation washed

over me. On the curiosity scale, my grandmother Amah says I'm off the charts. She thinks it'll get me in trouble someday. I respectfully disagree. What good is a librarian who isn't curious? I wanted to hear more about Maybelline's theory, and she was obviously bursting to tell me.

"Then you don't think she's been abducted?"

"No, more likely she's run off."

"Why do you say that?"

"She's a bad seed. Her parents, Jed and Dora Belcher, had trouble with her right from the get-go. Menopause baby. Only child. Spoiled from all that money Jed made with his nuts."

"Excuse me?"

"Her daddy owned the almond orchards at the south end of the county. You've probably seen them from the freeway."

"I have." Curious, I waited for Maybelline to continue.

"Well, Jed and Dora were good folks. Well-to-do, but they lived a simple life. Not Bonnie. She was fast. They sent her to one of those boarding schools for troubled teens, but she ran off with a delivery truck driver. Married at eighteen, pregnant, but lost it."

"How sad," I said.

"Maybe, but it didn't slow Bonnie down. Left her husband for a traveling musician. Anyway, she was home again a year later. Her folks got her marriage annulled and put her in a drug rehab center. She was picked up on a DUI the week after she got out. That's when Jed and Dora cut her off."

"And they never relented?"

"Not another dime. They sold out, retired to Florida, and lived off the proceeds. Both of them are gone now."

"How did Bonnie get by?"

"On her looks. She's a real beauty. She did some modeling and lots of local TV commercials." Maybelline paused for a sip of water, then went on. "After that, she got herself hired as a TV spokeswoman. That's when she changed her name. You can't be calling yourself Belcher on TV. I guess she thought Bonnie Belle was a good name for a celebrity."

"A spokeswoman? For what?"

"Animals. You know, save the stray cats. Neuter your pets. Things like that."

"So she liked animals?"

"I guess. But she liked money more. She wanted a bigger career. Still counting on her looks, she decided to get a boob job. She liked Dr. Beardsley's work, so she had him do her nose next. Not that there was anything wrong with the original. By that time, the poor man was hooked like a big, dumb sturgeon. He dumped his sweet wife Lorraine and married Bonnie."

"When was that?"

"About two years ago. Bonnie quit working, of course. Got in with the so-called society set. Tennis, charities, all that. Vane Beardsley makes bundles of money, but Bonnie has been doing her best to spend it."

"Sounds like she has it made. Why would she run off?"

"She's man-crazy. Being married didn't change that; it just made her sneaky."

"Do you think she was sneaking around on Dr. Beardsley?"

"'Course she was." Maybelline stabbed at her lasagna.

"Do you think he knew?"

"He had to. Everyone knew. He pretended not to. Shamed him, though. High price to pay for a trophy wife, if you ask me."

I had been wondering how Maybelline knew so much about Bonnie Beardsley, but apparently the hospital grapevine had worked overtime on the Beardsley gossip. *Everyone knew.* I would have pressed her for more, but one of her volunteer buddies stopped by our table to chat. I left the two of them and went back to the library.

Maybelline had given me plenty to think about. The police always suspect spouses first, and according to her, Dr. Beardsley had an obvious motive. I couldn't help but worry about the missing woman's fate, but in a flash of pure selfishness, I realized that the fate of my budding career might depend on whether Bonnie Beardsley turned up safe and sound.

On my way out at five o'clock, I was relieved to see Orrie Mercer replaced by a clean-cut young security guard who said a polite, "Have a nice night, Miss." Even better, the foul-smelling Dumpster in the alley was gone.

I stood outside my car with both doors open to let the interior temperature drop to a safe level. August in Timbergate was often the hottest spot in the entire country and I didn't look forward to my sweltering studio apartment with its temperamental swamp cooler. My budget was so tight I would need to work several months at my new job before I could afford to move out of my grandparents' llama barn and rent an apartment of my own in town.

In exchange for free rent, I did chores and watched the place for Amah and Jack when they were away on adventures involving Jack's career as an outdoor writer. Their Highland Ranch property was in Coyote Creek, a ranching community eight miles east of Timbergate in the Cascade Range foothills.

My petite and active Amah is my father's mother, on the Portuguese side of the family. She and Grandpa Machado were divorced before I was born, and she's been married to Jack Highland ever since I can remember. When I was a baby, she asked my mother about the Chinese word for grandmother. Mom explained that the word for paternal grandmother is pronounced *a-ma*, but it's sometimes confused with *amah*, a devoted family servant similar to a nanny. Amah joked that either name fit, since she was frequently called into service as a nanny when both my parents were working. She's been our dual-purpose Amah ever since. She and tall, lanky Grandpa Jack love the outdoors and frequently hike with their llamas. They're in their early seventies, but I can't see any signs that age has slowed them down.

After a few minutes, the interior temperature of my car had dropped to a level I could tolerate, but instead of heading home, I called Harry and told him I was on my way to his condo with Mexican take-out and wine. I wanted his perspective on the doctor's missing wife. Harry isn't just my little brother, he's my very best friend. At twenty-six, he's two years younger than I am and already making his fortune designing and constructing commercial buildings. He's a lefty with an ambidextrous brain. I think that gives him an edge. He decided on dual majors in architectural engineering and business when he was in the eighth grade, finished high school in two years, and college in three. What makes me most proud is that he hasn't let his success as a boy wonder architect or his reputation as a playboy go to his head.

We devoured our tacos in the cool comfort of his living room, where the air-conditioning never failed. With the world news on mute, I filled him in on my first day at work.

"Bouncy Bonnie's missing?" Harry grabbed the remote. "Wonder if we'll hear anything on the local news."

"Bouncy Bonnie? What are you talking about?"

Harry flashed his wicked grin. "Bonnie and I were in middle school together. She was a cheerleader—the first girl in sixth grade to develop in the chest area, if you get what I mean."

"I get it. And you can say 'breasts' in front of me."

"Guys don't say 'breasts.' Doctors say 'breasts.' Librarians say 'breasts.' Old, boring librarians."

"Okay, you've made your point. Any chance you can explain why she would go to Dr. Beardsley for a boob job if she was so well endowed?"

"Probably because they weren't the same size."

"How do you know?"

"Give me a break, Sis. You know how guys talk about stuff like that."

"In middle school?"

Before he could answer, the local news came on, and Harry turned up the volume. Milton Palmer, the genial evening anchor with a bad toupee, kicked off the six-thirty segment.

"A local doctor is questioned in the disappearance of his wife. More after these messages."

gutter evening another with a cold supper clicked off
the six thirty of stations.

"A local ducteria questioned in the divorce scandal
of her with Blackball of divorce-ways.

TWO

DURING THE BREAK, Harry muted the TV and filled me
in on what he knew about Bonnie Beardsley's television career.

"She started out doing freelance commercials, then
the station hired her to do feature stories for the eleven
o'clock news, but her segments were filled with so
many bloopers she only lasted two weeks."

"I heard she was a spokeswoman for animals."

"That's right. She did a few spots for the Humane
Society and the local animal shelter after the station
let her go. No one could understand how she got hired
in the first place until Milton Palmer's wife sued him
for divorce."

"Bonnie had a fling with Milton?"

"Yep." Harry looked puzzled. "I'm surprised you
don't remember all the gossip."

"I wasn't here back then. I was in New Haven."

I had chosen Southern Connecticut State University for my library degree so I could spend my week-
ends and holidays with our Grandpa Machado and his
wife in New York City. After he and Amah split up,
he moved there and worked as a doorman in a luxury
apartment building until he retired.

"That's right," Harry said. "You missed the whole
soap opera. Arnetta Palmer slugged poor love-sick Milton with a brutal property settlement. Soon as Bonnie

figured out Milton was broke, she dumped him and latched on to Beardsley."

Harry turned up the sound at the end of the commercial break, and we watched Milton Palmer report on the disappearance of his former paramour. The story didn't provide much insight. The police were following the standard missing person's routine. Palmer introduced Willow Underhill as an officer of Bonnie's favorite charity. The woman spoke tearfully about Bonnie and Everlasting Pets.

"Her support of our full-service pet cemetery—complete with interment, cremation, cloning and cryogenics—will never be forgotten," the woman said. "Bonnie was our greatest benefactor."

"That's cold," Harry said. "Their friend's missing, and she's turning it into a commercial."

"Cryogenics? They're freezing dead animals? Is anyone really that gullible?"

"Hey, leave the pet lovers alone. It makes them feel better. If they can afford it, what's the harm?"

I was trying to think of a good response when the meteorologist came on, predicting the next day's high at 115 degrees.

Harry turned off the set. "You're looking pretty grim considering you don't know the woman."

"I was thinking about something I heard at work. Her parents gave up on her and now they're gone. Who will care if something's happened to her?"

"Her husband, for starters."

"Maybe, but you know what they say about spouses. You can bet he's going to be a suspect."

"He probably won't be the only one," Harry said. "She isn't exactly a saint."

"She must have some redeeming qualities."

A pensive look crossed Harry face. "You know, now that I think about it, she used to do a thing that was nice in a weird sort of way."

"What do you mean?"

"She fed her lunch to the stray cats that hung around school. Almost every day, even in the rain."

"So she loved animals. That's probably why she hooked up with the pet cemetery people."

"I guess so. Too bad she didn't have that kind of rapport with humans." Harry disappeared into his bedroom and returned with a gym bag.

"Want to go to the dojo and work out for a while?"

"Isn't it a little hot for jujitsu?"

"Only for wimps. My fourth degree black belt test is only two weeks away. Come on. Mark Takamoto's out of town and I need another black belt to spar with me."

"Sorry, I don't have my gi with me."

"No excuse. There'll be an extra one in your size at the dojo."

I gave in because I needed the practice, too. I had earned my third degree belt a few months earlier but hadn't been working out lately. One of the advantages of growing up as mixed-race kids in our predominantly white community was a healthy respect for self-defense. Our father started each of us in jujitsu when we turned seven, making us promise to use the art only as a last resort. I slipped up once in second grade. I broke a nasty boy's little finger on the school bus. I got in a world of trouble, but the kid never asked me to show him my underpants again.

The temperature in the dojo was close to ninety degrees, but Harry didn't seem to notice.

"Come on, Aimee, we're not dancing here. Get serious."

Harry knew how squeamish I was about hurting anyone. He constantly reminded me that jujitsu was not just a sport, it was a weapon—the gentle art that could save my life. He thought I'd choke if I ever needed to use it for the real thing. I blamed that kid on the bus. I still got queasy thinking how ghastly his little finger looked sticking out sideways. I had to admit that Harry might be right. I could act the part in tournaments, but how would I handle myself in a life or death situation?

After an hour of randori, I'd been tossed, twisted, and slam-dunked until my dinner was threatening to come up. I gave Harry an ultimatum. "We quit now, or you loan me your Jaguar for a week." In five minutes we were in the car and headed back to his place.

"What are you doing with the rest of the evening?" Harry asked.

"Sleeping, if the swamp cooler in my apartment is working. Jack thinks it needs a new motor."

"I know. He asked me to have a look at it and I forgot. I could follow you out to Coyote Creek now if you want. See if I can do a patch job."

"No, it's too late. Almost nine thirty."

"You want to stay over in my guest room?"

"It's tempting, but I can't wear the same clothes to work two days in a row."

"Okay, it's your call, but I don't want the blame if you go home and die of heatstroke."

"What about you?" I asked. "Did you have plans for the rest of the evening?"

"Nothing important. Someone was going to come

by at ten, but I've been looking for an excuse to cancel. You're it."

Someone meant a woman. "Who is she? Someone new?"

I was always a week or two behind on Harry's love life. He had dated one girl all the way through high school and college, but she broke up with him a week after they announced their engagement. That was four years ago. Harry has been playing the field ever since. Once, after he'd had a few beers, he confided that his porcelain-skinned fiancée broke it off because her parents were afraid their grandchildren would look foreign.

"*Foreign*?" I'd said. "What does that mean?"

"Like me, I guess. Or they might have been homely, like you." Harry had laughed, but it sounded like something was breaking inside. He made me promise never to tell our parents. There were other things we'd never told them, and we had made a blood vow long ago that we never would. I remembered it as a noble and exciting pact: Harry and me against the world.

Back at his condo, he made his call while I sat on the balcony watching moonlight ripple across the Sacramento River below. A trace of breeze off the water had lowered the outside temperature.

Harry came out with two glasses of iced tea.

"I should go."

"Drink your tea first. It's decaf; it won't keep you awake."

"Thanks." I sipped. "Are you going to tell me about this woman who just got the brush-off?"

"Probably not." He leaned against the balcony rail, looking down at the river. "She's not important."

Would any woman ever be important to him? After

four years, it didn't look promising. With his dark good looks, he was never at a loss for a date, but his love life never got too serious.

We made small talk until I finished my tea and said I had to get home. I made a stop in the bathroom, and Harry went outside to retrieve his gym bag from his car. I was washing my hands when I heard his phone ring in the living room. I debated whether to pick up and let the caller know Harry was home. While I stood there undecided, the answering machine clicked on. I couldn't help hearing the caller's message.

> Hey Machado, it's Mark. I'm still in Sac at the convention. Heard a news flash about Bonnie Beardsley. Did she tell you she was going to split? Man, this is trouble you don't need. You better hope they find the crazy broad in one piece.

Harry opened his front door just in time to hear *trouble you don't need*. He read the expression on my face and replayed the whole message.

When it was finished, he shook his head. "Damn, I wish you hadn't heard that."

I sank into the nearest chair, afraid I might faint. "Harry, what's going on?"

THREE

"DAMMIT, HARRY, TELL ME. Do you know where she is?"

"No, I swear. Bonnie called me last Wednesday afternoon, out of the blue. I hadn't heard from her in years. She said she wanted to learn self-defense and she'd heard I taught at the dojo. She thought someone was stalking her, someone she met at the Natural History Museum. I told her to come to class Saturday morning."

"Why didn't you tell me any of this earlier?"

"There wasn't any point getting you all worried for nothing. Odds are she'll show up in a day or so."

"I'm your big sister, for God's sake. I'm supposed to worry." I couldn't sit still, so I got up and paced the room. "What are you going to do if she doesn't turn up?"

"Nothing, because she will."

"You have to call the police. Tell them about the stalker."

He grabbed me by the shoulders and backed me into the chair I'd just left. "Will you please sit still and listen?"

"I'm listening."

"I've already called the police. I told them everything I know."

"When did you call them? Why? How did you know

she was missing? It wasn't on the news until tonight, was it?"

"That's four questions. First, she didn't make it to my self-defense class Saturday morning. I wouldn't have given it much thought, but a couple of guys on the job were talking about her this morning. Their wives go to the place where Bonnie gets her nails done. Evidently she missed her appointment Saturday afternoon, and she didn't show up for a tennis lesson this morning. Put it together and she could have been missing for almost three days, so I called the police to tell them her stalker story."

"That's good. So what did they say?"

"They thanked me for the information and said don't leave town."

"Oh, great. You know what that means, don't you? You're a suspect, Harry. This is serious. It could affect your mall project. We should call Mom and Dad."

"No. This is exactly why I didn't tell you. It's too soon. Mom and Dad are thousands of miles away in the Azores. And don't worry about the mall project. I have a contract that says the project is mine unless I'm unable to fulfill my end of the agreement."

"Even if you're a murder suspect?"

"Yes. Even then. Basically, they can only cancel my contract and hire someone else if I become incapacitated or drop dead."

"What if you get arrested?"

"You're overreacting, Aimee. This is not nearly as bad as you think, so let's not get Mom and Dad involved. There's no point in worrying them when this case will probably be solved in a day or two."

He was playing the guilt card, and we both knew

it would work. Our parents had begun a construction business on a shoestring, and over the years, built it into a thriving enterprise. Along the way they had sacrificed plenty to bring us up with every advantage they could afford. When our father inherited property in the Azores six months ago, he and Mom decided to retire, so they turned the business over to Harry.

Always up for a challenge, my brother had not hesitated to bid on the design and construction of a new three-story shopping mall for the City of Timbergate. To his competitors' surprise, Harry's bid won. Without our father's exceptional reputation backing him, a multi-million dollar deal like that would never have gone to someone as young as Harry. The project would take three or four years to complete, and there were one or two disgruntled contractors in Timbergate who were betting Harry would not be able to see it through.

As soon as the mall contract was signed and Harry took over the reins of the family business, Dad and Mom moved to their property on the island of Faial, where money stretches about five times as far as it does in the states. Dad teaches jujitsu when he's not sailing. Mom is fluent in four languages, so she volunteers as a translator at the hospital in Horta, the island's port city. As long as we were healthy and happy here at home, they could relax and enjoy their new life. Harry was right; they didn't need us disrupting them unless we had a good reason.

"Okay," I said. "We won't call them. Yet. But you'd better not fib to me about any of this. And don't leave anything else out. Like Bonnie Beardsley's stalker story. Did she say who she thought it was?"

"I just told you everything I told the police." Harry

erased Mark's message from his answering machine. "Think about it, Aimee. I teach at the dojo every Saturday. Half the policemen in town have been in my classes. It's perfectly reasonable that Bonnie would call me if she wanted to learn self-defense, and they all know it."

"How did Mark Takamoto know Bonnie called you?"

"I mentioned it to him when we were sparring last Wednesday night. Now let's drop this."

I made one last attempt to pull rank on him. "I'll drop it for now, but only if you promise to tell me everything that happens. If the police talk to you again, or if you think of anything else Bonnie said. Especially about her stalker. I mean it, Harry, promise me."

"Okay, okay. You're acting like a lunatic, but I promise."

I DROVE HOME with Harry's story running through my mind. Here, again, was the major difference between us: whenever something went wrong, my first reaction was to panic and expect the worst. Harry was never oblivious to the possibility of trouble—no black belt is—but he always kept his cool and was prepared for anything. Not for the first time, I wished I were more like Harry.

Jack and Amah's house was dark when I pulled into the driveway and started down the lane to the barn. Sixty-five yards from the main house, my apartment was close enough for comfort, but far enough away for privacy. I parked in the stable yard and climbed the exterior stairs to the deck that wrapped around the north and west sides of the building. In the moonlight, the dark shapes of Jack's half dozen llamas dotted the field. They were settled in for the night, kushed with all four legs folded under their bodies, but that would change quickly if they sensed a predator. Llamas aren't just cute and wooly packers; they also make great watchdogs.

Inside the stuffy space, I opened all the windows to catch the meager breeze and took a cool shower, careful not to bang my elbows on the walls of the tiny cubicle. I left my hair wet and cool and crawled into my fold-out futon bed. With a legal pad and pen, I started to make a *To Do* list for the next day, but that proved futile. My mind kept switching to the Bonnie Beardsley mystery and Harry's unwitting involvement. I finally dozed off, lulled by the hum of my portable fan moving fusty air around the room.

THE DUMPSTER BEHIND the Happy Ox was back in place the next day when I pulled into the employee parking lot. Not *the* Dumpster, but *a* Dumpster. It was definitely a different container. Someone from the hospital must have contacted the restaurant owner. Had my comments to the hospital security guard been passed on? I walked near enough to take a better look. At close range there were very few flies, and the stench from the day before was gone.

I noticed a coppery glint winking in the weedy dirt at the edge of the alley and reached down with a tissue to pick it up, thinking it might be a lucky penny.

"Whatcha doin', Missy?" The gravel-voiced question rose from the Dumpster like some kind of ventriloquist's trick.

A skinny old man leaned against the side of the container taking a smoke break. His dirty apron displayed a graphic of a smiling blue ox kicking up its heels. The cook? One look at his dirt-lined fingernails and I promised myself I'd never eat at the Happy Ox café.

I slipped the tissue into the pocket of my skirt. "Nice Dumpster," I said, "is it new?"

"Ain't mine. City come by yesterday and took mine. Loaned us this one."

"That seems like a bargain. This one smells better, too."

"That ain't the point. City didn't ask, just took it away. Folks don't have no say about nothing anymore. If government wants it, that's the way it is." He ground out his butt under his ratty tennis shoe.

I was saved from further dialogue when a coughing fit seized him. I mumbled, "I'd better be going," and escaped before he could catch his breath.

When I reached the library, Dr. Beardsley was chatting with a snowy-haired little bird of a woman in the peach-colored uniform of the volunteers. She had to be my other volunteer. Less than five feet tall, her height had obviously been diminished by thoracic kyphosis, an increased curvature of the upper spine commonly called dowager's hump. I guessed her weight at less than ninety pounds.

"Miss Machado," Dr. Beardsley said, "this is your Tuesday and Thursday volunteer, Lola Rampley."

"I'm pleased to meet you, Ms. Rampley."

"And I, you, dear. Please, just call me Lola."

Dr. Beardsley asked how I had managed in his absence the day before. I assured him I'd been quite comfortable getting familiar with my surroundings.

"That's fine, just fine. Was Maybelline helpful?"

"Yes, she was a great help." *If he only knew.*

That seemed to satisfy him. I spent an awkward moment wondering if I should bring up the subject of his missing wife, but I thought of Harry and decided against it.

Beardsley asked me about my plan of action for developing the forensic component of the collection. I explained that I would start by researching the items that were recommended for a core collection of print and online journals, databases, and texts.

I'd already communicated with a forensic librarian in another state who was delighted with Beardsley's idea. I was shocked to learn that according to my source, there were only three official forensic librarians in the entire country, and that there were areas like ours all over the map in dire need of ready access to up-to-date forensic resource materials.

Beardsley and I talked about the consortium of users he envisioned and how it might be set up. When he left, I watched him walk away with his shoulders back and a spring in his step. I was struck by how upbeat he seemed for someone whose wife's whereabouts were unknown.

Lola Rampley proudly told me that she was eighty-one years old. She mentioned that she had been a public librarian back in the days of card catalogs and hand-stamped due dates. After we discussed her duties, she went to work on the boxes of books and journals marked for discard, removing them from our online catalog.

I heard her humming country tunes to herself while she worked, and eventually I realized that her repertoire consisted entirely of Marty Stockwell tunes. I had a good ear for Marty's songs because he made his home in Coyote Creek. For more than twenty years, all of Sawyer County had claimed the country music icon as its resident celebrity, but Coyote Creek locals had the privilege of shooting the breeze with Marty in the produce section of the Four Corners grocery market.

Thanks to his friendship with Jack, I'd heard Marty's music all my life. The Stockwell property was a few miles from Amah and Jack's ranch, and Marty and Jack went bass fishing together when their schedules allowed. Of course, Jack bought everything Marty recorded.

While Lola worked on the discards, I tackled the stack of binders and manuals that all new employees are required to read.

Jared Quinn, the hospital administrator, called me at eleven. He had been out of town on business when I was interviewed, and the two of us had never met. His voice was strong and clear, and he sounded amused. I had the feeling he was smiling as he spoke. He asked if I had been told I was required to facilitate the monthly meetings of the medical staff's Continuing Medical Education Committee, where all actions related to the library were addressed. In addition to supervising the library and establishing the forensic collection, I was to take charge of TMC's continuing medical education programs. Quinn said I should contact Dr. Beardsley whenever I wanted to add an item to the agenda.

After he hung up, I decided to make a good first impression by suggesting at least one agenda item. The meeting date was more than a week away, so I would have time to submit a preliminary list of forensic materials for the core collection, along with a cost estimate. I called Dr. Beardsley's office to tell him about my plan. A woman with the voice of a twelve-year-old answered, saying that Dr. Beardsley was out and that she didn't know when he would be back. With misgivings, I told her I was calling to discuss the CME Committee agenda and to please ask Dr. Beardsley to return my call.

"Okay, what's your name again?" she said.

I pronounced it for her again, and even spelled it. "It's Aimee *Ma-SHAW-do*. A-I-M-E-E M-A-C-H-A-D-O."

"Okay, just a minute." I listened while she mouthed the letters, presumably as she wrote each one down. "Okay, got it. Now what did you want me to tell him again?"

"It's about next week's CME Committee meeting. Please ask him to return my call." I gave her my extension number and hung up. So Beardsley's secretary sounded like Betty Boop on helium. Was he having a fling of his own? Did I file that under motive? Why not? Maybe he wanted Bonnie out of the way. Or maybe Bonnie had gotten jealous and split to teach him a lesson.

As it turned out, Dr. Beardsley would not return my call that day. I found out why when Lola and I went to the cafeteria for lunch.

The place was buzzing, and the lines were long. When we finally got served, we went to a table where two volunteers were waving us over to join them.

"What's all the hubbub about?" Lola asked.

An elderly gentleman wearing the male version of the volunteer's orange blazer leaned across the table in a stage whisper. "The police found the doctor's wife."

"Where?" I blurted. "Is she alive?"

"Nope. Not hardly. Dead. In a Dumpster just down the alley from here." He sat back, obviously satisfied that he had been the one to deliver the gruesome news.

My ears rang and my eyes blurred. So much for Harry's theory that Bonnie would turn up in a day or two. *Bonnie wasn't coming home.*

"How did they find her?" Lola asked.

He touched the side of his nose. "The smell. That's what I heard."

"Oh, my." The other woman glanced down and shook her head.

So Bonnie Beardsley's remains had been the source of the foul smell in the Dumpster behind the Happy Ox. Dead in a Dumpster. What a dreadful cliché.

I excused myself, threw my lunch away and headed back to the library where I spent the rest of the day working on autopilot and worrying about Harry. Near quitting time, I debated whether I should call him or just show up at his place after work. If he'd heard from the police again, I wanted to know every detail.

My stomach had been roiling for an hour, so I popped a piece of peppermint candy into my mouth. Before it had a chance to melt, TMC Administrator Jared Quinn came striding toward my desk from the library entrance. The photos I'd seen in the employee newsletter didn't do justice to the live version. I watched him walk toward me with powerful grace. His wavy black hair and dark blue eyes would have made him too pretty, but he was saved from that by a rugged jaw and a scar running horizontally through his left eyebrow. His lips had a sculpted, sensuous curve and his smile was engaging.

Earlier in the day, Lola had mentioned that Quinn

was single, comparing him to old-time movie stars like Clark Gable and Tyrone Power, but I had only a vague idea who they were. She said it was high time the dreamboat found himself a wife. Then without skipping a beat, she wanted to know if I had a steady beau. When I said no, she beamed. I knew a matchmaker when I saw one. She had walked off humming "You're Nobody 'til Somebody Loves You," which Marty Stockwell had recorded, of course, on his CD of old standards.

Lola had no way of knowing I was recovering from a break-up. Romance was the last thing on my mind. In any case, I would never allow myself to get a crush on the man who signed my checks. Amah had warned me about that years ago, the day I got my first job as a student aide in our local college library.

"It's a no-win situation," Amah had said. "Women who date the boss always lose when the break-up comes. They lose the man and they lose the job." It made sense, and I had followed her advice. Of course I was still single, but at least I had never lost a job. This was my brand-new dream job, and I wasn't going to risk it for any man.

I ducked down, pretending to search for something in a drawer so I could spit out the candy. It landed in my lap and stuck there. Quinn reached my desk just in time to watch me pick it off my skirt and drop it in the wastebasket. He seemed not to notice.

With my cheeks ablaze, I said, "Hello, Mr. Quinn. What can I do for you?"

He wore chinos and a pale blue shirt open at the collar. I tried to ignore the faint but tantalizing scent of carnations and spice that made me long to breathe deeply. The room suddenly seemed smaller and felt very warm.

"I thought it was time we met," Quinn said. "I dropped by to tell you Dr. Beardsley is going to need some time off."

"Of course. I heard about his wife. He must be devastated."

"We're all concerned for him, but I'm also wondering how you're doing. Losing your supervisor on the second day of your job is a tough break."

"I'm sure I can manage. Is there someone I should report to while he's gone?"

"Me, I suppose. Will that work for you?" He flashed his captivating smile, and for an instant I forgot about Bonnie Beardsley and Harry and the whole mess.

"That's…certainly, that's fine, Mr. Quinn."

His eyes sparkled with humor. "Why don't you call me Jared? I prefer first names if you don't mind."

"No, of course not." *Yikes, Amah definitely would not approve.*

"Good." He reached out his hand. His grasp felt strong and sensual. "Welcome aboard. I'm sure we'll get by while Dr. Beardsley is away."

"I'm sure we will. If you have any priorities for the library, please let me know."

"Just get the forensic stuff up and running. Law enforcement folks in the rural counties up north are begging for a resource closer than Sacramento. I'm not a librarian, and neither is Dr. Beardsley, so we're counting on you to make this work."

"I'm already compiling a list and a budget for the forensic collection. I'll send you a draft."

"Perfect. Other than that, I'd say just go with your gut and give me a shout if you need anything."

By the time he left, it was close enough to five o'clock for me to make my getaway. I called Harry's cell and left a message.

"We need to talk."

FOUR

I MADE TWO resolutions on the drive from work to Harry's condo. First, I would find a way to keep Harry out of trouble even if I had to find Bonnie Beardsley's killer myself. Second, I would keep my new job with or without Dr. Beardsley's support. Somehow, I would prove to Jared Quinn and Timbergate Medical Center that Dr. Beardsley's vision for the library was worth pursuing and that I was the person best qualified to bring it to life.

When Harry drove up, he didn't look pleased to see me sitting on the steps outside his condo fanning myself with a Country Pizza take-out menu I'd found on the floor of my car.

"I should have known," he said.

"Have you heard about Bonnie Beardsley?"

"I've heard."

"Well?"

"Well, what?"

I followed him up the stairs and into his condo. As soon as we were inside, I gave him an ultimatum. "We are going to talk about Bonnie Beardsley, so don't try to stonewall me."

"Fine. Can we eat first?"

"Fine."

I made veggie omelets while he opened a bottle of Cabernet. He wolfed down his dinner and took his wine glass with him to his home office to check his email. I loaded his dishwasher, then turned on the TV for a second airing of local news. Harry came into the room just as the broadcast began. Milton Palmer did not report the news. His co-anchor announced that Palmer was off on assignment. *Sure he was.*

The somber junior anchor reported that Bonnie's body had been found. Next came a recap of her disappearance, followed by clips of her less-than-stellar career at the TV station. Finally, a video showed a persistent reporter interviewing the police officer in charge of the case.

"Is it true the victim's death was due to strangulation?"

The officer's terse reply was noncommittal. "Cause of death is being withheld pending further investigation."

Again, I felt a twinge of pity for the much-reviled victim. Strangulation sounded like a gruesome way to go. I observed Harry while he watched the report and saw his face turn to stone. His ink-dark eyes, usually so alive with mirth, seemed to shut out the world. That was his poker face, and it set my alarm bells clanging. He was holding out on me.

"Harry, is there something you haven't told me?"

He headed for the kitchen. "Want some more wine?"

"No. Get back in here and answer me. I know when you lie. You know I know."

"I hate it when you do that." He realized he was busted.

"Tell me, or I'm calling Mom and Dad."

"You'd really do that?"

I took out my phone. "Damned right."

He dropped into an overstuffed chair and placed his wine glass gently on the coffee table.

"Put down your phone."

I put it down. "Now talk."

"She came over here last Friday night."

"What? The dead woman was here? In your home? And you don't think you're a suspect?" I heard my voice rising with each word. I wasn't usually a screecher, but this was a level of anxiety I rarely experienced. The victim's DNA would be all over the place. I envisioned crime scene investigators dusting and probing—and Harry in handcuffs.

Harry stayed calm. "I told the police she came by about ten o'clock Friday night. It was totally unexpected. I offered her a glass of wine. She said she wanted to start my women's self-defense class the following morning and could she do that, did she need to sign up or anything. I told her no, just show up at the dojo at nine in the morning." He stopped to sip his wine.

"Go on," I said. "What else?"

"I asked her if she'd told the police about the stalker. She said no, she didn't want her husband to know. She thought it might be a guy she'd flirted with a couple of weeks ago at the Natural History Museum over by the river. What kind of guy stalks a woman he meets in a museum, for Chris' sakes?"

"Oh, I don't know. Probably the kind of guy who trolls for promiscuous trophy wives like Bonnie Beardsley."

"Good point." His eyes shifted away from mine for a moment. *A red flag.*

"Anything else?" I knew there was something.

"She got a little weird with me as she was leaving."

"What do you mean?"

"I walked her out to her car and tried to convince her to call the police about the stalker. She acted pissed, said she didn't need me giving her orders. Then she went coy and apologetic, tried to get me in a lip lock. I disentangled her and practically shoved her into her car. Told her again to be at the dojo at nine the next morning."

"Jesus, Harry. Did anyone see that?"

"I doubt it. It was pretty late by then. Maybe eleven."

"Aren't you even a little freaked out? What if the police think you did it? What if they dig up the old excessive force incident?"

"That was different. You were being attacked. I was cleared." He shook his head. "I know they'll have to rule me out, but I don't know anything about what happened to Bonnie."

"What if Marco Bueller gets his teeth into this?"

"He can't. His brother is in prison because of you and me. His prior involvement in that case would keep him from being assigned to any new case involving either of us."

Harry held black belts in at least three martial arts. He wouldn't start a fight, but he had finished one in spectacular fashion one night a few years ago when I had a flat tire. He'd saved me from rape or worse by showing up just minutes after a couple of drunken thugs broke my car window with a tire iron, smacked me on the head with the damned thing, and started hauling me into the brush. I could have taken both of them if I hadn't been knocked senseless. Luckily I had already called Harry on my cellphone.

My brother arrived on the scene in time to take one

of them out at the knees and fracture the other guy's ribs. Taking the circumstances into account, the judge cleared Harry of excessive force charges. Excessive force is what the law calls it when a black belt beats the shit out of someone. They were both sent to prison. The guy with the crushed knees was Tango Bueller, who ended up with a permanent limp. Problem was, his big brother Marco was an investigator for the Timbergate Police Department. Marco tried to convince Harry and me to put all the blame on Tango's accomplice. He claimed his brother was high on coke and out for a joy ride, but he never would have assaulted me. At the trial, I honestly couldn't say which one of them had bashed me on the head, or whether they had both dragged me out of the car, but they were both convicted of aggravated assault with attempt to rape. When Tango went to prison, Marco lost his bid to become chief of police. He still blamed Harry and me for his stalled career.

"So Marco Bueller isn't allowed to participate in any investigation that involves either one of us," I said. "Do you really think that would stop him?"

"It won't come to that," Harry said. "The truth is out there. The police will find it."

"Maybe we can help things along."

"Aimee, leave it alone. Bonnie is dead. If you stick your nose in it, you could end up just like her."

"There must be something we can do."

Harry grabbed my shoulders. "Aimee, listen to me. Someone killed that woman. We don't know why, but whoever did it could do it again."

"I'm right there, working with her husband. I can—"

"No. Absolutely not." He got up and headed down

the hall toward his bedroom. "Go home and get some sleep. It's late."

The lights were out in Amah and Jack's house when I got home. I drove down the lane to the llama barn, hoping this mess would sort itself out before our grandparents discovered Harry might be involved. In my humid little studio apartment in the corner of the pasture, I tossed and turned until three in the morning, listening to my pulse pound in my ears.

FIVE

My HAIR WAS still drying when I reached the TMC parking lot Wednesday morning. I ran a brush through it and applied a fresh layer of power red lipstick. I headed for the employee entrance, but before I could open the door, I was stopped by the same security guard I'd met on my first day.

"Hold it, Missy." Orrie Mercer held out his beefy arm, barring my way. "You gotta get cleared by Administration."

Confused, I asked if he knew why.

"Not my place to say. I'm just following orders."

The administration suite occupied half of the fourth floor of Timbergate Medical Center's newly remodeled tower. It was nicknamed the penthouse and was as far from the Health Sciences Library as a person could get without leaving the hospital campus altogether. By contrast, the library operated out of the poorhouse, the oldest building in the complex. We coexisted with departments like Housekeeping, Maintenance, and Security. Since none of us produced revenue, we were at the bottom of the healing profession's food chain.

On my ride up the elevator, I puzzled over why I was being asked to report to Administration and came up blank. I managed to greet Varsha Singh, Quinn's elegant executive assistant, with a pretense of com-posure. She let him know I was there, and after a few minutes, he opened the door to his office.

"Aimee, come in."

His walls were papered in muted earth tones and adorned with photos and prints of exotic birds and animals. Large plants—bamboo, rubber, and a few others I couldn't identify—enhanced the tropical theme.

"Please have a seat." Quinn gestured toward a small teakwood conference table flanked by two Havana chairs with dark wood backs carved in a feather motif. He took one and I perched on the pristine white fabric of the other, afraid the chair would judge me unworthy of its elegance and dump me on the floor.

"What can I do for you, Aimee?"

"I don't know. Orrie Mercer said I should report to you. He didn't explain."

"Ah, I suspected as much. Let me assure you there is no problem."

"Then why am I here?"

Quinn shook his head. "You can imagine how rumors have been flying for the past three days. Now that Mrs. Beardsley's body has been found nearby, our security personnel are taking extra precautions. They seem particularly concerned with new faces. You're the third recently hired employee who's been denied entry this morning." Quinn stood. "I'm sorry you had to waste your time with this. Since I'm still your interim supervisor, I'd better let you get back to your job. If there's any more trouble, give me a call."

Alone in the hallway, I reassessed the situation while I waited for the elevator. I still had a job, Harry probably wasn't in trouble after all, and Jared Quinn was charming, single, and possibly even a decent human being. *Don't be too sure about that last one*, I thought. *He is a hospital administrator.*

On my walk back to the library, I told myself I had probably overreacted by thinking bigotry on Mercer's part had prompted him to single me out. From what Quinn said, all the security guards were acting with an excess of caution in the aftermath of Bonnie Beardsley's death.

I had worked my way through my morning email messages when Maybelline Black arrived at nine o'clock, carrying a potted plant in each hand.

"Morning, Miss Machado," she called as she came toward my desk.

"Good morning. I see we've acquired a few more plants."

"Oh, yes. I made the rounds this morning. Many people leave them behind, you know."

"You mean all of the plants in here came from patient rooms?"

"Only the orphans. Otherwise they might be thrown away. A terrible waste, don't you think?"

"Yes, of course."

She found shelf space for the newest arrivals, then started watering all the plants in the room, murmuring softly to them as she worked. Some hung from planters, others sat in pots on top of tables and file cabinets. They seemed to thrive in our quiet, scholarly setting.

Maybelline approached my desk and placed a gorgeous violet on the one empty corner.

"There, isn't she just the most beautiful thing? I've named her Veronica."

"You named the plant?"

"Oh, dear." She put her persimmon-polished fingertips to her lips. "I shouldn't have presumed. You can give her a different name, of course."

"No, no," I said. "Veronica is fine. Thank you."

Maybelline leaned close and dropped her voice. "I suppose you heard about Bonnie Beardsley."

"Yes, it was all over the hospital grapevine yesterday. When did you hear?"

"Last night on the news. I found it ironic."

"How do you mean?"

"She was trash, ended up where trash belongs." Maybelline obviously didn't have a problem speaking ill of the dead. I wondered what else she might say with a little prompting.

"It is sad, though," I said. "Poor Dr. Beardsley must be distraught."

"He'll get over it." Maybelline turned her back on me and began loading her book cart.

I tried again. "I understand he's taking some time off."

"Excuse me," she dropped another book into the cart. "I have work to do." Five minutes later, she and her cart were out the door. I wondered if she was feeling guilty about her theory that Bonnie Beardsley had run off with some man.

The morning passed quickly once I got absorbed in compiling a list of items to purchase for the core forensic collection. My shopping list was almost complete when my phone rang. It had been silent all morning, and I answered the call still a little tongue-tied, trying out my greeting.

"Aimee Machado, Librarian. How may I help you?" Dorky, but it would do.

"By having lunch with me," Jared Quinn said.

"There's something we need to discuss. Can you break free in half an hour?"

"Twelve thirty? Yes. I can do that."

"Good, I'll drop by and pick you up." The ever-present smile was there in his voice.

When I put down the phone, I discovered Maybelline hovering at my desk. "Sounds like you have a lunch date."

"Not a 'date,' an appointment. Mr. Quinn wants to meet for lunch to talk business."

"Well, don't mind my saying so, but you'd best watch yourself with that man." Her face pinked up and she fanned herself with an old issue of *Urology Today*.

Did I need advice to the lovelorn from a world-class gossip? Maybe. The best gossips usually dug up some pretty reliable dirt. She obviously didn't share Lola Rampley's good opinion of Jared Quinn.

"It's a meeting, not a date," I insisted.

"Hah." She waggled a finger. "He's a womanizer; you're a woman."

"I'm sure it'll be fine. I make it a rule never to date anyone where I work. That goes double for my boss." I waited a beat to see if she would dish up any dirt about Jared Quinn, and I wasn't disappointed.

"I can name half a dozen women who think he's crazy about them. A couple of them work here, and the rest are part of the so-called society set Bonnie Beardsley ran with after she married poor Dr. B."

"Mr. Quinn ran with the Beardsley crowd?"

"Doctors, lawyers, architects. All the educated folk rub elbows when there's anything high-brow going on in this town."

Architects? Some of them, maybe. I'd never thought

of Harry as one of the high-brow set. His idea of culture is a one-night stand with a ballerina when the San Francisco Ballet Company comes to town.

"Where's the lady killer taking you for lunch?" Maybelline asked.

"I don't know. Why?"

"If it's a fancy Italian place, it's just business. If he picks up fast food and takes you to the park, watch out."

Forty-five minutes later, Quinn and I were on our way to lunch in his gold-trimmed white Navigator. I watched with growing apprehension as he turned into the drive-thru lane at McDonald's.

"I hope you don't mind fast food. I thought we'd drive over to the park." *Score one for Maybelline.*

At the park we found a reasonably clean picnic table in the shade of a large oak tree near the river. The temperature had dipped to the mid-nineties, and the humidity was low, so we were able to eat in relative comfort.

I picked at my grilled chicken salad while Quinn tossed his necktie back over his shoulder and lit into his Big Mac and fries like a starving high school fullback.

"What time do you have to be back?" he asked between bites.

"By one thirty."

"Any appointments this afternoon?"

"No, but I had to close the library when I left for lunch." What was this about?

"Then you can take a long lunch. I'm pretty sure your boss won't mind." He licked at a dab of special sauce at the corner of his mouth. The brief glimpse of the tip of his tongue sent a shiver through my belly, reminding me I hadn't been kissed in a long time. I looked toward the sky, grateful for the diversion of a graceful hawk soaring above the river.

Quinn followed my gaze, tracking the hawk's flight. "Amazing birds, aren't they?"

"Are they? I've always taken them for granted."

"Most people do. Bald eagles get all the respect, symbol of our great nation and all that, but they're not so different from the hawk."

"Really?"

"Sure. They're both raptors, keen-eyed predators who do what it takes with one pure motive—survival."

I wondered if we were still talking about birds. It sounded like a metaphor for the life of a hospital administrator. Fresh out of conversation, I tackled the last few bites of my salad and drained my soda.

"Let me take those." Quinn got to his feet, looking around until he spotted a trash bin. "I'll be right back."

I stood, brushed off my skirt and checked my blouse for embarrassing blobs of dressing. I ran my tongue over my teeth. All clear. Quinn was walking toward me smiling that killer smile, and I still hadn't learned what this lunch was about. I could almost hear Maybelline saying, "I told you so."

"Let's walk over to the river," Quinn's fingers grazed my elbow.

"Shouldn't we be getting back to work?"

"This is work. It's a meeting. Why talk in a stuffy office when we can combine business with pleasure?"

"I'm a little confused about the purpose of this meeting."

Quinn picked up a stone and skipped it along the water. "Your résumé listed jujitsu as a hobby. I used to dabble at it myself. Are you any good?"

"Third-degree black belt. What about you?"

"Not that good. I'm impressed."

"Thanks, but what's that got to do with my work?"

He turned to me, squinting in the bright sunlight. "I need your help with something."

"What do you mean?"

"This Beardsley thing. It's picking up momentum. The corporate office is nervous about the bad publicity. They want it resolved pronto."

"How do they expect you to do that?"

"They want damage control. Dr. Beardsley hasn't been charged with anything. He's due to return to work next week. While the investigation is ongoing, I'd like you to pay attention to what he says, notice anything that seems off, that kind of thing."

"You want me to spy on him?"

"No, just observe." Quinn tossed another rock. "If I thought this would put you in any danger, even with your martial arts background, believe me, I wouldn't ask. Beardsley has been on the TMC medical staff for twenty years. During that time he's been a model citizen. Voted Chamber of Commerce Man of the Year back in the nineties. I'm sure he didn't harm his wife, but her sudden death has to be affecting him. Grief often causes temporary changes in behavior, so I want to keep an eye on him, and you're the obvious person to help me do it."

This kept getting worse, but what choice did I have? The man I worked for had just lost his wife, who was murdered. Now, after only two days on the job, I was to report on him to the hospital administrator. Although in a way, it made sense. I'd probably feel safer knowing he was being watched, even if I was doing the watching.

"Okay," I said. "I'll do it."

"That's great." His next stone skipped five times, and he gazed out at the river with a satisfied smile. Meanwhile, I noticed the hawk swooping down along the riverbed. It snatched a small squirrel in its talons. The rodent's screams raised goose flesh on my arms as the raptor gained altitude and headed home with the bacon. It struck me that death is never far away.

SIX

I HAD PROMISED to have dinner with Amah and Jack that night to hear about their latest adventure. They were planning a trip to Idaho for a llama exposition, and after that they were going over to Washington and Oregon to look at some llamas for sale.

I found them out back on the veranda. Amah jumped up and wrapped me in a hug.

"Dinner is all ready. We're eating out here. Don't say a word until I get back. I want to hear everything." She disappeared into the house.

Jack watched her, an affectionate grin softening his weathered face. In his early seventies, he had aged even better than Robert Redford or Clint Eastwood.

"She's so curious she's about to bust," he said. "We saw the story about that doctor's wife on the early news."

We gathered around the wrought-iron table where Amah had laid out a spread of barbecued chicken, steamed Korean squash, and fresh tomatoes from their garden.

"Now tell us about your day," she said, "and leave room for peach pie."

I told them what little I knew about Beardsley's deceased wife but said nothing about Harry's connection to the case. They filled me in on their recent hike in the Thousand Lakes Wilderness. The llamas had packed in without protest, and the trout were biting. It didn't get better than that.

We gathered in front of the TV after dinner for the local news. Bonnie Beardsley's death was the lead story. Milton Palmer was still "out on assignment." The lanky junior reporter said police were questioning employees of the Happy Ox café and Timbergate Medical Center who might have witnessed suspicious activity in the parking lot near the Dumpster. Officially, the cause of death was not yet determined, but unofficial leaks to the press mentioned the earlier rumors about strangulation. The reporter announced a gruesome new twist.

"According to an unconfirmed report, the body was found stuffed in a bloody deer bag."

"Big deal," Jack said. "Half of Sawyer County hunts deer."

Even Harry, I thought.

After we turned off the news, I helped Amah with the dishes and then walked down the lane to my little home above the barn. I hated holding out on them, but I didn't want them to worry. With luck, the Bonnie Beardsley mess would be resolved quickly, and they'd never know Harry had been questioned.

The llamas perked up as I neared the barn and began making the *mrrrr* sound that told me they were hoping for treats. I filled a small bucket with cob, their favorite mix of corn, oats, and barley. In the darkening twilight, I walked out into the field. As aloof as ever, the five adults came close enough to nibble treats out of my hand, but backed away as soon as the goodies ran out. One of the females had given birth to a snow white cria three months earlier. The little one looked irresistibly cute and cuddly. Her dam let me get pretty close because I offered cob, but touching her cria was not allowed. When I got within a couple feet, she gave me a spit warning with her chin raised high and ears flattened back.

Inside the apartment, my swamp cooler was on good behavior for a change. The studio was compact and convenient. It had seen little use after Jack sold off part of his acreage and quit hiring ranch hands. The paint on the walls was a dingy white, and the furniture was an eclectic mix of ugly but functional hand-me-downs. The small kitchen area was on the east side of the room facing Jack and Amah's house. The west side of the room was living space with a fold-out futon for sleeping. Two doors on the south wall opened to a closet and the tiny bathroom.

I tried to read in bed for a while, but I couldn't keep my mind off the Beardsley mystery. I finally gave up and turned on the TV to catch the local eleven o'clock news. Bonnie Beardsley's demise continued to be the lead story. According to the police, most of the blood on the deer bag was animal, not human. They wouldn't comment on whether any of it was the victim's.

A composite artist's sketch flashed on the screen. Police were asking help from the public. A witness had seen someone loitering near the Dumpster the night after Bonnie went missing. The sketch showed a figure wearing camouflage clothing, a hunter's billed cap and aviator sunglasses. Big help that was going to be, but it did give me an idea.

Hannah Roberts, one of Jack's granddaughters, was Sawyer County's on-call forensic artist. The only one. She must have done that sketch. Her day job was working as an art therapist at the county's mental health clinic. We had grown up as step-cousins, but her pale blue eyes and white-blond hair made it obvious we didn't share the same genes. I considered calling her, but eleven thirty was a little too late. Her husband, Johnny, was a landscape architect whose work day started at dawn in the summertime. Their family went to bed early.

The swamp cooler began making its usual ominous thumping noises, so I turned it off and opened the window above my futon. The room filled with a balmy, cedar-scented breeze and the croaking serenade of a hundred horny bullfrogs. I propped myself up in bed with a clipboard against my knees and contemplated a list of suspects who might have done away with Bonnie Beardsley.

The TV anchor Milton Palmer and his ex, Arnetta, had obvious motives, but so did Dr. Beardsley, even though he was my least favorite suspect—next to Harry, of course. Dr. Beardsley's ex-wife, Lorraine Beardsley, was a better bet—woman spurned and all that—but my heart wasn't in it. I really hoped the killer would turn out to be the mysterious stranger Bonnie told Harry she'd met at the Natural History Museum. I already thought of him as the museum stalker. It just seemed right. So I had five suspects with motive, but what about opportunity?

I would have ample access to Beardsley when he returned to work, so I put a check mark next to his name. Next to the ex-Mrs. Beardsley's name, I made a note: *pump Maybelline re Lorraine Beardsley.*

Cornering the museum stalker would be tough, since I had no clue who he was. A trip to the museum was a long shot, but I made another note: *Stalker at museum?*

Then came Milton and Arnetta Palmer. Harry had said the ex-Mrs. Palmer was pretty vindictive with the property settlement, but three years was a long time to wait for revenge. I needed to chat with her—get a gut feeling, but under what guise? I wrote, *Access to Arnetta Palmer?*

And what about Milton Palmer? Had Bonnie rekindled that flame? Maybe she had been sneaking around with him behind her husband's back. She seemed like the type to fall for a celebrity, and except for Marty Stockwell, TV anchors were the only celebrities around.

I doodled on my list for a while and finally recalled the people who were interviewed on the news about Bonnie's favorite charity: Everlasting Pets. The couple who ran the animal cemetery and cryogenics center professed to be close friends of the victim. They might be a source, but I needed a plausible reason to contact them. If I told them I was looking for a cryogenics gizmo big enough to freeze a llama, they'd probably agree to meet with me. Heck, they'd probably spring for lunch.

SEVEN

I SHOT OFF an email to my step-cousin Hannah Thursday morning, asking if she was free for lunch. She worked three blocks from the hospital in a former fifties-era school building that housed half a dozen county agencies and a pretty good Mexican restaurant called Casa Loco.

Hannah called just before noon. "What's up?"

"I'll tell you at lunch. Can you get away?"

"Sounds mysterious. Is it about a guy?"

"Yes, but I can't talk now." *Perfect.* She'd talk all day if it involved my pathetic love life, but she'd shut up like a clam if she knew I was going to pump her about the sketch she'd drawn for the police.

"Okay. How about the Happy Ox?"

"Not there," I said.

"Why not?"

"I've seen the cook."

"Then you choose."

"Order some take-out at Casa Loco. I'll pick you up out front in twenty minutes."

Hannah emerged from Casa Loco's front door when I pulled up. She dropped into the passenger's seat with bags of food and two sodas.

"I hope your A/C's working today."

"So far." I headed south on the freeway.

"Where are we going?"

"Nowhere. I'll drive while you eat." And talk, I hoped.

Hannah pulled a taco out of the bag, unwrapped it, and bit off a mouthful. My stomach responded to the aroma with an angry growl, reminding me I'd forgotten to eat breakfast.

Hannah swallowed. "So what's going on? Is this about Nick? Are you getting back together?" Hannah and everyone else thought I was crazy to break up with Nick, but they'd never met Rella Olstad, his co-pilot and ex-girlfriend.

"No, forget about Nick. He's probably back with Rella by now."

"Is it true she was a fighter pilot before she went to work for Nick's boss?"

"Probably, but I don't want to talk about either one of them."

"So who's the guy? Did you meet someone new?"

"I'll tell you about that later, but right now I need information, and we don't have much time. My lunch hour's half gone."

"Information? Oh no, Aimee. Is this about my forensic sketch of the Camo Man? Because if it is—"

"I know, professional ethics. You can't tell me anything. So how do you know it's a man?"

"Aimee, that's not fair. I didn't say it was a man."

"Camo Man. You said *man*."

Hannah's cheeks flushed, and she picked at her taco.

"Well?" I said.

"The witness didn't know for sure. She said the person she saw walked like a guy."

"So the witness was a she?"

Hannah dumped her taco in the take-out sack. "That's it," she said. "Take me back."

"Relax. No one's going to know we talked about this. I'm not asking you for the name of the witness."

"Wouldn't do any good, 'cause they didn't tell me her name. It's a secret."

"Must be someone who lives near the Happy Ox, huh? Out walking her dog or something?"

"Leave it alone, Aimee. We can't get involved." She stared out the window.

"You know, don't you?"

She glanced at me. "Know what?"

"That Harry's a suspect."

"Of course I know. I hear things."

"Then why didn't you say something?"

"I was waiting for you to bring it up."

"Did you also know the dead woman is my supervisor's wife?"

"No. That's.... Wow, no wonder you're freaked out."

"Let's stay focused on the problem. We need to help Harry."

Hannah was almost as protective of Harry as I was. Amah and Jack had been together since all of us were kids, and we were family in the best sense of the word.

I had driven about ten miles down I-5, so I took an exit that led to an overhead freeway crossing, then re-entered northbound, heading back to Timbergate.

Hannah reached out to put her soda cup into the beverage holder and pulled her hand back. "Ouch, darn. I just snagged a nail."

"Are you wearing the fake ones again?"

"Yeah, mine won't grow. I'm thinking about trying acrylic toenails, too."

"You're kidding. Toenails?"

"Someone in the crime lab said Bonnie Beardsley was wearing them. I guess the acrylic nail on one of her big toes was missing." Hannah pulled a clipper from her purse and trimmed her broken nail.

"I heard she missed her nail appointment, but I wouldn't have thought of fake toenails."

"Yeah, who knew?"

I got Hannah back to work on time and made it to the library only a few minutes late. The place was empty, which was par for the course every afternoon since I'd started the job. I hoped things would pick up when Dr. Beardsley came back to work. I ate my cold taco, washing it down with lukewarm coffee.

The sluggish afternoon hours passed while I fiddled with busy work. Hannah had been no help about the guy dressed in camo. All I got out of her was he'd been seen at night. Did that mean shortly after sundown or in the pre-dawn hours? Either way, wearing sunglasses in the dark suggested he was in disguise.

I arrived home that evening just in time for a farewell dinner with Amah and Jack. They reminded me they were leaving at four o'clock the next morning for their llama trip.

"Are you sure you can handle all of it?" Jack asked. "We'll be gone at least two weeks."

"All of it" included a vegetable garden, a few fruit trees, half a dozen llamas, and a flock of turkeys. The rest of their menagerie lived in their guest room. It included a king snake in an aquarium and an elderly, foul-mouthed cockatiel they'd inherited when their crusty bachelor neighbor died. Amah's semi-feral

Maine Coon cat, Fanny, wanted nothing more in life than to add the cockatiel to her list of feathered victims.

"You two go and have a great time," I said. "I'll take care of everything until you get back." *Including keeping Harry out of jail.*

Amah gave me a hug. "Okay, sweetheart, we'll leave you a little chore list on the fridge. Jack just fed the snake a lizard and a mouse, so you'll only have to feed him once. Be sure to check his water. It'll all be on the list. And don't worry, the herd will look out for you."

Llamas' senses are acute, and when they see, hear, or smell danger, their alarm cry is unmistakable. It's something like a high-pitched donkey's bray played double-time at top volume, but no description really does it justice. Llama owners know it when they hear it, and they take it very seriously. Llamas use it sparingly and never cry wolf.

The animals were fine for sounding an alarm, but Jack was the real reason I'd had no qualms about bunking alone out in the pasture. He woke at the slightest sound, and he was a crack shot. Now, with the folks gone, I'd be alone on the ranch for two weeks with half a dozen woolly, cantankerous bodyguards whose ammo was limited to huge green gobs of spit.

After I thought it through, I decided having Amah and Jack gone for two weeks was a stroke of luck in spite of the isolation and extra chores. They didn't know Harry had been questioned about Bonnie Beardsley. There was no way they would leave if they thought he was in trouble.

Jack walked me through the evening chores, giving me a refresher course on how to keep the Highland Ranch running smoothly in their absence. I felt a stab of guilt about keeping Harry's predicament from them, but I justified it by reminding myself that the Beardsley case probably would be solved by the time they got home.

Later that evening when I studied my list of suspects, I realized that all but one of them still lived in Timbergate. I had tried the phone directory and an Internet search for Arnetta Palmer with no luck. I stuck a note above my computer monitor. *FIND ARNETTA PALMER.* She had to be out there somewhere.

Meanwhile, I figured Bonnie Beardsley's favorite charity was a good place to start detecting. It was almost midnight and I was tired, but I pulled up the Everlasting Pets website. I couldn't get my mind around this animal cemetery/pet cloning set-up as a legitimate charity, but there it was. According to the home page, they had a nonprofit designation from the federal government. They were legit. The Underhills were the only two staff members listed. He was the Executive Director, she was the Clinical and Ethics Director. Whatever that meant.

Their fees for gene banking were lower than I'd have guessed. Only $500 for the first year, plus a $100 per year maintenance fee. Their fee for cloning pets was vague. According to their literature, the science was not yet perfected for commercial use. So I could get a biopsy of one of the llamas at my own expense and have the tissue sample frozen for $500 plus the annual $100 maintenance fee. At some date in the unspecified future, for an unspecified price, I might get a llama clone if the science was perfected before I was ready to have my own genes frozen. Nice racket for the Underhills. Only a creative genius could write the kind of hogwash that would get such a bogus application for nonprofit status approved.

ON FRIDAY MORNING when I called Everlasting Pets, Willow Underhill answered the phone. I asked for an appointment to discuss freezing a pet.

"How's three thirty this afternoon?" Willow said.

"I don't get off work until five."

"No problem. We're flexible. Come at five-thirty. Do you know our location?"

I assured her I did. I'd taken it from their home page.

Friday was my day without a volunteer. Maybelline worked Monday and Wednesday, Lola was Tuesday and Thursday. Friday was just me, and I was grateful. I spent the day drafting a protocol for interlibrary loan services related to the new forensic collection, then closed up shop and headed across town to Everlasting Pets. The place was smaller than I'd expected, housed in a former tanning salon next to a tattoo parlor called Needle Me. *Not in this lifetime.*

I walked into the empty waiting room and rang a bell on the scarred wooden counter. The poorly maintained furnishings reminded me of the shop where I took my car for oil changes. Old chrome-legged chairs. A cheap, laminated corner table holding a few outdated magazines. A coffee maker held the dregs of a pot brewed earlier and left to burn. The scorched smell of it lingered. I rang the bell again. This time Mrs. Underhill appeared from behind a partition. I recognized her from the publicity photo on their home page. The live version was a good ten years older.

"You must be Miss Machado," she said.

"Yes." If I'd thought of it earlier, I'd have given her a fake name.

She picked up a pen and pad. "Now tell me about your special needs."

"I'm interested in your cryogenics program, but the animal I have in mind is rather large."

"What is it?"

"A llama."

Her brow furrowed. "That *is* large. Perhaps cloning would be a better choice."

"You can clone a llama?"

"We can clone anything—when the technology is ready, of course."

"How soon will that be?"

"Very soon." She avoided eye contact, shifting her glance around the room. "Please don't judge us by these humble surroundings." She arched her penciled brows and twirled a lock of mistreated blond hair showing dark at the roots. "We're moving to our new location next week."

"You're moving? Are you leaving Timbergate?"

"Oh, no. Just across town. Thanks to the many generous donors to our cause, we'll be in a lovely location near the river. You must come by." She reached out to touch my arm with a lavishly manicured hand, light pink polish and a tiny black poodle painted on each nail. "May I ask how you heard about us?"

I stepped back out of reach. This woman was too darned friendly. "From your television interview about Bonnie Beardsley. After I saw it, I looked up your website."

"Poor Bonnie." Willow pushed out her lower lip. "We're devastated about her shocking death. And it's just so ironic. If we'd known she was going to pass, maybe we could have..." she sighed, "...but that wouldn't have been legal. We're only approved for animals."

Good thing, I thought. Seemed like the original Bonnie had been enough trouble. Cloning her would just be asking for it.

"Then you and Bonnie were close?" I asked.

"She and Grover and I were three peas in a pod."

"Grover?"

"My husband. Grover and I adored Bonnie. And she felt the same about us. We often remarked that we were soul mates."

"I'm sorry for your loss."

"I don't know how Grover and I will ever find another Bonnie." The appraising way Willow looked at me made me want to turn and run out the door, but just then I heard a man's voice from the back room.

"Come on, get your ass in the car. I'm starving."

Willow's face flamed. "In a minute, Grover. I'm with a client."

A moment later Underhill appeared at his wife's side, unruffled and oozing charm. He was a big guy, in his fifties, I guessed, with a thick seventies-style mustache and jet black hair styled in a pompadour.

"Sorry to interrupt. I didn't know Willow had an appointment." He flashed a mouthful of capped teeth and left the way he had come.

"I should let you go," I said.

"Don't worry about him, he'll wait." Willow beamed at me. "Would you like an application? Once the paperwork is done, we can proceed with a biopsy of your llama."

"I'd like to think about it a little longer," I said.

Willow gave me a brochure about their cloning program and extracted my promise to visit their new facility. I made my getaway, uncertain whether I had learned anything useful. I had determined to my satisfaction that the Underhills were an odd couple, and that when Bonnie was alive, they'd been an even odder threesome.

EIGHT

MY NEXT STOP was Harry's newest building project, a two-tiered mega-mall that would draw shoppers from at least three neighboring counties. If everything worked out, he would make enough money on this venture to retire before he was thirty. But he wouldn't. He loved his work far more than the lifestyle it afforded.

Living alone in a llama pasture had a certain quirky charm, but while the folks were away, I knew I'd sleep better at night with a deadbolt on my door. When I got to Harry's mammoth construction site, huge yellow earth-moving machines were prowling like prehistoric behemoths, biting into red clay dirt, rearing, twisting and turning, so like the bright yellow Tonka versions Harry had adored when he was a toddler.

In work boots, jeans, and hard hat, he stood alone at the edge of the excavation. The sight flooded me with so much love, it took my breath away. My little brother was carved deep in my heart, and I thought I'd die if anything happened to him.

Blinking away the moisture in my eyes, I plastered on a grin and called out to him.

"Hey, Brother."

He turned, looked a little surprised to see me, but broke into a smile and waved. "Hi, Sis. Come over here. This is awesome. Take a look."

We stood together staring at the spectacle. Harry's

eyes glowed with pleasure. "Remember how we used to do that? Build roads and construction sites around the edges of Jack's garden?"

"Is it still as much fun?"

"More. The playground is bigger now."

He took my elbow and we walked toward the site supervisor's trailer. Inside, the cool air goose-pimpled the skin on my arms. The custom-built Airstream Land Yacht housed a well-stocked pantry, TV, microwave, and three laptop computers. I'd asked once what it cost, and Harry would only admit to less than half a million. His job foremen took turns spending the night at the work site, and Harry sometimes stayed over if a major screw-up or set-back required immediate attention.

He opened his fridge and pulled out a bottle of raspberry tea.

"Here you go." He took a bottle of water for himself and plopped into the chair next to his scaled-down drafting table. After a long swig, he got around to asking why I was there.

I perched on his settee. "I need a deadbolt for my apartment."

"Why?"

"Jack and Amah are going to be gone for two weeks. Llama stuff."

"Ah, you're alone out there in the pasture without Jack around. Why don't you stay in their house?"

"Amah offered, but the guest room smells of snake and bird poop."

"Only to you with your delicate nose."

"That's not all. The house is too big and creaky, and not one of their doors has a decent lock, not to mention the windows. I actually feel more comfortable over the barn. I don't think they'd mind if we put a deadbolt on the door."

"Of course not. Do you have the hardware?"

"It's in my car."

He agreed to meet me at the ranch in an hour if I'd spring for dinner. I stopped off at Country Pizza, a little place tucked next to the grocery store at the Four Corners mini-mall in Coyote Creek. While I waited, it occurred to me that for the first time since Bonnie Beardsley's death, Harry and I had talked to each other without mentioning her name.

At home, I changed into shorts and a tank top and switched on my window-mounted swamp cooler. I had dropped off Jack and Amah's mail at the main house but brought the local paper with me. Bonnie Beardsley was back on the front page.

Socialite's Murder Investigation Continues. My stomach churned as I read the headline. Our local district attorney, Connie Keefer, was quoted as being unable to provide details of the investigation. Keefer wasn't particularly young or beautiful, but gossip linked her with several of Timbergate's high-profile bachelors. Maybe her position of power was the ultimate aphrodisiac, or maybe she was just awesome in bed.

Whatever the reason, the latest stud she'd been seen with was Police Investigator Marco Bueller, the brother of Tango, the thug who had cracked my head with a tire iron and tried to rape me. Bueller would never stop hating my brother. Harry rapped on my door, interrupting my thoughts.

After we ate our pizza, Harry installed the deadbolt in ten minutes flat.

"Anything else you need done around here?"

"Just the swamp cooler."

"It's getting dark. I'll do it this weekend." He spotted the newspaper on my table, picked it up, and read the headline, a smile playing at the corners of his mouth.

"Connie Keefer's grandstanding again. What a publicity hound."

"How can you be so cavalier about this? Have you heard who she's dating?"

"I've heard. It won't last. Marco Bueller is not going to get serious about a Botoxed prima donna like Keefer."

"It might last until she picks a prime suspect in the Bonnie Beardsley case."

"We've already talked about this. Marco won't be allowed to investigate this case."

"Not officially, but give me a break. He's sleeping with the DA and you're really not worried? Even if nothing comes of it, your reputation will be tarnished. What if the killer is never found? Our parents spent decades of hard work and sacrifice to build a business and make our family name stand for integrity and a strong work ethic. You're their only son. All Mom and Dad achieved will be lost if the Machado name becomes associated with an unsolved murder case." I choked up and couldn't go on.

"Don't you think I'm aware of that?" Harry said. "Why do you think I'm telling you not to call them? When Dad retired and turned the business over to me, he said the good Machado name would be my greatest asset. He made me promise to protect it."

"The family name is only part of it. God, Harry, you

could be arrested, even convicted and sent to prison. That would break all of our hearts."

"It's too soon to worry about that, Aimee. We have no idea where this is going." He picked up his tools and opened the door. "Tell you what, if Abe Edelman tells me to worry, I'll worry."

"But Abe does real estate law. He's not a defense attorney."

"He was a DA's investigator in Southern California before he got his fill of criminal law and moved to Timbergate," Harry said. "He's more than qualified if I need him. Now let it go."

"Okay. If you promise to consult Abe at the least sign of trouble, I'll let it go for now."

"Fine." He glanced out the kitchen window. "I'd better leave. It's almost dark and you have a barnyard full of critters to feed."

"How about some help?"

"Sorry, I have a date."

Of course. He always had a date. I watched from the top of the stairs while he shooed a turkey off the hood of his Jag and inspected the paint for scratches. Half a minute later he was headed down the lane toward the street. Our conversation had only strengthened my resolve to prove Harry's innocence.

The chores took another forty-five minutes, and by the time I finished, I was hungry again. I settled at my computer with a bag of microwaved kettle corn and a cold beer. Since I'd already met the creepy Underhills from Everlasting Pets, Bonnie's Natural History Museum stalker was next on my list. I decided to hang out there on Saturday morning.

That would leave all day Sunday to pursue other

leads. I was determined to learn the whereabouts of Milton Palmer's ex-wife, Arnetta. She had to be out there somewhere. Palmer might know where she was, but I had no plausible excuse for asking him. He'd been "off on assignment" from the evening news for several days, and that was starting to arouse my curiosity. Maybe it wasn't his spurned wife who I should be looking at. Maybe ol' Milton had carried a grudge all this time. Being in the public eye and all, it must have been pretty embarrassing being dumped by Bonnie. But why kill her now? Their affair had ended almost three years ago.

I booted up the computer and re-checked some people search sites for *Arnetta Palmer*, but came up blank again. I tried a truncated name search using *Arn* Palmer* and got thirty-two hits in the U.S. Most of them turned out to be Arnolds. Had all these people been named after a famous golfer?

There was only one candidate residing in California. An Arnie Palmer lived in Manton, a small mountain community east of Timbergate where the economy was sustained by apple orchards and marijuana farms. It seemed unlikely, but I supposed Arnie could be a woman. I made a note of the address and phone number and tried calling, but without success. No answer, no answering machine.

NINE

Saturday morning I checked my disguise in the mirror. In my shortest skirt, highest heels, blue contact lenses and a blond wig left over from a grad school Halloween party, I was ready to visit the Natural History Museum where Bonnie Beardsley had flirted with her alleged stalker. The odds of running into him, if he existed, were astronomical, but I liked the museum and had nothing better to do.

After an elderly gentleman docent gave me an absurdly detailed lecture on the skeletal structure of turtles, I wandered over to the aquarium's viewing wall to wait for a highly touted visitor attraction: fish feeding time. The gathering crowd squeezed together for a better view of the fishy antics. Feeling slightly claustrophobic, I tried to step back, but whoever was behind me didn't budge. Meanwhile the space in front of me had closed, and I couldn't step forward. The body behind me wasn't quite making contact with my backside, but I definitely felt my personal space being invaded. The miniskirt that barely covered my behind wasn't helping.

A low voice spoke near my right ear. "Awesome creatures, aren't they?"

I responded with a barely perceptible nod of my head. This was creepier than I'd expected. What would I do if this was the stalker?

After a few minutes of watching various forms of marine life snatching and gobbling their breakfast, the crowd dispersed. I wondered if the man behind me would make a move. I didn't have to wonder long.

He stepped alongside me, still watching the fish-viewing wall. I was surprised to see how harmless he looked. Probably in his late thirties, only a couple of inches taller than my five foot four, he was slender, clean-shaven, and handsome verging on pretty. His clothes were Eddie Bauer. His light brown hair was thick and well-cut. The term *metrosexual* came to mind. A straight guy, apparently, but with a flair for grooming and style. And not creepy in the least.

He turned to me. "Hi. Do you come to the museum often?"

"Once in a while," I said.

"Do you live in the area?"

"Uh-huh."

"I hope you won't think I'm too forward," he said, "but I haven't met many people since I moved here. Could I buy you a cup of coffee? Pick your brain about things to do in Timbergate?"

The museum café was a short walk in plain sight of staff and visitors. I figured that was safe enough, so we headed over and found a free table.

"I should introduce myself," he said. "I'm Arnie Palmer. No relation to the golfer. I suck at sports."

Holy crap. Of all the fish exhibits in all the natural history museums in the world, Arnie Palmer had walked into mine. He had to be the Arnie Palmer from Manton who popped up in my online search. And he was a guy, so he sure wasn't Arnetta, but was he Bonnie's stalker?

"And you are…?" he said.

My mind raced as I tried to invent a name for myself. What came out was really stupid.

"Ingrid."

"Ingrid…?"

Damn, I needed a last name. A lock of hair from my wig tickled my cheek.

"Wiggins," I said, feeling a little faint. "Ingrid Wiggins." A waitress came by to take our orders. I asked for coffee and apple pie. Arnie ordered green tea and pecan pie.

"Lots of apples where I live," Arnie said.

"Oh?" I played dumb.

"Manton. Thirty minutes east of here. Up in the pines. Do you know it?"

"I've heard of it."

"Not much to do there, but it's cooler than Timbergate, and the rent's reasonable."

I took a tiny bite of pie and washed it down with coffee. I was torn between the need to know more about this guy and a yearning to get the hell out of there, but there was one question I had to ask.

"We have a newscaster here named Palmer. Are you related?"

"No." He shrugged. "I get that a lot, though. It's a very common name."

True. I'd discovered that during all those people searches.

I glanced at my watch. "You asked about things to do in Timbergate. I have a couple of suggestions, then I have to be going."

"So soon?" His obvious disappointment was flattering, and just short of pathetic.

"We have a community theater, a concert series, a convention center, art exhibits, a sports arena, but you said you suck at sports, so I guess that's out." I took a breath, trying to slow my rapid-fire delivery. "Anyway, you can get more information at the Visitors Bureau. When you leave the museum parking lot, make a right at the intersection. It's just down the street."

"Any singles bars in town?"

"Probably, but I don't do the bar scene, so I'm not a good person to ask." Considering my miniskirt and four-inch heels, he probably found that hard to believe. "It's been nice meeting you, Arnie, but I really have to go." I stood. "I'm meeting my boyfriend for lunch at the gun club. He teaches marksmanship there."

"No problem. In fact, I'd like to meet your boyfriend. I just bought a gun and I could use some pointers. Can I get your phone number? I'd like to follow up on this."

Mr. Harmless just bought a gun? *Great.* "I just moved," I said. "I don't have a new phone number yet."

"No cellphone?"

"Sorry."

He looked disappointed, then brightened. "What's your boyfriend's name? I can call the gun club and ask for him."

Would this never end? "He doesn't like me giving out his name. He's a little paranoid. Besides, anyone at the gun club could help you."

I walked out of the coffee shop, pinched toes screaming in pain, stomach growling protest at the apple pie I'd left behind.

What a fiasco. Ingrid Wiggins with a paranoid, gun-totin' boyfriend. Not the alter ego I'd have imagined for myself. Worse, I had no hard evidence that Arnie Palmer was the museum stalker. And yet, there was the bizarre coincidence of his name. I sensed there was something connecting Arnie to Bonnie Beardsley, but short of seeing him again, I had no idea how to figure out what it was.

Back in Coyote Creek, I started the daily chores at Amah and Jack's house by collecting the mail and paper. The king snake's eyes were cloudy and its skin was dull, which meant it was about to shed and wouldn't need food for several days. Amah's cat stared hungrily at the cockatiel, which was hunched in a corner of its cage like a prisoner on death row. I didn't like the looks of that scenario, so I put the cat in its carrier, put the birdcage in my car, and took them both down the lane to my lonely little apartment where I could keep an eye on them. Truth was, I needed the company.

The llamas wandered over to watch while I lugged everything upstairs, but they lost interest when I didn't offer hay or grain.

The birdcage fit fine on top of my dresser, and the cat took over the futon as if she owned it. I changed into shorts, a T-shirt, and sandals, and made a tuna sandwich. Taking a bite, I picked up the paper. The tuna stuck in my throat when I read the headline: PROMINENT ARCHITECT QUESTIONED IN BEARDSLEY CASE. Heart racing, I scanned the article.

District Attorney Connie Keefer said local architect Harrison Machado, designer and builder of Timbergate's controversial Timber Mountain Mall, is one of several people being interviewed.

When asked if the victim's husband, Dr. Vane Beardsley, was a suspect, she had no comment.

MY PHONE RANG while I was reading the article for the third time. Harry, sounding subdued, said he was on his way over.

I met him downstairs in the stable yard. "I just read the paper. What's going on?"

"Nothing." He pulled a wire stripper from a tool box in his trunk. "I told you Keefer would milk this. She's got no leads, so she's manufacturing news stories out of nothing."

"But it makes you look like a suspect. Can she do that? Isn't that libel?"

"I doubt it, but I'm talking to Abe Edelman on Monday." *His lawyer.*

"Then you *are* worried." Tears stung my eyes.

"Sis, don't get upset. It's just a precaution." He took the stairs to my deck two at a time and went to work on my swamp cooler.

TEN

I HAD BEEN up Sunday morning just long enough to make coffee and fetch the paper when my phone rang. For the first time in days, the Beardsley case was not on the front page. A brief story in the local section recapped earlier accounts and quoted the chief of police saying that all leads were being pursued. The phone rang again, and Bosco, the unhinged cockatiel, responded with an ear-splitting squawk. I guessed the caller would be Amah, checking in from Idaho.

I picked up the phone, trying to shush the crazy bird while I faked a cheerful tone.

Just as I said "Hello," Bosco uttered one of his favorite quotes. "*Go ahead, make my day.*" As usual, he nailed his Dirty Harry impersonation.

The caller wasn't Amah.

"Hey, lady. Was that Bosco, or are you dating Clint Eastwood these days?"

"Nick?" Disoriented, I lost my breath for a moment. Then anger came to my rescue. "What do you want?"

"It's been eight weeks since Paris. I understand why you were upset, but I think you owe me a chance to explain. I thought we might get together and talk things out."

Tears threatened, but I was determined that he wouldn't hear the pain in my voice. I swallowed, took a beat. "What's the point? Aren't you and Rella back together?"

"Look, this is too complicated for the phone. Can I see you?"

"I don't think so, Nick. It's best if we both move on."

I hoped that would be true one day. With Harry in jeopardy and a new job to protect, I didn't have the emotional energy to deal with Nick. I couldn't afford the distraction until the Beardsley case was solved and Harry was in the clear.

"I'm not giving up on us, Aimee. We had something worth fighting for."

"I used to think so." I used to think Nick was the love of my life, but not anymore.

"Then think again. You know where to find me."

Bosco squawked again and boomed out his other favorite epithet in a gravelly voice no one in the family recognized, "*Hit the floor, asshole!*"

I heard Nick's soft laughter in my ear as I hung up.

If it hadn't been for Harry and Jack, I would never have met Nick. They had talked me into taking a gun safety course a few months after I moved home from New Haven. Even Amah was on their side; she'd taken the course several times.

Nick had been one of the volunteer instructors. That's why my lie to Arnie Palmer had come so easily. It might have been the truth if Nick and I were still together.

I'd had misgivings about dating a pilot, but Nick's expertise soon conquered my fear of flying. He conquered the rest of me with hands that could do no wrong and kisses so right that I still missed him every day and every night. We lived together for six months, but things changed between us after Nick's boss, Buck Sawyer, hired Rella Olstad.

Buck, a billionaire philanthropist with a small fleet of airplanes, needed another experienced pilot who could fly jet aircraft. He asked Nick, his chief pilot, if he had any suggestions. Nick recommended Rella, but he neglected to tell me they'd been a couple. Rella filled me in at a company picnic at Buck's house. The Nordic blonde looked down from her six feet in height and, fixing me with her steely blue eyes, assured me she was "no longer hot for Nicky." I'd seen the way she looked at him, and I wasn't sure I believed her. They shared an intimate past and a present that involved putting their lives in each other's hands in the cockpit of a jet plane. How was I supposed to compete with that?

Soon after Rella came on board, my relationship with Nick began to deteriorate. Our last three months together were like hiking up a long, steep trail with blisters on both heels. My twin blisters were jealousy and insecurity. Rella and Nick flew opposite shifts most of the time, and I believed Nick when he said he had recommended her only because she was the best pilot available. Flying together cross-country or overseas, Nick wanted a co-pilot he could count on.

It was Buck Sawyer's week-long trip to Paris that finished things off. Nick and Rella flew Buck there together, but they had nothing to do for a week except wait around in the world's most romantic city until Buck was ready to come home. While Nick wandered Paris with his ex-fighter pilot ex-girlfriend, I sat behind the Reference Desk at the Timbergate County Library answering questions about water levels in a sand slough and praying the hospital library job would come through.

Nick called from Paris every night, but on the last night, he didn't call. I got worried and called his room near midnight Paris time. Rella answered in a whisper clotted with alcohol and sex and told me "Nicky" was asleep and she didn't want to wake him. I hung up in shock. Until Nick, I had never been deeply in love. That phone call had fractured my heart.

I moved out of his apartment and into the llama barn the next day. Within a month I had pulled myself together, but I vowed never to put my heart and soul in the hands of another man the way I had with Nick. Harry told me Nick deserved a chance to explain, but I said it was pointless. No matter what story he came up with, I would have to decide whether I believed him. I wasn't ready to take that chance and risk that kind of pain a second time.

Nick's call derailed my Sunday morning game plan, but with a heroic effort, I put thoughts of him on hold. My love for him was history. My love for my brother was unconditional and forever.

I fed the cat and the bird, then poured a cup of coffee and walked out on the deck to do a head count. Six llamas grazing peacefully, a dozen turkeys pecking and strutting.

Whatever Harry had done with the cooler seemed to be working, even though his repair was makeshift. My original plan for Sunday had been to sleuth out Arnetta Palmer. My run-in with Arnie Palmer at the museum had convinced me that the only person in Sawyer County with a name similar to Arnetta's was a guy. The real Arnetta's whereabouts were still a mystery, and the Internet had been no help. That left a long shot—Milton Palmer himself. I tried the phone book first. There were a lot of Palmers, but he wasn't listed.

I called Vanza Vonderhausen, a friend who wrote romance novels under the pen name, Vanza Von. I remembered Vanza saying that she and Milton Palmer had dated a few times after Bonnie Beardsley dumped him. They had been paired up by a computer dating service for busy professionals. I asked her what she thought of Palmer.

"He was nice," she said, "but no sparks."

"Do you have his phone number?"

"Sure, but why do you want it? You and Nick were great together. And Nick is so hot. If I were you, I'd take him back in a New York minute."

"Nick's too hot for his own good," I said. "I got tired of the competition."

"I think you're nuts, but it's your life."

She read off Palmer's home phone number. "He's kind of sweet if you can get past the toupee. Just don't ask him about his ex."

"Why not?"

"He's not supposed to talk about her. Some privacy thing in their divorce agreement."

"Okay. I appreciate the heads-up."

Intrigued, I considered Vanza's warning. Palmer couldn't talk about his ex, and he sure wasn't going to confess to murdering Bonnie Beardsley, so how was I going to pry any information out of him? I'd have to get creative. I made a few notes so I wouldn't get off track and trip myself up. When I had a workable script, I picked up the phone. Was I calling a killer or a jilted lover with a vengeful ex-wife?

"Palmer residence." The voice that answered on the first ring was young and female. *Oops.* That wasn't in my script.

"Hello," I said. "May I speak to Mr. Palmer?"

"Who's calling?"

"Ingrid Wiggins." I couldn't keep track of more than one alias.

"Just a minute." I heard a muffled, "Dad, it's for you." *His daughter. Back to the script.*

More muffled words. "It's a woman. Wig-something."

"Milton Palmer, can I help you?" I recognized the mellow tones from the evening news.

"Mr. Palmer, I hope you won't find this incredibly forward of me, but I'm interested in computer dating, and a mutual friend suggested I call you to get your opinion on what service to try."

"What friend was that?" He didn't sound annoyed, just curious.

"I'm afraid I promised I wouldn't say. I hope you understand."

"Well, I suppose I do. What is your name?"

"Ingrid Wiggins. I'm new in the area. I was working as a lingerie model in San Francisco, but city life got too stressful. I'm looking for a career change."

"Model? That's...what kind of career change?"

"I'm thinking of opening a massage parlor. I'm very good, and I've saved up quite a bit of money from the modeling."

Milton cleared his throat. "That's wonderful. Did you say you're looking into computer dating?"

"Yes. I'm all alone in new surroundings, and it's so lonely, so difficult to meet someone *simpatico*."

The throat clearing again. "Perhaps we should get

together for coffee. Computer dating can be complicated. I could explain some of the things to watch out
for. Wouldn't want to see you get involved with the
wrong sort."

"Oh. I hadn't thought of that. Would your friend
mind?"

"Friend?"

"The woman who answered your phone."

"Oh. No. That was my daughter. She's visiting from
Miami."

"Miami?" I was about to ask if her mother was in
Miami when I remembered Vanza's advice. *Don't ask
him about his ex.* "Is it difficult for her? Being so far
from family?"

"Not really. She's busy with college. She's attend-
ing the University of Miami in Coral Gables. Making
her old man proud."

Nice, but it wasn't helping me find Arnetta. I needed
an exit line. "Oh, I think I hear someone at my door,
Mr. Palmer. I'm afraid I—"

"Yes, of course," he said. "About the dating service.
When can we get together for a chat?"

"Soon. I'm going out of town for a couple weeks.
May I call you when I return?"

"Please do. I'll be looking forward to it."

"So will I, Milton. Nice talking to you."

Okay. Now I knew the Palmers' daughter was in
college in Florida. Maybe her mother had moved there
after the divorce. That put her a continent away from
the Bonnie Beardsley scandal.

I kept busy until mid-afternoon washing my car and
doing my laundry at Jack and Amah's house. Then I
did the only thing I could think of to keep my mind

off the Beardsley case and Nick's sudden reappearance. I went to the dojo and worked out with anyone who would spar with me. Four hours later, I was tired enough to limp home, shower, and zone out in front of the television with a glass of wine and Amah's peevish cat, Fanny.

ELEVEN

MY SECOND WEEK at Timbergate Medical Center was my first week as a company spy. Simple, really. Observe Beardsley without being too obvious. Report anything suspicious to Jared Quinn.

Orrie Mercer was at his post at the employee entrance when I arrived Monday morning, but he was engrossed in conversation with Maybelline Black. Trading gossip, no doubt. Mercer turned his back and studied the tips of his shoes when he caught sight of me. I breezed by with a quick wave to Maybelline.

A dark, empty library greeted me. Veronica, the orphaned violet, seemed to be thriving on the corner of my desk. The room had an expectant look, like the set of a play before the first act begins. I needed to fill that stage with TMC's doctors and other health professionals, and soon.

I used the first quiet minutes at my desk to make notes: 1. Work up list and budget for core forensic component. 2. Log all library visits and services. 3. Find Arnetta Palmer.

I couldn't help feeling sorry for poor Milton Palmer. After his nasty divorce and Bonnie Beardsley's shabby treatment, he had definitely paid his relationship dues. That didn't mean he hadn't killed Bonnie, but the guy didn't seem like the murdering kind. His shadowy ex-wife, however, moved up a notch on my suspect list.

I looked up from my notes to see Maybelline walk in wearing a smear of persimmon-colored lipstick across her two front teeth.

"Good morning, Miss Machado. Did you have a nice weekend?"

"It was fine. And you?"

"The usual. Bingo on Saturday. Senior brunch at the smorgy on Sunday. I had Swedish meatballs and two helpings of tapioca."

"How nice." *Pitiful.* I figured that would be my fate in a few years if I didn't start working on my social life.

Maybelline pulled a small mirror from her pocket and checked her makeup. I was about to mention the lipstick on her teeth, but she discovered it for herself and attacked it with the tip of her tongue. Satisfied, she put the mirror away.

"Is there anything I can do for you before I start my rounds?"

"Not a thing," I said. "You go ahead."

She began loading her delivery cart with reading material. She had just disappeared with the cart when Dr. Beardsley entered, looking grim. He approached my desk with a wary expression, as if he thought I might be afraid of him, potential murder suspect that he was.

I took the initiative. "Dr. Beardsley, welcome back. I am so sorry for your loss. Please let me know if I can help."

I saw genuine gratitude in his eyes. "Thank you. I'm happy to be back. So sorry about all this uproar. Your first week here and all. It has been…it's been gruesome."

"Are you sure you're ready to come back to work?"

"I must come back. Staying home doing nothing would drive me insane. I'm not scheduling surgeries yet, but I will catch up on my committee work."

He asked if I was happy with Maybelline's help, and I assured him she was doing fine. We compared notes on my progress, and he left for his plastic surgery office across town.

My observations so far were of a man with strong professional values. Vane Beardsley was not only the hospital's chief of staff, he also chaired its Continuing Medical Education Committee. The committee responded to reports of weak areas in the care of hospital patients by providing opportunities for upgrading the doctors' skills. This was usually done by scheduling on-site continuing medical education programs. As was the case in most hospitals, TMC's health sciences librarian served a dual role as coordinator of the medical staff's continuing education department. Quinn had confirmed that among my other duties, I was to help Dr. Beardsley facilitate the CME Committee's efforts.

Some of the minutes I had reviewed led me to believe Vane Beardsley took his work seriously. That was a plus. As for his dark side, the only vice I'd observed was a weakness for pretty young women.

An hour passed without interruption before my phone rang. Jared Quinn wanted to get together. Beardsley was back at work, and Quinn wanted a report. He suggested lunch at Casa Loco.

Before Nick's call on Sunday, the thought of another lunch with Quinn might have set my pulse racing. Now it just depressed me. The only attractive men in my life were off-limits. I saw my future in line behind Maybelline at the smorgy, hoping for second helpings of tapioca. No, that was wrong. Even Maybelline might have a man in her life. She and Orrie Mercer had seemed engrossed in each other when I noticed them earlier.

Maybelline returned from her book delivery run with letters and newspapers she'd retrieved from the hospital mail room. The library subscribed to half a dozen newspapers, including the *Timbergate Times-Record*, which carried a new headline: SEARCH WARRANTS ISSUED IN BEARDSLEY CASE. The article didn't name names, but warrants had been issued for searches of the homes and vehicles of at least two individuals.

I called Harry's cellphone. He didn't answer, so I left an urgent message: *Call me.*

Next I called Hannah. Because of her forensic sketches, she knew people on the inside. I had to learn more about Bonnie Beardsley's autopsy. What had prompted the warrants? I asked if she'd seen the newspaper. She had. I told her we needed to talk, and she suggested we meet for lunch.

"I can't. I'm supposed to have lunch at Casa Loco with Jared Quinn."

"Who's Jared Quinn?"

"TMC's administrator."

"Oh. The big boss. Then do lunch with him at Casa Loco, but come by my office first." She sounded worried.

I called Quinn, saying I needed a bit of exercise and wanted to walk the three blocks to Casa Loco. He agreed to meet me there at twelve thirty. Hannah was waiting for me in her basement office when I arrived at noon.

"You can never, ever tell anyone about this." Her voice was low, her blue eyes intense.

"Of course not."

"If it was anyone but Harry, I'd never do this."

"What is it?"

"I overheard some talk about Bonnie's autopsy. Apparently there was evidence of recent sexual activity."

"She was raped?"

"That wasn't clear. Apparently it could have been consensual. Even the bruises on her neck might have been caused during rough sex play."

"Her death might have been caused by rough sex gone wrong? Why are you telling me this? Surely you don't think Harry—"

"Of course not, but there is something worrisome about the bruises."

"What about them?"

"The medical examiner thinks they were inflicted by someone left-handed."

"Oh, God. Harry's—"

"A lefty, I know. Don't panic. Think of all the left-handed people we know."

"Is one of the search warrants for Harry?"

"I don't know. All I know is the theory about the bruises. You'll have to ask Harry about the warrant."

I left Hannah's office and went upstairs to the restaurant. Growing up with Harry had raised my awareness of lefties. They were everywhere. Jack was a lefty. Hannah's older sister and father were both lefties. It didn't mean anything, really. Nevertheless, Marco Bueller must be jumping for joy. Harry's good left hand had wreaked havoc on Marco's brother. Now Connie Keefer, the DA, had Harry in her sights.

I waited for Quinn in Casa Loco's foyer, watching

with envy the carefree lunch patrons chatting happily while they walked to their tables.

"Aimee, I hope I'm not late." Quinn came through the restaurant's front door wearing khaki slacks and a short-sleeved shirt in a subtle shade of olive green. On his lean, lithe body, casual looked better than a tux.

I mumbled something about having just arrived, and we followed the hostess to a table. I arranged my napkin and pretended to study the menu while I waited for Quinn to break the ice.

"See anything you like?" he asked.

"The Caesar salad looks good."

Quinn gave our orders to a waitress who blushed prettily when he smiled at her. Hoping food might distract me, I bit into a chip loaded with salsa. I couldn't ponder Harry's dilemma, and I didn't want to think lustful thoughts about Jared Quinn, the man who was second on my personal *least eligible* list, after Nick of course. The heat level of the salsa was intense. I managed to swallow it, but nearly choked in the process, provoking a coughing fit that left my eyes watering.

By the time our food arrived I had managed to convince Quinn that I didn't need medical attention. What happened next drove every other thought from my mind.

Quinn picked up his fork...with his left hand.

TWELVE

THE CASA'S SPECIAL Caesar crab salad languished on my plate while I watched Quinn fork into his enchilada verde. Definitely a lefty.

"Is your salad okay?" he asked.

"It's fine." I managed to chew a small mouthful and wash it down with a sip of water.

"So, give me your thoughts on Dr. Beardsley," Quinn said. "How did he seem this morning?"

"He was subdued, said the past week had been gruesome." I squirmed in my chair. *Tattletale at work.* "He said he isn't up to doing surgery yet, but he wanted to catch up on committee work to keep his mind off things."

"That's good, I suppose. Although you'd think he'd take more time off. It's only been a week since he lost his wife."

"They say we each grieve in our own way." I poked at my salad so I wouldn't have to look Quinn in the eye. My guess was that Beardsley's grief was mixed with a big dose of gratitude. Whoever killed his wife had saved him from a scheming gold digger with a roving eye.

"You're not eating," Quinn said. "I hope you're not one of those women who starve themselves for the sake of fashion."

"Not me." I managed another mouthful.

"Good. I saw too much of that in Paris. Young women walking around like stick figures because that's what they saw in magazines. What a waste."

"A waste?"

"Of fine French cuisine."

"You lived in Paris?"

"Not exactly, but I spent some time there. My former wife was Parisian. That was several years ago." He changed the subject abruptly, asking if I'd like coffee and signaling a passing waiter.

He didn't elaborate on his marriage, but I filed the disclosure away for further speculation. All along I'd been thinking of Quinn as a confirmed bachelor. Now there was a former wife and a life in Paris. What else would I learn about the man?

Quinn had an afternoon appointment across town, so he dropped me off at the hospital on his way.

"Thanks for your help, and keep up the good work." He gave my shoulder a tentative pat and I tried not to flinch.

"No problem." My shoulder burned from that light touch. It was sad, really. Everything I liked about Quinn was tainted now by the way he had picked up his fork.

If anyone knew about Quinn's past life, it would be my favorite gossip. Back in the library, I called the auxiliary director's office to ask for a phone number for Maybelline, but I was told she had no number on file.

No message from Harry, so I went to work on a list of forensic journals I wanted to discuss with Dr. Beardsley. Their subscription prices ranged all over the place from a few hundred dollars to more than two thousand dollars a year. The average online article could cost between thirty-five and forty-five dollars, so requests for multiple articles for a particular case could quickly become prohibitively expensive. I suspected this project was going to involve more work and more expense that Beardsley had anticipated.

With that done, the rest of the afternoon lay ahead of me in a jumble of routine busywork. None of it could distract me from worrying about Harry. I went to the library's tiny break room and made a fresh pot of strong coffee. Most of an hour and three cups of coffee later, Harry finally called.

"Sis, what's going on?"

"Where have you been? I called hours ago."

"Marathon meeting with the Planning Commission. I didn't check messages until just now."

"Have you read today's paper?"

"Haven't had time."

"It's about search warrants. Have you been served?"

"Let's not talk about this on the phone."

"Can you come out to the ranch after work?"

"It's going to be late. We're working overtime tonight."

"How late?"

He said he could make it by ten o'clock, and ended the call with a hasty, "Gotta go, Sis."

I toyed with the idea of leaving work early. With the amount of caffeine I had on board, nothing I did in the next half hour was going to make much sense anyway. I checked emails one last time. Only one message required immediate action. It was from Nick.

Have dinner with me. I'll pick you up at work at five.

I looked at the clock: four forty. I deleted Nick's message, shut down the computers and hit the door at ten minutes to five. When I got to the employees' lot, Nick's hybrid SUV was parked next to the old Buick I had inherited from Amah. He was leaning against his front fender, looking better than my best memory of him. I could have ignored the fair hair and powerful shoulders, but the look in his blue-gray eyes stopped me short.

"Dammit, Nick. Are you stalking me? I could have you arrested."

"Go ahead." He laughed. "But Harry would bail me out, so why bother?"

"Who told you where I work? I've only been here for a week, and Harry wasn't supposed—"

"Not Harry. I ran into your writer friend, Vanza."

"I should have known. If I agree to have dinner with you, will you leave me alone?"

"Depends."

"On what?"

"Let's not talk here." He opened his passenger door. "Come on, get in."

"Give me one good reason."

"Harry."

My heart knocked. "What about him?"

"I'll explain over dinner."

"Okay," I said. "For my brother."

Nick saw me wipe at a tear and took me in his arms. I should have pulled away, but the tender way he held me said this wasn't about sex, it was about comfort.

"Don't turn me away now, Aimee. Reject me if you want, but let me be here for you and Harry." The faint lime scent of his aftershave triggered a flood of erotic memories. Another minute and I'd have melted in his arms, devouring him with kisses.

"Excuse me, folks." Jared Quinn's voice snapped me out of my trance. "Oh, hello, Aimee."

Phenomenal bad timing. While I'd been wrapped in Nick's arms, I hadn't noticed Quinn walking toward us.

"Mr. Quinn. Is something wrong?"

"Nothing major. Security has been hounding me about unauthorized parking, so I thought I'd take a walk through the employee lots. When I saw a car in the employee lot without a permit, I thought I'd have a look. Now that I know he's a friend of yours...."

"Nick Alexander." Nick put out his hand.

"Jared Quinn." Quinn shook the offered hand.

Nick took a step toward his car. "I apologize for the parking violation, Mr. Quinn. I had urgent business with Aimee and didn't want to miss her. It won't happen again."

Quinn's grin stopped just short of malicious. "Just don't let our security crew catch you. They're not as understanding as I am."

"Thanks. I'll remember that."

"Aimee, I'll see you tomorrow," Quinn said. "Mr. Alexander, nice meeting you." He walked on, whistling softly. His story about checking on parking violations seemed lame, but I let it go for the moment.

"Nice guy," Nick said. "He your boss?"

"Sort of. He's the administrator."

"Ah, the big boss. Seems to like you."

I ignored that. "Let's get this dinner over with. You said it had something to do with Harry."

I followed Nick across town to an eatery called Stone Soup. It wasn't generally known, but the place had been established to provide re-entry jobs to graduates of local drug rehab programs. Nick's boss, Buck

Sawyer, had donated seed money for the project. The décor was an eclectic combination of booths, tables, and chairs donated by restaurants on their way up or on their way out of business. As a condition of employment, all of the employees were enrolled in a food service program at the local community college.

We gave our orders to a tattoo-covered waiter with a shaved head whose name, according to the tag on his shirt, was Gore. He looked as if he could bench press a cement truck. On his recommendation, we each ordered one of the specials. I chose the avocado shrimp bisque, and Nick settled on the lobster chowder.

As soon as our bruiser of a waiter left, I pounced. "Okay, what's this about Harry?"

"He asked me for backup."

"What does that mean?"

"It means he's worried. He wants to make sure there's someone to look out for you in case—"

"Oh, damn. In case he's arrested? Is that what you mean?" Tears flooded my eyes just as Gore appeared with our soups.

He placed the bowls in front of us. "Everything all right here?"

"Fine," I sniffled.

Gore gave Nick a threatening look. The coiled snake on his right bicep undulated. "You sure, Miss?"

"Yes," I said. "Something's in my eye. I'll be fine."

With one more glare at Nick, the tattooed man took a couple of steps backward, turned and walked slowly away.

"Holy crap," Nick said. He wasn't easily intimidated, but he clearly didn't relish the idea of tangling with Gore. If I hadn't been so scared for Harry, I'd have laughed.

"Forget about him," I said. "If I don't get some straight answers from you, you'll wish that over-protective waiter was your only problem." I took a sip of my soup, expecting it to taste like bilge. It was divine.

"Here's the deal," Nick said. "Harry told me that your grandmother and Jack are out of town and you don't have anyone else... I mean, he asked me to keep an eye on you in case this Beardsley thing gets out of hand."

Great, Harry had portrayed me to Nick as Aimee the helpless little wallflower, implying there were no men in my life, as if I hadn't had a date in the three months Nick and I had been apart. It was true, but that was no excuse for his telling Nick. Once Harry was out of danger, I'd make him pay for that.

"How do you propose to keep an eye on me if I don't want you to? And what about your job? How can you be here for me if you're flying?"

"I'm on paid leave. Buck's not doing any trips this month that Rella can't handle on her own." Nick hesitated for a moment, probably regretting his mention of Rella, then went on. "Aimee, with any luck, the truth will come out and all of this will go away. Maybe I shouldn't have said anything. Harry didn't want me to tell you he's worried, but I owed you that much."

Tears burned my eyes again. I told him what Hannah had said about the bruises on Bonnie's neck and the theory about rape or rough sex gone wrong. "They think whoever was involved was left-handed."

"Damn," Nick said. "Like Harry."

I nodded. "I'm afraid they're going to arrest him. I can't bear to think of him in jail."

"Then let me help."

"I don't trust you anymore."

"But you never let me explain. Why?"

"Because I'm afraid I won't believe you."

He reached across the table, took my hand, traced his thumb across my knuckles with a light caress. "Before the fiasco in Paris, had I ever done anything to betray your trust?"

I allowed myself to make eye contact. He held my gaze until I felt faint. "No, never."

"Thank you. That's all the collateral I have to offer. Will it do for now?"

I pulled my hand away. "It will for as long as Harry's in trouble and needs your help. I'll do whatever it takes to keep him from going to prison."

"That won't happen. And when this is over, you and I can—"

"No, I'm afraid we can't."

"We'll see." Nick signaled for the check.

THIRTEEN

LUNCH WITH QUINN and the early dinner with Nick left me feeling bloated and burned out, in no mood for a late-night confrontation with Harry. His rapping on my door startled Fanny. She flew off my lap and leapt at the door, hissing. As I let Harry in, the cat shot out into the night.

Harry glanced at his watch. "Sorry I'm late," he said. "Helluva day."

"Tell me about it." I poured myself a glass of wine. "Want some?"

"Will I need it?"

"What's that supposed to mean?"

"You summoned me. I assume you're going to rant about something."

I poured him a glass. "Let's sit." I curled up on the daybed.

He took the old rocker. "Okay, hit me."

"Maybe we should watch the eleven o'clock news first. It'll be on in a minute. Let's see if your name comes up in the Bonnie Beardsley segment."

"Damn reporters. They actually came to the construction site today. I had to call security to get rid of them." He picked up the remote and clicked on the TV.

The lead story concerned an air tanker that had missed its target, a small fire in the hills east of town. Its load of retardant had landed on the freeway, caus-

ing a commuter's nightmare. Traffic on I-5 was backed
up in both directions for miles. Aerial shots of vehicles
shrouded in orange retardant were meant to convey the
seriousness of the accident, but the visuals were unin-
tentionally comic. The reporter on the scene seemed to
be having trouble keeping a straight face. Back in the
studio, the only mention of Bonnie Beardsley's case
was a brief comment from District Attorney Keefer,
asking the news media to refrain from publicizing further details about the case.

The rest of the newscast was the usual depressing
fare: petty theft, an attempted rape, and a small-time
meth lab bust, complete with toddlers taken to Child
Protective Services while their repulsive parents were
booked into the county jail. When the meteorologist
came on, Harry clicked the TV off. Anyone in the
county could predict hot and dry.

"Okay, Sis, let's get this over with. What's important
enough for you to summon me at this hour?"

"Shall I start with a search warrant, or shall we talk
about Nick Alexander?"

"No warrant so far."

"Really? I was so afraid you'd be the first on their
list."

"I'm pretty sure they'd start with her husband, but
even then, they have to show a judge probable cause.
I don't know about Beardsley, but they certainly don't
have anything to justify searching my place. And if
they did do a search, there's nothing to find. I didn't
kill Bonnie. Her blood isn't smeared on my walls."

"They might find something else. Hair or a fingerprint—"

"They already know she was at my place on Friday

night. If they find evidence of that, so what? You're getting carried away, Aimee. I know you're putting together a forensic collection for the hospital, but that doesn't make you a crime scene investigator."

"No, but it does give me a pretty good idea what the crime scene people will be looking for, and I know forensic evidence can be manipulated. What we don't know is what kind of bogus evidence might turn up— or what might be ignored once it gets to Keefer's investigator. Tell me that doesn't worry you."

"I don't like it, but that doesn't scare me nearly as much as you do. If you don't stop trying to protect me, you're going to get in over your head."

"Is that why you sicced Nick on me? To play body-guard?"

"What are you talking about?"

"I had dinner with him tonight. The conversation was fascinating."

"So, you had dinner. That's great. Are you two getting back together?"

"No, dammit. That's over. He's never going to be your brother-in-law."

Harry stood, took my hand and pulled me out of my chair. "Sis, I have to go. I get that you won't take Nick back. I think you're wrong, but I get it. At least let him keep an eye on you."

"Why? You're the one who's in trouble."

He studied me for a moment and heaved a world-weary sigh. "I hate telling you this, but you're worried about the wrong Bueller. Marco may be after my ass, but his little brother Tango has been paroled, and I'm afraid he'll come after yours."

I felt a distinct clunk somewhere in my abdomen. I

think it was my heart dropping all the way to my pelvis. My wannabe rapist Tango Bueller was out of jail? That was tantamount to turning loose a rabid dog.

"What about the other guy?"

"Dead. A gang hit in prison."

"How long has Tango been out?"

"A couple of weeks. I heard about it this afternoon."

"Is he here? In Timbergate?"

"I don't know. But you'd better forget about that little kid you hurt on the school bus. So you twisted his finger...big deal. He was bullying you, and you taught him a lesson."

"More than twisted. I broke it."

"You were in second grade. That's ancient history. You need to get over it and get serious about your workouts. You're dealing with grownups now."

"What's that supposed to mean?"

"You know what it means. You've been going through the motions at judo tournaments for years, but you're still a sissy when it comes to a real fight."

"You don't know that. I've never needed to fight. The Tango Bueller incident doesn't count. He caught me off guard."

"It might count next time. You'd damn well better decide what you will and won't do."

"Like what?"

"If he comes after you again, you're going to have to hurt him. Are you ready to gouge his eyes out if that's what it takes?"

"Of course." But the thought of gouging eyes from their sockets made me feel faint. I left the table and took our wine glasses to the sink so Harry wouldn't notice.

He went to use the bathroom while I was rinsing the glasses in hot water. I reached for a dishtowel hanging on a rack near the door. I stopped in mid-reach when I saw the doorknob jiggle. I stood very still, holding my breath. Call out for Harry? Find a weapon? The knob jiggled again, more forcefully. What kind of prowler would be that obvious?

When Harry came out of the bathroom, I put my finger to my lips to shush him and pointed toward the doorknob. It jiggled again, then we heard a plaintive *meow* just outside the door. Fanny! Harry's face broke into a grin. He cracked the door open, and Fanny charged in with a disgusted cat noise somewhere between *meow* and *it's about damn time*.

I'd forgotten about the old firewood box next to the door. A perfect height for a smart cat that knew tapping on a doorknob would magically cause a door to open.

After Harry left, I locked up, poured another glass of wine, and crawled into bed with Fanny. While I waited for sleep, sinister visions of the Bueller brothers danced in my head. Spit-and-polished Marco with the buzz cut, and Tango, the loose-limbed, mop-haired gypsy.

FOURTEEN

TUESDAY MORNING BEGAN with a sunrise assault on my sleep-deprived senses. Jack's tom turkeys strutted below my window, greeting the day with a cacophony of alpha male gobbling that set my ears ringing. Fanny jumped on the bed and tried to roust me by kneading my back with surprising force. I enjoyed the massage until she worked her way south and sank her needle-sharp toenails into my left butt cheek. I yelped and jumped out of bed, vowing to clip her claws as soon as I got home from work. She dropped to the floor un-fazed, shook her great gray plume of a tail, and stalked off toward her food dish.

I dressed for the day's predicted heat in a cotton shift and low-heeled sandals. No worries about get-ting too chilly at work; the air conditioning was as old as everything else in the antiquated building that housed the library.

It took my entire allotment of self-discipline to put my personal troubles on hold once I reached the hos-pital. The possibility of Harry being arrested took first place on my list of worries, but Tango Bueller's parole came in a close second. A shiver crossed my skin, raising pimply flesh on my arms every time I thought about him.

I passed the main parking lot and checked the small lot closer to my building, where I got lucky and found an empty space. When I reached the library door, my luck soured. Orrie Mercer was manning the entrance. What was he doing there? Then I recalled seeing him with Maybelline. Maybe they were an item and he'd requested a duty change to be closer to her. Whatever the reason, he was the least of my worries, so I acknowledged his presence with a nod and went inside.

Lola was due at nine o'clock. That gave me an hour to get organized. I started by checking messages. The first one I heard took my breath away.

"Hi, *Ingrid*. This is Arnie Palmer. I enjoyed meeting you at the museum last Sunday. I'll bet you're surprised to hear from me. I understand about the fake name; a woman can't be too careful these days. I hope you'll call me." He left a number with a Manton prefix.

I was beyond surprised. Stunned was more like it. How had he found me? I called the gun club and asked for Russell West, who had worked there for years.

"Yeah," Russell said, "a new guy just joined the club. We got to yakking, you know, about women who shoot. I told him you were the only woman I knew who had dated one of our instructors. But I said your name was Aimee Machado, not this Ingrid chick he was looking for."

"Did you tell him where I worked?"

"Nope. I said I didn't even know if you were still in town. Did I screw up? He seemed like an okay guy, you know? Kind of puny and harmless."

I reassured Russell he'd done nothing wrong, and hung up. Add Arnie Palmer to my list of things to worry about. He might be smitten with *Ingrid*, or he might be Bonnie Beardsley's stalker. Possibly both. He certainly had gone to a lot of trouble to track me down.

My second message was from my romance author friend Vanza Von. No doubt she was curious about Nick and me, since she was the traitor who had told Nick where I worked. I called her back, planning to give her some grief. She stopped me before I warmed to the subject.

"Listen, girl, you need to cut Nick some slack. He's one of the good guys."

"How would you know?" I said. "All the men in your books are macho misogynistic narcissists."

"I may write trash, but I've done my research. My heroes are domineering and powerful, sultry and charming. Granted, they're the worst husband material a woman could dig out from under a rock, but that's what my readers want."

"What's your point?"

"Nick's a hunk, and definitely eye candy, but trust me, sweetie, he's the real deal. Give him a chance."

"Is this why you called?"

"Partly. The other reason is Milton Palmer. What's with him?"

I'd almost forgotten about the jilted news anchor. "What about him?"

"Haven't you heard? He's in your hospital."

I nearly dropped the phone. "What? Why?"

"If I knew that, I wouldn't be calling you. Last I heard, you were thinking about dating him."

I told Vanza that hadn't worked out and got off the phone.

When I checked the hospital's online roster showing the day's new admissions, there he was: Milton Palmer. His room number indicated he was on the surgical floor. Just then Lola appeared, tiny and hunched, her white crown of hair looking freshly coiffed. She wore lipstick in a cheerful shade of red, and her cheeks were lightly blushed.

"Morning, Aimee. What lovely tasks do we have today?"

I pointed out a stack of new journals to be shelved. She went off into the stacks humming a Stockwell tune while I focused on the calendar on my computer screen. It highlighted my morning appointment with Dr. Beardsley—the one I would be late for if I didn't make tracks. Beardsley was waiting for me in a small conference room adjacent to Jared Quinn's office. He greeted me with a look that suggested he was envisioning me in a kimono. It might have been my imagination, but I wasn't seeing much evidence of grief in this man. He showed no sign that he was worried about the police investigation, either.

We took care of library business in five minutes. He listened to my proposals about the forensic collection and how best to spend the allotted funds, nodded enthusiastically and approved everything I suggested. Good news, as I could make headway with the job I'd been hired to do. I was crafting a graceful exit line when Jared Quinn materialized in the open doorway. His Cheshire cat qualities were unsettling. He seemed to materialize as if by magic, and his quizzical smile lingered after he was gone.

"How are you two this morning?"

"Jared, come in," Beardsley said.

"Don't want to interrupt."

"Nonsense. We're finished with our little meeting."

"That's right." I rose from my chair. "I was just leaving, so if you two have business—"

"Nothing like that," Quinn said. "Just my morning rounds. Would you like to walk with me, Aimee? You don't get to spend much time in this building. I'd like to give you a tour of the tower."

"I should be getting back to the library. Lola may need me."

"Lola is a capable woman." Quinn smiled at the thought.

"You know her?"

"I know all the volunteers. I attend their monthly meetings. You would be surprised how much I learn about this place."

I tagged along while Quinn strode the halls looking in on various department heads, offering upbeat comments, asking about families, dropping a compliment here and there and introducing me along the way. No wonder he was a popular administrator. I had no idea he put such stock in building morale.

On the surgical floor I spotted Milton Palmer's room number. It was a single room, and the door was closed. As we walked toward the nurses' station, I heard snippets of a conversation, which I assumed concerned Palmer.

"Toupee glue? Hair grower?"

"...scalp was covered in boils."

"...debridement took two hours."

Quinn leaned on the counter. "Hello there. How's it going this morning?"

"Not bad," the older nurse replied. "Our celebrity is pretty uncomfortable, but we're keeping him medicated."

"Good. Refer any inquiries about his condition to Public Relations."

"We know," the nurses answered in unison.

"You do good work," Quinn said. The nurses beamed.

I left Quinn to finish his rounds and went back to the library where I pondered what to do about the message from Arnie Palmer, the man I suspected of being Bonnie Beardsley's stalker. After a moment, I realized the answer was obvious. I'd already told him I had a boyfriend. I called the number he'd left, praying I'd get a message machine. Another prayer went unanswered.

"Arnie Palmer here." My day for Palmers, but the name was common, and Arnie was obviously no relation to the pitiful patient. He sounded pleasantly surprised even before I spoke, as if he didn't get many calls. Words like *stalker* and *pervert* spun in my mind, but they just wouldn't come to rest on this innocuous but persistent man.

"Arnie," I said. "This is Aimee Machado. How clever of you to find me."

"Then you're not upset?"

"Of course not, I'm flattered."

"Whew, that's a relief. I'm not too good at this yet."

"Good at what?"

"Meeting women. I guess I'm what you'd call a late bloomer."

"Here's the thing, Arnie. You may recall my telling you I have a boyfriend. The one who works at the gun club?"

"Yes, I do. But let me tell you why I called you earlier. I have tickets to the ballet tomorrow night. *Giselle*. I was hoping you might know someone who would like to join me."

It was my turn to be disappointed. I adore ballet.

Nick hates ballet. And worse yet, Nick wasn't really my boyfriend; therefore, there was no reason I shouldn't go with Arnie, except that he might be a stalker and/or a murderer.

But then maybe a date with Arnie wasn't such a bad idea. How could I assess him as a suspect if I didn't learn more about him? Like Russell West at the gun club had said, he seemed puny and harmless.

"You know, if we make it a platonic thing, I'm sure my boyfriend wouldn't mind. That is, if you need someone to use that extra ticket."

"Really? That would be wonderful. I mean, great. Platonic it is. Tell me where you live and I'll pick you up. We can have dinner first."

"Um, that might be pushing it. How about I meet you at the Civic Center? What time does the ballet start?"

"Eight. Meet me in the lobby about seven thirty?"

"Sounds perfect." I jotted a note on my desk calendar.

"Right. Then…goodbye for now." He sounded pensive, a little sad, and anything but menacing. I considered the odds of being attacked while surrounded by balletomanes and decided they were slim to none. On the other hand, this was a chance to find out whether Arnie was Bonnie's museum stalker, and I would get to see *Giselle* in the bargain.

"I finished shelving the journals, Miss Machado. Do you have any special tasks for me this morning?" I looked up from my desk to see Lola smiling at me. The smile told me she had overheard me making the ballet date.

"No, Lola, nothing special."

"All right, then, I'll just do some mending." She went to work on repairing textbooks with loose pages. The mending skills she had acquired during her long-time career at the county library still served her well.

FIFTEEN

LOLA LEFT AT NOON, and I spent the rest of my workday on small but critical details only a librarian could love. Harry's dilemma, Tango's parole, and my date with Arnie Palmer vied for my attention. There was nothing I could do about any of them at the moment, but Milton Palmer's proximity could not be ignored. If only I could drop in on him. But how? Use my Ingrid persona? Call him expressing concern? No. Ingrid had told him she was leaving town.

I couldn't afford to miss the opportunity, so I closed the library at five o'clock and trekked to the third floor of the main tower where pre- and post-surgery patients were housed. Celebrity or no, as soon as Palmer's IV line was pulled, he'd be discharged. Health insurers have a reputation as heartless bean counters for a reason.

When I reached Palmer's room, I squared my shoulders and stepped inside. A young brunette woman sat on a chair next to his bed holding his hand. Although I was sure we'd never met, she looked familiar.

"Hello," I said. "I'm Aimee Machado, TMC's librarian."

The slender woman stood and smiled, showing a dimple in her right cheek. "I'm Penny Palmer." *The voice on the phone. His daughter.*

"I hope I'm not interrupting," I directed my words to Palmer, whose head was swathed in white bandages. The rest of him was covered by white sheets. *The Mummy Returns*.

Palmer slurred, "Iz ah righ."

Penny murmured, "Excuse me. I need to make a call."

She left me alone with a heavily medicated Milton Palmer, so I decided to go for it. Chances were good he'd never remember I'd visited him.

"Mr. Palmer? Would you like me to bring you something to read? We have a nice collection of bestsellers in the hospital library."

He turned toward my voice, but stared through me at something only he could see. "Netta? That you? So…sorry."

Netta? That had to be his wife, Arnetta, whose revenge for his adultery had been a bitter legal battle over their property settlement. According to Harry, she got the lion's share, and yet the man was still racked with guilt.

Penny Palmer returned to the room. She bore only a slight resemblance to her father, but she definitely looked familiar. She sat next to him and nodded with relief when he closed his eyes and slipped off to sleep.

"It was nice of you to come by." She patted his shoulder. "Dad's been through so much."

I was touched by her concern for him. "Have you had any dinner?"

She shrugged, looked embarrassed. "I don't think so. It's been a long day. I ate a vending machine snack while he was in surgery… I mean, I guess it wasn't an operation."

"Casa Loco is close," I said. "Do you like Mexican food?"

"I'm not very hungry."

"You need to keep up your strength. Are you the only caregiver your father has?"

"Yes, at the moment."

"What about your mother?" I faked ignorance of their family situation.

"No, she's...not available."

Penny Palmer's reluctance reminded me of what Vanza had said. There was some condition in the Palmers' legal agreement prohibiting them from talking about the circumstances surrounding their divorce.

"I didn't mean to pry," I said.

"I wish I *could* talk to someone." Penny's eyes filled. "It's so hard, loving both of my parents, seeing what's happened to them."

Wicked anticipation sat on my right shoulder and guilty conscience on my left. Blessed with loving, happy parents myself, I truly felt sad for this girl. And I wanted to know more. *Needed to know.*

"Let's get you away from here for a while. I'm guessing your father will be out for hours."

The Casa dinner crowd was light when we arrived at six. We were seated right away. The waiter brought our chips and salsa and took our orders—two Caesar salads with shrimp—in less than ten minutes.

Penny picked at her food, sighing occasionally. She didn't offer conversation. I decided I'd get nowhere without some gentle prodding.

"How long can you stay with your father?"

She looked confused. "What do you mean?"

Oops. I wasn't supposed to know anything about her. Milton had told *Ingrid* that his daughter was going to college in Florida, but neither he nor his daughter had told me.

"I thought I'd heard you were living out of the area."

"I was here on school break from the University of Miami when this happened. I brought him to the emergency room. He was so miserable, his scalp was all broken out in those…it was so…." She looked down at the fleshy pink shrimp curled on her salad. Her face went pale and she pushed her plate away. I did the same.

"It's going to be okay, you know. He'll be better soon and you can go back to school." I took a chance. "Does your mother live with you?"

"I live in Coral Gables, where the campus is. Mom lived with me at first, right after they separated."

I waited for her to explain. She nibbled on the edge of a chip. The devil on my left shoulder prodded. I felt the pitchfork jabbing me in the neck. *Ask her. Ask her.*

"Is she still in Florida?"

Penny looked surprised. "Who?"

"Your mother."

"I'm not supposed to say where she's living."

"Oh. I'm so sorry." A flush of guilt burned my cheeks. The angel on my right lit up with approval. "I shouldn't have pried. It's just that you said earlier you wished you had someone to talk to."

"Mother's not a bad person, you know. Not like the gossip that went around back then."

"I wasn't living here then. I didn't hear it."

"That selfish, greedy woman started it. She broke up their marriage, and then she said terrible, untrue things about my mother."

"Are you talking about Dr. Beardsley's wife?"

"Yes. The second one. The one who's dead. You

should ask the first Mrs. Beardsley what she thought of her replacement. Lorraine Beardsley and my mother were both victims, and who knows how many other lives that hateful woman ruined? I'm not surprised someone killed her."

At this point I hoped Penny Palmer had a good alibi, because my suspect list was already crowded with people who had it in for Bonnie Beardsley.

"Even so, it must have been a shock to your father."

"It was. He called me and I flew out here the next morning."

So Penny was in Florida when Bonnie died. Cross her off the suspect list. Penny was anxious to get back to the hospital, so I asked for our check.

When we reached Palmer's room, a uniformed policeman stood guarding his door. Penny spotted him and murmured, "Oh, no."

SIXTEEN

THE OFFICER STANDING outside the door to Palmer's room crossed his arms on his chest and blocked our way. "Sorry, ladies. You can't go in there right now."

Penny's eyes filled with tears. "What's wrong? Has something happened to my father?"

"Nothing like that. He's being interviewed. You can go in when we're finished."

Penny's eyes widened, panic dilating her pupils. "Interviewed about what?"

"Who authorized this?" I asked. The officer didn't answer.

Penny stepped up to the nurses' station across the corridor and demanded to speak to the administrator immediately.

The nurse picked up her phone. I couldn't hear what she said, but she looked determined. She put the phone down and addressed Penny. "Mr. Quinn will be here right away."

I put an arm around Penny's shoulders. "Try not to worry."

"My father would never hurt anyone. This is crazy."

I reached in my purse. "Here's my card. Call me at my office if you need anything at all." I wasn't keen on explaining why I had paid a visit to Milton Palmer. With luck, I'd be gone by the time Quinn arrived. My spying was supposed to be limited to observing Dr. Beardsley.

At the elevator I pushed the down button and turned back to give Penny a wave and a reassuring smile. The doors slid open, and I stood face to face with Quinn.

"Aimee," he said.

"Mr. Quinn."

"Jared," he corrected. "What brings you here at this hour?"

"Visiting a friend." I stepped into the elevator.

"Can I keep you for a few minutes?"

"Sure," I said. Stuck, I stepped out and followed him. He went straight to the nurse in charge.

"What's the problem?"

"Palmer's daughter. She asked for you." The woman nodded toward Penny, who was slumped in a chair outside her father's door. The powerfully built officer stood rigid beside her, arms crossed, eyes fixed on an imaginary horizon.

Quinn walked over to Penny and introduced himself. She stood up, a spark of hope in her eyes.

"This officer won't let me see my father."

"Would you like me to go in?" Quinn said. "See how much longer this will take?"

"Yes, please."

The officer side-stepped until he stood blocking the door.

"You can't go in there, sir. This is a police investigation."

Quinn pointed to his ID badge. "You people are here at my discretion. I suggest you step out of my way."

"Please," Penny interrupted. "Please tell them to

leave my father alone. He's sick, and he's on heavy medication. How can they question him that way?"

"She makes an excellent point," Quinn said. "When I was asked about interviewing this patient, I expected to be consulted beforehand."

The door to Palmer's room opened and Marco Bueller stepped out and addressed the guard.

"What's all the commotion out here?" I backed against the wall and turned my face away. It was no good; he spotted me. "What's she doing here?"

"She works here," Quinn said. "Are you the investigating officer?"

"No, but...." I saw Marco wondering if I knew he wasn't allowed to work the Beardsley case. Saw him struggling to come up with an excuse for being there.

"Well?" Quinn said. "Why are you here?"

"It was a mix-up," Marco said. "I was asked to fill in at the last minute and didn't realize this wasn't one of my cases."

"So we're done here, right?" Quinn said. "You and your officer are leaving?"

"Right." Marco tilted his head at the officer guarding Palmer's door. They began walking toward the elevators.

"Just a minute," Quinn called after Marco. "You seemed to recognize Ms. Machado. How do you know her?"

"I don't." Marco shot me a malevolent look. "I thought she was someone else—a friend of my brother's."

Misery. Marco knew he'd hit home.

With Marco and the officer gone, Penny stationed herself at her father's bedside. Quinn and I left the building together. His concern for Penny and her father nearly made me forget he was one of my suspects. Outside, he asked where I was parked.

"I'm over in Lot 4, by the library."

"Mine's closer, I'll give you a lift." His car was in his reserved space near the VIP entrance to the penthouse.

"That's not necessary. It isn't quite dark. I can walk over."

He held the door open for me. "You'd be doing me a favor. I want to know what was going on in Palmer's room before I got the call. It appears you were there with his daughter."

I accepted the lift and told him a friend had asked me to look in on Palmer. I explained that I'd ended up having dinner with Penny because she was worried and needed a friend. I said we had spotted the guard at the door when we returned from dinner. I stopped short of telling him Marco was most likely lying, deliberately overstepping his authority.

Quinn parked his Navigator next to my hand-me-down Buick in the lot near the library and cut the engine.

"What was all that about you and the policeman who thought he recognized you?"

"It's a long, ugly story."

"I have nothing else to do."

I sat for a moment, still unnerved by the encounter with Marco. A low-riding hot rod rumbled up the street, rap music throbbing at maximum volume as it passed by.

"Aimee? Is it really that ugly?"

"The worst thing that's ever happened to me."

"Does it have anything to do with the death of Beardsley's wife?"

"It could have some bearing on the investigation."

"If there's a chance it does, I think you should tell me about it."

"It happened a few years ago, before I went back east to school."

I told him my story. About the taste of blood in my mouth from biting my tongue when the tire iron came down on the top of my head. How I heard the labored breathing of the two men as they pulled me from my car. The smell of drink on them, the gravel, then the rough undergrowth scraping skin off my arms and legs as they dragged me down the embankment and into the brushy cover alongside the road.

"I was too stunned to fight," I said. "In spite of my years of training, I realized they could do whatever they wanted to me."

"Jesus, Aimee." A shudder went through Quinn's body. "You don't have to say any more."

But I went on. About Harry appearing like an avenging angel, rage contorting his fine features, his powerful leap breaking both of Tango's legs, destroying one of the knees beyond repair. About the other man on his hands and knees, groveling. *It was his idea, man, I didn't do nothin'.*

"The road was in county jurisdiction. Harry called for help, and a sheriff's patrol car pulled up within minutes, followed by an ambulance."

"And you. Were you okay?"

"Thanks to Harry's good timing, I only suffered some scratches and bruises, but I hated going to the ER. They checked me for a concussion and took my vital signs. The worst was they wouldn't believe I hadn't been raped. They wanted to examine me. They even asked for my consent to do a rape kit. I refused, but I'm not sure they ever believed me. Harry sat there holding my hand through the whole thing. When they finally let me go, Harry stayed up with me the rest of the night checking my pupils, watching for signs of a brain hemorrhage."

When I finished my story, I sat staring at the dashboard of Quinn's car, angry that I'd shown weakness to a man I hardly knew.

"I'm so sorry," he said. His voice was ragged. "I had no idea. This Tango. Where is he now?"

"Out on parole."

"Here in Timbergate?"

"I don't know."

"What does this have to do with the murder of Beardsley's wife?"

"My brother crippled Marco Bueller's brother. Marco hates Harry. I'm afraid he hates him enough to want him arrested for this crime."

"Just to get even? Would he do that? It seems pretty extreme. If it had been my brother, I'd feel like apologizing to you for the rest of my life."

"Marco doesn't see it that way. He's never apologized to me or Harry. He can't feel regret for what his brother did to me. He can only relate to what's been taken from him—his family's good name and his chances for promotion. He might want revenge, and I think he would relish putting Harry and me through hell."

"Back there...was he was lying," Quinn asked, "about the mix-up and not knowing it wasn't his case? I'm no policeman, but I do know he wouldn't be conducting an interview if he hadn't reviewed the case file first."

"It seems likely he was lying. But what I don't understand is why he was there. How would talking to Palmer build a case against Harry?"

"Palmer is a suspect. Maybe your friend Marco was feeling him out to see if he might make a deathbed confession."

"Palmer's hardly on his deathbed, but you may be right. A confession would definitely throw a wrench in Marco's case against Harry."

"Tell me about this guy's brother. Tango, is it? Is there a chance he had anything to do with Beardsley's wife's death?"

The question spun me in a new direction. "I don't know. That never occurred to me."

"So you're telling me that your brother saved your life, and now you want to save his?"

"Yes, I owe him my life. I'll do whatever it takes to clear his name."

"Try not to worry about Harry. This crime is going to stay in the spotlight until it's solved. It's so high profile, the DA wouldn't dare charge anyone unless the evidence was overwhelming."

"My brother didn't do it."

"Of course not," Quinn said. I wished I'd heard a stronger note of conviction in his voice.

We sat in his car in silence for a few moments while the sun finished its slide behind the mountains to the west. Floodlights switched on in the parking lot.

"I need to be going," I said. "I have chores to do."

Quinn came around to open the door for me. "Do you want me to follow you home?"

"Why?"

"In case this Tango character is around."

"No. I'm a few miles out of town. I'm sure it's out of your way."

"It's really no trouble."

"Please don't worry. I've learned a lot about taking care of myself since…since it happened."

"Do you have someone at home?"

"Yes. There's someone." A cat was someone. A bird was someone.

"Ah, well…." Quinn seemed to grope for something else to say.

I got into my car and started the engine. I lowered the window. "Thanks for helping with the Palmers."

Quinn gave a little wave. "Just doing my job." He forced a smile. "Big bucks, you know."

"Right. See you."

"See you."

Driving home I regretted my decision to tell Quinn about Tango. My professional relationship with my boss had been altered by my personal baggage, and nothing I could do would change it back. I had let my fear of the Bueller brothers cloud my judgment.

As I approached my little apartment over the barn in dusky light, the llamas raised their heads. All six galloped to the barn, eager for their evening meal and hoping for a handful of cob. When I stepped out of my car, Fanny ran up and dropped a dead field mouse on my open-toed sandal, then rubbed against my leg, purring. Two feline gestures of love. She must have missed me. I didn't have time to change out of my work clothes, so I stepped out of my heels and slipped my feet into my barnyard muck boots. I made quick work of the feeding and watering, but stars were already winking in the sky when I finished.

I locked up and changed into sweat shorts and a T-shirt, a sleepwear habit I'd acquired after the Tango Bueller assault. Since that wake-up call, I had taken other measures, too. I always kept an industrial-strength flashlight by my bed, along with my purse, car keys, and running shoes. I'd stopped short of buying a gun. Now I was sorry.

I had just put a bag of popcorn in the microwave when Harry called. The police hadn't been in touch with him again, which meant no search warrant so far. He asked about my cooler.

"Any more funny noises?"

"No problems so far," I said.

"Good. I'll feel better when I can put in a new motor, but meanwhile let me know if it acts up again."

We hung up without mentioning Bonnie Beardsley's murder or the Bueller brothers. We seemed to have reached a tacit understanding. If either of us had anything useful to say, we would say it. Otherwise, let it alone. I had decided not to tell him about Marco's visit to Milton Palmer unless things started looking a lot worse.

SEVENTEEN

AFTER MY BRIEF conversation with Harry, I sipped a glass of lemonade and munched popcorn from the microwave bag while I surveyed my closet for something appropriate to wear to the ballet the following evening. I had no desire to make an impression on Arnie Palmer, but it *was* the ballet. I reminded myself that I'd accepted the date not only for love of the dance, but for the chance to learn more about the peculiar man from Manton.

A dress would require heels, and since I was going on a date with a possible killer, I wanted to be able to use my feet—either as weapons or for running. I settled on black slacks, a simple white silk blouse, and low-heeled walking shoes. With my hair up in a twist and jade earrings, I could achieve casual elegance, thanks to a little makeup and Mom's Asian genes.

The sultry air of a hot August night had me heavy-lidded at ten thirty. Five minutes after I went to bed, I heard a high-pitched blast from one of the llamas. The shrill combination horse's whinny and donkey's bray jerked me out of bed. Jack and Amah had warned me that since becoming a mother, Princess had taken to sounding alarms at the least provocation. She gave another half-hearted blast, then seemed to settle down. Reassured by the quick return to silence, I plumped my pillow and got comfortable.

Before long I heard another noise—this time out on the deck. Fanny? Was she outside? She definitely wasn't on the bed with me. I picked up my brawny flashlight and tiptoed to the door, but I kept the lights out.

I listened for her meow. Heard the scuffling noise again. I listened harder. My heart thumped in my chest. *Calm down. It's the darn cat.* I looked out the peephole. No cat. No prowler.

With a ferocious feline growl, Fanny shot out from under the dinette table and flung herself at the door. Crazed, she then leapt onto the kitchen counter, pawing at the window and howling bloody murder. I shushed the cat and peered out the same window just as three raccoons—audacious masked bandits—made their getaway across the moonlit field. I watched until they scrambled under the fence and disappeared into a manzanita thicket. Two of the llamas had jumped up as the critters passed by, but none sounded another alarm. Not even Princess.

What had drawn the bushy-tailed marauders to the deck? I never left cat food or garbage out there, but it had to be something edible. Wide awake and morbidly curious, I knew I wouldn't sleep until I figured it out. I locked Fanny in the bathroom and pulled on my muck boots. I took my little hammer from the kitchen drawer and hung it on the waistband of my shorts. That and my flashlight were the only weapons I could come up with.

Pitifully armed and pulsing with adrenaline, I turned on the outside light to illuminate the deck. Nothing showed through the peephole, so after a couple of deep breaths, I opened the door—and nearly screamed. Lying motionless in an elongated S shape just outside my door was a rattlesnake. A big sucker, no less than two and a half feet long, with at least eight rattles.

I'd heard stories of raccoons killing a rattler but never expected to see it myself. Judging from the reptile's hide, several of them had sunk teeth into it before Fanny and I interrupted their meal. But why was it on my deck? I couldn't imagine the raccoons dragging it up there.

Maybe they hadn't. Maybe they had simply followed its scent and discovered it there. A far-fetched idea came to mind. Had someone tossed it on my deck to frighten me? I thought of Tango Bueller. Maybe he was back in town and bent on revenge. Maybe he'd used a poisonous snake to make a point. If so, that meant he knew where I lived. The thought set my ears ringing as if he'd bashed me on the head again.

Then I realized there was a more likely explanation. There was a halfway house for troubled boys a couple of miles up the road, and in the past few weeks, there had been several pranks and incidents in Coyote Creek blamed on the older teens who lived there. A series of mailboxes knocked over, toilet-papered yards, and other typical acting out. I had shooed a couple of them away from Jack and Amah's mailbox a few days earlier. Maybe the snake was retribution. Not a pleasant thought, but I preferred troubled teens to a vengeful Tango.

I stepped inside and shot the deadbolt. My blinds were drawn and my windows locked, but I checked them again. Fanny began to howl when she realized I was back inside. I opened the bathroom door and grabbed her in a hug that set her struggling for freedom.

I went back to bed, despairing of getting enough

sleep to work eight hours the next day and sit through the ballet in the evening. Before long, it occurred to me that I had to dispose of the snake's carcass before some hungry scavenger showed up to finish the buffet. If I threw it out into the barnyard, I'd invite more nocturnal predators. I had no choice but to bring it inside until I figured out how to get rid of it. I got up, pulled on my boots again and poured a glass of wine, which I chugged. I had no rubber gloves, so I dug out my ski mittens. No way was I going to touch that defiled reptile with my bare hands. I found a plastic grocery bag in my kitchen waste basket and pulled a pair of old barbecue tongs from my utensil drawer.

Flipping on the porch light, I edged out the door. Starting with the head, I stuffed the limp snake into the bag inch by inch. When my tongs gripped the snake near the tail, the rattles buzzed, and I panicked. I dropped the tongs and jumped back. The snake slipped out of the bag head first and slithered into my apartment through the open door.

I shut the door behind it and stood on my deck, paralyzed. From inside I heard Fanny growl deep in her throat. She and Bosco were in there with that monster. I scrambled downstairs to the barn, looking for a weapon. Hay hooks? No good. Shovel? Possible. I scanned the tool storage area in the dim light. No shovel. No hatchet. Heart hammering, I opened the enclosure where Jack stored hay. Pitchfork. Not as good as a shovel, but better than nothing.

I ran back up the stairs and tried to look in a window, but of course the shades were all drawn, and the windows were locked. I went to the door and opened it a crack. No sign of the snake. I opened the door a few more inches and slipped inside. Fanny was perched on my kitchen table staring toward the open bathroom door. I followed her sight line and saw the snake curled at the base of the toilet.

Its spade-shaped head was twice the size of the head on Jack's pet king snake. The markings on its mid-section looked like brown blotches with light-colored edges. The creature's posterior section was ringed with black and white bands, which gave way to the impressive set of rattles. In a lethargic, undulating movement, it receded behind the toilet toward the back wall.

I closed the bathroom door, pulled a damp towel out of my hamper and stuffed it in the crack below the door. Bosco was in his cage, so I grabbed it, and Fanny, and shut them both in the closet. They immediately set up a ruckus of screeches and howls.

I took a moment to calm down, but I had to get the rattler out of my bathroom pretty soon. I was going to need my toilet. The racket in the closet continued until I opened the door and let the cat out. She wasn't much in the way of backup, but I'd heard somewhere that snakes and cats are natural enemies. That was good enough for me.

With the pitchfork hoisted in my right hand like a javelin, I opened the bathroom door and flipped on the light. The rattler stirred and tasted the air with its forked tongue. Fanny erupted in a blood-curdling, deep-throated moan. Her back went up and her tail bushed out. The snake slid out from behind the toilet and began to coil itself. My arm trembled with the weight of the pitchfork. My best shot would be to aim at the coils. I had no idea how far the rattler's striking distance was, but it seemed to me I was well within range. When the rattles began to buzz, I thrust the pitchfork.

Three out of four tines hit their mark. The snake writhed and lashed, but it was fatally pinned. I shut the bathroom door and sat on the edge of my bed trembling while I waited for the miserable creature to finish its death throes. When I finally peeked in the bathroom, there was no sign of life, and I really needed to use the toilet. I stared at the impaled snake while I emptied my bladder. No mistake this time; it was dead. Just the same, I left it pinned to the bathroom floor while I had another glass of wine, and then another. Then I went outside to scrub the deck where the raccoons had drawn rattler blood.

At one o'clock, half-looped and smelling of Pine-Sol, I dropped into bed and drifted toward oblivion with my flashlight in one hand and my little hammer tucked under my pillow.

WEDNESDAY MORNING CAME too soon, and with it, the problem of disposing of a rattler carcass. I didn't have time to bury it, and even if I did, the vultures that patrolled the skies above Coyote Creek would likely catch its scent and dig it up. I decided to put the reptile's remains in a plastic garbage bag and shove it into the freezer compartment of my fridge until I could tell Hannah about it.

Her father, Jack's younger son, was an avid fossil hunter who enjoyed bleaching and mounting the skeletons of small animals and reptiles. They were quite artistic and beautiful, and he donated many of them to the Natural History Museum. He never killed a creature just to mount it, so we all checked with him when we came across a carcass, in case he wanted it for his collection.

I had no appetite for breakfast, so I made a quick stop for coffee at Starbucks and managed to reach work on time.

When Maybelline appeared, her orange jacket and matching carrot-colored hair made my bleary eyes ache, but the sight of her reminded me of my lunch with Jared Quinn two days earlier. If my chatty volunteer knew anything about the administrator's former Parisian wife, odds were I could coax it out of her.

"Morning, Ms. Machado," Maybelline said. "Do we have any special projects today?"

How to broach the subject of the former Mrs. Quinn? I knew she thought Jared was trouble. As she'd warned me earlier: "He's a womanizer, you're a woman."

"There's something I'd like to ask you," I said. "Mr. Quinn did a favor for a friend of mine last night. I'd like to find some way to thank him, but I know so little about him. I thought you might have a suggestion."

Maybelline's protruding eyes gleamed with curiosity. "Are you thinking of a gift?"

"Something like that, but I wouldn't want to make it too personal. He is single, at least that's what I heard, and I don't want to give the wrong impression."

"Oh, he's single, all right." Her reply was heavy with innuendo. *There's more, but you'll have to drag it out of me.*

"Then it's true he's never been married?"

"Never married? Oh no, that's not right. Vane says there's a wife in Mr. Quinn's past. A sad story."

"Vane?" She used Beardsley's first name, but wouldn't use mine?

"Yes, Dr. Beardsley." Maybelline blushed. "All of us old timers call him Vane in private. He's very dear to us."

"I see. But you said there's a sad story about Mr. Quinn's wife."

"Yes. Very sad. A stunning beauty by all accounts. French, you know. She worked in television in Paris. Talk show. Like Oprah."

"What's her name?"

Maybelline frowned. "I don't think I ever heard, but it doesn't matter. She's dead now."

That news ramped up my curiosity. "How terrible. Was it an illness? She must have been fairly young."

"A tragic, violent death is what I heard."

"Did you ever meet her?"

"Heavens, no. It happened before he came to work here. That's all I know. The way he carries on now, with every kind of woman, seems an insult to her memory."

"You mentioned before that he dates a lot."

"I should say. Even that man-eating Bonnie Beardsley a time or two."

Hold the phone. What was she implying? "Are you saying Jared Quinn was involved with Bonnie Beardsley?"

"Involved? Nothing that official, and it was quite some time ago. Bonnie set her sights on Quinn, but he dropped her after a couple dates. Didn't take him long to see her for what she was. That's when she moved on to poor, gullible Vane. She had better luck there." She laid a hand on my arm. "Mind you, this is all off the record. I don't believe in spreading gossip."

"Of course not," I said.

"And don't worry, dear. I'll work on that gift thing. You came to the right person."

EIGHTEEN

I WATCHED MAYBELLINE fill her book cart and head out on her morning rounds. Supplying reading material to our patients seemed to be the extent of her skills. She ignored any technology more complex than the telephone. She never volunteered for any chores that required complicated thought or attention to detail. The concept of Library of Congress call numbers was foreign to her. She resisted any attempts from me to teach her the combination of alphabet, whole numbers and decimals used to shelve books in their correct order.

I was shelving a few medical texts myself when Arnie Palmer called just before noon to confirm our ballet date. I assured him I would be in the Civic Center lobby by seven thirty that evening. He sounded so innocent and eager I felt a little guilty about suspecting him of murder. As I hung up, I noticed Maybelline had come back from her rounds. The gleam in her eye convinced me she'd been eavesdropping, so I confessed I had a date for the ballet.

"Not with Mr. Quinn, I hope."

"No. Someone else."

"Lovely," she said.

Maybelline's shift ended at noon. After she left I spent my lunch hour napping on the ratty old chaise lounge crammed into the library's employee restroom. I hung a PLEASE KNOCK LOUDLY sign on the library door, but not a soul interrupted my snooze.

I woke up feeling refreshed enough to concentrate on a tutorial handout I was creating to help patrons use our new online forensic databases. The subscriptions had cost Dr. Beardsley big bucks, so the least I could do was make sure their use justified their cost. It would also show administration and the medical staff what my job could do to support their work. That kept me busy until quitting time.

At home, I checked messages. Amah had left one saying the usual wonderful time was being had, but the good news was they'd been invited on a once-in-a-lifetime llama packing trip into Washington's North Cascade Mountains. Instead of heading home, they would be gone several more days, probably out of cell-phone range, so not to worry if I didn't hear from them.

"Don't forget Fanny's fur ball medicine," Amah said. "And Jack says don't forget to feed the king snake." That made my day.

Their prolonged absence would buy some sorely needed time. Maybe enough to figure out what had happened to Bonnie Beardsley. I still hoped the mystery would be solved before Amah and Jack returned.

I walked up to the main house and checked on their snake. It was my least favorite task, but even more so since my encounter with the rattler the night before. Their reptile had finished shedding, so he was going to be hungry. The feeding instructions were taped to the aquarium. I would need to stop by the pet store for a live mouse. I counted llamas on my walk back down the lane to the barn. The little white cria named Moon-beam frolicked in circles around her mama, looking more like a fluffy wind-up toy than a real animal. I tossed hay, replenished poultry feeders and provided fresh water to the entire menagerie. I finished with less than an hour to get ready for the ballet.

Showered, dressed and primped, I had groomed myself for a man I barely knew, who might or might not be planning to commit mayhem or worse on my person before the night was over.

Judging by the number of cars in the Civic Center parking lot, *Giselle* was sold out. Happy memories of my childhood ballet classes came to mind as I hurried to the lobby entrance. Arnie was already there, studying his wristwatch. When I spotted him and waved, he looked confused until I got close enough for him to recognize my face.

"Hi Arnie, it's me, Aimee Machado." His face brightened with relief. Poor guy, I wondered how often he got stood up.

"Hi. I didn't recognize you for a moment. I was looking for a blonde."

"I was wearing a wig when we met. Sorry."

"Don't be. Dark hair suits you better."

It was thirty minutes before the curtain rose, so Arnie suggested we have a drink. We strolled to the bar at one end of the lobby.

"You look lovely," he said. "I hope you'll thank your boyfriend for me."

I'd almost forgotten about my boyfriend. "He should be thanking you," I said. "He hates ballet."

"His loss."

"You look very nice, too." I would have said it just to be polite, but it was true. Arnie had gone all out. His tux was the ultimate in good taste and fit like a custom job. His skin had a healthy glow, and I could have sworn he was taller than I remembered.

With our wine glasses in hand, we stood people-watching as balletomanes entered the building. Arnie held his glass in his right hand, then switched to his left. I couldn't be sure which hand was dominant. He seemed to enjoy making witty, sometimes catty, observations about various people in the lobby.

"See that couple coming in?" He jutted his chin in the direction of Willow and Grover Underhill. I'd nearly forgotten about the Everlasting Pets proprietors and their connection to Bonnie Beardsley. I turned my back to them.

"Do you know those people?" I asked.

"I know they have a reputation as swingers."

"I'm not certain how you mean that." I had a pretty good idea, but I wanted him to say it.

"Wife-swapping, ménage à trois, that sort of thing."

Bingo. I recalled Willow's odd, almost seductive behavior toward me the day I visited Everlasting Pets. And these swingers had considered Bonnie Beardsley a soul mate.

"That sort of thing doesn't appeal to me."

"Me either," Arnie said. "Sex is complicated enough when it's just two people."

I didn't respond. We passed a moment in awkward silence, broken when the lobby lights flashed.

"Maybe we should find our seats," I said.

I was filled with excitement as we made our way to the dress circle. What a difference a day made—from dead rattlesnake to *Giselle.* I read the synopsis of the ballet to refresh my memory. Giselle's untimely death and Albrecht's subsequent broken heart led me back to Maybelline's recounting of Jared Quinn's ill-fated marriage. At least the Quinns had made it to the altar. I reminded myself to research the deceased Mrs. Jared Quinn the first chance I got.

Arnie and I parted in the crowded lobby during intermission, heading for our respective restrooms. My line was longer, of course, so I expected to find him waiting for me as I descended the stairs from the mezzanine. I stopped halfway down the staircase to scan the crowd. No Arnie.

Lobby lights flashed, warning patrons to return to their seats, but there was no sign of Arnie. I headed back toward our seats and spotted him standing in the aisle chatting with none other than Willow and Grover Underhill. Odd, after his comment about their lifestyle. Arnie spotted me, waved me over and did the honors.

"Willow and Grover Underhill, I'd like to introduce Aimee Machado."

Thank God I hadn't given them a fake name when I'd visited them in a professional capacity.

Willow's eyes narrowed. "I think we've met. You have the emu, right?"

"Camel," Grover corrected.

"It's a llama," I said. "They're related to camels, but smaller."

"Yes, of course." Willow persisted. "Have you decided about the cloning?"

"Not yet." I glanced at Arnie. His curiosity was obvious, but he kept quiet. I wasn't the only one who hadn't acknowledged knowing the Underhills.

Grover hung an arm over Arnie's shoulders, and another over mine. "Say, why don't we all go out for drinks after?"

"Yes," Willow gushed. "You two are such a darling couple, and it's so hard to meet people with similar interests in this town. We must get to know each other better."

Most of the audience had returned to their seats. I shot Arnie a *get us out of this* look.

"Thanks, but we've made other plans," he said.

"That's too bad." Willow pulled a business card from her purse and pressed it into my hand. "Miss Machado, you must visit us in our new location. You do want to make plans for that special pet of yours, don't you?"

The Underhills departed for the balcony, and Arnie and I returned to our seats. By the time Albrecht survived the dance of death and Giselle drifted out of his life forever, I was emotionally exhausted. I thought I had been prepared because I knew the story line, but watching the inspired performance by this troupe had an unexpected emotional impact. The heartbreak and finality of the couple's loss of love reminded me of Nick and brought me close to tears.

NINETEEN

APPLAUSE FILLED THE theatre at curtain call. House lights
came up and we began our halting progress toward
the exit. Arnie and I found ourselves stalled behind a
group of folks who were too busy critiquing the performance to notice that they were blocking traffic. While
we waited for the exodus to pick up speed, I heard a
familiar voice.

"Yoo-hoo, Ms. Machado. Wait up."

It seemed impossible, but I recognized the voice of
Maybelline Black as she and Orrie Mercer descended
from the nosebleed seats in the balcony. Maybelline's
choice of formal wear might have been surprising if
I hadn't already been familiar with her flamboyant
taste: a black velvet tunic trimmed with a wide collar
of black ostrich feathers. Her spindly legs were encased
in leopard print tights, and on her feet she wore metal-
lic gold ankle boots with three-inch heels. She had a
fake beauty mark glued to the corner of her upper lip.

Stunned as I was, I managed to grasp the piece of
knowledge this chance meeting confirmed. Maybelline and Orrie were indeed an item.

"One of the auxiliary girls came down with shingles, so she gave me her tickets," Maybelline explained.
"Wasn't that a stroke of luck?"

I doubted the woman with shingles saw it that way.
I made introductions, all the while ignoring the blatant

curiosity in Maybelline's enormous eyes. She was giving Arnie an examination only slightly less thorough than a full body CT scan.

Orrie's maroon leisure suit fit him like a sausage casing. The bolo tie circling his enormous neck was fastened with a replica of the Confederate flag. There was a surreal quality about the moment that left me dazed.

As soon as I had performed introductions, Orrie announced, "I gotta take a leak." He turned to Maybelline. "Meet me at the truck." With that, he elbowed his way through the slow-moving crowd, leaving the three of us behind.

"Are you new to the area, Mr. Palmer?" Maybelline asked Arnie.

"You could say that," he replied.

"Your name is so familiar. There's a celebrity—"

"I don't play golf," Arnie said.

"No, no, not that celebrity. I'm thinking of our local luminary, Milton Palmer. Any relation?"

"I'm afraid not. It's a common name."

True. I remembered asking Arnie the same question and recalled seeing a lot of Palmers listed when I looked for Milton Palmer's number.

"Well, any friend of Ms. Machado's is a friend of mine," Maybelline said, as if she were bestowing knighthood on Arnie.

The crowd finally began to move, and the three of us progressed to the lobby. I turned to say goodnight to Maybelline, only to have her say, "Oh, look, there's Lorraine. She adores ballet. Let's go say hello."

Lorraine? Could she mean the ex-Mrs. Beardsley? This was an opportunity I couldn't let pass.

"Woo-hoo, Lorraine. Over here, dear."

Several heads turned, but Maybelline continued waving and calling out until the poor woman had no choice but to come our way. The attractive man who accompanied her wore an amused grin. He looked a bit younger than Lorraine, and very fit in an open-collared white shirt and navy blazer.

Lorraine was no slouch, herself. Slender, tastefully dressed in a two-piece white brocade dress, she wore a diamond bracelet and earrings, and her blond hair was cut and colored in a style that flattered her California tan.

Maybelline introduced me as Vane's new librarian and Arnie as my boyfriend. Lorraine introduced her companion, Troy Bilkowsky.

Maybelline lifted Lorraine's left hand. "Is this what I think it is?"

Lorraine smiled up at Troy. "Yes, it is."

The rock on her third finger sparkled in the light from the lobby chandeliers. Her betrothed obviously had some bucks. Some women got all the rich guys. So much for Lorraine as a suspect. Living well was definitely the best revenge.

The lobby was nearly empty, and the staffers were giving us meaningful looks. *Get out so we can close up.*

Arnie walked me to my car with Maybelline trotting at our heels until she reached Orrie's truck, parked two spaces away. Orrie sat in his cab with the engine running. Maybelline stood on her side of the vehicle glaring at him until he figured out what was wrong. He exited his side, walked around, and opened the door for her. He looked so chagrined that I almost felt sorry for him. As soon as Maybelline scrambled in, he gave the door a shove, catching her floppy ostrich feather collar and pulling her face until it was scrunched against the window.

She let out a screech.

Orrie muttered, "What the—"

When he saw the problem, he opened her door again to free her collar. She rubbed her throat and gasped, "What's your hurry? You could have killed me."

Orrie jumped into the driver's seat, gunned his engine and pulled out.

Arnie and I stood outside my car for an awkward moment. Since this was not a real date, there was no need to make decisions about seeing each other again or initiating a good night kiss.

"Drive home safe," he said, "and thanks for coming."

"It was my pleasure." As I voiced that polite response, I realized it was true. Arnie had shown me a lovely time in spite of zero chemistry between us. If it turned out he was as innocent as he seemed, he was the sort of person who would make a great friend. He insisted on waiting until my car started and my doors were locked, then he gave a little salute and strode off.

He had not mentioned the Underhills, and neither had I. It wasn't important, since I didn't plan on seeing Arnie again. I put Alicia Keys in the CD player and headed home. Five miles out of town, I noticed my steering wheel pulling to the right. I flashed back to the flat tire three years earlier. It couldn't be happening again.

But it was. I nearly lost control and had no choice but to stop on the shoulder. The moon gave enough light for me to check my surroundings. The embankment to my right sloped upward at a forty-five degree angle for about fifteen feet, topped by a screen of manzanita bushes.

I'd been a sitting duck waiting in my car the last time. Never again. I activated my hazard lights and scooted out the passenger side door. Scrambling up the bank, I hunkered down behind a screen of manzanita bushes and called road service on my cellphone. I was given an estimate of thirty minutes. Meanwhile, three cars slowed when they saw the Buick's hazard lights, but none stopped.

I was about to dial Harry when passing headlights illuminated a familiar-looking old Trans Am pulling up behind my car. The driver got out and stood for a moment, looking at my tire. Just then a pickup slowed down and seemed to catch the other driver's attention. Two good Samaritans or two bad guys in cahoots? After a brief exchange, the pickup moved on.

The Trans Am driver reached into his car and pulled out a long stick. Now what? He leaned on the stick, and it suddenly dawned on me. The stick was a cane, and the man was Tango Bueller. No wonder the car looked familiar; it was the same one he had driven that night three years ago. I expected a rush of fear, but it didn't come. Neither did anger. Tango's limp was so severe, a child could have knocked him over with one push. No wonder he'd waved the other driver on. What was he going to do?

He shone his flashlight on my license plate, then looked around, probably wondering where I'd gone. I ducked low behind the brush. Maybe he hadn't recognized the car before he stopped, but I couldn't be sure. Had he been following me?

Tango limped to the driver's side door, opened it and popped the trunk open. Great, in my hurry to get out and hide, I'd forgotten to lock the car. What did he expect to find? Whatever it was, he would be disappointed. I watched in fascination while he searched. Sorry, Tango, there's nothing there to sell. You'll have to get your drug money from some other poor chump.

Tango set his cane on the hood of his car and used both hands to lift something out of my trunk. My spare tire. He was taking my spare. Now I was angry. Who would parole a dirt bag like that? No question he was planning to make my life hell. He set the spare down and reached back into my trunk. When he stood up, I saw my jack in one hand and my tire iron in the other. For a moment, my vision blurred. Three years ago, a tire iron had nearly killed me. What Tango did next brought tears to my eyes.

He changed my tire.

When he finished, he put the flat tire and tools back in my trunk and closed it. Then he walked to his car and sat inside for a moment. I couldn't see what he was doing, but when he got out, he limped around to my windshield and tucked something under my wiper. He gave my front fender a gentle pat, got into his car and drove away.

I crouched there in disbelief until something rustled in the brush behind me. Time to get moving. I scrambled down the hill and pulled the piece of paper from my windshield wiper. I jammed it in my purse, got in the car and drove home, convinced I'd slipped into a parallel universe.

Inside the bunkhouse I shot the deadbolt and pulled my shades. I took the piece of paper from my purse. It was a brochure from the Helping Hand Rescue Mission. In a spidery scrawl, two words were written in the margin with a pencil: *Amends, Tango*.

Tears flowed, and I gave in to them, whether from relief or confusion I wasn't sure. One thing was clear. If Tango Bueller had found a higher power, there was hope for the rest of the world.

TWENTY

THURSDAY MORNING HARRY met me at the tire shop. We left my car there, and as he drove me to work in his Jag, I told him my astonishing Tango Bueller story.

"It was dark, Sis. Are you sure it was Tango?"

"Trust me. I'd know him in any light."

"I'll do some checking."

"Start at the Helping Hand Rescue Mission." I took the brochure out of my purse. "Maybe he's living there."

Harry braked the Jag to let a trio of laughing teenage girls cross the street. "If Tango's clean and sober, he doesn't need to live at the Rescue Mission."

"What do you mean?"

He pulled into the parking lot next to the library building. "There's more to Tango than a rap sheet."

"So tell me."

"Neither of us has time right now. I'm sorry I wasn't there for you last night, but I'm impressed as hell about Tango. Maybe he really is on the road to redemption. If you want to know more about him I suggest you talk to Nick." *Nick again.*

"Why Nick?"

He sighed. "He knows Tango's history better than I do. Now get out, I'm late."

"Wait," I said. "Have you heard anything more about a warrant to search your place?"

Harry expelled a long breath. "Not yet, but I suppose it's still a possibility. They're not exactly keeping me informed." He nodded toward my door. "Out, Sis. I've got to go. Try not to worry. I'll pick you up at lunchtime and take you back to the tire shop."

I made an effort to be friendly to Orrie Mercer at the library entrance. It seemed the socially correct thing, seeing as how his relationship with Maybelline had been confirmed at the ballet the night before.

"Hello, Mr. Mercer," I said.

He allowed me an almost imperceptible nod, but underscored the greeting by spitting a brown streak of tobacco juice into a potted begonia near the door.

Once I was inside, things looked up. With Lola on the job, the morning passed smoothly. Twenty years Maybelline's senior and her opposite in attitude, Lola embraced new technology. Her arthritic fingers flew over the computer keyboard as she explored our software programs and databases. She had been a public librarian in the days of card catalogs, hand-stamped due dates, and constant shushing of noisy patrons, so the ease of online research struck her as nothing short of a miracle. Lola's lips moved as she worked, and occasionally I caught a hushed verse of Stockwell's newest song. Her experience and dedication made her an ideal advocate for what I was trying to accomplish in the library.

I checked the daily patient list and saw that Milton Palmer was still in house. It struck me again that two of the men I suspected in Bonnie Beardsley's case had the same surname. Palmer was a fairly common name, but it still seemed like a coincidence in a town the size of Timbergate. I checked the phone book and stopped counting at twenty, only a fourth of the way down the list. Okay, there were at least a hundred Palmers listed. I let it go and got back to analyzing my date with Arnie.

The only significant observations I had made were his knowledge of the Underhills' swinging lifestyle and his lack of reaction when Willow mentioned my interest in llama cryogenics. Most men would be thinking *nut case*, yet Arnie had seemed unfazed. During intermission I'd wanted to ask how he had hooked up with the Underhills, but I hadn't had a chance. Not after the ballet, either, what with Maybelline tagging along to the parking lot. Watching Lola's diligent attention to her tasks reminded me I had better quit musing and apply myself to library business.

At noon I went outside to look for Harry's Jag. Instead, I saw Nick leaning against his hybrid SUV, arms crossed. His fair hair gleamed with sparks of light in the brilliant sunshine. His smile drew fine, crinkly lines at the corners of his eyes. I used to touch those lines with my lips. But that was before Rella, when Nick was someone else—the man I trusted.

"What are you doing here?" I asked.

"Harry sent me."

"Figures."

"He's tied up. Said you needed a ride."

I needed a ride.

The atmosphere in Nick's car grew thicker with every mile on our way to the tire shop. My resentment and mistrust clotted the silent air.

Nick finally spoke. "Harry told me about Tango."

"He would."

"He said it might help if you heard the rest of his story."

"And why are you the one to tell me?"

"It'll become obvious."

"All right. I'm listening."

"For starters, Tango went to U.C. Davis on a full scholarship."

"You're kidding? I thought he was developmentally disabled."

"This was before the meth."

"What kind of scholarship? Football?"

"He was a science major. Biology, botany, one of those. Maybe both."

"What happened?"

"He graduated with honors. Came home. Worked for Buck Sawyer for a while as an environmental impact consultant while he started work on his master's."

"Sounds like he had a good thing going. What happened?"

"A woman."

I didn't like where this was headed. "Please tell me it wasn't Bonnie Beardsley."

"It wasn't."

"Who, then?"

"Buck's daughter."

"Buck has a daughter? I've never heard anyone mention that."

"She's dead. A meth-induced stroke killed her, but not before she got Tango messed up. He dropped out of his master's program about that time."

"And you know all this because…?"

"Buck and I are pretty close. After his first wife died—before he remarried—he went through a pretty rough time. A lot of soul-searching."

"Another rich guy who made a fortune at the expense of his family?"

"Let me finish."

"Did he have any other children?"

"No. Just the daughter, Sam. A surviving twin. Among his other regrets, he was so grief-stricken when the boy died at birth that he saddled his daughter with the name he'd planned for his son."

"Samantha is a fairly common girl's name."

"Not Samantha. Samuel Buckeye Sawyer the Fifth. He told her when she married, she was to keep her maiden name and insist her children be raised as Sawyers. For the sake of the family line."

"That's pretty harsh."

"True, but not unheard of."

"Why didn't Buck and his wife try for more children? A boy?"

"Apparently that wasn't an option. Sam wasn't born until his wife was in her forties, and there were some medical complications with the birth."

"Adoption?"

"Buck wanted a blood heir."

"So Sam Jr. was his only chance?" I asked.

"Yep, and once she was introduced to meth, he lost her."

"Imagine having all that money and no one to leave it to. Did Buck ever say how his daughter got involved with meth?"

Nick pulled into the parking lot at the tire store. "He figured it was her junior year in high school. About the time she started running around with Bonnie Belcher."

Bonnie again. It seemed she had crossed paths with everyone in Timbergate. Once more I wondered who had most wanted her dead—or who among the many people she'd offended or hurt had homicidal tendencies. My conversation with Nick had begun as a window into Tango's past. I wanted to hear the rest of his story, but first I had to pay for my repaired tire.

I got out of Nick's car and headed inside the shop to put the bill on my already strained credit card. Nick followed me in, which annoyed me.

The clerk nodded to Nick. "What can we do for you?"

"We're here for Miss Machado's Buick."

"I can do this myself," I muttered.

The man behind the counter looked at my work order and pursed his lips. "Oops," he said. *Not a good sign.*

"We're not quite finished with your car."

Nick spoke up. "What's the problem?"

"Oh, no problem with the car. It's just—" His shoulders drooped a notch. "I don't know how this happened, but the job got overlooked. We're on it right now if you'd care to wait."

Before I could object, Nick took over. "Tell you what, give her a twenty percent discount and deliver her car to the TMC parking lot when it's finished."

The tire man brightened. "No problem." He took my work phone number, promising to deliver the car well before my quitting time.

We left the shop, me storming ahead of Nick. "That's great, Nick. Just take over. I'm not helpless, you know."

"Hey, I'm sorry. Old habits."

"Well, you need to get over it. And I need to get back to work."

"I thought we might grab a sandwich. You still have most of your lunch hour left, don't you?"

"I wasn't planning to eat." I had a peanut butter sandwich in my desk at work, but I wasn't about to tell him that was all I could afford.

"My treat," he said. "Come on. Don't you want to hear the rest of Tango's story?"

We ended up at Stone Soup again. Gore, the server with the tattoos, wasn't around. Instead, a thirty-something woman with pasty skin and lank brown hair took our orders. She barely moved her lips when she spoke. When she walked away, I mentioned it to Nick.

"Did you notice how she talks without opening her mouth? She's like a ventriloquist."

"Meth mouth." He looked grim. "She's trying to hide it."

"What's meth mouth?"

"Meth rots the teeth. Doesn't take long, either. There's probably nothing in there but little black stubs." He shook his head. "Meth's been a real boon for denture makers."

"I'm surprised she got hired."

"She has the right résumé. Stone Soup doesn't hire anyone who isn't in a drug rehab program."

"You seem to know a lot about this place."

"It's one of Buck's philanthropic projects."

Before I could reply, our soup arrived, served with trembling hands by the tight-lipped waitress. She seemed relieved and a little surprised when they touched down on our place mats without any spillage. The tantalizing aromas set my stomach gurgling.

Nick dipped into his beef goulash and I tasted my cream of asparagus soup.

"Well, if it isn't alias Ingrid Wiggins." I looked up to see Arnie Palmer standing at our table. "We meet again, Aimee."

Hard to believe this was a coincidence, but if Arnie was stalking me, he was pretty brazen about it. Apparently he wasn't going to move on until I introduced Nick.

Nick looked at me deadpan and said, "Ingrid who?"

I kicked at him under the table, my first shot hitting the center post, which was painful, because I was wearing open-toed sandals. The second try connected with Nick's shin. He set his spoon down and waited.

"Arnie Palmer, I'd like you to meet my boyfriend, Nick Alexander. Nick, this is the man I told you about."

"Umm," Nick said. "Remind me." He was enjoying my predicament far too much.

"The ballet," I said, "remember? You said I should go with Arnie so you wouldn't have to take me."

Nick nodded. "Of course." He stood and reached out a hand to Arnie. "Put it there, Buddy. You did me a favor."

Arnie winced, and I knew Nick's handshake had been the *I can beat the shit out of you any time I want to* version he favored for establishing dominance.

At that point Arnie took his leave, and I followed his progress, wondering if he was eating alone or meeting someone. I was doubly surprised when he approached a table where Lorraine Beardsley sat alone. She brightened when she saw him and offered her cheek. He gave her a quick air kiss and sat. They looked far too chummy to have met for the first time the night before.

"Are you going to tell me what that was about?" Nick asked.

"I'd rather not."

He looked toward the table where Arnie sat. "Christ, Aimee, he shakes hands like a girl."

"I'm not dating him."

"Fine." He was silent for about two seconds, then asked the question I was dreading. "Who the hell is Ingrid Wiggins?"

"It's my alias. I'm a single woman. I don't give out my real name to every man I meet."

"Okay, that's probably a good idea. Where'd you meet that guy?"

"Can we change the subject?" I couldn't go into detail without confessing my bait-the-stalker museum escapade. And besides, Nick's tone sounded way too proprietary.

"All right." Nick put up his hands in surrender. "Let's get back on track. We were talking about Tango before your little friend showed up. When do you have to be back to work?"

I checked my watch. "Twenty minutes. And he's not that little."

"Eat your soup."

I ate while Nick related Tango Bueller's story.

Tango had returned to Timbergate quietly several weeks earlier. Early enough to have been in town when Bonnie disappeared. Having a respected officer of the law as his nearest relative had worked in Tango's favor, but it put considerable pressure on Marco. His reputation, and probably his career, depended on Tango's parole remaining unblemished.

Tango's redemption was not making me feel better

about my brother's future. DA Keefer needed an arrest, and from the way Marco behaved toward me at the hospital, he hadn't gotten over his grudge against Harry. A lot depended on how much his prowess between the sheets could influence the DA. Satisfying her libido was one thing, but what if she had fallen in love with him? He'd surely use that to his advantage—a frightening scenario.

I drew my attention back to Nick, who was detailing the remarkable feats Tango had accomplished during his two-plus years in prison. He'd kicked his meth habit and finished his dual master's degrees in biology and botany through a correspondence program. Once he was out of prison, the leg injury Harry inflicted would have qualified Tango for disability, but Buck Sawyer offered him a job, and he took it. Tango was currently on staff at Recovery Ranch, a plot of agricultural land in the foothills east of Timbergate.

"Recovery Ranch?" I asked. "Didn't I read where Buck had donated that property?"

"Buck's money is helping support every anti-drug effort in the county, even that soup you're eating. Stone Soup was his brain child. Recovery Ranch is an experimental farming project that supplies all the produce and most of the other food served here."

"How does Helping Hand fit into the picture?"

"Recovery Ranch operates under the umbrella of the Helping Hand Rescue Mission."

"That's why Tango had the brochure in his car?"

"Most likely," Nick said. "He probably keeps stacks of them on hand to dispense to the down-and-outers in his old haunts."

"How does that explain where he was headed last

night when he saw my car along the side of the highway?"

"He was headed home. He lives at Recovery Ranch."

"So he was simply playing Good Samaritan when he stopped?"

"It's what he does now. Atonement. Harry said you thought Tango recognized your car."

"He must have. He wrote the note. 'Amends, Tango.'"

"Twelve-step language. Buck says he attends meetings every day. Wouldn't accept the job unless he could fit them into his schedule. Tango probably thought finding your flat tire was serendipity. An unexpected opportunity to apologize."

"Does Harry know what you've told me about Tango?"

"He does now. Tango has a right to some privacy, but he did leave the note, so I suspect he won't mind if you know his story. He couldn't tell you himself. He'd be ill-advised to approach you in any way, considering you were the victim of the attack that sent him to prison."

His words triggered a shudder of recollection. Nick noticed. "Sorry."

"Forget it." I checked the time. "Let's go, I'm already late."

On the drive back, I asked Nick the question everyone in Sawyer County would have asked, given the opportunity.

"How did Buck Sawyer get so rich? Was it lumber?"

"No, but that's the common misconception about Buck, because most of the wealthiest families between northern California and Canada got their start with lumber."

"Then what was it?"

"Fish. Buck's great, great granddaddy Salmoneus Sakellaridis emigrated from Greece, changed his name to Samuel Sawyer, and started a fishing business over on the coast."

"So the family fortune is all from fishing?"

Nick shook his head. "Hardly. The first Samuel built up quite a fleet, but wise investing down through the generations played a major role. Now Buck owns a piece of nearly every commodity on the globe."

"So how did he end up here? I thought Sawyer County was named for his family."

"Not true, but that's an interesting story. He met his first wife in college over on the coast. She told him she was from Sawyer County, and he took that coincidence as a good sign. They dated all through college, but when he proposed, she had one condition. She hated the ocean climate, couldn't get used to the fog. She wanted to live where the sun shines from morning to night, and where summers are hot and dry. Buck promised if she would marry him, they'd have a second home here."

"I thought he lived here year-round?"

"He has for the last twenty years, since he took over the reins of the business."

"It sounds like he was devoted to his first wife. What happened to her?"

"After their daughter died, she insisted they start a foundation dedicated to drug rehab programs and fighting drug trafficking. She was devoted to the cause, but her spirit was broken. Her health failed over the next few years. Officially, she died of congestive heart failure. Buck says that's medical jargon for a broken heart."

"Close enough," I said. "Speaking of medical jargon, here we are."

Nick stopped at the entrance to my building, where Orrie Mercer stood guard. His face glistened with a sheen of sweat, and his features bore the familiar look of challenge.

"What's his problem?" Nick asked.

"I don't know. The heat, maybe. He always looks like that."

"Let me park the car; I'll walk you inside."

"That's not necessary." I opened the door and got out. "I suppose I should thank you for lunch."

"Not unless you mean it," he said.

I shut the door a little too hard. He put the car in gear and drove away a little too fast.

TWENTY-ONE

MY CAR WAS delivered that afternoon by the manager of the tire shop. He came inside to take my credit card number and get my signature on his paperwork. I wondered why he had come himself instead of sending one of his employees. Forgetting to fix the flat didn't seem like that big a deal. After we finished our transaction, I asked if he'd found a nail in the tire.

He handed me my receipt. "That's the thing. That's why I came instead of sending one of my crew."

"What do you mean?"

"How long were you driving on that low tire?"

"It wasn't low when I left the Civic Center. I went about five miles before I noticed the problem. Why?"

"It looks a little fishy."

"Fishy how?"

"Like tampering. We see a lot of nails in tires. Usually the tire won't go flat right away. In this case, the air leak wasn't coming from a nail. There was a puncture wound in the tire. That's why it went flat so fast."

"What kind of puncture?"

"Hard to say. Ice pick, something like that."

"Are you saying someone punctured my tire deliberately?"

"It's possible. I thought you should know."

I felt my face flush. *Damn.* Had Tango set this up?

How could he have known my car was parked at the Civic Center?

"Were you able to repair it?" I asked.

"Sure. It's fine. Lots of good tread left." His duty done, he left with poorly chosen parting words. "Have a nice day."

I had almost convinced myself that the rattler on my deck was the work of hungry raccoons. Now, with a suspicious flat tire, I wasn't so sure. These supposedly unrelated incidents smelled *fishy*, to use the tire guy's word. If they *were* warnings, veiled threats, then someone out there knew where I lived and what I drove, and suspected I was snooping into the Bonnie Beardsley case.

My *nice* day took another turn for the worse when Dr. Beardsley strolled into the library an hour before quitting time. For a man on the wrong side of middle age with a recently deceased wife, Beardsley seemed to get younger and more amiable every day. His charisma quotient was definitely on the rise. He looked around my deserted domain with satisfaction. Why that should please him soon became apparent.

"Ms. Machado, I'm happy to find you alone. We haven't spoken for several days. I was hoping we could catch up."

"Of course. I have some time now."

He cleared his throat. "Unfortunately, I do not. I had hoped you might be free for dinner tonight."

There it was. One of those moments every working woman dreads.

He picked up on my reluctance. "Strictly a business dinner, I assure you. Please don't misinterpret my intentions."

"I understand," I said, "but I'm afraid my fiancé wouldn't be comfortable with that. We always spend our evenings together."

Disappointment clouded Beardsley's countenance for a moment, but he quickly reverted to his usual good-natured affect.

I pulled my desk calendar close and picked up a pen. "Do you have any free time tomorrow?"

"I'm afraid not. My schedule is hectic, trying to make up for lost time."

After he left, I blew out a breath, relieved that I'd dodged that bullet. With any luck Nick wouldn't find out he'd been promoted from fictional boyfriend to fictional fiancé. I was still staring after Beardsley when I heard the door to the library employees' restroom open.

"Had to take a leak," Orrie Mercer said. He adjusted his crotch and banged out the front door. Apparently he had come in while I was distracted by Vane Beardsley's problematic dinner invitation. The courtship of Orrie Mercer and Maybelline had evolved from oddly amusing to exceedingly annoying. There were public facilities in the building. He had no business using the library staff's private restroom. I resolved to have a talk with Maybelline first thing in the morning. At the moment, there were more important things on my mind.

I had an hour to fill before quitting time, so I went online to follow up on what I'd learned from Maybelline the day before about Quinn's late wife. The woman had been a television talk show host in Paris. That struck me as an odd coincidence, since Quinn had dated Bonnie Beardsley during her run as a TV celebrity here in Timbergate.

I used the most obvious search terms to get started:

Female talk show hosts in Paris. Nothing helpful there. I refined the search to *French television talk shows.* I scanned the hits until I saw something in French: *Blanche Montague tragédie.* I clicked that link and found myself at the Blanche Montague fan club home page. Also in French. I clicked on the English language version.

As far as I could tell, this woman's show had been as popular in France as Oprah's had been in America, and she had been just as politically active on the world stage if not more. Her show frequently featured blistering denunciations of the world's most wretched offenses against women: female circumcision in Sudan, brutal Hudood laws in Pakistan, and unconscionably negligent maternity care in remote Ethiopian villages.

I left the Blanche Montague site long enough to look up the Hudood reference. It seems in Pakistan a woman who reports a rape must provide four male witnesses to the crime or risk being whipped and imprisoned for adultery. A horrific predicament in a country where a woman is raped every two hours. I shuddered, recalling my near rape at the hands of Tango and his accomplice. I couldn't imagine going through that nightmare as a Pakistani woman, knowing how much worse my fate would be if I reported it.

My esteem for the late Blanche Montague grew with every word I read. Her fan club considered her a martyr, slain for her campaign to eradicate these atrocities against women. A series of photos showed her to be a striking brunette with sensual features and a radiant smile. Her eyes were large and dark; her straight nose had the flared nostrils of a supermodel.

Was Blanche Montague the late wife of Jared

Quinn? Puzzled, I scrolled down the page. One small photo captured her standing on a portable ramp of stairs framed by the open hatch of an airplane. A tall man with dark hair stood next to her. Both were waving to the camera. The caption read:

Talk show personality Blanche Montague and American relief worker Jared Quinn, one week before Montague's fateful trip to Ethiopia.

SO THERE IT WAS. I checked the date of her death. Five years ago. How long had Quinn been employed at Timbergate? What had brought him from Paris to a small rural hospital in the far reaches of northern California?

A patron came in, so I bookmarked the fan club home page. I helped the young male nurse find and print several articles on wound care, which put me past quitting time. I still had errands to run before going home. Jack's king snake needed dinner, so I called the nearest pet store to check on their supply of feeder mice. They were well stocked and open until seven.

First, I wanted to squeeze in a second visit to Milton Palmer's hospital room. Two days had passed since Penny Palmer and I interrupted Marco Bueller's devious visit to her father. With any luck, Palmer would be off the heavy meds this time—and alone.

I closed the library and headed for the third floor of the main tower, arriving just as the dinner trays were being served. Feeding time in the hospital always smelled like meatloaf no matter what was hidden under the domed covers that kept the meals warm and soggy.

Milton Palmer's room had no guard at the entrance. None of the surgical floor nurses so much as glanced

at me, so I walked right in. Palmer had the TV tuned
to our local station. His five o'clock news slot was in
full swing with his female co-anchor running the show.
Palmer turned when he realized I was in the room. The
white bandages on his head reflected soft blue light
from the TV screen.

"Who are you?"

"I work here," I said, "in the library. I came to see
you two nights ago, but you weren't ready for visitors."

"Oh." He turned the volume down. "I don't remember. The medications, you know."

"Yes, but you seem much better today."

"I am, thanks. Why are you here?"

"Routine. I try to visit patients. Let them know we
have services available in the library other than our
book delivery."

His eyes widened. "The rather colorful woman with
the cart? She belongs to you?"

"I'm afraid so."

"She left some things for me. They're on my bedside table."

I glanced at the titles: *Valley of the Dolls, War and
Peace, 100 Ways to Win at Bingo.*

"Looks like she's using the shotgun approach. I'll
take those back. Is there anything I can bring you? That
is, if you're going to be staying with us for a while."

"Another day or so, they tell me." He shifted his
rump in the bed. "Can you bring me something on
dissecting cellulitis of the scalp? It seems that's my
diagnosis. It's a disease of unknown cause, they say,
but still, I'd like to read up on it."

"I'll search our databases and print out what I find."

"Will the cart woman be delivering it?"

"I'll deliver it myself."

"I'd appreciate that."

A silent moment followed, with Palmer expecting me to depart. For lack of a better segue, I asked if he was expecting any visitors.

"My daughter. She'll be here soon."

A moment later, Penny walked into the room arm in arm with Arnie Palmer, who was wearing a dress.

"Dad, look who's—" When she saw me, she broke off and clamped her mouth shut.

TWENTY-TWO

"HELLO, MILTON," ARNIE SAID. "It's been a long time."

Why was Arnie wearing makeup? And a dress? And why was he here? Nothing about this scene made sense. Was Arnie related to Milton after all? A cross-dressing brother? I'd read about transvestites, and I'd even had one as a classmate while I was in school back east, but I had never expected to find myself dating one. I groped helplessly for something to say.

Penny finally broke the awkward silence. She put her hand on Arnie's arm. "Mother, I'd like you to meet Aimee Machado."

"We've met," Arnie said.

Could it be? Was my Arnie the missing Arnetta Palmer after all? That would explain why Penny had looked so familiar when we first met—she took after her mother.

Arnetta crossed to Milton's bed, sat next to him and picked up his hand. Penny's eyes brimmed and a solitary tear slid down her cheek. "We should leave," she said to me.

Arnetta tore her gaze away from her husband to smile at her daughter. "That would be nice, darling."

Penny and I left her parents to work out what appeared to be the first tentative step toward a reconciliation. We caught an elevator to the basement, raided the vending machines, and found a quiet corner in the cafeteria.

"I'm so sorry I misled you," Penny said. "I wasn't at liberty to tell you the truth."

"And now?"

"Mother likes you. She trusts you and so do I. We felt we should explain."

My cup of vending machine coffee grew cold while I listened to Penny's telling of the Palmer family saga. After Milton's seduction by Bonnie Beardsley broke up the marriage, Arnetta took a nosedive into depression and hooked up with a third-rate psychologist who convinced her she wasn't attractive to men because she was a man trapped in a woman's body.

The psychologist referred Arnetta to a sex-change clinic in Miami. Arnetta and Penny moved to Miami, and Penny enrolled in the university at Coral Gables while her mother enrolled in the Institute for Transformation. Arnie, as she began calling herself, was conflicted, but she eventually decided to start hormone therapy and live as a man for a year.

I was still puzzled. "Why did she come back here? And why didn't she change her last name? For that matter, why 'Arnie'?"

"She was lonely in Florida. Miserable. And the name thing? Mom is clueless about sports celebrities. She doesn't even know who Tiger Woods is. She wanted to keep her name as close to the original as possible until she was sure about the change. Living out of town in a little community like Manton, she figured no one would make the connection to Dad. Palmer's a pretty common name."

"I've noticed that," I said.

"I think deep down she always had doubts about the gender switch," Penny continued, "whether she and Dad got back together or not."

"Do you think they will?"

"He's desperate to have her back. It's up to her now. At first, Dad wouldn't let me tell her he was ill, but after a few days, when I saw how miserable he was, I told her anyway."

That answered my unasked question. Arnetta hadn't known Milton was in the hospital the night she and I were at the ballet. This revelation also debunked my theory that Arnie was Bonnie's stalker. Because if I'd recognized Arnie in a dress, wouldn't Bonnie have recognized Arnetta in men's attire?

"It sounds like their getting back together would make you happy," I said.

"They're good people. I love them both." Penny unwrapped a Milky Way bar and took a bite.

I glanced at the wall clock. The pet store would close in fifteen minutes. I needed a mouse. I wasn't paying any rent, so the least I could do was feed Jack's pets as promised.

"Will you be okay if I leave you here?"

"Sure. I'm going back upstairs pretty soon. Mom is going to spend the night with me at Dad's place. We have a lot to talk about."

"Then I'd better be going."

Two questions came to me on the drive to the pet store. First, why had Arnetta been lunching with Lorraine Beardsley? Lorraine must have been in on Arnetta's secret identity. The two women were members of the same club, Victims of Bonnie Beardsley. Was that what drew them together? Had they joined forces to put an end to Bonnie's home wrecking? The second question involved another link to Bonnie Beardsley. At the ballet, Arnetta, still in Arnie mode, had mentioned the Underhills' swinging lifestyle, then struck up a conversation with them. What was that about? For Penny's sake, I hoped her mother was in the clear, but I couldn't count on it just yet.

At the pet store I did the grisly job of choosing the unsuspecting mouse that would be sacrificed that evening to a hungry three-foot king snake. When the clerk asked if I wanted a male or female, I was too squeamish to come up with an answer.

"I don't want to know," I said. "You decide."

I picked up a bag of cockatiel food for the demented bird and a catnip toy for Fanny while I was there. On my drive home, the little mouse scrabbled around in its take-out box, niggling my conscience with its scritchy noises.

As I slowed to turn in at the entrance to Jack and Amah's property, a dark green pickup pulled out of the driveway onto the road. The heap looked so dilapidated I couldn't determine the make or model. As it passed I tried to get a look at the driver, but the sun was in my eyes. All I saw was a flash of camo and dark glasses as the driver sped away, a cloud of noxious black smoke roiling in his wake.

Hannah's forensic sketch came to mind: the suspicious character who had been lurking in the alley behind the Happy Ox the night before Bonnie Beardsley's body was found.

If the pickup driver was Camo Man, what was he doing at the Highland Ranch? When I reached the likely conclusion, my mouth went dry. Camo Man was looking for me.

I stopped in Jack and Amah's driveway, picked up the little cardboard takeout box with the mouse skittering inside, and unlocked the main house. I checked every room until I was satisfied there hadn't been a break-in, then dropped the live morsel in the snake cage and left the guest room immediately.

I backtracked to Jack's office and contemplated his gun safe. I don't like guns. I can hit a target, but I can't imagine aiming at a person, or any living thing, and actually pulling the trigger. Before Jack and Amah left, he'd written the safe's combination on a scrap of paper for me.

"Not likely you'll need it, but just in case," he had said.

I'd thanked him, stuffed the paper in the pocket of my jeans and forgotten about it. Those jeans had since gone through Amah's washer and dryer, but maybe the scrap had survived in my pocket. Much as I hated the idea, I had to look for it.

Driving down the lane to the barn, I scanned the property for any sign of vandalism. The llamas raised their heads and looked my way, but none of them seemed agitated or injured. Little Moonbeam nursed greedily, her white pom-pom tail wagging in gustatory bliss. The turkeys scratched and pecked, which was pretty much all they ever did.

I parked and checked in my rearview mirror. No one in sight. Up on the deck the door to my bunkhouse apartment was secure. I walked around the deck to check each window. Nothing broken. No sign of forced entry. Maybe the man in the pickup had been someone looking for Jack. Most of his friends were hunters, and they wore camo as everyday attire. I held on to that thought.

Inside my hot little apartment, I turned on the water to the swamp cooler and flipped the switch. Nothing happened. I turned the switch off and back on again. Still nothing.

The kitchen light worked. So did the TV. I'd missed all the evening news programs, so I turned the TV off again. No power outage, so the problem must be what Harry predicted: the cooler's motor had conked out. The wall thermometer showed the temperature at ninety-five degrees. If I didn't get the thing fixed, I'd have to sleep with my windows open to catch whatever scant breeze the night might offer.

I called Harry about the cooler and got his machine but didn't leave a message. He didn't answer his cellphone either, but I did leave a message there. It finally occurred to me he must be screening his calls because of the Beardsley case. That thought wrenched like a knife in my heart. No matter how brave his talk, he was worried. That he might end up wrongly accused kicked my resolve up another notch. Bonnie Beardsley's killer had to be found, and soon.

After I changed into shorts and a T-shirt, I pulled both my pairs of jeans out of the closet and dug through the pockets, looking for the combination to Jack's safe. Nothing in the first pair, and in the second, all I found were a few shredded bits of white paper.

It was almost nine o'clock by the time I finished the chores, and I was hungry. I sat at the little dinette table contemplating whether to read the newspaper first or open a can of soup.

Harry called while the soup was heating.

"Hey, Sis. I got your message. Want me to come out and check the cooler?"

"Not tonight. I can get by with a fan. Do you still have the spare key?"

"In my wallet. I'll get out there tomorrow. You sure you can wait?"

"I'll be fine. Any news? I was just about to read the paper."

"Nope. Nothing new. You doing okay out there?"

"Sure." I thought about Camo Man in the pickup pulling out of Jack and Amah's driveway. "By the way, do you happen to know the combination to Jack's gun safe?"

"No, why?"

"No special reason. He gave it to me, in case of coyotes or something, and I lost it."

"Give me a break," Harry said. "You wouldn't use a gun if you had one. Buy some bear spray."

"Good idea, thanks." It was a great idea. I'd kept pepper spray with me for the first year after Tango's attack, but I hadn't ever needed it, and eventually fell out of the habit. "I'd better go. Fanny wants in."

The cat was outside my door meowing her disgust at being ignored long past her usual feeding time. Bosco, who had nodded off on his perch as soon as the sun went down, protested the commotion with his shrill, relentless squawking. When he dared me to make his day, I covered his cage with a towel.

I let Fanny in and heaped her bowl with extra kibble. She scarfed half of it, lapped at her water, and hopped up on the dresser next to the birdcage, startling Bosco, who squawked and flapped under his towel until I moved the cat to the daybed. With the pets finally quiet, I got ready for bed. The more I thought about the stranger in the pickup, the less I liked the idea of leaving my windows open. Instead, I propped my rickety oscillating floor fan on a chair and aimed it at my bed. The fan squeaked and the chair beneath it vibrated, but the feeble imitation of a breeze allowed me to sleep sporadically, despite the night's sticky heat.

TWENTY-THREE

FRIDAY MORNING BEGAN at five o'clock with black coffee to help me wake up and a cold shower to counter the oppressive air in my apartment. When I arrived at work, things started to look up. Orrie Mercer was missing from the entrance to the library. He had been replaced by a buff young black woman I knew from the dojo. We exchanged greetings and chatted briefly about black belt class. Her name was Shelly Hardesty, and she was filling in for Mercer.

"Where is he?" I asked.

"Taking a day off, I guess. I just got the call this morning."

Maybelline was off on Fridays, so I figured she and Mercer must have made spur-of-the-moment plans together. A romantic trip to Reno? Or a day of bingo at the local casino? I reminded myself not to sneer at other people's tastes in entertainment, since Timbergate's gambling enthusiasts far outweighed fans of the ballet.

The library was quiet, as usual. I checked my email. TMC's daily online newsletter held nothing relevant to my job. Also as usual. The rest of my email consisted of two items. First was a reminder from Dr. Beardsley about the CME Committee meeting, where I was to present an overview of the library's anticipated forensics collection. The other was a request from Jared Quinn to contact him at my convenience.

Widower Quinn, whose political activist wife had died five years ago. According to Maybelline, Quinn had played escort to a diverse range of available women since arriving in Timbergate.

I couldn't deny the sour grapes in my thoughts about Quinn's social life. Not because I cared, but because my ego was bruised. My radar had picked up something beyond the professional interest of an employer in his employee. Either I needed my radar checked, or Quinn had backed off after he witnessed my embrace with Nick Alexander in the parking lot.

There was no going back. According to my rules for romance, both these men were off-limits. Nick's close working relationship with his ex-girlfriend Rella was a definite red flag. Ditto Quinn's position as my boss. Meanwhile, the only man I'd actually dated in ages turned out to be a woman. This dismal train of thought reminded me of Vane Beardsley's awkward dinner invitation. I sighed and turned my attention to library business.

I started by replying to Dr. Beardsley's email, attaching a copy of the agenda for the CME Committee meeting and a second attachment describing the concept he and I had discussed for creating a forensic resources consortium, including hospitals and law libraries in California's seven northernmost counties.

My next obligation was to contact Quinn. He had said *at my convenience*, which on a day this slow was pretty much anytime. Before I placed a call to his office, I reviewed everything I knew about the man: his status as my boss, his great looks and sex appeal, and his wife's untimely death. I wondered how deeply he had been involved with Bonnie Belcher before she became Mrs. Beardsley. Was it coincidence that his late wife and Bonnie both worked in television, or did he have a thing for glamorous women in the public eye?

What I most wanted to know was how his wife had died. For that, I returned to the bookmarked fan club site where I had originally found references to Quinn's late wife. I discovered that Blanche Montague had begun her career as a journalist and photographer, and progressed to TV anchorwoman and finally to talk show personality. Her show became a lightning rod for criticism from several world leaders, particularly those whose political interests were in conflict with Montague's campaign for global recognition of women's rights.

Montague had received her share of death threats, and her show's producers had been pressured to take her off the air, but until the time of her death, she remained a compelling voice. There were references to her tragic death, but no details about the actual cause.

My searching finally turned up a remarkable site called the World Association of Newspapers. Under the heading of Press Freedom was a link showing the number of journalists killed in the course of the past several years. The deaths were listed by country and year, so I searched for Ethiopia and found an article dating back five years where the following paragraph appeared:

> The body of Blanche Montague, star of a popular French television talk show, was found 25 July on a roadside fifty miles from Addis Ababa with three gunshot wounds to the head. She had been filming a documentary exposing the appalling

lack of maternity care for women in the country's
remote villages. Montague had received death
threats demanding she abandon the assignment.
Her American husband, Jared Quinn, a consultant on the project, was beaten and shot by the
unidentified assailants, but survived the attack.

I CALLED QUINN's office with a new attitude. The man
had lost his wife, and nearly his life, in a ruthless,
volatile world far removed from the relatively banal
simplicity of Timbergate Medical Center. The least I
could do was accept him for what he was: a widower
trying to get on with his life.

"Aimee, good timing," Quinn said in that amused
tone that gave me a pleasant little buzz. "Do you have
plans for lunch?"

"Not really, but—"

"Good, I'll swing by in half an hour."

Thirty minutes later, I locked up and met Quinn in
the parking lot. He pulled his Navigator into traffic
then glanced over at me.

"I hear congratulations are in order."

The comment stumped me. "I'm sorry. I'm not sure
what you're talking about."

"Your recent engagement."

Chagrined, I realized my lie to Dr. Beardsley had
been passed on to Quinn.

"Oh, that." My cheeks flared hot. "I'm afraid that's
not quite—"

"Is it the fellow from the parking lot?"

"No." I debated another lie. I could say I had called
it off, but that would leave me fair game for Beardsley.

"I see." Quinn's lips curled in amusement. "You're certainly a popular woman. Who is the lucky guy?"

"I hate to admit it, but I lied. I do that sometimes, to avoid awkward situations."

"Beardsley asked you out?"

"I'm afraid so. To be fair, he called it a business dinner."

"You don't have to explain."

"I didn't want to embarrass him with a rejection."

"Or anger him?" Quinn leveled a quick look at me.

"He seems harmless, but—"

"But his wife is dead."

"Do you think he could have done it?"

Quinn took a moment before he replied. "It's hard to imagine. The police are handling it with kid gloves. Beardsley's been around a long time. He's a civic leader, generous with gifts to the hospital, and very good at his work. An impressive list of Sawyer County women have shaved years off their faces and various other body parts in Beardsley's operating room."

"So a high-profile citizen like Dr. Beardsley wouldn't be arrested and hauled in unless there was overwhelming evidence?"

"Not a chance. Although Beardsley's late wife was no angel. She gave him plenty of grief, and the police seem to know that."

I played dumb. "Did you know his wife?"

"Someone fixed me up with her before she hooked up with Beardsley. It wasn't pleasant."

I waited, hoping he'd say more, and after he turned into the Burger King drive-up, he did.

"She had recently broken off a relationship with

someone and had her feelers out. A mutual friend introduced us."

Quinn pulled up to the take-out order box. "What's your pleasure?"

"Iced tea and a cheeseburger, please," I said.

Minutes later Quinn's car was filled with mouth-watering aromas as he pulled back into the stream of traffic. "What do you say we try another meeting in the park?"

Maybelline's warning about fast food and trips to the park surfaced, but I chose to ignore it. "Fine with me," I said.

"Where was I?" Quinn asked.

"Something about your dating Dr. Beardsley's wife. Before they were married," I hastened to add.

"Oh, right. There's not much to that story. She was a knock-out of a woman, but our only topic of mutual interest was my late wife, and that wasn't one I wanted to pursue."

"Most women would want to know something about your past relationships. Maybe she was concerned you were still grieving." I was trying to keep my questions subtle.

He shook his head and a wry twist crossed his lips. "It was nothing like that." He parked and pulled a blanket from the cargo space.

We walked down the sloping green lawn to a large oak tree near the river. Quinn spread the blanket under its canopy. I leaned against the trunk of the oak and sipped tea in silence while he bit into his burger. Between bites, he returned to his story.

"She wasn't concerned about whether I was still grieving. She wanted to know if I could help her get a gig on a talk show. She thought she had great potential, but she needed someone to manage her career."

"She wanted you to make her a star?"

"It seemed that way to me. She had the wrong idea about who I was...." He broke off in mid-sentence. "I'm sorry. I guess none of this makes much sense out of context."

"Can you put it in context for me?" I had no intention of giving away what I knew about Blanche Montague.

Quinn picked a daisy and began pulling off its petals one at a time. *Tell her, tell her not.*

TWENTY-FOUR

I HAD NO doubt that Quinn was contemplating the wisdom of continuing the conversation. While the silence between us grew, a slight breeze stirred through the branches of the oak tree above our heads. It carried the pungent scent of river grasses and the happy shouts of children playing at the nearby aquatic center.

"Maybe we should change the subject," I said, praying he wouldn't do that.

"You confided in me the other night, Aimee, on an intensely personal level. You trusted me enough to do that. The least I can do is reciprocate."

"Only if you want to," I said.

"I'll be right back." Quinn gathered our wrappers and paper bags and walked to a waste bin several yards away.

Something tickled my ankle and I spotted an ant crawling up my leg. I flicked it off, but the rest of its regiment was marching toward our blanket, so I moved to a nearby picnic table. Quinn came back and sat down across from me. In a navy blue polo shirt and pressed khaki slacks, he looked more like a golf pro than a hospital administrator. His muscular forearms rested on the picnic table between us. He studied the rough wooden surface, tracing carved initials and other graffiti with the pad of his index finger. *Left hand.*

"She was French, from Paris." He looked up at me. "You already knew that, I think."

"Yes, you told me she was Parisian."

"Her name was Blanche." His gaze returned to the tabletop. "We were married for six days. If she hadn't died, we might have lasted another six."

That was the last thing I had expected to hear. "I don't understand."

"Of course not. How could you? The Blanche Montagues of the world are made of different stuff from the rest of us. Her charisma was off the charts. Her fans adored her, and cameras loved her."

I recalled the photo of the stunning, sensual woman standing and waving in the open hatch of the airplane. I hadn't noticed the expression on Quinn's face. Blanche Montague had simply overshadowed him.

"I've heard the same about Dr. Beardsley's deceased wife."

"She did have stunning looks, and a certain kind of charisma, but no soul—at least none that I could discern. In contrast, Blanche had a soul devoted to women's causes. Her causes had become obsessions by the time I met her."

"How did you meet?"

"I had finished what seemed like a lifetime of college and postgraduate work in health administration. It was time to continue a family tradition. My siblings and I were expected to do a stint of humanitarian work in a developing country before settling into a comfy life of luxury back home.

"My mother is French, and well connected. She had heard about Blanche Montague's work. Some strings were pulled, and I became a consultant on a project in Ethiopia."

"Your wife was already a major celebrity when you met?"

"I'm afraid so. Much as I hate to admit it, I was star-struck. She was ten years older, and her sophistication was a heady aphrodisiac. Since we were together constantly in some pretty primitive circumstances, things heated up between us right away. I figured once the project was finished, she would drop me and move on. The last thing I expected was her proposal."

"But you went through with the wedding?"

He nodded. "We flew to an American consulate. Very spur of the moment and romantic. I suppose you could call it an elopement. Within days, both of us came to our senses. It would have been annulled if she had lived." He paused, working his shoulders to relieve tension. "We were part of a small convoy. Blanche had been warned off by every kind of government official, but none wanted publicly to refuse help to the women she was trying to reach. They finally washed their hands of us and said we could proceed at our own risk."

"She must have been fearless." I thought of Rella Olstad and Nick. What was it with these two men and their fearless women?

"I don't find that trait as admirable as I once did," Quinn said. "Fearless is a close cousin to reckless."

"Was anyone else killed?"

"No. The guerillas targeted Blanche and ignored the other three vehicles, which scattered immediately. I was hit," he ran a finger along the horizontal scar that split his eyebrow, "but I'm sure the bullet was intended for her. When the gunmen closed in on our jeep, their only apparent goal was to make certain Blanche was dead."

Quinn paused again. He shook his head and looked out across the river. I waited.

He went on. "The thugs entertained themselves for a while by using me as a soccer ball, but they left me alive. The other vehicles in the convoy eventually came back for us. They knew the mission was risky. I think many of them resented Blanche, partly because she offered so much money. They simply couldn't afford to turn her down."

"This was several years ago, wasn't it?"

"More than five. Going on six, now."

"I don't recall hearing anything about this in the news back then."

"Blanche's death wasn't a big story here in the states, but it caused a sensation in Europe. As her next of kin, I spent a lot of time in Paris trying to put her business affairs in order. I was able to make some progress, but in the end I turned it over to her law firm and returned home to San Francisco."

"I'm surprised you ended up here. Timbergate must seem so provincial to you."

"With Blanche's death, my career stalled before it began. I needed a job, and this looked like a place where I could make a fresh start."

We were distracted when a gray squirrel hopped across the lawn and stopped near the oak tree next to our table. It reared up on its hind legs and cocked its head to one side then the other, sizing up Quinn and me.

"Hi, fella," Quinn said. The squirrel dropped to all fours and ran off across the grass.

I stood and smoothed my dress. "I guess we should be getting back."

"Right, but I had intended to ask if you've noticed anything new in Beardsley's behavior. You've already mentioned his dinner invitation. At this point, I think you were wise to turn him down. Has there been anything else?"

"No, not really."

"Then I'm afraid our working lunch turned into the story of my life," he said. "I'm sorry I monopolized the hour."

"At least we're even now. I don't feel so bad about unloading on you the other evening."

"Aimee, wait."

Quinn gripped my shoulders, turning me to face him. "I hope I haven't made you feel uncomfortable about our working relationship. You came to TMC with stellar recommendations. We were incredibly lucky that you wanted the position. Don't worry for a moment that befriending me will harm your career. I wouldn't let that happen." As an apparent afterthought, he added, "I don't seem to have many friends."

Lately, I had been feeling the same way. The only true friend I had was Harry, and he was in terrible trouble. If he went to prison, I was sure my heart would break. How would I find the strength to help him survive behind bars? I thought of Blanche Montague's incredible courage and wondered about my own.

TWENTY-FIVE

WE HAD ALMOST reached the hospital when Quinn suddenly turned up the volume on his car radio. "Damn, that's Benoit Blue Boy." He must have seen my confusion. "French blues harmonicist. I didn't think any DJ in this part of the world had ever heard of him."

"His name isn't familiar to me," I said, "but I had no exposure to blues until I spent some time back east. Out here it's mostly country."

"Country's okay. Some of it isn't so different from blues. They both make good use of the harmonica." He smiled to himself. "One of my favorite instruments."

"You play?"

"Occasionally. Some of us at the hospital have formed a blues combo."

Another unexpected facet of Jared Quinn. Before I could digest it, the music ended and news came on as we pulled up to my building, I heard a mention of the Beardsley case:

Sawyer County District Attorney Connie Keefer announced today that an arrest is imminent in the murder of a prominent physician's wife. Keefer declined to comment further.

Quinn's apprehensive glance telegraphed his thoughts. He reached over and patted my hand.

"Aimee, I won't tell you not to worry. Just keep me in mind if you need a friend."

"What'll I do if they arrest Harry? I'll have to call our parents. They'll be devastated."

"Where are they?"

"The Azores. They're retired, they—"

"Slow down a minute. We don't know if this is about Harry, but in case it is, does he have a lawyer?"

"Yes."

"Then wait a bit before you worry your family. Sometimes these things get sorted out quickly."

"I suppose you're right," I said. "I'm so shaky right now, I can't think."

"Do you want to take the rest of the day off?"

"No, I'd rather keep busy."

"It's your choice."

I closed the car door and he pulled away, heading toward the VIP lot on the other side of the hospital complex. I still didn't have a clear picture of how things had been left between Quinn and Bonnie Beardsley. There must have been occasional social contact, since TMC played a large part in the careers of both Quinn and Dr. Beardsley. Was there more than social contact?

I texted Harry, asking if he had any news. He didn't reply. For the rest of the afternoon, my brain seemed short-circuited. I dusted shelves and mended a few torn journals. What would I do if Harry was arrested? I dreaded the prospect of calling Mom and Dad.

Inside my apartment that afternoon, the atmosphere was pleasant, thanks to Harry, who had come as promised to repair the swamp cooler. I looked on the table for a note.

It's fixed. Check the fridge. H.

In the refrigerator, I saw two bottles of his favorite dark beer. I wasn't crazy about the taste, but I opened one immediately and drank half of it down. Knowing he'd been there, instead of handcuffed and sitting in a cell, raised my spirits a notch. The beer raised them another notch.

I changed my clothes and did the routine chores. The little cria started toward me when I held out a handful of cob. One of the geldings tried to horn in, and Moonbeam's dam sprayed him with a gob of foul-smelling green slime. Llama spit isn't pleasant, but they have other aggressive tactics that do considerably more damage. One is a vicious, lightning-fast kick. And under enough duress, they charge forward at full throttle, slamming their chest or shoulder into their perceived foe with the force of a stoked-up NFL linebacker. Any unsuspecting person who didn't know this about llamas would be knocked senseless before he knew what hit him.

After chores, I scanned the newspaper. It rehashed the Beardsley investigation, but I knew it had gone to press before the radio announcement about an impending arrest. The local TV news was beginning its second edition when I turned on my television. I took the other bottle of Harry's leftover beer from the fridge. Milton Palmer's co-anchor began with a teaser: "DA promises arrest in Beardsley case. Stay tuned."

A dozen commercials later, the newswoman continued her Beardsley story by replaying footage of the Dumpster in the alley where Bonnie's body had been discovered, the bloody deer bag she'd been wrapped in, and a clip of Hannah's forensic sketch of Camo Man. Viewers were told to tune in again at eleven o'clock for late developments on the story.

I picked up my phone to call Harry, and it rang in my hand. It was Hannah.

"Are you okay?" she asked.

"Not really. Why? Do you know something?"

"A couple of friends at the department are keeping me informed. They think the police are going to bring Harry in. I wanted to warn you."

My eyes filled and the phone trembled in my hand. "Damn. What shall we do?"

"Trust Harry's lawyer. From what I hear, the DA's evidence is feeble. Bonnie's fingerprints were on something in Harry's condo, which was to be expected, since Harry's the one who told the police she'd been there."

"*That's* the evidence they're using?"

"Apparently. It's pretty flimsy, but Keefer is forcing the issue."

"When did they search his condo? He said there hadn't been a warrant."

"No warrant. Apparently he gave them consent to search his home."

"Why?"

"He said he wants to get this over with, and figured it would speed things up. He knows he's innocent, so he figured there's nothing in his place to suggest foul play."

"Hannah, have you talked to him?"

"Johnny and I just left his condo. Abe Edelman is there." Abe. Harry's lawyer.

"Did he say anything about Mom and Dad?"

"That's the only thing he's worried about. Besides you. He said to tell you he'll call you as soon as he can. He's insisting he doesn't want you to call your mom and dad yet."

"What do you think?"

Hannah was silent too long before she answered. "There's still time. The real killer will be found."

"Not if no one's looking for him."

For a long while I sat staring at the muted television screen. I would have to kick my pursuit of Bonnie Beardsley's killer into high gear. To do that, I needed a clear head. Food and coffee would be required to counteract the two beers.

I started the coffee and built a fairly healthy dinner salad with a mixture of veggies from Jack's garden, some sliced mozzarella cheese, and a handful of walnuts. When it was done, I went out to my deck. I sat in a camp chair and ate slowly while I watched the sunset bring a blush to the sky and turn the blue hue of the Yolla Bolly Mountains to deep indigo. One by one, the turkeys flew up to the high branches of a blue oak, where they could roost in safety.

I heard my phone ring and jumped up, tangling myself in the chair. I nearly fell, but reached the phone while it was still ringing. *Harry.*

"Hi, Sis, is the cooler still working?"

"It's perfect. Thanks."

"Did you find the beer?"

"Drank both of them. What's going on?"

"I need to tell you something, but I don't want you to worry."

I kept the fear from my voice. "Are you going to be arrested?"

"Maybe. Abe thinks there's going to be an arraignment, but it's no big deal. He's sure it won't stand. If the DA doesn't show probable cause, the judge will release me."

"Oh, God, Harry. What shall I do?"

"Just try not to worry. And don't call Mom and Dad. If you need someone to talk to, call Nick."

"Why Nick?"

"Because I trust him. Please, Aimee. Abe's here for me. We're working this out, but you need someone, too." I heard a voice in the background. "Abe's asking for me. I have to go."

The food and a shower did away with the last vestiges of my beer buzz but left me wide awake at bedtime. Fanny and Bosco were snoozing peacefully. I sat at my kitchen table with a notepad, but the only note I'd made was *bear spray*. I couldn't get Harry's news off my mind. All my efforts to save him from an arrest had been in vain. Worry was my constant state of mind, but I still had to function somehow. I couldn't do my job or help my brother if I panicked.

I needed a mundane chore to distract myself, so I decided to organize my clothes closet. When I got to my favorite skirt, I noticed a bulge in one of the pockets. I pulled out a crumpled tissue, and when I tossed it toward the wastebasket, I heard a click as something hit the floor. I remembered I'd been wearing that skirt the day I found a penny near the Dumpster.

The shiny thing on my floor was the size and color of a penny, but the shape was wrong. I looked at my bare foot planted next to the little copper scrap. My big toenail was exactly the same shape. Hannah's comment about acrylic toenails rushed back to me.

I'd never heard of them either, until someone in the crime lab said Bonnie Beardsley was wearing them. I guess the acrylic nail on one of her big toes was missing.

Please, God, I thought, let this be the one.

I ran for my tweezers, picked up the toenail and slid it into a small paper bag. I stapled the bag shut and put it in the kitchen cupboard. At last I had a clue. Or I would have, if Bonnie Beardsley's assailant had grabbed her foot while he was dumping her body. He might have left a fingerprint on that nail.

I called Nick. He picked up on the first ring.

"Were you sitting by the phone?"

"Yes," he said. "Where are you?"

"Home."

"At your grandparents' house?"

"Not exactly. I'm in the studio apartment over their barn."

"Jesus, that's where you're living?"

"It's not that bad, and it's only temporary."

"It's a hovel."

"Never mind about that. Harry said to call you if I needed help."

"What kind of help?"

"I want you to find out if Buck Sawyer has any influence with a crime lab somewhere out of the area."

"Why?"

"I think I found a false toenail from Bonnie Beardsley's body. It was at the Dumpster site the day after her body was found."

"You're thinking someone's fingerprint could be on the toenail? That's a whopper of a long shot, isn't it?"

"It's better than nothing," I said. "Someone dumped

her. What if he wasn't wearing gloves? Hannah said she was wearing acrylic toenails, and one from her big toe was missing. What if this is it?"

"What about prints on the rest of her body? And what about the deer bag they found her in?"

"I don't think Sawyer County's crime lab is sophisticated enough to recover prints from flesh or fabric. They would have to send her remains and clothing to Sacramento, where there's bound to be a backlog. If Marco and Connie Keefer are convinced Harry's the killer, they might not have bothered."

"So what do you want to do?" Nick asked.

"I want to find out as soon as possible if there's a print on this acrylic toenail."

"Seems pretty improbable, but if you're right and this ever goes to trial, you'd have to give it up at discovery."

"I know, but I can't give it to the Timbergate PD before we get it analyzed. I'm afraid Marco Bueller would find some way to bury it. I'm sure he has friends on the force who owe him favors. I don't want to take that chance."

"Okay, I see your point, but don't get your hopes up. I'll have to get back to you. How late will you be up?"

"Doesn't matter."

I paced the apartment, opening and closing the cupboard, staring at the paper bag. If there was a print, would it be complete enough to confirm a match? Would the owner of the print be in any data base? Whopper of a long shot was right. But in spite of Nick's warning, it gave me hope at a time when it was sorely needed.

My phone rang and I pounced on it. "Nick?"

"Yep. Pack an overnight bag. We're flying to San Francisco in the morning."

"Why there?"

"Buck's late wife was a patient at a medical center in the city. She was treated well, and he thanked the institution with a sizeable donation."

"How will that help? We need a crime lab."

"Buck knows someone at the hospital there who knows someone at a forensics lab in the Bay Area. Don't ask any more questions. Just meet me at the muni airport tomorrow morning at seven. I'm flying the Citation."

"Doesn't sound familiar."

"It's Buck's newest Cessna. Mustang Citation. Seats six. It's more plane than we need, but it's what's available right now."

"What time will we be back? I still have to take care of the ranch."

"We might be gone overnight. Call Hannah. She knows what to do."

"I can't just—"

"Aimee, work with me. If we're going to do this, we don't have a lot of time. Call Hannah, then get some sleep. On second thought, make some notes. You work with Beardsley, the dead woman's husband, and I know how nosy you are. You've probably been snooping like crazy. I'm guessing you know more about his dead wife than the police do."

"I'm not nosy, I'm curious." He didn't need to know I was spying for Jared Quinn.

"Right," Nick said. "Do you want me to come out there? I could sleep in the main house."

"No, I'm fine alone." With him that close, I'd have

been awake all night for sure, longing for the old times and wishing I were lying in his arms.

Hannah didn't answer when I called, so I left a message saying I'd call again early in the morning.

I poured a cup of coffee and listed the names of everyone I knew who had a connection to Bonnie Beardsley. Her not-so-grieving husband topped the list. Much as I disliked the idea, I added Quinn's name next. He had dated Bonnie, however briefly. Then came Milton and Arnetta Palmer, followed by the swinging Underhills of Everlasting Pets, who had had some kind of kinky relationship with Bonnie Beardsley. The last person I could think of was Dr. Beardsley's ex-wife, who was days away from becoming Mrs. Troy Bilkowsky. I was still searching for a clear motive for Bonnie's killer, and Lorraine Beardsley was unfinished business.

Penny Palmer's words came back to me. *You should ask the first Mrs. Beardsley what she thinks of Bonnie.* I searched my mind for what I knew about Lorraine Beardsley. The scene in the civic center lobby came to mind: Maybelline Black gushing about Lorraine's engagement. Lorraine had too much class to snub her ex-husband's eccentric library volunteer. I made a note: *Learn more about Lorraine. From Maybelline?*

Arnetta Palmer had a connection to Lorraine as well. At the ballet, they'd behaved as if they'd never met, but the very next day at Stone Soup they'd acted like the best of chums. I wondered again what that was about. Was it really possible they had teamed up to rid the world of Bonnie Beardsley?

Around midnight, I thought I might be able to sleep. I tucked my notes in my purse and pulled a small overnight bag out of my closet. I packed a bare minimum, mainly underwear and toiletries. I put out a light turtleneck, jeans and low-heeled boots for the plane ride, along with a denim jacket. San Francisco could be cold in the summertime. I left my bag near the front door and set my alarm for six o'clock.

TWENTY-SIX

"YOU'RE SPENDING THE weekend with Nick?"

Hannah's shout through the phone early Saturday morning set my right eardrum vibrating. I switched to my other ear and tried to explain that the trip was about helping Harry and had absolutely nothing to do with Nick and me.

"Just toss some hay to the llamas this afternoon, and make sure everyone has water. The turkeys won't need more food before I get back."

"What about Fanny and Bosco?"

"I've been keeping them in the apartment with me, but I'm putting them back in the main house with the A/C on low. You might need to adjust it if we get another scorcher tomorrow."

"Got it. Do you want me to check your apartment?"

"No need...wait, I almost forgot. There's a dead snake in my refrigerator. Your dad might want it for his collection."

"What kind of snake?" Hannah asked.

"Rattler."

"Good. He could use another one of those."

"It's in my freezer compartment," I said, "in a plastic bag."

"Care to explain why?"

"It was on my deck the other night. I had to kill it."

"On your deck? How?"

"I think raccoons dragged it up there." I hoped that was what happened. I didn't want to think about other, more troubling, explanations.

"Why would they do that?" Hannah asked.

"I don't know, but that's where I found it."

"Wow. That's unusual…and kind of creepy. I'll take it over to Dad tonight."

"Thanks. And Harry just changed my locks, so I'll leave my extra key in a baggie in the cob bin. Just dig around for it."

"Got it. You'd better get moving if you're meeting Nick at seven."

"Okay. I'll call you tomorrow if we're running late getting back."

"I hope you *are* late," she said. "It's about time you two—"

"Stop it. We're not getting back together." She was as bad as Vanza when it came to Nick and me. I checked the time. Six thirty.

I drove to the airport, parked in the overnight lot and entered the small terminal with a few minutes to spare. Nick stood at a car rental kiosk chatting with a pretty clerk who didn't look a day over fifteen. When he spotted me and called out, "Hi, Honey, I got you a coffee," the pretty clerk's face fell.

We walked to the hangar where the Mustang Citation waited. It was magnificent, even by Buck Sawyer's billionaire standards, with sleek, futuristic exterior lines and a leather interior done up in champagne tones.

"Holy Cow," I said.

Nick smiled. "I thought you'd like it."

"How much is this trip costing us?"

"Nothing. It's on Buck."

"Why?"

"He likes Harry."

Nick went through his final checklist before he taxied onto the runway and executed his usual perfect takeoff. We reached altitude and he set the autopilot for what promised to be a short hop. I doubted we would cruise more than thirty minutes before starting our approach to SFO. Riding shotgun, I fell into my old habit of scanning the sky for other air traffic.

Nick and I couldn't carry on much of a conversation with headsets on, so I rummaged through his CD case and listened to the score of *Les Misérables* until we reached San Francisco. We had to wait for permission to land, so Nick circled above a low ceiling of clouds that obscured the runways. I passed the minutes by tracking the Citation's shadow play on the white blanket below us.

When our turn came, Nick touched down so smoothly that I had to look out at the runway to confirm that our wheels were on the ground. We taxied to the private aviation terminal where he had arranged to leave the plane overnight; then we walked to the terminal's long-term parking lot where Buck's Prius waited. As we drove north toward San Francisco, the clouds broke and sunlight drenched the majestic hills of the city.

Nick kept pace with the swift-moving northbound traffic, driving as expertly as he flew.

"Do you have your notes handy?"

"Right here." I pulled them from my purse.

"What do you have so far?"

I described the various suspects and their connection to Bonnie Beardsley. I reviewed everything I'd written the evening before, ending with Dr. Beardsley inviting me to go out for a so-called business dinner.

"Did you accept?"

"No. I told him I was engaged."

Nick smiled, but kept his eyes on the road. "Are you?"

"Of course not."

He laughed out loud. "Hey, last I heard, you had a boyfriend. I thought things might have heated up since then."

"It might seem funny to you, but lying to a murder suspect is outside my comfort zone."

Nick sobered. "Damn, I'm sorry. You were right to turn him down. Don't let him change your mind."

We had reached the heart of downtown San Francisco, so I opened my window to draw in the bouquet of the city: diesel smoke from the city buses, the heady fragrance of the flower stalls, the mouth-watering aromas from hot dog carts and pretzel vendors. Encompassing all of it was a briny breeze from the bay.

"Hungry?" Nick asked. The hot dog aroma must have gotten to him, too.

"A little, but I can wait." I watched the flow of people and traffic on the city streets and sidewalks.

"You're quiet. What are you thinking?" Nick asked.

"Harry has absolutely no motive," I said. "Do you think this is all Marco Bueller's doing? Has he convinced Keefer that Harry is the killer?"

"That's what Abe is up against. Marco's bias against Harry."

Nick drove into the underground parking garage at the med center. I held the little bag with the fake toenail as we walked toward the elevator.

Nick pushed the button. "What do you know about those Everlasting Pets people?"

"The Underhills? They're creepy and sleazy, but they're a legitimate nonprofit from what I can tell. The woman said Bonnie Beardsley was their soul mate, whatever that means."

I started to tell him how the Underhills were schmoozing Arnetta Palmer and me at the ballet when Arnetta was passing as Arnie, then realized I'd never told him the rest of her story. I filled him in on Arnetta Palmer's gender confusion and her true identity.

"So your ballet date was a woman passing as a man? That explains a lot." He managed to keep a straight face, but I could tell it wasn't easy.

"Right. They thought she was a guy and hinted about the four of us getting together. I'd rather have my skin peeled off."

"Why?"

"If you met them, you wouldn't have to ask."

"I plan to. You can arrange a double date when we get back to town."

"You can't be serious."

Nick laughed. "I'm dead serious." He didn't elaborate, so I let it go for the moment.

We rode the elevator to the main lobby, where Nick asked for a Dr. Larry Tipton. I handed the little paper bag to Nick.

"Oh, yes," the receptionist said. "He's expecting you."

Dr. Tipton came out a few minutes later and shook hands with both of us in turn. Apparently, all necessary communication had taken place earlier, because the doctor simply took the bag Nick offered and said, "I'll be in touch."

As we made our way back to the garage, I turned to Nick. "That's it? What do we do now? Wait?"

"Yes. But we have a nice place to wait."

"Where?"

"Sausalito. We'll drop off our bags and get some lunch."

"We're staying in Sausalito?"

"Don't worry, Buck's yacht has three staterooms."

"We're staying on the yacht?" I'd heard about the luxurious Sawyer yacht but hadn't seen it.

"Buck hasn't been able to use it all summer. He promised Delta he'd take her and some of her friends out next weekend. He said we'd be doing him a favor if we spent the night on it and stocked the larder. He gave me a grocery list. I was hoping you'd go to the market while I start the engine and inspect the rigging and sails."

We crossed the Golden Gate, driving headlong into a picture postcard. Excited tourists walked the bridge, stopping every few feet to snap photos. Billowing white sails dotted the gray-green water below us, and puffy white clouds rode the cool bay breeze.

Nick took Bridgeway Drive to the north end of Sausalito. Turning on Harbor Drive, he parked near the business office of the harbor where Buck's yacht was moored. He went inside and emerged moments later with a key to the marina. Whistling softly, he led the way down the dock through a forest of masts. Buck's pampered yacht, one of the largest in the basin, was at the end of the slip. Its brass trim shone, and the deep umber color of the teakwood decks suggested they had been freshly oiled.

Down below, the portholes flooded the cabin with sunlight. The curtains and cushions in plaid fabric of red, white, and blue accentuated the nautical tone.

"Which stateroom do you want?" Nick held out my overnight bag.

"The smallest." I dropped my bag on the V-shaped berth in the bow, farthest away from the other two in the stern. I made a show of fingering the door's lock and checking to make sure it worked. Nick noticed, as he was meant to.

"You don't really think you're going to need that, do you?"

"You never know."

"Let's get back to our detective work." He tossed his small duffel on the bed in one of the aft berths. "Some of your suspects sound like oddballs, but I haven't heard anything that makes me think *killer*."

"Well somebody did it, and it wasn't Harry."

"Hey, take it easy. I'm on your side."

"Sorry."

"Never mind. Let's go get some lunch."

We walked to a combination deli and bait shop near the harbor office, where we both opted for the fish and chips and beer.

I spread my notes on a small table and we rehashed the information I'd gathered on my suspects: Dr. Beardsley, Jared Quinn, the Palmers, and the Underhills. After repeating everything I'd already told Nick about them, I felt we were getting nowhere and said so.

"Then let's assume for a moment that they're all innocent," Nick said. "We know Harry's innocent. Where does that leave us?"

"Nowhere."

"What about the guy in the camo clothes?"

"That could have been any of my suspects."

"What if it wasn't?"

"Then we're back to looking for a mysterious stranger."

"Not necessarily," Nick said. "How about Tango Bueller?"

"You're the one who told me about Tango's amazing effort to redeem himself. It's hard to believe a guy who's trying that hard would—"

"I agree, but we can't overlook any possibilities. You said Bonnie had sex with someone just before she died."

"Are you suggesting Tango raped and killed her?"

"It's possible, isn't it?"

"Barely possible," I said, "but after what I saw the night he changed my tire, he's the last person I'd suspect."

"Then who else? Any idea who she might have been intimate with?"

"No, but Hannah's friend at the TPD says there was no concrete evidence of rape, so the sex could have been consensual. If it was, why would her lover kill her?"

"If there was sex, especially if it was unprotected, there's probably a specimen. What about DNA?"

"It's been checked against Beardsley and Harry. It's not a match with either of them." At that I swallowed hard. Damn them for subjecting Harry to that embarrassment.

"That should work in Harry's favor," Nick said, "but prosecution could argue Harry killed her because he discovered she was cheating with someone besides him."

"This seems hopeless. We're going around in circles and getting nowhere."

After finishing our lunch, we were halfway back to the dock when Nick's cellphone rang. He stopped and answered. His expression changed from mild interest to intense curiosity. He turned to me. "Pen. Paper. Quick."

I dug in my purse and handed over a pencil and notebook. He scribbled and said, "Right, got it. Thanks." Closing the phone, he faced me with a look of triumph. "Do you know anyone by the name of Verna Beardsley?"

"No, why?"

"Because her fingerprint was on the acrylic toenail."

"They identified the print?"

"Unofficially. Don't get your hopes too high. We don't know if this is evidence we can use if Harry were to go to trial, but at least we finally have a clue."

"But who's Verna Beardsley? She must be related to Dr. Beardsley, but I've never heard anyone mention that name. Did the lab have any details on her?"

"Some," Nick said. "But it's so unofficial that it never happened. Dr. Tipton suggested we make a stop at Green Pastures Psychiatric Facility. He arranged an appointment for us with the administrator there."

"Where is this place?"

"Near Larkspur. It's a few miles up Highway 101. Apparently Verna Beardsley was an inpatient there several years ago. They fingerprint all of their patients."

"With all the privacy laws in place these days, I'll be surprised if they'll tell us anything."

"Maybe not, but we're in the neighborhood, and this is the best lead we have. We're damn lucky the woman's prints were on file."

"She could be anywhere if she was discharged several years ago."

Nick pulled out his phone. "Let's see if we can find her online."

It was worth a try. Even though the name sounded uncommon, there was probably more than one Verna Beardsley out there. I looked up my own name once, and found several other Aimee Machados. Until then, I thought my name was unique.

"Any results?" I asked.

"Three, but two are obituaries and the other one is in Kentucky and only ten years old."

We headed up the highway toward Larkspur.

TWENTY-SEVEN

We reached Green Pastures Psychiatric Facility in mid-afternoon. The place looked as bucolic as its name, except for the eight foot high chain link fence surrounding the property. Nick stopped at the closed entry gate where a uniformed security officer leaned out the guard shack window and asked the nature of our business. Nick showed his identification and said we had an appointment with the administrator. The guard spoke into his radio, nodded, then aimed a remote at the gate.

"Main building, first office on the left." The gate rolled open. "Have a nice day."

The compound consisted of a two-story brick building and several clapboard cabins, all shaded by towering eucalyptus trees and nestled against a hillside dotted with oaks and populated with a herd of black-and-white dairy cattle.

The lobby's décor mirrored the compound's pastoral setting with grass-green carpet, wallpaper sporting rural scenes, and pale green gingham upholstery on the couches and chairs. Goldfish swam in a stone pond dominating a corner of the lobby.

Nick checked in at the reception desk, and we were told to have a seat, that Mr. Delacruz would be right out.

"Why is the administrator here on a Saturday?" I whispered.

"Maybe he's the weekend guy," Nick said. "Someone has to be in charge if the inmates get restless."

"Inmates? Come on, they're patients."

"They're that, too."

"What do you mean?"

Before Nick could elaborate, a fireplug of a man with horn-rimmed glasses, a black moustache, and receding hairline marched toward us, offering his hand to Nick. We both stood.

"Anthony Delacruz." He shook Nick's hand, then mine. "Please, let's talk in my office." We followed him down a spotless corridor into a tidy office of modest proportions. Delacruz sat at his desk, and we took the two visitors' chairs.

"You're interested in Verna Beardsley."

"We are," Nick said. "Larry Tipton said you might be able to help us."

Delacruz lifted a folder from the top of his desk. "Up to a point. Are you familiar with the Health Insurance Portability and Accountability Act?"

When he heard Delacruz rattle off that mouthful, Nick shot me an inquiring glance.

"HIPAA. Yes, of course," I said. "It protects patient privacy." I had been wondering how Nick would clear that hurdle. A tense moment passed, then Delacruz spoke.

"I understand you work for Samuel Sawyer?" The question was directed at Nick.

"That's right." Nick waited calmly.

"I see." Delacruz tapped his pursed lips with his index finger. "Mr. Sawyer's philanthropy is quite admirable. Larry Tipton tells me his endowments have enriched many worthy institutions."

Nick remained silent.

Delacruz cleared his throat. "I must say the world could use more men like Samuel Sawyer."

Nick handed the man a business card. "He is a generous man, all right. Never says no to a good cause. That's the number for his private foundation, if you should want to inquire about a grant for your facility."

Delacruz stood. He dropped the file folder on his desk. "If you two will excuse me, I have a matter of importance to discuss with my nursing supervisor. Her office is rather a long trek, but if you'll bear with me, I should be back in say, twenty minutes?"

Nick smiled. "Twenty minutes is fine with us."

"Tell you what. If I'm not back in twenty minutes, just let yourselves out. We can reschedule if necessary. I'm off tomorrow, but I'll be here every day next week."

"Sounds good," Nick said.

As soon as the door closed behind the administrator, Nick shot out of his chair and walked around the desk. He lifted the cover of the file with the point of a pen.

I walked over to watch out the small square of glass in the door while Nick went to work. He took a small digital camera from his pocket. "It's not complete, just a few pages, but it's better than nothing." He snapped pictures of each page.

"What does it say?"

"For starters, she's no longer an inpatient, but she still checks in from time to time for evaluation of her condition and adjustment of medications."

"Does it say where she's living?"

"Nope."

"Next of kin?"

"No. Verna Beardsley was admitted eleven years ago with a diagnosis of manic-depressive illness."

"It's called bipolar disorder these days. Does it say why she was committed?"

"She must have committed some kind of crime. This place only treats patients referred by the courts. Hence the fingerprints. Are bipolar people violent?"

"They can be. In severe cases the disorder destroys rational thought. Some patients commit what the text-books call dreadful behaviors."

Nick flipped through the remaining pages of the scant file. "Nothing here about that. Delacruz didn't give us everything."

"But it's her fingerprint on the toenail?"

"Yes. Larry Tipton's forensics source was positive." Nick checked his watch. "We'd better leave. I have a feeling Delacruz won't want to see us here when he gets back."

"I agree. Even if the end justifies the means, what we're doing could make trouble for all of us. I just hope Buck Sawyer comes through if he gets a grant request from Delacruz."

"He probably will. This place fits right in with his foundation's mission."

We left the compound heading south, surrounded by a steady flow of traffic on 101.

"It's pretty likely this Verna Beardsley is related to the doctor," Nick said. "Have you heard anything about his family?"

"Just the ex-wife and the dead wife. But this woman must be family. If she killed Bonnie, what's her motive?"

"Money or passion," Nick said. "My guess is money."

"There's talk the deceased was a world-class gold-digger," I said. "If Verna is some kind of heir, maybe she was about to be left out in the cold."

Back in the harbor, a salty afternoon breeze set the rows of sailboats and cruisers rocking. Riggings on a forest of masts tinkled like the high notes on a piano keyboard. I hugged myself against the chill until we reached the yacht. We climbed aboard and went below.

Nick opened a bottle of Cabernet, poured two glasses, and handed one to me. "Want to go out to dinner or eat in?"

"In. This weekend isn't a date. We're here to work."

I sounded snarky, even to myself, but Nick ignored the barb. He took out his wallet and handed me his credit card and Buck's shopping list.

"Do you mind doing the shopping while I putter here?"

"Sure you trust me with this?" I dropped his card into my purse.

"You're the one with trust issues."

"With good reason," I replied.

"I disagree," Nick said, "but now's not the time to go down that road." He handed me the keys to the car and the dock. "You can use one of the carts at the basin gate when you get back with the groceries."

Food shopping at the Harbor Market in Sausalito was a delight. I bought everything on Nick's list, then indulged in some exotic cheeses, fruits, and pastries I would never find in Timbergate's big box supermarkets.

Nick was finishing his inspection of the sails and riggings when I returned, so I stowed the groceries and arranged a snack plate of brie, crackers, and grapes. We sat at the dinette table munching food and sipping wine in a silence that was too comfortable, too much like the good days in our past. I broke the mood by taking two large notepads from my tote bag and handing one to Nick.

"Let's brainstorm the Verna Beardsley puzzle," I said. "Where do we start?"

"We start with where is she?"

"If she's mixed up in the murder, she must live in or near Timbergate."

"But our Internet search for Verna Beardsley didn't turn up anyone on the west coast," Nick said, "so she's probably using an alias."

I wrote *Alias?* on my pad. "Isn't it more likely she simply goes by a married name? Someone she met after she left the psych center?"

"I think Delacruz would have left that information in the file for us. Remember, she's still on their rolls as some kind of outpatient under her real name. If she's using an alias, Delacruz probably doesn't know about it."

"Then how do we find her? And what if she doesn't live in Sawyer County at all, much less right under our noses?" I threw my pen on the table. "This is hopeless. Harry's going—"

"Stop." Nick picked up the pen and handed it back to me. "Don't panic now. We're just getting started. This Beardsley woman must have something to do with your Dr. Beardsley. The name isn't that common."

"What if I ask Beardsley about her when I get to work Monday?"

"No. Absolutely not. If he's the killer and the woman is an accomplice, you'll be their next target."

"Maybe there's another way. There's a gossipy woman, a volunteer who works for me two mornings a week. Monday and Wednesday. She seems to know a lot about Beardsley and everyone else at the hospital."

"It's worth a try." Nick picked up his pen. "For now, let's make a list of every woman you can think of with any connection to Beardsley or his dead wife."

The first three names on my list were Arnetta Palmer, who was looking less likely as a suspect, her daughter Penny, who hadn't been anywhere near Timbergate when the crime was committed, and Lorraine Beardsley.

"Who else?" Nick said.

"I'm thinking."

"What about that Underhill couple?"

"Right. I keep forgetting about them."

"Well, don't. It sounds like there was something deviant going on between the Underhills and the promiscuous victim."

"And you actually expect me to set up a double date with those two perverts?"

Nick reached out and touched my arm. "Aimee, they run what's most likely a scam, and from what you've said, they were into something kinky with the deceased woman. We need to know more about them."

"I agree, but I don't like your plan. They invited me to visit their new facility. Why don't I just do that?"

"That might work, but if they're the kind of people I think they are, we'll learn more by arranging a private get-together."

"The thought gives me the creeps."

"Too bad. You took a hell of a chance dating your friend Arnie. You're damn lucky that turned out as well as it did. I don't want you getting chummy with

the Underhills by yourself. Any contact you have with
those people is going to include me."

"Nick, I'm not helpless. I met you at a gun club, remember? I'm a third degree black belt—"

"Fine, but none of that saved you from Tango."

"That's not fair. Tango was a fluke. No one could
have been prepared for that."

"You could have been killed. I can't let—"

"Enough about Tango. I don't care what you promised Harry. You're not my bodyguard, okay?"

Silence filled the cabin. Nick went to his stateroom
to make a phone call. Checking in with Buck Sawyer,
I presumed. Or maybe Abe Edelman, Harry's attorney. The sooner Abe knew about the mysterious Verna
Beardsley, the better.

"Well?" I asked, when he came back out.

"Harry's been released. The judge ruled there wasn't
probable cause for his arrest."

"Thank God."

"It's a break, but it isn't over. He's been instructed
to stay in town, and you know Keefer isn't going to
let up." Nick reached out to touch my cheek. "Try not
to worry, Sweetheart. We'll keep at it until we figure
this out."

I pulled back. "No touching. No sweetheart stuff."

"Fair enough. Let's get some sleep."

The cradle-like rocking of the yacht lulled me toward sleep, but with Nick so near I couldn't stop wishing that things between us were different and that Paris
had never happened.

TWENTY-EIGHT

NICK'S FLAWLESS LANDING at Timbergate Municipal Airport on Sunday morning brought me back to earth in more ways than one. He taxied to the hangar while my spirits sagged under the weight of our task. To save my brother from a vindictive police investigator and an ambitious DA, we had to find the killer of an amoral woman with a past full of shady characters.

Nick walked me to my car. I didn't need the grim set of his jaw to remind me we were running out of time.

"Call me as soon as you make contact with the Underhills," he said. "We need to set something up right away."

"I know. I'll take care of it." I slipped into my car and lowered the window. "What will you be doing?"

"Meeting with Harry and Abe. Keeping an eye on you."

"I hate that."

"Get used to it. You're stuck with me until this is finished."

When Harry was out of danger, would Nick and I be finished as well? I had been ready to move on, but working as a team to help my brother had put a dent in my resolve to forget Nick. At least he had kept his promise the night before. No touching. No sweetheart talk. Neither of us referred to our night in separate bunks or asked how the other had slept.

Everything looked peaceful and normal back at the ranch, if a pasture filled with llamas and turkeys could be considered normal.

Inside my little apartment, I found a welcoming committee. Hannah had obviously made an early morning visit and returned Fanny and Bosco to my domain. I spotted a note on my table:

Found the rattler. Took it to Dad. Thanks, Hannah.

I left messages on Harry's landline and cellphone. If I didn't hear back soon, I planned to drive by the mall project. Even on a Sunday, accused of murder and out on bail, that's most likely where I'd find Harry.

I spread my notes on the table and started prioritizing. Nothing was more important than finding Verna Beardsley, but our Internet search down in Sausalito had turned up no one by that name anywhere near Timbergate. I would have to wait until Monday morning to see if Maybelline Black could help.

Reluctantly, I wrote entry number two: *Arrange double date with Underhills*. Just thinking about it made me want to take a hot, soapy shower.

My third item was a visit with Lorraine Beardsley. When was she getting married? At the ballet she had said in two weeks. One of those weeks was almost gone. Very soon she would probably be on an extended honeymoon in some exotic locale. I needed to get to her right away.

Lorraine wasn't listed in the phone book, but I figured I could get her number from Arnetta Palmer if I could come up with a good reason to ask for it. I called the hospital and discovered Milton Palmer had been discharged. If the reconciliation was working, I might reach Arnetta at their family home.

If I did manage to arrange a meeting with Lorraine Beardsley, I wasn't about to invite Nick. I had no worries about holding my own against a pampered society matron twice my age.

Jared Quinn was farther down the list, but still under consideration. If the mysterious Verna Beardsley had done away with Bonnie, she must have had help, and Quinn had a history of getting himself involved with complicated women. The question was, where would he draw the line?

I changed from my boots and jeans into a pair of shorts and a tank top. Fanny circled my legs, emitting her purr-meow combination that either meant she'd missed me or she wanted out. I picked her up for a quick hug, but she pushed off my chest with all fours and hit the floor, heading for the door. So much for feline affection. With her safely outside, I tried Bosco next. I opened his cage door and offered my finger as a perch. He hitched a ride to my shoulder, where he bit my earlobe in the process of trying to pull off my earring.

"Bad bird," I said, waving my hand at his beak.

"*Go ahead, make my day,*" he rasped. Eerie, how much he sounded like Clint Eastwood. I soon felt the telltale warmth of bird poop dripping down my back, so I put the annoying little mimic back in his cage and changed into a clean T-shirt.

That left me pretty much alone and friendless, but I didn't have the luxury of feeling sorry for myself. I still had Milton Palmer's home phone number, so I decided to call the Palmers and see if Arnetta would talk to me.

Penny answered. I asked how her father was feeling, and after being assured he was doing well, I asked to speak with her mother.

Arnetta came on the line. "Aimee, I'm glad you called," she said. "Penny explained how kind you were to her when the police were harassing Milton."

"It was nothing," I said. "Have the police bothered any of you again?"

"No. They've determined Milton is no longer a person of interest—I think that's how they say it. Neither am I for that matter."

"That's wonderful." I couldn't force much enthusiasm into my words.

"I suppose you're calling about my deception."

"Deception?" She lost me for a moment, then I realized what she meant. "You mean our ballet date?"

"Yes. Penny told me she explained my situation, but I still feel I owe you an apology."

I laughed. "To tell you the truth, you were the best date I've had in months."

"Then you're not angry?"

I assured her I wasn't, but I took advantage of her eagerness to make amends.

"Arnie… I mean, Mrs. Palmer, I called because I need to ask for a favor."

"Certainly. And please call me Netta. I've had enough of Arnie. What's the favor?"

"It's not easy to explain."

"Then let me treat you to lunch. The phone is so impersonal."

It turned out the Palmers lived on a two-acre ranchette not far from Jack and Amah's property. We agreed to meet in an hour at the Four Corners Pizza Parlor, which split the distance between us. I showered, slipped on a clean pair of jeans, and pulled my hair back in a ponytail.

Arnetta and I reached the parking lot at the same time. She waved and came over to my car wearing white slacks and a ruffled pink blouse. Her hair was highlighted and tousled in stylish curls, and silver hoop earrings hung from her ears. As a woman, she was every bit as attractive as she had been as a man. Next to her, I could have passed for an orphaned refugee.

We walked into the pizza parlor together, found a clean table and ordered beers. I showed my ID, and we eventually got served. I stared at her face as it morphed back and forth between Arnie and Netta. She had the kind of androgynous beauty that made actors like Johnny Depp so fascinating.

"It takes a while, but you'll get used to it," she said.

"I'm sorry, I'm being rude."

"No. You're adjusting to a new reality." She took a sip of her beer.

I took a hefty swallow of mine. "I should explain why I wanted to talk to you. It's rather complicated, but I think you can help me."

"I'll try. What is it you need?"

"A friend of mine is in trouble, and I think Lorraine Beardsley can help. I'd like to talk to her, but I don't have her phone number. It's unlisted, and she's getting ready for her wedding and all. I thought you might be able to arrange something."

"And why do you think I have her number?"

"You were lunching with her at Stone Soup. The two of you seemed friendly, even though you acted as if you'd never met when we were introduced at the ballet."

My observation evoked a wry smile from Netta. "That was for Maybelline Black's benefit. She doesn't know about my gender change experiment, and I'd like to keep it that way."

"I understand completely. How do you happen to know Maybelline?"

"I met her once in the pre-Bonnie days, when Milton and I attended a TMC volunteers' fundraiser at the Beardsleys' home. Fortunately, she didn't recognize me at the ballet. I hope you'll keep my secret."

"Don't worry. I'd pluck my eyes out before I'd give you away to Maybelline."

Netta responded with a throaty laugh. "Apparently Maybelline has been a loyal TMC volunteer for years. She's particularly fond of Vane, so Lorraine made an effort to befriend her. I don't know how she found the patience."

"Tell me about it."

Netta gave me a sympathetic look. "I suppose you're stuck with her now."

"Twice a week," I conceded. "She takes some getting used to. I can understand why you didn't want her to know you were Arnie. She's not good at keeping secrets."

"Thank heavens Lorraine is. She's known all along, and she's been fully supportive. We're members of a very exclusive club, you know."

"Victims of Bonnie Beardsley?"

"We prefer the term 'survivors.'"

"Do you have other members?"

"I'm sure Bonnie preyed on any number of married men, but Lorraine and I are the only wives in Timbergate who have been humiliated so publicly by the late Mrs. Beardsley."

"But you both survived; she didn't."

"True. And neither of us is a suspect in the case, so we're free to get on with our lives."

"Lorraine has been cleared, too?"

"She and Troy were eliminated early on. She thinks the police have a promising suspect."

My heart sank.

"We're hoping it isn't Vane," she continued. "He's such a hopeless romantic. He actually thought Bonnie was in love with him."

"He seems to be handling it well enough."

"Lorraine has talked to him. Apparently he's confident the real killer will be found. Meanwhile, he's already beginning to appreciate his new single status."

"Sounds like everyone benefited except Bonnie."

"Sad, but true," Netta agreed.

"You almost sound sorry for the woman who broke up your marriage."

"I am, actually. I'll tell you a little secret. You're not the only woman Arnie met at the museum."

My whole body tingled as if I'd put my finger in a socket, but I managed a cool, "What do you mean?"

"I—Arnie, I should say—spotted Bonnie at the museum one day, just a couple weeks before she died. I suppose it was morbid curiosity, but I struck up a conversation with her. I thought if I was really meant to be a man, some part of me would respond to her so-called irresistible sexuality."

"How did that work out?"

"She flirted, but I could tell her heart wasn't in it. It was pathetic, really, as if she were set on autopilot to seduce any man she met. She obviously wasn't saving her love for Vane Beardsley. I took her number, told her I'd call, then left, wishing there was some way to save her from herself."

If she was telling the truth, "Arnie" Palmer had flirted with Bonnie, but according to her, at least, her behavior did not constitute stalking.

"And you never saw her again?"

"No. I'd done what I needed to do about Bonnie. Closure, if you'll pardon an overused term."

"You and your husband are back together, and Lorraine Beardsley is marrying a great guy. The survivors are thriving."

"True. Lorraine and Troy are blissfully happy. As for me, I'm luckier than most people with gender confusion. I let myself be influenced by a well-meaning but biased therapist. Ironically, what I've been through did help me find myself. I know who I am now. I love Milton, and I want to be his woman, his wife." Netta studied her pearl-polished nails for a moment. "You know, anyone who thinks the opposite sex has it easier should try it for a while. That goes for both genders. A little give and take could go a long way in most relationships."

For some reason, that reminded me of the Underhills. "There's one other thing I wanted to ask you. It's about the couple we met at the ballet. The Underhills."

"The people who are cloning your llama? What about them?"

"I'm not really having it cloned. That was a fiction."

"I'm glad to hear that. Considering my own situation, I try to allow people their eccentricities, but that surprised me. You seem so normal."

"Thanks," I said. "But about the Underhills. How well do you know them?"

"Milton and I have been at social functions occasionally where they've appeared. Of course that was a few years ago, before we separated. When I saw them at the ballet, I was curious whether they'd recognize me, so I struck up a conversation while you were in the powder room."

"Do you think they did recognize you?"

"No. Willow was undressing me with her eyes. Wouldn't she have been surprised? And by the way, I was serious about their reputation. If they ever invite you to spend time with them, run like hell in the other direction."

"Sounds like good advice." Too bad I was about to do the opposite.

Netta swallowed the last of her beer. "I'd better get back. Milton still needs a lot of looking after." She took a pen from her purse and wrote on a napkin. "Here's Lorraine's private number. I'll call her to pave the way as soon as I get home. She's the salt of the earth. If she can help your friend, I'm sure she will."

We hugged goodbye and promised to keep in touch. After she left, I sat staring at the phone number, torn between heading home and ordering another beer. I started toward the counter and heard a man say, "Gimme a beer" in a horribly familiar croak. I was standing directly behind Orrie Mercer.

I did an about-face and sped out the door. Mercer was the last person I wanted to run into on a day off. It was bad enough I had to see him every day at work. The way my luck was going, Maybelline's disagreeable beau would turn out to be one of Jack and Amah's neighbors.

There were two messages waiting on my machine at home, but I didn't listen to them. Instead, I waited fifteen minutes, then called the number Netta had given me, hoping Lorraine had already been told to expect my call.

A man answered. A household employee, I guessed. I gave him my name and said Mrs. Beardsley was expecting my call, that I was a friend of Arnetta Palmer.

"Right, I'm Troy Bilkowsky," the man said. "We met at the ballet. I just got off the phone with Netta Palmer. She said you'd be calling. I'm afraid Lorraine isn't here."

"When do you expect her?"

"Not until Thursday. She's visiting family out of state."

"Her daughter?" I figured it was worth a shot. He had said out of state.

"Daughter? No, she has no children. Her father is quite ill, so her parents can't travel out here for the wedding. She went to New York to spend a few days with them. After the wedding this Friday, we'll be abroad for several months."

Bad news.

"I'm sure this sounds like an imposition, but it's extremely important that I talk with her. Does she have a cellphone number I could call?"

"I'm sorry. I can't give out her number. She asked not to be disturbed."

"She won't be home until Thursday?"

"That's right. If you'll tell me what this is about, I'll see what I can do when I talk to her this evening."

"Please, just tell her I called and give her my number. Ask her to call me as soon as she can."

TWENTY-NINE

WITH THAT OUT of the way, I checked the first of my two
messages. It was Harry, sounding inappropriately upbeat. "Hi, Sis. Don't call Mom and Dad until you call
me first. Call my cell. I'm at the job site."

My other message was from Mom in the Azores.
"Hi, honey. We miss you. Call us. We want to hear
about your new job at the hospital." *Oh, boy.*

I called Harry. As soon as he picked up I said,
"What's going on?"

"Have you talked to Mom and Dad?"

"No, I got your message first. Have you talked to
them?"

"Yes, but I didn't mention this Beardsley thing.
Aimee, I don't know how much longer we can keep it
from them. The Azores aren't that backward. At least
Faial isn't. Mom says the yacht club in Horta has a
cyber bar now."

"Darn, I keep thinking they're out of touch with
the world."

"So do Mom and Dad, and except for talking to us
once a week, they prefer it that way."

"They're going to hear about all this anyhow, as
soon as Amah and Jack get home."

"When's that?" Harry asked.

"I'm guessing Saturday."

"Almost a week." I could hear the wheels spinning

in Harry's brain. "Abe thinks he can keep DA Keefer off my back for a while. We can do a lot by Saturday." Harry, ever the cockeyed optimist.

"I won't say anything to Mom and Dad before Saturday."

"Okay. By then Bonnie's real killer should be in jail. Considering the number of registered sex offenders in this area, I can't believe they're wasting all this effort on me."

"I can. Marco hates you."

"That reminds me. Is Tango keeping his distance?"

"As far as I can tell. I honestly haven't had time to worry about him."

"Keep your eyes open. If he gets anywhere near you, I want to hear about it."

"You will. Anything else while you're giving orders?"

"Yeah, Nick told me about the lead you two brought back from Larkspur. He said you promised you wouldn't snoop around on your own again."

"Nick and I are working on it together."

"Good. I love you, Sis. Hang tough." I nearly choked on the lump in my throat. He never said stuff like that.

"I will," I whispered.

Working with Nick involved my making a call to Grover and Willow Underhill. Willow had given me their Everlasting Pets business card at the ballet. I searched through my purse and found it in the bottom stuck to a Snickers wrapper.

The face of the card was crowded with hot pink embossed lettering and a sketch of what appeared to be a poodle romping in some sort of doggy heaven. In the bottom right corner, I noticed an arrow drawn in green ink. I flipped the card and read the hand-written message. *Call 530-555-4FUN.*

This was a call that required false courage. I checked the fridge. No wine, no beer, no nothing. I needed to go shopping. I taped the Everlasting Pets card to the door of the fridge. The Underhills could wait a little longer. I drove to the market.

When I returned, I stashed my groceries and checked messages again. Only one, and it was from Nick, nagging me to call the Underhills and try for the next night. With a twinge of guilt, I thought about the call from Mom. I had put off calling back, and now they'd be asleep.

I opened my newly purchased bottle of Chardonnay and poured a hefty helping into an old juice glass decorated with a sketch of a rooster. When I raised it to my lips, my stomach growled, reminding me I hadn't eaten since the brie and crackers with Nick on the yacht. I'd skipped breakfast, and lunch had been a beer with Netta Palmer.

I would need my wits about me when I called the Underhills, so I set aside my wine glass and surveyed my new purchases. Cooking would take too long. I was tired of kettle corn, so I settled for apple slices and Triscuits spread with peanut butter. Bosco perked up when he saw me sitting at the table with my snacks, then fluttered and squawked until I gave in. I made sure Fanny was outside, then opened the cage and let the bird join me at the table. My rosy-cheeked dinner date pranced around on his little claws, pecking at Triscuit crumbs and bits of apple while I polished off my feast.

I was almost finished when my phone rang. No doubt it would be Nick hounding me about the Underhills, so I let it ring. When my machine picked up, he left a terse message: "Quit stalling."

I cursed the machine but made the call. Willow answered. "Underhill residence, Willow speaking."

"Hello, Willow, this is Aimee Machado. With the llama? I hope you don't mind my calling your private number. It was on the card you gave me at the ballet."

"Of course not. I'm thrilled to hear from you. Are you still seeing that lovely man we met at the ballet?"

"I'm afraid not. He's involved with someone else."

"I see," she said. "Then you're unattached at the moment?"

"Not exactly. I made up with my ex-boyfriend. I told him about you and Grover, and he thought it might be fun to get together."

She made a breathy "Ahhhh" sound. I heard her whisper, "Grover, pick up." A muted click told me I had two fish on the line.

"What's your boyfriend like?" Willow asked.

"He looks a little like Robert Redford did thirty-five years ago. Did you ever see *Butch Cassidy and the Sundance Kid*?"

"Yes, but I never can recall which was which."

"Redford was the blond one, Sundance. That's what I call Nick when we're feeling playful."

"Oh," Willow sighed. "And what does he call you?" I heard breathing on the extension.

I spouted the first thing that came to mind. "He calls me Princess Moonbeam."

"I get it," Willow said. "He's the sun and you're the moon. That's quite clever."

"Thank you." I wished I had thought of it. I made

a mental note to tell Nick about our new terms of endearment.

"Grover and I call each other—"

I dropped the phone at that point. I wasn't about to hear what Mr. and Mrs. Disgusting called each other in the throes of passion.

"Oops, sorry, dropped it," I said, then rushed on. "So anyway, Nick and I were wondering if you two are free tomorrow night."

"It so happens we are. What did you have in mind?"

"Tell you what, now that I know you're available, I'll run it by Sundance and get back to you."

"When?" Willow asked.

"Suppose I get back to you tonight? No later than ten."

"Lovely, just lovely." Her eagerness would have been flattering if the circumstances hadn't been so revolting.

I put Bosco back in his cage and then called Nick and ran the conversation by him. He suggested we meet them for dinner at Chez Philippe, Timbergate's most elegant restaurant.

I called Willow back with the details, and we agreed on the following evening at eight o'clock.

"Have a nice night," I said.

Willow giggled, "Same to you, Princess Moonbeam."

THIRTY

I PARKED NEAR the library in Lot 4 on Monday morning feeling as if I'd been gone for weeks. Orrie Mercer was back in place guarding the library entrance. I thought of mentioning that I'd seen him at the Four Corners Pizza Parlor, but he barely acknowledged me with a faint nod so I didn't bother.

My workplace looked considerably brighter than when I'd left on Friday. The burned-out light fixtures in the ceiling had been replaced, and the windows were clean. I took this newfound interest as a sign that someone had enough faith in the library's future to sign a work order. Jared Quinn or Vane Beardsley?

I tackled the flurry of Monday morning email. A message from Quinn topped the list. He wanted to meet at my convenience. I called his office. He was out, but Varsha Singh assured me he would return my call.

Maybelline arrived at nine. I asked if she'd had a good weekend.

"Lovely. And you? Did you do anything special with your nice man?"

"Nice man?"

"From the ballet, dear." She meant Arnie Palmer, of course. Her eyes protruded more dramatically than usual. The woman was eager for details.

"We're not dating anymore."

Maybelline's affect changed radically with that news. She fixed me with an angry scowl.

"You're a fool."

"I'm sorry?"

"That was a good man. I know one when I see one. I can read people, you know. I have a knack. Pretty women like you take advantage. You probably broke his heart."

"Actually, it was his decision," I explained. "He's in love with someone else."

Maybelline's disposition underwent another lightning transformation. "Oh, you poor thing. How sad. Are you all right?"

I would be, once I got Maybelline out of my hair.

"I'm fine. Thanks for asking."

Apparently satisfied, she loaded her book cart and sailed out the door. Maybelline had just disappeared when Dr. Beardsley popped in. He wore an off-white linen summer suit, tailored to whisper "expensive" rather than shout it. A red silk handkerchief decorated his breast pocket, and a matching carnation in the buttonhole of his lapel gave off a pleasant, spicy scent.

"Miss Machado. Good morning. You're looking lovely."

I had chosen a fitted white sleeveless dress with red frog fasteners and red piping trimming a mandarin collar. I'd piled my hair up high in a twist anchored with combs. Apparently Beardsley was a sucker for the exotic. I hadn't dressed to impress him, but his reaction worked right in with my plan. Harry and Nick would be furious if they knew what I had in mind, but the moment was right, so I plunged ahead.

"I've been thinking about your suggestion that we

have a working dinner meeting. I'm free tomorrow night if that's convenient for you."

Beardsley beamed. "Tuesday? Why, yes, I am. That's a wonderful idea." A furrow of concern crossed his brow. "Wasn't there a problem about your being engaged? Will your fiancé object?"

"I'm sure it'll be fine. I've already cleared it with him."

Beardsley looked a little uncertain. "You're sure?"

"Of course." I leaned toward his carnation and took a long sniff. "Your boutonnière smells wonderful, by the way." That did the trick.

We arranged to meet in the lobby of the Timbergate Golf and Country Club Tuesday evening at seven. No sooner had he left than Orrie Mercer slammed out the door of the library's private restroom and barged out the entrance door without a word. That transgression was the last straw. I was going to have to talk to May-belline about her boyfriend.

Quinn strolled in around eleven o'clock. His first concern was for Harry's predicament.

"He's not out of the woods," I said, "but at least he's not in jail."

"That's a good start." Quinn picked up the framed photo on the corner of my desk. "Is this your brother in the photo?"

Tears threatened. I nodded. Blinked.

Quinn saw. "He's quite a handsome guy." He put the photo down. "Are you free for lunch?" He smiled. "Strictly business, of course. I wouldn't want to anger your imaginary fiancé."

I ignored his little joke. "It depends on the time.

I have to deal with a situation before my volunteer leaves at noon."

"Oh? Anything I should know about?"

"Nothing I need to bother you with."

"Try me."

I relayed my frustration about Mercer. I mentioned his using the library staff's private restroom, but it sounded so petty, I regretted bringing it up and said so.

"Not at all. You were right. The guards are supposed to use the public facilities. It's written in their contract. Do you want me to deal with it?"

"I'd rather handle it myself."

"Then I'll trust your judgment. I'll swing by to pick you up for lunch at noon."

Maybelline returned half an hour later looking as if she'd had a melt-down somewhere along the way. Mascara ran down both cheeks. Her bright orange hair hung limp and damp, as if she'd been caught in a downpour.

"Good heavens," I said. "What happened to you?"

"Not to worry, dear. Just an unhappy patron. He threw water on me. Emptied his whole pitcher." She waved a shaky hand in the air.

"What? That's terrible. We should report this to Dr. Beardsley."

Her eyes flashed. "No. Don't tell Vane."

"At least tell me why it happened."

"He didn't like the books I brought him."

"That's *it*? He threw water on you because he didn't like the books? What's the man's name?"

"I don't know. He's just old and senile. Not to worry."

"Do you remember his room number?"

"I didn't notice."

I recalled the eclectic mix of titles she had delivered to Milton Palmer. Heaven only knew what she had come up with to trigger the fury of the water thrower.

"Maybelline, did anyone witness the patient's outburst?"

"No, no one. Please don't tell. I don't want any trouble." I heard the hope and apprehension in her answer and wondered if there was more to the story. Had she unwittingly provoked the patient with one of her tactless remarks?

"All right, I'll let it go this time, but if it happens again, we'll have to report it."

She brightened. "Of course," she said. "I bear no malice toward the crazy bastard."

With that, I figured I'd better ask her about Verna Beardsley before she got any wackier.

"Maybelline, I need your advice about a man."

She lit up at the prospect, as I'd guessed she would. "Ask away, dearie, if there's anything I know about, it's men."

"This is strictly between us girls, but Dr. Beardsley has asked me to dinner, and I wanted—"

"No, no, no, no."

"Wow," I said. "I thought you'd have an opinion, but I didn't expect this."

She shook her finger in my face. "He's too old for you. Find someone your own age."

"I don't mind his age, but there's one thing that does bother me. I don't want to get involved with someone who's been married several times or has grown children who might try to run his life. I hate complications like that. You understand."

"Of course. Very wise."

"So I wondered if you might know."

"Know what?"

"How many times he's been married. Or whether he has children."

"Only two marriages. Sweet Lorraine and the dead tramp. No children. But you still shouldn't date him. He's a fool for women. A bad risk."

"You're probably right. I suppose there's nothing to the rumor, then."

Her eyeballs danced. "Rumor?"

"Something about another ex-wife, a woman named Verna Beardsley."

"No. That's wrong." She gave me an appraising look. "I must say, you're a nosy little thing, aren't you?"

"Curious," I said. "It's in my job description."

"Don't get involved with Vane Beardsley," she said. "That's my advice."

"And I appreciate it. You've been a big help."

"Don't mention it, dearie." Maybelline pulled a comb and a small mirror from the pocket of her damp volunteer's jacket and began wiping mascara from her face and rearranging her damp mop of persimmon-colored hair. I dreaded setting her off again, but I was running out of time, so I risked broaching the problem of Orrie Mercer and the restroom.

"Maybelline, I wonder if I could have your advice on another little problem."

She slipped the comb and mirror back into her pocket. "What's that? More man trouble?"

"In a way. It's about your friend Orrie Mercer."

"What about him?"

"I'm afraid he's going to get in trouble unless we help him out."

Maybelline's head whipped around. "Lower your voice," she said.

"It's all right. There's no one in here." But I did drop my voice.

"What is it?" Maybelline whispered. "Is he blaming me for something?"

"Not at all, but you might have accidentally contributed to the problem. I was wondering if you might have given him permission to use the library staff's private restroom."

Maybelline looked confounded. "Why would I tell him something like that? I don't talk to him about bathrooms."

"I see. What with him being your boyfriend, I thought you might have—"

"He's a lying dirt bag. And he's not my boyfriend."

That was more information than I'd bargained for. Intrigued, I continued. "Then you won't be upset if I tell him to use the public restrooms?"

"That's the problem? Telling Orrie where to go potty?" She looked at me as if I were demented.

"Well, yes." I felt my face flush. "I thought you might want to tell him, but—"

"Tell him what you want. My shift is over. I have to go."

I helped Maybelline out of her soaked volunteer's jacket. She hung it on a coat tree near the entrance on her way out. I made a mental note to drop it off for laundering and to pick up a fresh one for her to wear on Wednesday.

I was still puzzling over Maybelline's scathing remarks about Orrie Mercer when Quinn walked in wearing his Cheshire cat smile.

THIRTY-ONE

QUINN DROVE THE two blocks to Casa Loco, saying he had to be back at one thirty for a meeting with the Timbergate police chief. What little appetite I had vanished.

Quinn asked for a booth in the back. We were seated in a corner, private enough to talk without being overheard. He waved away the menus and asked for two of the day's specials.

"Why are you meeting with the police chief?" I asked.

"The corporate office wants an update on the Beardsley case. I thought I'd ask if he has any leads on new suspects."

"Good. It's about time they stopped railroading Harry and looked for someone who might actually be guilty."

We went quiet while our waiter delivered two orders of crab enchiladas.

"Aimee, you can't accuse the police department of targeting Harry. A lot of people have been questioned. Even me."

"Really?"

"Of course. I told you I dated Bonnie. I told the investigators every detail I could remember. Bonnie Beardsley was a self-centered, unscrupulous woman with a long list of reasons to get herself bumped off. I provided proof that I was out of town when she went missing. They were so thorough, I began to wonder if I was going to be charged with murder for hire."

"Are you still being considered?"

"I don't think so, but I'll be relieved when this thing is over. Not just for myself, but for the bad press it's brought to the hospital."

I was reminded that his first loyalty was to Timbergate Medical Center. For Jared Quinn, protecting Vane Beardsley's reputation—and the hospital's—trumped keeping my brother out of jail.

I cut into my enchilada. "Are you saying you don't believe Dr. Beardsley is involved? If they eliminate him, that leaves only Harry."

"I understand, but I can't implicate Vane Beardsley just to protect your brother."

I felt heat rush to my face. "Well, understand this. My brother is innocent. He isn't going to jail to keep Timbergate Medical Center out of the headlines."

"Aimee, don't make me your enemy. It doesn't have to be Beardsley or Harry. There's still a long list."

"Then tell that to DA Keefer and her lover."

"I intend to, if it comes to that." Quinn reached across the table and touched my hand. "Aimee, if you know anything—if you have any ideas, this is the time to tell me."

I wasn't ready to tell him what Nick and I had discovered about Verna Beardsley. "My ideas are skewed toward protecting Harry. They'd be invalid on that basis alone."

"What is it you're not telling me? Has Beardsley said something? Done something?"

"Not yet."

"What does that mean?"

"I'm having dinner with him tomorrow night."

"What?" Quinn shook his head. "Are you crazy?"

"It's not a date. I thought you wanted me to spy for you."

"I wanted you to report anything suspicious." His lips compressed to a thin line and he shook his head. "This is a bad idea."

"It'll be fine. I'm meeting him in the Timbergate Country Club dining room. We'll be surrounded by people the entire time."

"Including me. What time are you meeting him?"

"Seven. But he'll be suspicious if you're there."

"I'll be discreet."

Great. Another babysitter.

We returned to TMC, and Quinn pulled into Lot 4 near the library entrance. When he spotted Mercer standing guard, he asked if I had resolved the restroom problem.

"Not yet."

"Then let me take care of it."

"No need. It's my problem."

"Not anymore," Quinn said. "You stick to running the library. I'll take care of Mercer."

"Then he's all yours." I didn't want to waste any more energy arguing. I still had to psych myself up for my date with Nick and the swinging Underhills. I exited the cool interior of Quinn's Navigator without another word. The midday heat sucked the breath out of me as soon as my feet hit the pavement. As I passed Mercer, he dipped his head in an unexpected attempt at cordiality. I wondered why, then realized he'd probably noticed Quinn watching him.

NICK CALLED JUST before quitting time to confirm our plans for dinner with the Underhills. I took a shot at convincing him to meet me at the restaurant, but he insisted on driving out to Coyote Creek to pick me up. He pointed out that the Underhills might think it was odd if we arrived on a date in separate cars.

Orrie Mercer was not at his guard post when I left the library. I was surprised to see Shelly Hardesty, my black belt friend from the dojo, standing in his place.

"Are you working nights now?" I asked.

"No. I got called in a couple hours ago. I'm just subbing for the rest of Orrie Mercer's shift."

"Any idea what happened to him?"

"They didn't say."

Quinn must have worked fast if Mercer wasn't allowed to finish his shift.

I stopped at the market in Coyote Creek for milk and eggs and some of the other staples I'd forgotten to pick up in my haste the day before. I wouldn't put it past Nick to examine my fridge and pantry. He believed in keeping a well-stocked larder.

I gathered Jack and Amah's mail and checked things in the main house. It looked a little dusty and forlorn after the more than two weeks they'd been away. I made a mental note to do some cleaning later in the week.

I parked at the barn, girding myself for the weird evening ahead. The llamas seemed a little uneasy, pacing with heads up, ears forward and nostrils pulsing. I tossed out hay and most of them came running, but

Princess and little Moonbeam hung back in a shaded corner of the pasture.

I walked toward them, and little Moonbeam scampered in my direction, but Princess hung back, calling to her cria with an urgent moaning sound. Moonbeam stopped, and when she turned back to look at her mother, I saw a ragged red bull's eye spray-painted on her pure white wool. It covered most of the left side of her small body.

In a fit of fury, I ran to the barn for a halter and lead rope. Angry tears blurred my vision. My heart thudded in my chest. What was wrong with people? Who would vandalize a helpless little cria? I tied Princess first, then secured Moonbeam close to her. The distraught mother moaned and hummed to her baby while I used a pair of shears to clip off the stained wool. When I'd removed the worst of the paint, I untied both llamas and they trotted off to join the herd.

By then I had calmed down enough to wonder how anyone had gotten close enough to spray paint on the cria. I walked the pasture until I spotted a patch of ground scattered with cob. *Llama candy.* So hard for them to resist. The sound of grain shaking in a can is as irresistible to llamas as a siren's call to a lonely sailor.

That's how the vandal had coaxed the cria to come close. I ran back to the barn and checked the cob bin. The lid was off. That confirmed it. The bin was made of varmint-proof metal and we always secured the lid to keep mice and ground squirrels out.

I replaced the lid and secured the door to the feed storage closet with the combination padlock we rarely bothered to use. Only then did I remember the groceries I'd left in the car. They were still in pretty good shape, so I hoisted a bag in each arm and trudged up the steps. When I saw the message scrawled in crooked red lettering on my door, the grocery bags hit the deck.

THIRTY-TWO

BUTT OUT OR ELSE.

Or else what? This monster would use the cria for target practice? What kind of sick excuse for a human being would do such a thing?

I stumbled over the wrecked groceries and checked my doorknob. Still locked. The smell of fresh paint tainted the scorching afternoon air. I touched a two-inch rivulet of red running below the L in ELSE. Still damp. The brute had not been gone long. Or was he gone? Had I walked into an ambush? Was it Camo Man—the intruder I'd seen leaving Jack's driveway the week before?

I inched along the outside wall and peered around the corner. No one there. My windows were all locked and there was no sign of tampering or broken glass. I managed to maneuver my groceries through the door without smearing paint on my white dress.

After satisfying myself there was no evidence of an intruder inside, I changed into an old pair of shorts and a tank top and tried to clean the door before Nick showed up. If he saw the scrawled warning, he'd tell Harry, who already had enough to worry about. I scrubbed my fingers nearly raw before I gave up. Although I'd managed to smear it into a barely legible blob, the paint would not come off.

A few groceries survived the free-fall, so I put them

away and checked the time. Six thirty. Nick would show up in half an hour expecting me to be dressed for our date. I agonized over leaving the llamas alone while Nick and I participated in this ridiculous mate-swapping charade.

I wasn't ready to tell Harry about the vandalism, so Hannah was my best hope. She and Johnny were planning to adopt the cria when it was old enough. I called and explained about the spray paint and mentioned I had a date with Nick that couldn't be broken.

Hannah was torn between worry about the vandalism and excitement over the prospect of my date with Nick.

"Johnny and I will bring a DVD over to grandpa's house and keep a lookout until you and Nick get home."

"Are you sure you don't mind? What if the creep comes back?"

"We'll sic Rufus on him." Rufus being their lily-livered Doberman.

"You're kidding. What's he going to do, slobber the guy into submission?"

"All Rufus has to do is show up and bark a couple times," Hannah said. "Which reminds me, you shouldn't be staying out there alone. Why not let Nick spend the night?"

"I'm hanging up now."

With worry about the cria simmering on the back burner, I contemplated my closet. What in my meager wardrobe would send the necessary signal to the Underhills? *Have mate, will swap.*

I settled on a sheer white silk blouse over a black lace push-up bra. I left a few extra buttons open, allowing a view of what little cleavage there was to see.

A floor-length red shantung skirt slit above the knee on both sides, and the red satin three-inch sandals I'd bought on impulse and never worn completed the costume. I pulled my hair back over my left ear with a fake magnolia blossom attached to a comb. The right side hung free, making what I hoped was a seductive curtain over my eye.

By the time I had applied lipstick and used a tissue to clean a red smear off my teeth, Nick was pounding on my door, yelling like a madman.

"Aimee? What the hell's going on?"

I yanked the door open and nearly got a face full of Nick's fist. "Bring it down a notch, will you?"

He stood staring at the smeared message on the door. "What is this bullshit?"

"Just what it looks like," I said. "Do you want to come in?"

He stepped into the kitchen and started to speak, but then stopped with his jaw hanging open. I figured he'd finally noticed my getup.

"Close your mouth," I said.

"Sweet...you look...." At that point he must have aspirated some saliva, because he choked and proceeded to have a coughing fit that left his eyes streaming with tears.

"Water," he gasped, when he could speak.

Nick dragged the rest of the story out of me on the way to Chez Philippe, but only after I had extracted his promise not to tell Harry. We agreed the person responsible for the red paint had to be our murder suspect. If that were true, it became less likely that either or both of the Underhills were guilty. Unless they were desperate enough to drive out to Coyote Creek to spray paint a cria just before getting gussied up for a double date. Guilty of fraud and sleaziness, no question. Guilty of murder? Doubtful.

"So let's stand them up," I said. "I'll call the restaurant, make some excuse, and offer apologies."

Nick shook his head. "Not yet. They told you they were thick with Bonnie up until she died. Let's try to find out what they know."

"Good point, but we can't pretend to be swingers one minute then suddenly start pumping them like a couple of amateur detectives."

Nick grinned. "Haven't you ever heard of pillow talk?"

"Don't be disgusting."

"We can divide and conquer," Nick said. "The restaurant has a dance combo. Maybe you and old Grover can take a turn or two around the floor while I do my best to charm the lovely Willow."

"You have no charm."

"You've been vaccinated," Nick said. "I'm guessing Willow's not immunized."

As we pulled into the parking lot, I realized I hadn't briefed Nick on our pet names—something I dreaded, since he was already enjoying this caper entirely too much.

He walked around and opened my door. I stepped out and scanned the lot. No sign of Willow and Grover.

"There's something I forgot to mention," I said.

"Oh?" Nick shut the door behind me and locked it.

"I told them you and I have pet names for each other."

"You vixen." Nick's look would have done the devil proud. "What's mine?"

"You're Sundance."

"Ah, Redford. I like it," Nick took my arm. "And you are?"

"Princess Moonbeam." Wobbly on the three-inch heels, I stepped on a small rock and stumbled, catapulting myself into Nick's arms.

He held me close. "Umm, the sun and the moon. How'd you come up with that?"

I pushed away, regaining my equilibrium. "It seemed cheesy enough to fit the situation."

Inside, Nick confirmed our reservation while I slipped into the restroom to check my hair and makeup. So far, everything was still in place, even the fake magnolia.

No sooner were we seated with our menus open, than a piercing voice called from across the room.

"There they are, Sundance and Moonbeam."

Anxiety danced a tarantella in the pit of my stomach as the Underhills advanced toward us. Willow was in the lead, wearing a snakeskin print miniskirt and a black tube top that revealed way too much of the crinkled skin on her arms and upper chest. Grover brought up the rear in faded jeans riddled with phony rips and tears, and a fringed suede jacket he must have stolen from a Buffalo Bill museum. His lofty pompadour and luxuriant moustache both looked as if they'd been touched up with black shoe polish.

"Damn," Nick whispered. "*They're* the Underhills?"

"Still think this is funny?" I murmured.

Before he could answer, our dinner companions reached the table. Grover sat down without bothering to help his wife into her chair.

She seemed not to notice, plopping down and scooting close to Nick.

"Hi, you must be Sundance," she cooed.

"And of course we already know our little Princess Moonbeam." Grover reached over and gave my hand a squeeze.

Willow curled her fingers around Nick's bicep. "Wow," she said. "I'll bet you work out."

"I keep in shape," Nick said. His bicep flexed under the sleeve of his gray silk polo shirt. I glanced down at the table to hide a hot rush of jealousy.

Willow licked her lips. "Would you like to know our pet names?"

I kicked at Nick's leg under the table, but missed.

"Sure, why not?" he said.

"I'm Honey Pot," she pointed at Grover, "and he's Pooh."

She's got that right, I thought. Neither of them asked for Nick's real name. He didn't volunteer it, and neither did I.

Grover waylaid a waiter who was en route to another table with a tray full of meals.

"Can we get some service here?"

The waiter assured us someone would be right over. I wanted to slide under the table, but when I caught Nick's glance, his message was clear. If we were going to learn anything about Bonnie Beardsley, we had no choice but to humor these socially handicapped perverts.

Grover ordered a bottle of the house red and poured for all of us. He and Willow each finished their second glass before the entrees arrived. Dinner seemed endless. Willow ordered lobster, which she proceeded to rip into with both hands while melted butter made trails from her wrists to her elbows. Grover tackled a prime rib the size of Arkansas. I sipped tomato bisque, hoping it would stay down, while Nick devoured our chateaubriand for two.

"So how's the pet cloning business?" Nick asked. "Aimee tells me you've expanded into a larger facility."

"It's not a business," Grover said. "It's a nonprofit. We serve a great need in these troubled times. People crave the solace their pets provide."

"Yeah," Nick said. "If I had the right pet I could forget all about terrorists and genocide."

"And the price of gasoline," Willow beamed. "There's just too much to worry about these days. That's where we come in. We offer people happiness in place of all that worry."

"That we do." Grover nodded his head toward me. "Our Princess Moonbeam here is on the road to such happiness."

"She certainly is." Willow wiggled her butt in her chair. "Did she tell you we're going to clone her camel?"

"Llama," Grover corrected.

Nick looked at me.

"That's right," I said, "Old Doolittle."

"Thank goodness." Nick didn't miss a beat. "I don't know how she'd get over the loss of that animal."

"Well, now she won't have to grieve," Willow said. "As soon as we've perfected our large animal cloning technique, she'll have a brand new Doolittle in the barnyard."

"And if that doesn't work," Grover chimed in, "we'll still have Old Doolittle in cold storage. Our cryogenics lab is up and running. All we need is a little more time to work out the kinks, and we can bring that old carcass back to life, good as new."

"Have you worked with llamas before?" Nick asked.

"No, but the process is about the same for most animals. They're what, something like a sheep? Hell, this whole cloning deal started with a sheep." He looked at Willow for backup. "Dolly, the sheep, right?"

"Sheep. Right." Willow wasn't really listening. She was staring at Nick like a hungry barnyard cat.

By the time dessert came—caramel pecan cheesecake all around—there were three empty wine bottles on the table. Nick and I had paced ourselves, but Pooh and Honey Pot were sloshed.

We hadn't really learned anything useful, and my energy was fading. I used what little remained to set the conversation on a new course.

"I'm sorry," I said. "I haven't asked how the two of you are coping with your loss."

"Loss?" Willow frowned and glanced at Grover, who drew a blank.

"Your friend, Mrs. Beardsley," I said.

Light dawned on their faces. Grover spoke first. "Of course we are deeply saddened. She was our largest contributor and most loyal advocate."

Willow blinked. "Damn straight, we're sad. We're going to have a hell of a time finding another—"

"Never mind, Honey Pot," Grover said. He tried for a sad face, but only managed to look dyspeptic. "She gets pretty upset thinking about poor Bonnie."

"Who would do such a thing?" Willow whined.

Nick leaned back in his chair. "Let's hope the police can answer that."

Willow suddenly raised her hand. "I gotta pee."

"Me, too," I said. "Let's go together."

In the women's room, we hit the stalls. While we washed and touched up our lipstick, I took another stab at the Bonnie Beardsley connection.

"I'm sorry if talking about Bonnie upset you," I said.

"Naw, that's okay. Grover's the one who really misses her. They were simpatico, but her husband wasn't part of the deal."

"And you didn't mind?"

"Heck, no. Vane Beardsley doesn't appeal to me. He's no Sundance."

"So you and Grover and Bonnie had a thing?"

"It was okay with me. We had ourselves some awesome champagne parties."

That got my attention. In literature about street drugs, I'd seen the combination of cocaine and marijuana referred to as *champagne*.

"That's cool," I said. "I love champagne parties." I gave her a conspiratorial nudge with my elbow. "You're not talking about the bubbly stuff, are you?"

"No way," Willow giggled. "Grover and I supplied the pot, and Bonnie brought the coke." She listed toward me. "The real deal. Liquid." *Another bombshell.*

"How'd she get access to liquid cocaine? Did her husband get it for her?"

"Heck no, he's a big prude. Bonnie used to say the old fart would crap his pants if he ever found out what she was doing."

"Can you still get the coke?"

"I doubt it. Bonnie was the one with the connection. She said she'd take care of us." Willow hiccupped. "Well, that ship has sailed."

"When did you and Grover last see Bonnie?"

"That's the sad part. We must have been about the last people to see her alive." Willow looked in the mirror, widened her eyes and pursed her lips. "We'd better get back before Sundance and Pooh get lonesome."

"What do you mean about being the last to see her?"

"We had a late date that Friday night. We didn't do much, just got high. She complained about how stingy her husband was getting. He wouldn't let her donate any more money to our cause."

"So the three of you got high. How did she get home?"

"She drove. Left around two in the morning, according to Grover. I fell asleep early."

I thought that might explain why the autopsy found evidence of recent sexual activity. Maybe Grover and Bonnie had a little fling while Willow slumbered.

"You didn't hear from her over the weekend?" I asked.

"Not a peep. Next thing we knew, the police found her in the Dumpster."

"Did the police ever question you and Grover?"

"Why would they? They don't know about Bonnie and us. Except how she supported our cause, of course."

"So you didn't contact the police—tell them she'd been with you that Friday night?"

"'Course not. That would bring up a lot of questions. We'd have to explain stuff that's nobody's business." She reached out and touched my cheek. "You understand about that, don't you, Princess Moonbeam?" Her words chilled the air, and her touch chilled me.

"Absolutely," I said.

Honey Pot adjusted her tube top for maximum exposure and gave me a wink. "Let's get back to those naughty boys, shall we?"

On the way back to the dining room, I silently cursed myself for agreeing with Nick's dim-witted plan. I double-cursed myself when I realized I hadn't asked Willow about Verna Beardsley.

Nick and Grover were deep in conversation when Willow and I approached the table. I was dying to get Nick out of there so I could tell him what I'd learned from Willow, but at the same time, I didn't want to leave until we could explore the Verna Beardsley angle.

"Hi, Moonbeam," Nick said. He pulled out my chair, and after I was seated, took my hand and kissed my fingertips. "Missed you."

"D'ja fall in?" Grover said to Willow.

She jerked out her chair and flounced down.

"Grover and I were just talking religion," Nick said.

"Oh?" Where was Nick going with this?

"I was telling him about our vow of celibacy."

I played along. "Oh, that. It's kind of personal, don't you think?"

"Sure, honey, but it came up in conversation."

"Celibacy?" Willow squeaked.

"You know," Grover growled. "That's when you don't have sex."

"Not with anybody, or just not with each other?" she said.

"Nada, zip, zilch," Grover said. "They don't do it."

"Well, shit," Willow said. She grabbed her wine glass and drained it. "How long does that go on? Is it like something you give up for Lent?"

"Lent doesn't start until next March," Nick said.

"Our vow lasts until we get married, right, Moonbeam?"

"That's right," I said. "Only two years to go."

"So what the hell are we doing here?" Willow asked.

I shot a look at Nick. He shot one back. I had no idea what to read into it, but figured he had his reasons for throwing a curve ball at the Underhills.

"We were hoping we could get the two of you to join our church," Nick said. "Shall we join hands and pray?" He grabbed my hand with his right, and Willow's with his left.

Willow pulled her hand away and stood up. "What are you, some kind of sicko missionaries?" Her shrill voice echoed off the far wall of the restaurant.

Grover signaled the waiter, who rushed over, obviously willing to do whatever it took to be rid of us.

Nick reached for his wallet. "This one's on us. You can pick up the tab some other time."

Grover turned to me with a sorrowful gaze. "Some other time."

Willow grabbed her husband's arm. "Let's go, lover boy."

We gave them a good lead, then made our way out to the parking lot.

THIRTY-THREE

NICK DROVE WHILE I filled him in on what I'd learned from Willow in the restroom.

"Bonnie was their source for liquid cocaine. I just wish I'd had time to get to the Verna Beardsley angle. Why did you create that story about celibacy?"

"I'd heard enough from the husband," Nick said. "I wanted to get you away from that creep."

"What did you hear?"

"We assumed there was sex involved, but Underhill hinted at videotapes. I think they've been selling them. That takes it to a whole new level." Nick headed east on the freeway toward Coyote Creek. "And don't kick yourself about the Verna Beardsley thing. I ran it past Grover while you women were busy in the powder room."

"And?"

"He never heard of Verna Beardsley, but he did say Bonnie hated her sister-in-law. He didn't know the woman's name."

"That's a start. Now we know Dr. Beardsley has a sister."

"Not necessarily. Maybe Bonnie had a married brother."

"Nope. No brother," I said. "She was an only child."

"Then who besides Bonnie would know about this sister of Beardsley's?"

"I already asked Maybelline about Verna Beardsley. She didn't recognize the name, but there is someone who might. Beardsley's first wife, Lorraine."

"Where's the first wife?"

"Visiting family back east. She's due home late Wednesday night, according to her fiancé. They're getting married Friday, then traveling abroad for three months."

"But she'll be in town Thursday?" Nick asked.

"Yes, and I'm already on it. I talked to her future groom over the weekend. He said he'd have her call me Thursday."

"She can't call you from back east?"

"I tried that, but he said she didn't want to be disturbed. Apparently her parents are elderly and frail."

BACK IN JACK and Amah's house, Nick and I brainstormed with Hannah and Johnny about the Verna Beardsley mystery. Johnny asked if we were going to tell the sheriff's office about the vandalism incident with the cria and the paint on my door.

"I'll report it, but with all the recent pranks out here involving the halfway house, I doubt it will get much attention." I told them about the kids I caught trying to tip over our grandparents' mailbox.

"What about those people you had dinner with?" Hannah asked. "Are you going to tell the police about their connection to the Beardsley woman and the porn?"

"We have no evidence," Nick said, "just Grover Underhill's drunken innuendo."

"What about the woman's claim that Bonnie supplied them with drugs?"

"Again, we have no proof, but I'll run all of this by Abe Edelman. He might have some ideas."

After Hannah, Johnny, and the cowardly Doberman left, Nick walked with me down the lane to the barn, where he insisted on checking inside my apartment and inspecting the locks.

He hesitated on the deck after we said good night. "I don't like leaving you out here on your own, Aimee. I'm not convinced the bull's-eye painted on that little cria was done by malicious kids."

"Who else?" I asked.

"Someone with a far more dangerous agenda. Specifically, someone who wants you to butt out of the Beardsley case. If you'll give me the keys to the main house, I'd like to camp out there, at least for tonight."

"It's not necessary. I appreciate everything you're doing for Harry, but he can't ask you to spend your days and nights being my bodyguard."

The warmth left Nick's eyes. "Is that what you think? That I'm only doing this for Harry?"

I felt a jolt of apprehension, as if a powerful undertow were pulling me into a conversation I wasn't ready for. One that I dreaded.

Nick leaned back against the deck rail and glanced up through the dark tangle of oak branches. "See those stars?"

"I do. They're magnificent."

"There are a lot of women out there, Aimee. Not as many as stars in the sky, but there are a lot of women out there who are looking for the right man. I've met a few of them, liked some more than others, but when I met you, I knew I'd found someone extraordinary."

"What do you mean?" I felt tears pooling in my

eyes. Somehow, this didn't sound like a declaration of love. It sounded like a prelude to *goodbye*.

"I mean I had found someone I could trust. There were no games, no pretenses, no manipulations. Just two people being themselves and being honest with each other. Do you know how rare that is?"

"Yes." The tears were flowing now.

"Then imagine how I feel, knowing that you think I've betrayed your trust when the opposite is true. And knowing if you hear the truth, you'll still wonder if it's a lie."

"I'm sorry, Nick." The words got stuck in my throat, and I swallowed. "I've been hurt before by men I trusted, but nothing ever hurt as much as hearing Rella answer your phone in the middle of the night in Paris. I can't imagine how you could explain that away, but even if you could, now is not the time. Until I know Harry's safe, I don't have the heart for anything else."

"Then I'll let it go for now." Nick stepped away from the deck rail toward the stairs. "But don't wait too long, Aimee. I feel the gap between us growing, and one of these days, it's going to be too wide to cross."

With that, he ran down the steps and got into his car. As he drove away, I tried to take a deep breath, but I couldn't. I'd felt like the wind had been knocked out of my midsection by an unexpected blow.

I WOKE TUESDAY morning with the same hollow feeling that had greeted me every day for the first month after Nick and I broke up. As time went by I'd managed to overcome it. Now it was back. All the while I was telling him I didn't want him, he was there asking for another chance. Now that it seemed he was get-

ting ready to move on, the pain had returned. I wanted
things to return to the way they'd been before Paris, but
that was childish, wishful thinking. I saw our future
was hanging by a thread called *trust*, and wondered if
it took more courage to give Nick another chance or to
let him go. No matter how things worked out between
us, I knew Nick would be there for Harry. At the moment, that was all that mattered.

When I got to work I was able to distract myself
from thoughts of Nick by ever-increasing demands on
my time. My efforts to boost library usage were paying off. The first trickle of doctors, nurses and other
health professionals had spread the word. I was seeing
a definite rise in the volume of patrons. They delved
into databases for information on everything from bio-
terrorism to the stock market. The initial steps toward
developing the forensic component added to my work-
load. In spite of Harry's predicament and the chaos in
my personal life, I was getting on with my job.

I was helping an orthopedist print an article on
smoking and osteoporosis when Dr. Beardsley dropped
by. He seemed downright jovial, considering his wife
had yet to make it into her grave—at least I assumed
the investigation had delayed her burial. Waiting for
toxicology reports, no doubt, which could take weeks.

"Miss Machado, how are you?"

"I'm fine, thank you." With that huge white lie, I
steered Dr. Beardsley toward my desk, signaling Lola
to take over with the orthopedist. My elderly volunteer relished any chance to tutor the docs on the use
of our databases.

Beardsley wasted no time getting to the reason for
his visit.

"I felt I should confirm our dinner plans." He rubbed his palms together like Henry VIII about to devour a roast suckling pig. "Shall I pick you up at your home?"

"That's not a good idea. I'd better meet you at the country club."

The eager light in his eyes dimmed a few watts, but he persisted. "It's no trouble, really. I'd be more than happy to drive you."

"I really couldn't," I said. "My fiancé might be uncomfortable with that."

"Ah, yes, your fiancé." Beardsley took a backward step. "Well, then, I'll meet you in the country club dining room at seven o'clock. Strictly business." He glanced around the library. "Is everything going well here?"

"Couldn't be better."

"Carry on, then." He waved to Lola and the orthopedist and shuffled out.

I watched his back and wondered if I would discover over dinner that the bipolar Verna Beardsley was his sister.

When Lola's shift ended at noon, she announced she was off to buy Marty Stockwell's latest CD. Her ardor burned brighter than ever. Fortunately for Marty, Lola thought he still lived in Oklahoma. I wasn't about to tell her he resided in Coyote Creek, a mere nine miles east of Timbergate. Lola was a sweetheart, but she had a mighty crush on her idol, who frequently shopped for organic veggies at the Coyote Creek grocery store. If Lola knew that, she might be tempted to seek out poor Marty right there among the artichokes.

She waved an arthritic goodbye and hung her orange blazer on the coat rack near the door, next to the

one Maybelline had left soaked and rumpled the day
before. That reminded me I'd planned on having Maybelline's jacket laundered. I took it off the hook, hung
a *CLOSED* sign on the door and headed for the Housekeeping Department.

The woman in charge of laundry promised to have
the jacket ready first thing in the morning. She checked
for stains, then felt inside the pockets. She found a
folded slip of paper, unfolded it, and frowned.

"Want this?" She held it out to me. It looked like
a page from a medical prescription pad. It must have
taken a direct hit when Maybelline got doused. The
thing was too smudged to read.

"Thanks," I said. I took it from her without mentioning that the garment wasn't mine. It was unlikely
that the woman had ever been in the library. She had
to assume I was a volunteer.

"Probably ought to get that filled. Looks like it was
written some time ago."

I glanced at the scrawl. "You can read this?"

"Only the date."

She was right. The date was smeared, but legible on
closer examination. The prescription was almost three
months old. I jammed it into the pocket of my slacks,
planning to give it to Maybelline first thing Wednesday morning. Probably her thyroid medication. I recalled noticing her protruding eyeballs on my first day.
I hoped she had not been going without her medicine
for three months, and debated whether I should invade
her privacy by asking.

Back in the library, I put the prescription slip in
my purse. For the rest of the day, a relentless proces-
sion of worries marched through my mind to the beat

of a throbbing headache. Save Harry. Protect the cria. Catch the killer. Suspects had been dropping off my list until only a few remained. Quinn, Tango, and the Palmers all seemed remote possibilities. The Underhills were unlikely. I suspected it was Grover who'd had sex with Bonnie before she died, but he couldn't be the intruder who sprayed paint on the cria and on my door; the timing was wrong. And why would he kill Bonnie? That would be killing the goose that laid the golden eggs.

The mysterious Verna Beardsley still seemed to be the key. If I played it right with Dr. Beardsley, I'd soon know if he had a sister squirreled away somewhere. Unless he caught on to my charade and got suspicious. Was Quinn right? Was I crazy to try to match wits with a suspected wife-killer?

THIRTY-FOUR

I STOPPED OFF at a sporting goods store on the way home to pick up a canister of bear spray. Everything was secure when I checked the main house. The llamas chewed their cuds peacefully, and I saw no evidence of further vandalism. The only sign that someone had been on the property was a new coat of red paint on my bunkhouse door. Nick's handiwork, no doubt. Considering the way we left things the night before, I was surprised he had bothered, but the door looked great.

As I marveled at Nick's thoughtfulness, I heard the taunting echo of Rella's slurred voice on the phone from Paris. *Nicky's asleep. I mustn't wake him. He has to fly tomorrow.* Would I be a fool to believe nothing had happened between them that night? Could I bring myself to try?

I put the bear spray on the kitchen counter and after a quick shower, found myself in a rerun of the previous night, picking through the contents of my closet for something to wear to dinner with Beardsley. Seductive was out. Prudish was too far in the other direction. I settled for a short denim skirt, calf-hugging leather cowboy boots, and a faux buckskin camisole trimmed in turquoise and coral beads. With my hair in a long braid and silver hoops dangling from my ears, the transformation from Mulan to Pocahontas was complete.

I ARRIVED AT the country club dining room ten minutes early. Vane Beardsley was nowhere in sight. The maitre d' took my name and offered to seat me, but I declined and headed for the powder room. I spotted Quinn loitering at the bar. He had made good his promise to spy on my date. I passed him on the way to the women's room and muttered, "Beardsley is going to spot you the minute he walks in."

I killed as much time as possible in front of the restroom mirrors before two skinny blondes stumbled in. They reeked of sickly sweet perfume and alcohol.

"Wow, do I ever have to pee," the platinum blonde in the blue dress said.

"Me, too. It's the diet pills." This from the champagne blonde in the white lace pantsuit.

I headed back to the dining room where the maitre d' told me Dr. Beardsley had just been seated. A glance toward the bar confirmed that Quinn had found cover. I spotted him partially hidden behind a fake ficus.

Beardsley rose from his chair when he saw me approach, but he caught the table edge with his thigh and nearly overturned the thing. We both groped for water glasses, silverware, and the lighted candle. We managed to avoid setting the room on fire, but that was small consolation. Anyone who hadn't noticed us before was surely aware of our presence now. We'd be fodder for every malicious tongue in Timbergate's country club set.

"Sorry," Beardsley said. "I'm acting like an old bull in a china shop."

"Forget it. This place needs sturdier tables."

"You look very nice tonight." He held out my chair. "Lovely, in fact. Like an Indian Princess. American Indian, I mean." He colored. "I don't mean to offend, to dwell on your ethnicity…but you seem to change from time to time…like a chameleon. It's bewitching."

"Thank you. And please don't worry. I'm not offended in the least."

I opened my menu, tried not to gasp at the prices, and wondered if I could swallow a piece of dead salmon that cost six dollars a bite. After we ordered, Beardsley began to talk shop.

"Well now, how have you enjoyed your first two weeks on the job?"

"Very much," I said. "Except for your personal tragedy, of course. I'm sorry for your loss."

"Yes. It has been devastating, but life must go on, you know. We in the medical profession are well acquainted with death."

I doubted that applied to his specialty. If plastic surgeons were well acquainted with death, there would be a lot fewer face-lifts on the TMC surgery schedule.

We discussed the library, our food, and the weather. It took all the restraint I could muster to keep from glancing toward the foliage where Jared Quinn lurked. Beardsley had just forked in a mouthful of mashed potatoes when I realized he was using his right hand. I was torn between relief and disappointment. Maybe he wasn't a wife killer after all. But if that were the case, the focus on Harry would be even more intense. Unless Beardsley had hired some thug to do his dirty work.

In spite of his being right-handed, I had to know if there was a connection to Verna Beardsley. I decided to try the direct approach.

"Do you have any family in Timbergate, Dr. Beardsley?"

He dropped his fork, pointed at this throat and croaked out, "Down the wrong pipe. Back in a jiffy." He left the table coughing and headed toward the restrooms.

Once again I was the focus of all eyes in the dining room. Sinking under the table wasn't an option, so I lowered my gaze to the chunk of overpriced and undercooked orange flesh cooling on my plate.

I recalled my first day at Timbergate Medical Center when Beardsley had promised to be back in a jiffy and hadn't returned at all.

He returned this time, but I didn't get an answer to my question about family. He claimed he had been paged by his answering service on his way back from the men's room. "I hope you don't mind. They need me in the ER for a consult."

"Not at all," I said. I'd definitely hit a nerve asking him about family. I suspected the story about being needed in the ER was fiction.

He looked uncertain, but eager to be let off the hook. "Well, then, I'll take care of the tab on my way out. Are you sure you don't mind finishing your meal alone?"

"I'll be fine." I forked into the cold fish to prove it.

"Another time, then." He hurried to where the waiter hovered, scribbled a signature, and left.

A moment later Quinn strolled over to my table. "May I join you?" His amused grin made my teeth itch.

"Would it do any good if I said no?"

He sat in Beardsley's vacant chair.

"You two put on quite the floor show. I don't think I've ever had a more entertaining evening in this boring joint."

"You're not helping matters. How is it going to look if *we* leave together?"

"Hey. You're a damsel in distress. Your date walked out, didn't he?"

"He said he got paged."

"You believed him?"

"Not necessarily," I said, "but it could be true."

"Did you get anywhere with your amateur sleuthing before he ditched you?"

"No."

Beardsley's so-called page to the ER had spoiled my chance to find out whether he had a sister, but I still wasn't ready to discuss the Verna Beardsley connection with Quinn.

"He didn't try to intimidate you?"

"Not in the least," I said. "No warnings, no veiled threats."

"So he really wanted to talk shop?"

"It's possible. What about you? Did you learn anything new from your meeting with the police chief?"

"No. I asked if they were broadening the list of suspects, but he said they're staying on the same tack."

"Still going after Harry?"

"I'm afraid so, but Vane Beardsley is first runner-up." Quinn pointed at my plate. "Are you going to finish that?"

"No. Let's get out of here."

"I'll walk you to your car."

Outside, the twilight air stirred, whispering across my bare arms. An overhead light in the parking lot cast a fluorescent glow, illuminating my old Buick. Something didn't look quite right. When we got closer, it hit me. All four tires were flat down to the rims.

"Damn." Quinn took a close look. "They've been cut."

"Oh no, not again."

"What do you mean, *again*? Has this happened before?"

"Not exactly."

"Aimee, what the hell are you talking about?"

"I had a flat tire about a week ago. The man from the tire shop thought it might have been done deliberately."

"So your tires have been cut twice?"

"Maybe. Except last time it was only one, and it wasn't so obvious."

"Any idea why?"

"To scare me, I suppose."

"Has there been anything else?"

I was tempted to tell him about the bull's-eye on the cria, when an awful thought struck me. How stupid I had been, leaving the ranch unguarded. I'd thought it was safe to keep the rendezvous with Beardsley because he couldn't be in two places at once. Now I was stranded, and if Beardsley really was the nasty piece of work who cut my tires and painted the cria, he might make good his threatened mayhem before I could get home.

"Where's your car?" I spotted the Navigator and ran for it.

Quinn strode after me, frowning. "Take it easy, Aimee. I'll give you a ride, but shouldn't we get your car towed first?"

"There's no time. We have to go."

"I've never seen you this frantic. What's the hurry?"

I jerked on the door handle. "Unlock this damn thing. I'll explain on the way."

THIRTY-FIVE

I GAVE QUINN directions to the ranch and told him about the incident with the cria.

"A bull's-eye? The sick SOB." He slammed his hand on the steering wheel and proceeded to singe my ears with a string of expletives that would have filled a quarter jar.

"Keep cursing if it'll get us there faster."

"Sorry, but this guy sounds dangerous. Hard to believe it could be Beardsley. Maybe you should call 911."

"What am I supposed to tell them? Someone might be assaulting a llama?"

"Good point," Quinn said, "but no matter what we find, I'm not letting you stay out there alone."

"Letting me? Who made you the boss of me?"

In the light from an oncoming car, I saw his lips twist into an ironic grin. "The TMC Governing Board."

"This is my personal life," I said. "I only answer to you at work."

"In case you haven't noticed, that line has blurred. You're trying to protect your brother, but he's in trouble because Beardsley's wife is dead. You can't separate this situation from your job, Aimee."

"I'd give up a thousand jobs if it would keep Harry safe, so don't try to pull rank on me."

"Understood. Now you have to understand where

I'm coming from. I'm not as cavalier about my career as you are about yours."

"So you're trying to protect Vane Beardsley and Timbergate Medical Center to save your career? How noble."

"I can't afford to be noble. I'm one of five siblings and my parents kicked every one of us out of the nest after we finished our educations. My stint in Ethiopia and my six-day marriage cost me more than a scar on my eyebrow. There were legal bills and medical bills, and this job allows me to keep my head above water. I've grown to like it and I want to keep it. This Beardsley mess is not going to send me back to dodging bullets in some third world desert." He glanced over at me. "How much farther to the exit?"

"It's coming up now. Then go left, under the overpass."

We rode in silence the rest of the way. Quinn cut his lights as we pulled into Jack and Amah's driveway. There were no strange vehicles on the property.

"Stay in the car," he said. "Keep the doors locked."

"Forget it." I opened my door. "If the scumbag is here, he's mine. I'm the one he's been harassing."

We crept around to the back of the main house. The doors and windows all looked secure. I counted six woolly mounds—five large and one small—settled for the night in the dark pasture.

"Let's look around inside," Quinn said.

I unlocked the house and we checked every room. Nothing was disturbed.

"Which room is yours?" Quinn said.

"None. I don't live in this house."

He looked at me as if I'd lost my mind. "Then what the hell are we doing here?"

"This is Jack and Amah's house."

"Who are they?"

"My grandparents."

"So where exactly *do* you live?"

"In the llama barn."

"You're shitting me."

"No. It's a studio apartment. Above the barn."

Quinn sighed and shook his head. "Let's have a look at your apartment."

We walked down the lane under the light of a crescent moon. A distant coyote howled, prompting a muted chorus of barking from the dogs on a neighboring ranch. The scent of clover sweetened the balmy night air as we approached the barn.

We checked outside and saw nothing suspicious. Quinn went first up the stairs to the deck where he pronounced the door and windows secure. I unlocked the door and we stepped into the kitchen. Fanny trotted over to Quinn and rubbed against his legs. Behind the room divider, out of Quinn's line of sight, Bosco delivered his Dirty Harry impersonation with more malice than usual.

"Go ahead, make my day."

Quinn pushed me behind him. A pistol appeared in his left hand.

"Don't shoot," I yelled, "it's a bird."

Quinn lowered the gun and drew a deep breath.

"Mother of God, woman, you're going to put me in my own cardiac care unit before this night is over."

"And whose fault is that? I don't recall asking you to spy on Beardsley and me."

"I suppose you didn't ask me to drive you out here to your crazy animal farm." He slipped the gun into what looked like a holster inside the waistband of his pants.

"Why are you carrying a gun?"

"Ask the murdering thugs who killed my wife."

"Do you always carry it?"

"No. I thought tonight might be special. Do you have a gun?"

"No." I pointed to the kitchen counter. "I have bear spray."

"Good." Quinn checked the bathroom and closet. "This place is clear. Now what?"

"Now you leave, and I call a tow service."

"How will you get to work tomorrow?"

"I'll call my brother for a ride."

"It makes more sense for me to stay," Quinn said. "If your tire-slashing friend decides to show up, who-ever he is, I want to be around. I'll go get the Naviga-tor and park downstairs."

In spite of my attempt at bravado, the idea of Quinn and his gun guarding me held major appeal. I needed sleep, and I wasn't going to get it if he left me home alone. And I didn't want to call Harry to act as a body-guard. That would mean telling him about my date with Beardsley, which he'd pass on to Nick. It made sense to let Quinn stay over and drive me to work in the morning.

"Do you want to sleep in the main house?" I asked.

"No. It's too far away."

"Then you'll have to sleep in your car. All I have in here is a fold-out futon."

"No problem, the car's big."

I made a pot of decaf while Quinn drove his car

down the lane and parked in the stable yard. He came up and sat at my kitchen table with Fanny on his lap while I called the twenty-four-hour tow service and arranged to have them deliver the Buick to the tire shop in the morning. I'd already paid for one tire repair on credit. The thought of buying four new tires made my eyes water. I was going to be living in the barn a lot longer than I had expected.

I'd just sat at the table with my coffee when Quinn jumped up and looked out my kitchen window toward the main house.

"Turn off the light," he said.

I flipped the switch. "Why?"

"I saw headlights. Someone turned into your lane."

"I don't see anything."

"The headlights just went out. When did you say your grandparents are due back?"

"Not until Saturday."

"Any chance they'd come back early?"

"Not this early."

"Look." Quinn pointed out the window. I saw the silhouette of a pickup making slow progress down the lane toward us. Then it stopped abruptly, its headlights flashed on, and it reversed, wheels churning dirt and gravel, until it reached the street.

"Hell and damn," Quinn said, "he must have spotted the Navigator." He opened the door and took the stairs two at a time. He crouched behind his car and watched the pickup as it backed onto the street, slammed into forward gear, and sped away.

By that time, I had reached ground level. "Could you make out the plate number?"

"No. Too dark. Too far away." He shook his head in disgust.

"Color?"

"Sorry."

Quinn followed me back up the stairs. "At least we know the tire slasher was up to no good."

"I wonder what took him so long to get here."

"Maybe he had trouble finding his way. It's not exactly on the beaten path."

"Assuming it's the same guy, he was here before. To paint the cria and spray the message on my door."

"Good point. Maybe with your four flat tires, he thought he had plenty of time."

"He would have, if you hadn't been at the country club tonight. If I'd had to call a taxi, I'd still be waiting."

"What I'd like to know is how the slasher knew your car would be at the country club tonight. Who knew you were going there?"

"You and Dr. Beardsley." I hesitated. "That's not what you wanted to hear, is it?"

Quinn looked out the kitchen window into the darkness. "No."

"Sorry," I said, "but Beardsley must be involved. Maybe he cut the tires himself and called an accomplice to show up here."

"It's hard to imagine, but if he is involved, I'll do everything I can to keep you safe and to see that your brother is cleared."

"Thank you." I blinked and felt a tear roll down my cheek.

He reached out and touched it. "No tears, Aimee. It's going to be all right."

I read the look in his eyes and felt my cheeks turn

warm. I had to clear my throat before I could say anything more. "So, we'd better call it a night. Do you need a pillow or blanket or anything?"

"For sleeping in the car, right?" The husky quality of his voice tested my will power, and made me wonder if I would feel the same spark of desire for Quinn if Nick and I were still together. I hoped not.

"Right. In the car."

"It's a warm night," Quinn said. "The blanket's optional, but a pillow would be nice."

I took a pillow from my daybed and pulled a blanket from the top shelf in my closet. When I walked toward Quinn, he took them from me and put them on the table. He looked into my eyes for a long moment, and a fleeting wave of longing rushed through me. He enfolded me in a gentle, lingering hug, then just when I thought he might try to kiss me, he pulled away.

"Sorry," he said. "For a moment there you looked so forlorn, I couldn't help myself."

"It's okay. I'm sorry you have to sleep outside, but—"

He touched a finger to my lips. "Don't apologize. Just get some sleep." He opened the door and stepped out onto the deck. "I'll see you in the morning."

I went to bed and eventually slipped into a dream where Jared Quinn and Nick Alexander were conjoined twins, one dark and one fair, and I was dating both of them.

THIRTY-SIX

WEDNESDAY MORNING BEGAN with the surreal experience of having breakfast with my sexy, enigmatic boss. It was a dicey way to cement an employer-employee relationship, but I was stuck, so I buttered toast while Quinn poured coffee.

The intimacy left me more tongue-tied than if we'd actually slept together. I had never shared a morning-after breakfast with any man except Nick Alexander. Starting the day with Jared Quinn served as a painful reminder of what I'd lost.

On our drive to town, the atmospheric pressure in the car felt too close to sexual tension for comfort. Our conversation consisted of long, awkward silences interrupted occasionally by banal observations about the weather and the traffic.

None too soon, Quinn pulled up at the entrance to the library where Orrie Mercer stood guard once again. The guard's gaze skipped from me to Quinn and back to me. He squinted at his watch. I read his mind. *At seven-thirty in the morning, the new TMC librarian is arriving at work with Administrator Jared Quinn.* How fast could he spread that prime piece of gossip? At the speed of light, if he mentioned it to Maybelline.

Quinn angled his head toward Mercer. "I spoke to him about the library's private restroom. Told him it was off limits. If he so much as steps foot in the library, I want to hear about it."

"I'll let you know."

As Quinn pulled away I called out, "Thanks for the lift," for Mercer's benefit. When I walked past him, I said, "Flat tire," annoyed with myself that it mattered what he thought.

I had just locked my purse in a desk drawer when Dr. Beardsley appeared. He covered the distance from the library entrance to my desk with his right hand hidden behind his back. "Miss Machado, I'm sorry to be the bearer of bad news, but Maybelline left word that she will not be in today. Can you manage without her?"

Two thoughts sprang to mind in quick succession. Relief that I wouldn't have to put up with her increasingly bizarre behavior, then guilt for feeling relief at her suffering.

"I hope she isn't ill."

"Nothing serious. Would you like a replacement? Someone to fill in for Maybelline?"

"No, that's not necessary."

"Fine, then. There's one more thing."

"What's that?"

Dr. Beardsley beamed, and with a flourish produced an exquisite bouquet of pink roses from behind his back.

"These are for you. To make up for abandoning you at dinner last night." He seemed so genuinely contrite, so pleased with himself for his thoughtful gesture, that I would have been charmed if I hadn't had other things on my mind.

"I hope you can find a vase around here somewhere." Beardsley glanced around the room. "I'm sure

Maybelline has some extras tucked away. She does enjoy plants and flowers."

I glanced at Veronica, the hand-me-down violet in glorious bloom on the corner of my desk. "Yes, she does. Don't worry, I'll find something. And thank you, they're lovely."

"Think nothing of it." He hesitated at the door and glanced at the coat tree. "I almost forgot. Maybelline mentioned something about her volunteer's jacket. Apparently she forgot where she left it. Do you know where it might be?"

"It got soiled on her last shift, so I took it to be cleaned."

"Ah. That's probably why she asked about it."

"Shall I let her know?"

"Don't bother. I'm sure it's not important."

After Beardsley left, I opened a low cupboard in the library's tiny break room and found it crowded with dozens of vases. Remains of orphaned floral arrangements Maybelline had confiscated from patient rooms.

I filled a cut-glass vase with water from the restroom sink and arranged the bouquet. As I carried it back to my desk, my appreciation for the gesture evaporated. I thought about the events of the previous evening. When Beardsley left, he had encouraged me to stay behind and finish my dinner. Did he have an ulterior motive? Had he planned to lie in wait at the ranch and silence me? Or had he sent someone else to do the job?

I had forgotten to retrieve Maybelline's jacket and have it ready for her next shift, so I made a quick run to housekeeping. I returned with the cleaned and pressed garment and hung it on the coat tree where Maybelline had left it.

Her prescription was still in my purse. I took it out and considered whether to remind her to get it filled. I decided to put it back in her jacket pocket and mind my own business. After all, I wasn't responsible for Maybelline's medical care. She was a grown woman, capable of fending for herself.

Or was she? Now that I knew she'd mentioned her jacket to Beardsley, I was even more curious about the rumpled, ink-streaked prescription she had left unfilled in her pocket. What if Maybelline *wasn't* capable of fending for herself? What if she suffered from a mental problem? If she'd gone off her meds, that would explain the strange incident with the patient who had doused her with water. Maybe she had antagonized him somehow. She had said some off-the-wall things about Orrie Mercer, too. *He's a lying dirt bag, you know. And he's not my boyfriend.*

Instead of being amused by Maybelline's strange antics, I should have looked beyond the humor for something that would explain her personality quirks. I spread the paper flat on my desk and took another look. I couldn't help thinking of Verna Beardsley, who was also on medication. Verna Beardsley, who could be involved in the death of Vane Beardsley's wife. With a whopping head rush, I followed this train of thought to a staggering conclusion. *Maybe the Verna Beardsley we're looking for is right under my nose. Maybe it's Maybelline!*

I needed to know what drugs she was on. The name of the medication was badly smeared, and the handwriting was terrible, but it might be legible to a doctor or a pharmacist, someone familiar with the name of the drug. I was fresh out of friends in either profession who would decipher it for me if they knew it wasn't mine.

I photocopied the original before returning it to her jacket pocket. What to do with this new and potentially crucial information? For starters, I wasn't going to mention the mysterious prescription to Dr. Beardsley. If Maybelline Black *was* Verna Beardsley, she wasn't strong enough to strangle Bonnie, stuff her limp body into a deer bag and hoist her into a Dumpster by herself. She had to have an accomplice. Her cuckold brother had my vote.

In a perfect world, I would simply take my theory to the police. Unfortunately, in my imperfect world, there was Marco Bueller to consider.

THIRTY-SEVEN

THE MANAGER OF Topper's Tires called shortly before noon to say my car was ready, the bill was nine hundred dollars, and how did I want to pay? I left a message on Harry's cellphone saying I needed a ride to the tire shop. He called back five minutes later.

"Tires again? What's going on?"

"I'll explain later. Can you give me a ride?"

"I can't get away now. How about later?"

"They close at five."

"Hold on." I listened to a few seconds of silence, then Harry was back. "Okay. Your ride will be there in ten minutes."

I didn't like the sound of that. "You'd better not send Nick."

Nick strode into the library ten minutes later.

"I knew it," I said.

Nick frowned. "Look, this has nothing to do with you and me. I'm doing Harry a favor. He's worried about you, and he can't get away right now."

"So I heard. Why did you paint my door? Another favor for Harry?"

"Yep. I get bored when I'm not working. I like to keep busy."

"What's so important that Harry can't take off for half an hour at lunchtime?"

"Let's talk on the way. You can explain the latest tire incident, and I'll explain about Harry."

"God, Nick, I'm so worried about him. Sometimes I can barely breathe."

Nick reached out and took my chin in his hand. "You have to stay strong."

Just then Quinn walked in. I jerked away from Nick and stumbled backward until my rear hit the front corner of my desk. Veronica the violet slammed to the floor. The ceramic planter cracked in two, and the plant's root ball spewed potting soil on the floor in a dark circle the size of an extra large pizza.

All three of us stared at the mess on the floor.

Quinn spoke first. "I came by to see if you needed a lift to the tire shop. Apparently not." He reached his hand toward Nick. "Good to see you again. It's Alexander, isn't it?"

Nick shook Jared's hand. "That's right. You have a good memory, Mr. Quinn."

"As do you."

I couldn't stand listening to the two of them try to out-polite each other. I grabbed my purse.

"Nick, we need to get going." I pointed to the ruined violet and said to Quinn, "I'll call housekeeping when I get back from lunch."

On the way I told Nick as little as possible about the previous night. A business dinner with Dr. Beardsley at the Country Club and afterward, four slashed tires.

Nick pushed for details. "How did you get home?"

"I caught a ride with a friend."

"What friend?"

"What difference does it make?"

"It was Quinn, wasn't it?"

"I'm not answering any more questions." Next he'd be asking how I got to work in the morning.

Nick parked at the tire shop and cut the engine. "Are you falling for that guy?"

"Don't be ridiculous. He's my boss." I opened my door and got out. "Thanks for the ride. I can take it from here."

I shut the door a little too hard and hustled into the office. Watching out the window while Nick's car pulled into traffic, I experienced a sensation like walking on an undulating sidewalk in a fun house. Only it wasn't fun. It was scary and sad at the same time.

The clerk finished up with another customer and turned to me. I faked a friendly smile while Topper's Tires maxed out my credit card.

I spent the rest of the afternoon at the library leaving messages on all of Harry's phones. I called Hannah, but she hadn't heard anything. By quitting time, Harry still hadn't called back, and I could think of only one reason. When the judge dismissed the case against Harry at the first arraignment, Abe Edelman had warned us the DA might try again.

After work I drove the eight miles to Coyote Creek with my shoulders hunched up to my earlobes. My tension level had spiked dramatically between worry about Harry and concern about the creep who was harassing me and assaulting the llamas. Each time I left the ranch unprotected, I worried until my shoulders burned and my jawbone ached from grinding my teeth.

I pulled into Jack and Amah's driveway and stopped, yo-yoing between relief and resentment. Nick's car was parked in the driveway. He sat on the front porch in a rocking chair reading the paper and looking as if he owned the place. A pizza box and a six-pack of beer sat on the table next to him.

I parked my car and climbed the porch steps, afraid Nick had come with bad news about Harry.

"What are you doing here?"

"Reading the paper." He wore a look of wide-eyed innocence.

"I see that. Is Harry okay?"

"He's okay. He's going over things with Abe right now. He said he'd call later." Nick opened the pizza box. "Why don't you sit down and eat?"

"First let me tell you about my lead on Verna Beardsley."

"So tell me."

"She could be one of my volunteers. A woman who calls herself Maybelline Black."

Nick burst out laughing. "You think some pink lady murdered Beardsley's wife?"

"Stop laughing and listen to me. I found a prescription in her pocket."

"You picked her pocket?"

"No." I explained how I'd found the prescription. "It could be significant. What if she's on the same drugs Verna Beardsley takes?"

"Okay, we'll check it out. But don't get your hopes up. I doubt your pink lady has been out here raising Cain with the livestock."

"Okay, maybe it's far-fetched, but I don't see you coming up with any better ideas."

"True. Now will you eat?"

"I need to do the chores."

"The chores are done."

"I'd like to change my clothes and check on Bosco and the cat."

"Okay, get out of your work duds and come on back."

I parked at the barn and took a quick look around. Nick had put out hay, replenished the salt licks, and filled the turkey feeders. The water in the troughs was clean and fresh. He must have spent all afternoon on the ranch. Not because he liked doing chores, but because he expected the vandal to strike again and wanted to be around.

The adult llamas munched hay and little Moonbeam performed her usual antics, bouncing around the pasture on her spring-loaded legs. Princess raised her head between bites to track the cria's whereabouts.

The apartment door was still locked. Good, at least Nick hadn't taken the liberty of going into my personal space. When I tried my key in the new deadbolt lock, it jammed. I wiggled it loose and tried again. After three tries, I managed to get the door open. When I did, my knees buckled. I grabbed the kitchen counter to keep from falling. Hanging by one leg from the light fixture over my dinette table was a dead turkey. On the table just below its dangling, severed neck was a dark crimson pool filling the stuffy room with the coppery scent of blood.

THIRTY-EIGHT

THE WORDS SCRAWLED in blood on my white kitchen wall sent a clear message:

LAST CHANCE QUIT SNOOPING

"Did you touch anything?" Nick circled the small table, snapping pictures of the crime scene with his phone.

"No, I called the sheriff's office, then I ran back to the house to get you."

"Good." He put the phone in his pocket. "Let's go back and eat while we wait."

We followed our long evening shadows up the lane to the main house and sat on the front porch. The pizza's mouth-watering aroma overrode my usual reaction to distress. I wolfed down the first slice, chugged most of a beer, and waited for the buzz. I wanted that now; I needed to let go, to dull my fear and worry down to a manageable level. I took another mouthful, closed my eyes and swished, letting the bubbles tickle the insides of my cheeks.

When I opened my eyes, Nick was watching me. "I heard from Harry."

"When?"

"Just after you went to the barn to change your clothes."

"Why didn't you tell me?"

"I got sidetracked by the scenario in your apartment. Then I thought I'd give you a little time to calm down."

"What did Harry say?"

"There's going to be another arraignment."

"When?"

"Maybe tomorrow, by Friday for sure. Harry's been in meetings with the city most of the day about his contract for the mall job. That's why he couldn't help you out earlier."

"What does that mean? Will they put Harry in jail this time?"

"It's up to the judge. He might dismiss the case again, or Harry might go to jail."

"If he does, can we bail him out?"

"On a murder charge? It depends."

"What does that mean?"

Nick hesitated too long before answering. Fear punched the air out of my midsection. "Nick. What do you mean? Tell me."

"Dammit, Aimee." He stared for a moment into the dark branches of the oak tree above our heads. "They might charge him with a capital crime."

I knew what that meant. Suspects charged with capital crimes usually aren't allowed out on bail. Or the judge might set the bail impossibly high. A capital crime is one that can be punishable by death.

"Stop. I don't want to hear any more." A sob tore out of me. "This can't be happening."

Nick swore under his breath while I blew my nose on a napkin and sucked in a deep breath of tepid summer air.

We sat without speaking as a chorus of frogs croaked

their evening serenade. The sound of nature doing what it was meant to do eventually calmed me and brought me back to the business at hand.

"Okay, I'm over my hysterics," I said. "Why are they refiling?"

"New evidence, maybe? We don't know."

"Why are they telling Abe and Harry ahead of time?"

"Because Harry is a prominent citizen, not a likely flight risk. It's a courtesy, to give him time to make some arrangements."

"Damn, Nick. What if the city takes the mall contract away from Harry? It would destroy his reputation and ruin him financially."

"Abe says they can't void the contract unless Harry is unable to fulfill it."

"Harry told me that, but if he's in jail and tied up for a long time with a murder trial, how can he fulfill his contract? Even if he's proven innocent, it will be too late, won't it?"

"We're not going to let that happen," Nick said. "We have to trust Abe."

The sun had dropped behind the mountains to the west, tinting the evening a cheerless shade that matched my dismal mood. The prospect of Harry in prison filled me with grief. If he survived, he would be someone else, a shell of my beloved little brother. I'd rather die than see that happen.

"I might be all wrong about Maybelline," I said, "but we're running out of time. Someone thinks I know something and wants to scare me off. We have to find out who's been trespassing here and how Verna Beardsley fits into the picture."

"It could be dangerous."

"It already is. So either help me or get out of my way." I drained the last of my beer.

"You mean that, don't you?" He leaned toward me, took the empty beer bottle out of my hand.

"Absolutely."

"Okay, what's your plan?"

"I need the pictures you took of the Verna Beardsley file. I want to see if you got any shots of the meds she's on. Do you remember?"

"Not really. I was in a hurry, so I just pointed and clicked."

"Are the photos still in your camera?"

"Sorry. I changed memory cards this morning. The one I used at the rehab facility is in my desk at Buck Sawyer's spread."

"That's where you're staying?"

"In the pool house. For now."

My insides took a hit. "What happened to your apartment?"

"Rella's using it." *Rella.* Another sucker punch. "Aren't you going to ask me why?"

"Only if you want to tell me."

"Her brother's in Europe on a political assignment for a few months, so his two young sons are staying with her. The pool house is small and she needed a kitchen, so we switched."

"Where's their mother?"

"Out of the picture. I don't know the details, but Rella's hired a live-in Nanny for when she's away working. She needs the space until she can either rent or buy something with enough room."

So Rella had a domestic side and possibly even maternal instincts. That news was more than I cared to think about.

"Let's get back to the photos," I said. "I need you to email them to me as soon as you can."

"Okay, what else?"

"I need to find out what medications Maybelline's taking so we can compare them with what Verna Beardsley is on."

"How are you going to do that?"

"I don't know yet, but I made a copy of Maybelline's prescription."

"Is that legal?"

"Not exactly."

Through a wash of deep purple twilight, the headlights of a sheriff's patrol car arced off the road and into the driveway. The officer walked over to the porch where we sat.

"Evening, folks, what seems to be the problem?"

I told him about the turkey and watched him struggle to keep a straight face. The three of us trekked down the lane to the bunkhouse in the glow of the patrol car's spotlight. When the deputy saw the carcass dangling from the light fixture and the threat scrawled on the wall, his demeanor changed. The pool of drying blood shored up the notion that this was indeed a crime scene, even if the deceased was poultry. He took photos and wrote copious notes.

We walked back to the main house and sat on the front porch.

"Any idea who might have done this?" the officer asked. "Any known enemies?"

"Who, me?"

"Yes, ma'am."

"No. I can't think of anyone."

"Have there been other incidents?"

"Her tires were slashed last night," Nick said.

The officer's eyes widened. "And you have no idea who's harassing you?"

"Not really, unless it's kids from the halfway house."

"What's your address here?"

I gave him the address. "This is my grandparents' home. I live with them."

"Then I'll need your grandparents' names."

"Jack and Rosa Highland."

The officer's eyes lit up. "Jack Highland, the outdoor writer?"

"Yes. Do you know him?"

"I read his stuff all the time." He put his little notebook in his shirt pocket. "If you have any more trouble, give us a call. Tell your grandfather we'll keep an eye on this place. Set up some extra patrols."

I thought I heard him murmur, "Jack Highland. I'll be damned," as he slid into his vehicle.

Nick and I watched the cruiser's taillights disappear into the night.

"Why did you tell him about my tires?"

"The tires weren't a prank by delinquent teens and neither was the turkey. They were warnings. You're a target. That's not something you keep to yourself."

"You think telling him is going to do any good?"

"Extra patrols can't hurt." Nick glanced up at the stars. "What do we do now?"

I stifled a yawn. "You'd better go home. I need to get some sleep."

"You can't be serious. You're not staying here."

"I have to. I'm not leaving this place unprotected.

Have you forgotten about the cria? She'll be this maniac's next victim."

"No, Aimee, *you* will. You have to give this up."

I twisted the lid off another beer and chugged. "I'm not quitting. We can solve this. We have clues no one else has. Are you in or not?"

"Of course I'm in. If anything happened to you, I'd lose my best friend."

"I'm not your best friend anymore."

"I was talking about Harry," Nick said. "He'd never forgive me."

THIRTY-NINE

NICK REFUSED TO LEAVE, so I tossed him a pillow and sleeping bag to use on the family room couch. I needed Nick as far away as possible, and the family room was on the opposite end of the house from where I would be bunking with the king snake.

I was trying to read myself to sleep with Fanny curled next to me when I realized I'd forgotten to check on Bosco after discovering the gruesome scene in the bunkhouse. I resigned myself to one more trip to the barn, hoping that whoever had butchered the turkey had spared the elderly little bird. Nick was sound asleep in the family room, but I didn't really need his help, so I closed Fanny in the guest room, slipped out the front door and headed down the lane to the barn, making my way by starlight.

I left the lights off when I got to my apartment in case Nick happened to wake up and look outside. Using a flashlight, I began my search. The birdcage door was open and the cockatiel was missing. Another vile act on the part of my tormentor? What had he done with the little guy? I opened the closet hoping to find him shut inside. No luck. In the studio's small space, it took only minutes to know that Bosco was nowhere to be found. I opened the door to leave and saw a shadowy figure on my deck.

"Do you have a death wish?"

Nick stood there looking as if he'd like to throttle me.

"Damn, Nick. You scared the crap out of me."

"Good. What the hell are you doing out here?"

I leaned back against the kitchen counter, hugging myself. "Looking for Bosco."

"Did you find him?"

"No. He's gone. His cage is empty."

"Why would your intruder bother with him?"

"Who knows?"

Nick nodded at the turkey, still hanging in my kitchen. "The guy who did this is nuts, and he's going to keep coming after you. He thinks you can link him to Bonnie Beardsley's death. If he's right, we have to find out why."

"That's the problem. I don't know why. He doesn't know we know about Verna Beardsley. We haven't told anyone about her fingerprint on the toenail."

"Someone's threatening you and there has to be a reason," Nick said. "This is about more than Verna Beardsley. You know something else. You have to figure out what it is. Now let's get out of here. We can talk back at the house."

"What about Bosco?"

"He's not here. We'll have to deal with that later."

We locked the apartment and walked up the lane to the house. The starry night and balmy air made a perfect backdrop for lovers, but the setting was lost on us. Nick and I were more than an arm's length apart, each of us isolated in our own thoughts.

We continued brainstorming at Jack and Amah's kitchen table.

"Tell me about this Maybelline," Nick said. "The

woman who might be Beardsley's sister. What do you know about her?"

"She's the right age. She's crazy about Vane, as she calls him, and her behavior has gone from gossipy and outspoken to erratic in the short time I've know her. And there's the prescription. It was in her pocket the day she was drenched by an angry patient."

"When did that happen?"

I thought back, amazed it had been just two days earlier. "Monday. She works Monday and Wednesday mornings. She didn't work today. Beardsley came by to tell me she wouldn't be there, but he didn't say why."

"Do you have the prescription with you?"

"I have a copy in my purse." I ran down the hall to the guest room.

Back in the kitchen, I handed the sheet of paper to Nick. "We have to find out if it's the same medication prescribed for Verna Beardsley."

Nick studied the copy. "I can't make anything out of this." He folded the page and put it in his wallet. "I'll get it to Abe first thing in the morning."

"Shall we call him? Give him a heads-up?"

"Now? It's almost midnight."

"So what? They might arrest Harry tomorrow."

"Abe can't do anything about this in the middle of the night." Nick stood. "Will you go to bed now and try to sleep?"

"What about Bosco?" His disappearance seemed like the last straw, and I was suddenly overwhelmed by sadness, thinking about how much Amah and Jack cared about the silly little bird and how tickled they were by its shocking, profane outbursts. "I know it's just a bird, but I'm supposed to be taking care of things here, and instead, it seems like the whole world is falling apart." I bit my lip, trying to hold back tears.

"Damn." Nick came to me and pulled me up from where I sat. Enfolding me in his arms, he said, "You're exhausting yourself with trying to keep it all together."

I couldn't find the energy to back away from his embrace. It felt like coming home from a long, lonely journey. We stood there in silence until Nick kissed the top of my head, then gently put me at arm's length.

"Better?" he asked.

I nodded. "Sorry about the meltdown. I guess I'm not as tough as I thought."

He laughed. "Don't worry. You're tough enough. But you're also human, so try to give yourself some slack once in a while."

"But we still don't know what happened to Bosco."

"Let it go for now. Wherever he is, he's probably in better shape that you are."

I fell into an exhausted sleep, thinking about giving myself some slack and wondering if it was time to give Nick some slack as well.

FORTY

NICK CAME KNOCKING on the guest room door at six o'clock Thursday morning.

"Coffee's ready."

I roused myself and opened the door just wide enough for him to hand me a steaming cup. Fanny slipped out and shot down the hall.

"Thanks, I'll be right out."

"Bacon's in the skillet," he said. "Toast is almost ready."

"I'm not very hungry."

"Suit yourself."

After a quick shower, I put my hair in a damp braid, then realized I'd have to go back to my apartment for something to wear to work. I rejected that idea and slipped into Jack and Amah's bedroom. In Amah's closet I found a flowered cotton dress with a flared skirt, and a pair of low-heeled sandals.

Nick had taken me at my word. The hot breakfast was nowhere in sight. I rummaged in the cupboards. All I found was stale All-Bran. Nick saw the box and took pity.

"Here." He pulled a warm plate of bacon slices and toast from the oven. While I munched, he scribbled on a notepad.

"What are you writing?"

"Things we need to do today." He put the pencil down.

"We? I have to go to work."

"That's on the list."

"I would have remembered that," I said. "What else is on your list?"

"We have to get your volunteer's prescription deciphered. What's her name again?"

"Maybelline Black. There are labs in Sacramento and San Mateo that do miracles with things like blurred writing." I used my cellphone to go online for the contact information, which I wrote down for Nick. "Here. See if Abe has influence with either of them."

"Can they work with a copy?"

"I hope so. It's amazing what they can do."

"I'll drop by Abe's office first thing." Nick took our plates to the sink. "More coffee?"

"No, thanks. And don't forget to email those photos of Verna Beardsley's medical record to me right away. All of them, so I can look for notes about her prescriptions."

He refilled his cup and came back to the table. "If they match, you're convinced the volunteer woman is our prime suspect?"

"Not necessarily," I said. "Verna Beardsley and Maybelline Black might simply be taking the same medication."

"Right. Maybe they both have acid reflux. It's popular."

"This is serious."

His eyes narrowed in a cunning squint. "You know, Maybelline Black's fingerprints are bound to be all over your library."

"Are you suggesting we ask the police to drop by and dust the library?"

"I see your point, but you could bag up something small. Can you think of anything she handles?"

"There's a cupboard full of empty vases. She washes them and stores them in there. That's the only thing I can think of that would have her prints and no one else's."

"That sounds good. Can you get me a couple of those?"

"That shouldn't be a problem," I said.

"Meanwhile, maybe you'll learn something when you meet with Beardsley's ex. She must know whether your Maybelline is his sister."

"Right, but we're not sure she'll tell me anything."

"Her husband dumped her for a younger woman. She's not going to protect him if he's involved in a murder."

"She's a classy woman. I'm not sure how she'll respond to my prying into her private life."

"You can bet the police have already done that."

"But they didn't know about the Verna Beardsley fingerprint. I doubt the fact that Vane Beardsley has a sister even crossed their radar."

"Probably not," Nick said. "We're going to beat this thing, Aimee." He knocked back the last of his coffee and got up to leave. "We'll go to lunch and compare notes." He winked at me from the open door. "By the way, I forget. Are we still engaged?"

I flung a piece of toast at him, but he ducked and it sailed out the door.

I fed the rest of my breakfast to Fanny and let her out. A few bacon scraps would barely whet her appetite for her day job as Jack's field mouse exterminator.

I called Harry before I left for work.

"Hi, Sis. What's up?"

"Where are you?"

"On the job, why?"

"No reason. I miss you. I thought we might get together later. After work."

"Sounds good. I'll drop by the ranch. Want me to bring food?"

"No, thanks. I'll pick up something for us." My spirits lifted. "Then you're not expecting to be arrested?"

"Not that I've heard. Gotta go," he said. "See you at six…no, better make that seven."

He broke the connection before I remembered the mutilated turkey carcass in my apartment. I'd have to get rid of it before Harry arrived. I called the sheriff's office to ask permission to clean up the mess and got an okay, but I wouldn't have time to take care of it until I got home from work.

The library entrance was unguarded when I arrived. That cheered me further. Any workday that started without Orrie Mercer was a gift.

Dr. Beardsley's ex didn't answer when I called, so I left a message saying I'd call back. I had just finished the call when Lola arrived. She wore a blue T-shirt and a tiny pair of jeans she must have purchased in JCPenney's children's department. Her orange volunteer's jacket was draped across her arm.

"Hello, dear," she said. "Do you like my new shirt?" She twirled like a model on a runway. "I ordered the three-shirt combo from Marty Stockwell's website. Only fifty dollars. A real bargain, don't you think?"

"Ahh…." Words failed me.

"The picture of Marty is supposed to be in front." Lola peered at her reflection in the glass covering a print of Van Gogh's *Portrait of Dr. Gachet*. "I think he shows up better if I wear the shirt backwards, don't you?"

Her beaming face demanded a response. "Marty has never looked better, Lola. He'd be proud to know a fan as devoted as you."

"Really? I hope so." She put on her jacket with obvious reluctance. "I'd like so much to meet him someday. Perhaps you could help."

"Me? How?"

"Is it true Mr. Stockwell lives right here in Sawyer County? In Coyote Creek?"

Oh, oh. "Now that you mention it, I might have heard that."

Lola beamed. "I understand you also live in Coyote Creek."

It kept getting worse. "I do, but I don't know Mr. Stockwell personally. I'm sorry."

A wistful look replaced her smile. "I have all his CDs. My late husband Joseph was such a fan. We played Marty's songs at our wedding. We married late, you know, but we had twenty wonderful years before he passed." Lola stared out into the stacks.

"I'm sorry for your loss," I said.

"Thank you. It *was* a great loss, but I found a way to cope. I played Marty's music at Joseph's funeral, and it brought me such comfort that I've gone on listening to Mr. Stockwell. He has kept my Joseph close to me these past five years."

At that point, tears threatened. Mine, not hers. I wanted to help, but there was nothing I could do.

"Maybe if you called his people and explained what you just told me, they'd invite you to meet him."

"Oh, I doubt that would work," Lola said. "I'm nobody special, and famous people have to be careful of their privacy these days. Stalkers and all that. I thought it would be lovely to bump into him at the grocery store. Just to shake his hand and thank him, you know. For Joseph and me, and for all the wonderful memories."

"At the grocery store? You mean in Coyote Creek?"

"Yes, at the Four Corners. I've heard he shops there. Is that true?"

"I suppose it is." I didn't elaborate. If she knew that Jack and Marty were acquainted, who knew what she'd ask me to do? Lola wasn't a stalker—she was merely a harmless fan—but I wasn't about to get involved. "Have you thought of writing a nice letter instead of trying to meet him?"

"I thought of that, but it wouldn't be the same. He must get lots of mail. I'd never know if he read it."

"Tell you what, Lola. I'll think about this. If there's anything I can do, I'll let you know."

Her lips pursed in a wry smile. "You're humoring me, I know, but I don't mind. I shouldn't have tried to impose on you."

My cheeks flamed in embarrassment. "I'm sorry. I wish I could do more."

Lola went to work putting protective plastic covers on a newly arrived batch of medical journals. I shook off my guilt for not telling her all I knew about Marty Stockwell and focused on my own problems.

I opened the cupboard where Maybelline had stored the vases. It was empty. I opened all of the cupboards. The vases weren't there. Lola noticed and walked over.

"Is something amiss?"

"No. I was looking for a vase. They were here a couple days ago and now they're gone."

"Oh. I can explain that. The volunteer from the gift shop came to collect them so they could be used again."

"All of them?"

"I suppose so." Lola smiled. "The gift shop people know about Maybelline and her flowers."

After I left a message for Nick about the vases, I put in a call to Hannah asking if she knew anything more about why the DA would go in front of a judge again. Did she have something concrete? A witness? Forensic evidence?

"There's a witness," Hannah said, "but they're not sure she's reliable."

"Do you know who it is? What is she saying about Harry? If she says she saw him hurt Bonnie, she's lying."

"No. Not an eyewitness to the murder. The witness claims she saw Harry and Bonnie arguing around the time Bonnie disappeared."

I recalled Harry telling me Bonnie had come on to him outside his condo that Friday night. What had he said? Something about telling Bonnie to call the police. *She acted pissed, said she didn't need me giving her orders. Then she went coy and apologetic, tried to get me in a lip lock. I disentangled her and practically shoved her into her car.* Had one of Harry's condo neighbors witnessed that scene and read it wrong?

"Who is she, this witness?"

"No one knows," Hannah said. "The police and the DA are making darn sure no one finds out."

"Can they do that?"

"Not indefinitely. If she's a witness, the defense has to know."

"Why hasn't DA Keefer already gone back to the judge?"

"Apparently they're still checking the woman's credibility."

A woman. I thought back to the night Harry had so casually broken a date. How many other women had he disappointed that way? He was a catch, and some of the women fishing for husbands in Timbergate didn't take rejection gracefully. Still, testifying against Harry in a murder case seemed like extreme revenge for a broken date. Why else would a witness implicate Harry? I could think of only one reason: to divert suspicion from the real killer.

FORTY-ONE

I CALLED LORRAINE BEARDSLEY at eleven o'clock Thursday morning.

"Troy tells me you'd like to meet with me," she said. "Why is that?"

"I think you can help me save my brother."

"That's extraordinary. What's wrong with your brother?"

"He's a suspect in the murder of Bonnie Beardsley."

An eternity of silence followed before she finally spoke. "I see."

"Please meet with me," I said.

"You work with Vane? At Timbergate Medical Center?"

"Yes. In the library. I began two weeks ago."

"He's a suspect, too, of course."

I had no idea how that would influence her decision. How did she feel toward her ex? Charitable, vengeful, or simply indifferent?

"Please, my brother is innocent, but the DA is trying to pin this crime on him."

"I won't promise I can help, but I'll hear you out. As a favor to Netta Palmer."

"Thank you. That's all I ask."

We arranged to meet at twelve thirty, and she gave me her address. I called Nick and canceled our lunch date. He told me Abe had managed to have the prescription from Maybelline's jacket examined. I reminded him again to email all the photos from Verna Beardsley's Green Pastures medical record, then told him what Hannah had said about a potential witness. We agreed to get back in touch if we had anything new to report.

I tried to concentrate on library business. I was afraid my dream job was slipping through my fingers while I fought for my brother's life.

Jared Quinn hadn't called or stopped by the library since he dropped me off at work on Wednesday morning. Although little more than twenty-four hours had passed since then, it seemed much longer. He had made it clear on Tuesday night that he wasn't going to jeopardize his career to keep Harry out of jail; his loyalty was tied to Timbergate Medical Center. In spite of asking me to keep an eye on Beardsley, he had to be hoping someone else looked good for the crime.

If Quinn wouldn't help Harry, he had at least tackled the problem of Orrie Mercer. Shelly Hardesty stopped by the library just before noon to tell me she was filling in for Mercer again. She had been called late in the morning when someone finally noticed Mercer hadn't shown up for work.

Maybelline was off, too. Now that I suspected her of being accomplice to a murder, I preferred knowing where she was and what she was doing. I reminded myself that she might simply be a lonely oddball. Maybe she and Orrie took the day to patch things up. The two of them having make-up sex wasn't a pretty picture, so I put that out of my mind and concentrated on Lorraine Beardsley.

If she could answer the Verna Beardsley question,

we might win by a toenail. If Maybelline *was* Verna, odds were good that she and Vane Beardsley killed Bonnie. With that argument, Abe Edelman could counter DA Keefer's evidence against Harry and argue that Dr. Beardsley should be the prime suspect in his wife's murder.

I found Lorraine's home five miles west of town in the posh Silver Hills community where Timbergate's real estate prices reached their zenith. The house was brick, trimmed in gleaming white. The front yard was manicured to perfection. Two BMWs parked in the driveway—one white, one silver—completed the picture of unapologetic affluence.

The door opened immediately when I rang the bell. I had been expecting a housekeeper, but it was Lorraine herself, dressed in spotless white slacks and a powder blue cotton shirt. In minimal makeup, with her crown of golden hair tucked behind her ears, she definitely did not look like a woman in her sixties.

"Let's talk in my study," she said.

We walked through a great room with a vaulted ceiling, down a corridor the width of a freeway, and up a flight of stairs. After a few more twists and turns, we finally reached a cozy, book-lined study. I hoped she wouldn't leave me there alone. Without a trail of breadcrumbs, I'd never make it back to the front door. A bowl of cinnamon potpourri filled the room with the aroma of fresh apple pie.

"Troy is in the backyard doing something with the pool," Lorraine said. "He wouldn't interrupt in any case. He's thoughtful and discreet. Two of the many reasons I'm marrying him."

I wondered why Troy wasn't at work. Either he had inherited wealth, or he expected to inherit Lorraine's.

"I'm sorry to intrude," I said. "I know it's an inconvenient time, but I'm afraid this is a matter of life and death."

"You mentioned your brother's unfortunate situation. You have my sympathy, but I don't see how I can help."

"By telling me if you know a woman named Verna Beardsley."

Surprise disordered the smooth façade of her face for only an instant, but it was enough.

"I wish you'd asked anything else." She pulled aside a window curtain to look down into her backyard.

"Why is that?"

"I'm under a legal obligation to remain silent about Verna. Part of the terms of my divorce."

"Then you do know her?"

"Of course. She is Vane's sister."

The breath I'd been holding rushed out. "That's what I hoped you'd say. Do you know where she is?"

"That's the sticky part."

"The part you're not supposed to tell?"

"Yes. If I say more, I place myself in some legal jeopardy."

"Please hear me out. If I can find Verna, I might be able to save my brother."

"How so?"

"I think she knows something about Bonnie's death."

"What gives you that idea?"

Time for a white lie. "Harry's attorney. He's not giving details, just that her name has come up and he'd like to interview her."

"Is she a suspect?"

"No. More likely a witness."

"Then Vane is the suspect?"

"I'm sorry. I can see I'm out of line coming here, but I know my brother is innocent. I'm desperate to help him."

"Why are you so sure he's innocent?"

"My brother would never do what they're accusing him of." I swallowed against the tightening in my throat. "Aside from that, someone is threatening me. Someone who thinks I know something. Obviously, it isn't my own brother. It's someone who wants to see him framed."

"Are you in danger?"

Her question brought me up short. Denial had been my modus operandi for two weeks. It was time to be honest with myself and with her.

"Yes. Whoever killed Bonnie is coming after me. I'm sure of it."

"Why don't you take what you know to the police?"

"The investigator and my brother have a history." I told her about Tango Bueller.

Lorraine's shapely lips curled into a sneer. "Do you know District Attorney Keefer?"

"No."

"I do. She had designs on Troy before he and I were a couple. She decided his money would help her get re-elected. She hasn't a thought in her head that isn't tied to her political career. Including her choice of bed partners."

I waited to see where this was going.

"Miss Machado, if clearing your brother helps expose Keefer's shoddy professional and personal ethics, I'd be delighted to help."

"What if it puts your ex-husband in her sights?"

"Vane doesn't have a violent nature, but he has expressed his frustration with Bonnie more than once."

"He came to you to complain about her?"

"He had no one else to talk to. I suppose at the beginning—when he realized he'd made a terrible mistake—he had some hope of our getting back together."

"How soon after their marriage did he regret hooking up with Bonnie?"

"I think the hunting fiasco was the final straw. That was about a year into the marriage." She seemed amused by the memory.

"Hunting?"

"Bonnie's father is a deer hunter. Bonnie wanted Vane to take up the sport. She liked anything macho. Vane bought all the gear and went out one weekend with Bonnie's father and her uncle." Lorraine stopped, cleared her throat. I wanted the rest of the story.

"Did Vane shoot a deer?"

"No. He shot Bonnie's uncle in the foot."

"That's awful."

"Yes. Vane was horrified."

"What did he do?"

"Apparently there was a lot of blood. Vane administered first aid, wrapped the man's foot in a deer bag until they could get to a clinic somewhere in the mountains. The uncle recovered after a time…except… I believe he lost a toe. Vane tried to make amends by getting the man a job at TMC."

"Bonnie's uncle works at the hospital?" My internal wiring began to zing. "Where does he work?"

"I don't recall, but I doubt it's anything white collar. Apparently he's a bit thick."

I filed that away for further thought. I needed to know who the uncle was, and soon.

"Was Bonnie upset with Dr. Beardsley about her uncle's injury?"

"No more than usual. She was always upset with him. She criticized everything he did, especially if it had to do with money."

"But he has a successful practice."

"It was never enough for her. He'd have left her, but he said he couldn't discard her unless he paid her off with an obscene amount of money. She threatened a terrible scandal that would ruin his reputation."

The Underhills came to mind.

"Then he wasn't independently wealthy?"

"No. He had to work for every penny. I was born into more money than Vane will ever earn. When we divorced, I didn't need anything from him. Bonnie would have been a different story. Apparently her parents had disinherited her."

I recalled hearing the same story from Maybelline.

"So Dr. Beardsley wanted to be rid of Bonnie?"

"Oh, yes, but don't misunderstand," Lorraine said. "I do not believe that Vane murdered her. He said her drug use had escalated. She flew into rages, and sometimes he had to physically restrain her. If she had been hurt in that kind of confrontation, he'd have done anything to save her."

"You sound very sure of that."

"I'm certain. Vane is a doctor first, last and always."

"But a plastic surgeon."

"Don't believe the bad press about his specialty. He spends more time correcting deformities and injuries than he does making spoiled women look beautiful."

"Thank you for what you've been able to tell me. There's one last question."

"Yes?"

"How well do you know Maybelline Black?"

Lorraine's eyes narrowed. "Why do you ask?"

"She's been edgy lately. There was a rather volatile incident with a patient a few days ago. I wondered if there was something I should know about her."

"Why ask me?"

"She's particularly fond of you, and she seems unusually devoted to Dr. Beardsley. I mean, for a volunteer."

"Have you discussed her behavior with Vane?"

"No. Maybelline made me promise not to."

Lorraine walked to the window again, looked down toward the yard where her fiancé puttered. "There is very little I can tell you about her. If her actions become a problem for you, you'll have to talk to Vane."

"I'd hate to break my promise to Maybelline."

Lorraine turned away from the window. "I wish I could help you, but I'm not at liberty to discuss Maybelline Black." She looked straight into my eyes. "I hope you understand."

"I think I do. Thank you." I hoped I was right.

"I suppose you should go now." She escorted me back through the maze of her luxurious home. At her front door she took my hand. "Good luck, Miss Machado. Your brother is very lucky to have you on his side."

"Thank you. I'd do anything for him."

"I believe you. Brothers and sisters can be very loyal, even in the most trying circumstances."

"Like a death in the family?"

"Yes, I would think especially then." She closed the door gently.

I walked to my car weighing every word Lorraine had spoken. She had used hints and innuendo, but the subtext was clear. I now felt almost certain that Maybelline Black was Verna Beardsley. I'd feel even more certain if the prescriptions bore that out.

FORTY-TWO

I WAFFLED BETWEEN doubt and certainty on the drive back to work. Lorraine hadn't come right out and confirmed that Maybelline was Verna, but she hadn't denied it, either. I'd half expected that response. What I hadn't expected was her bolt from the blue: Bonnie's uncle worked at TMC. Who was he? Orrie Mercer came to mind. That would explain how someone so uncouth had gotten hired. If I was right, and Maybelline Black turned out to be Beardsley's sister, it would also explain her inconsistent relationship with Mercer. Had they become shoestring relatives when Vane Beardsley married Bonnie Belcher?

Curious, I checked the TMC staff roster, but there was no one listed with Bonnie's maiden name: Belcher. An online search for obituaries turned up brief death notices published several years earlier by a newspaper in Florida, where Jed and Dora Belcher had died within a year of each other. There were no formal obituaries mentioning survivors, and Dora's maiden name was not mentioned. It seemed Bonnie had not felt compelled to commemorate the lives of either of her estranged parents.

My search was interrupted when an internist dropped in to research a paper he was writing on a possible connection between cocaine use and early male-pattern baldness. If his premise proved sound, there were going to be a lot of conflicted yuppies when the paper was published. By the time he left the library, it was close to five o'clock.

I was shutting down my computer when Lola walked in, bringing a faint scent of lilacs to the room. My elderly volunteer was the last person I expected to see at quitting time.

"Hello, Miss Machado. I'm so glad you're still here. I was so worried the library would be locked."

"Lola, what brings you here so late?"

"I forgot my iPod." She walked over and plucked it off the volunteers' desk. "It has all of Marty's songs on it. I was afraid it was lost."

"I'm glad you found it."

"So am I. The weekend would have been lonely without my music." As she walked toward the exit, I regretted again that I couldn't help her meet Marty Stockwell, then realized there was something I had wanted to ask her earlier that day.

"Lola, wait."

She turned. "What is it, dear?"

"How did you know I live in Coyote Creek?"

"Why, Maybelline told me. She's very well-informed."

"When did she tell you?"

"A week or so ago. Is there a problem? I do understand you can't help me about Mr. Stockwell, dear. I don't mind."

"No, no, there's no problem. I was just curious, that's all."

"Well then, have a pleasant weekend." She fixed the iPod's ear buds to her ears, caught a beat and two-stepped out the door.

I grabbed a vending machine soda on my way out

and left the TMC parking lot in high gear, ticking off what I had to accomplish before Harry showed up for dinner at seven. I had less than two hours to eliminate all traces of the decapitated turkey. I couldn't swear Nick to silence about the turkey incident, but I could make sure Harry didn't see the crime scene firsthand.

I mulled over my conversation with Lola as I drove. Maybelline had told her where I lived. Lola described Maybelline as well-informed. What an understatement. World-class busybody was more like it. She seemed to know everything. Did she know who Bonnie's uncle was? Of course she did—if she was Dr. Beardsley's sister.

I rearranged the players in the morass of my mind until an unsettling idea surfaced. Had Bonnie's uncle been Dr. Beardsley's accomplice? Had they conspired to do away with Bonnie? Whether the uncle was Mercer or someone else, I found that hard to accept. Why would an uncle plot against his own niece? For money? I hoped not, but then again, what kind of uncle was he? Lorraine said he was "a bit thick." Maybe he was that and something far worse. Maybe he had been offered a deal he couldn't resist.

After a stop at the Four Corners Market for Harry's favorite beer, deli fried chicken and potato salad, I collected the mail and newspaper and checked inside Jack and Amah's house, where everything looked undisturbed. I freshened the king snake's water, then I hightailed it down the lane to the barn, counting llamas and turkeys along the way. I suspected Nick had been doing random drive-bys. That, along with the extra patrols by sheriff's deputies, seemed to have discouraged any further vandalism.

Hoping the carcass would be gone, I pulled out my keys. I reasoned that Nick, who had painted my vandalized door, might clean up after my tormentor. But painting the door hadn't required entry into the apartment. Still, he could easily come up with an excuse to borrow a key from Harry or Hannah. Almost convinced, I opened the door and inhaled a blast of putrid air that knocked me backward into the deck railing. I managed to set the six-pack and the bag of deli food on the floor of the deck before I hung my head over the side and chucked up the soda I'd consumed on the drive home.

Inside, I wrapped a bandanna around my nose and mouth, cranked the swamp cooler's fan to its highest setting and opened all the windows in the apartment. Then I changed into my oldest shorts and T-shirt and my hiking boots. The ski gloves I'd used a week ago still bore some traces of dried rattlesnake blood, but they were plenty good enough for this chore. I cut down the carcass and dropped it into a thirty gallon garbage bag, along with the towels I used to wash the blood off my kitchen table and wall.

My plan was to bury the remains by digging a hole in the farthest edge of the pasture. That required a pick and shovel. After three months with no rain, Coyote Creek's soil was rock hard.

It took precious minutes to tote the garbage bag to a corner of the field thick with manzanita and other scrub vegetation. I raised the pick over my shoulder and brought it down with a mighty *thwack*. It hit hard pan, bounced out of my hands, and slammed into my shin before it came to rest deep in a thicket of poison oak. I hopped on one leg and let loose every swear word I'd

ever heard. I wasn't about to climb into poison oak for
the pick, so I tossed the bag of evidence behind a thick
screen of brush and hurried back to the apartment to
shower and change clothes.

Fanny waited for me on my deck, pacing in im-
patient little figure eights—kitty body language for
open the damn door. I put fresh kibbles in her bowl
and watched her scarf them, wondering if I'd ever see
Bosco again. I pondered the vanishing cockatiel mystery while I emptied a can of air freshener into the
apartment. There was no evidence Fanny had eaten
him. When she ate birds she always left something
behind. Usually the liver. Sometimes a tiny head with
open eyes and a hopeless expression. There were no
spare Bosco parts to be found anywhere, but he was
still missing. He must have fled the apartment during
the turkey-slaughtering incident. Or worse, the poor
little guy might have been taken by the intruder.

By six-fifteen I had scrubbed the wall with bleach
one last time and sanitized every surface in my little
studio. I thought the air had cleared, but I didn't trust
my sense of smell. I wouldn't know for sure until Harry
arrived. I beat my all-time record for speedy showers,
lathering my entire body in shampoo and rinsing in
three minutes flat. Since it was just Harry, makeup and
hairdo were of no concern. He wouldn't notice what I
looked like unless I had a black eye or a missing front
tooth. As long as he didn't see the hematoma forming
on my shin, I'd be okay. I wore jeans for that reason,
although the evening was hot and humid, and I would
have preferred cotton shorts.

With a few minutes to spare, I sat down to check
my email. No messages from Nick. I sent him a text:

Where are the photos? Harry was due at seven. Ten minutes to go. I checked the landline phone again for messages in case someone had called while I was in the shower. There was one. I punched the play button.

"Hi, sweetheart, it's Amah. Surprise! We'll be home a day early. We're planning to spend the night in Eugene. We'll see you tomorrow afternoon. Can't wait to get home. Love you."

Oh, hell. They'd arrive at the very apex of this mess. If Harry was arrested, Amah would call Mom and Dad in the Azores and Grandpa Machado and Tanya in New York. The whole family would be in an uproar. Harry had done nothing wrong. He didn't deserve this and neither did our family.

At that moment I knew how it felt to loathe another human being, and it wasn't DA Keefer. She didn't have it in for Harry; she simply had a politician's penchant for the version of reality that suited her agenda. The real villain in this travesty of justice was Marco Bueller. Our only hope was to fight the law. Someone wrote a song about that once.

As I recalled, the law won.

FORTY-THREE

HARRY'S RED JAG rolled down the lane toward the bunkhouse at seven o'clock with the low-lying sun reflecting off his windshield. He took the stairs two at a time. I met him on the deck and suppressed an impulse to grab him in a desperate hug. It seemed so long since we'd talked face to face.

"Hi," I said.

"Hi, yourself."

"Have you heard anything more?"

"Nothing new." He glanced around. "Looks like you're turning into quite the ranch hand."

Fanny trotted over to rub her head against Harry's ankle. He leaned down to scratch the top of her head, and she hacked up a slimy fur ball on the toe of his shoe. I ran inside and grabbed a handful of paper towels.

Harry shook the gunk off the edge of the deck to the ground below, and wiped his shoe clean. "Did you forget her fur ball medicine?"

"I'm afraid so. I'll do it tomorrow before Amah and Jack get home."

"Tomorrow? I thought they were coming home Saturday."

"So did I, but Amah just called. They're due back tomorrow afternoon."

"Damn. Bad timing." He side-stepped Fanny, who was rubbing his ankle again, and we went inside.

I handed him a bottle of beer and waited for a sign that he detected the dead turkey smell. He inhaled and asked what we were having for dinner.

"Fried chicken," I said. "Why?"

"Smells a little different."

"I know. The Four Corners deli is trying a new recipe."

He gave me a skeptical look and took a long draw from the bottle. I pulled the chicken from the oven where I'd been keeping it warm and put some pieces on paper plates with the potato salad. We sat at my recently scoured dinette table and started eating.

Dusk had settled on Coyote Creek, and the darkening room created an eerie disconnect between Harry's mood and mine. Harry munched away, content without conversation, while I floundered in uncertainty. I had never kept secrets from my brother. I was dying to tell him what I suspected about Maybelline and my theory about Bonnie's uncle being in cahoots with Dr. Beardsley. I was less eager to tell him about my stalker's progression from spray paint to bloodshed.

"Hey, earth to Aimless. I'm talking to you."

"What?" I'd been so deep in thought I'd tuned him out.

"Where's Bosco?"

"He's lost. I think he ran away."

Harry's lips twitched. "You lost Jack's foul-mouthed bird? How'd you manage that?" Harry got up and wandered through the studio's living space, looking under furniture and behind the stuff on my bookshelves.

"As if you didn't know. Nick must have filled you in on the whole catastrophe."

"What's he got to do with it?"

"You're the one who sicced him on me as a babysitter. Doesn't he report to you?"

"Yeah, but he hasn't reported lately. Last I heard you two were going out to dinner. How'd that turn out? I thought maybe you were getting back together."

"Sorry to disappoint you, but it looks like he's never going to be your brother-in-law."

"Too bad. He's still my best friend." Harry walked back to the kitchen and opened the cupboards.

"Save yourself the trouble. The bird's not here. I've looked everywhere."

Harry sat and picked up another drumstick. "Fanny?"

"I don't think so. She always leaves a messy crime scene. There's nothing linking her to his disappearance. Not a single feather."

"When did you notice he was gone?"

With that perfect opening, I forged ahead. "Something happened here last night. I think Bosco got out during the...thing that happened."

Harry stopped eating and leaned forward, elbows on the table. "What happened?"

"A break-in."

He shot out of his chair. "What kind of break-in? Were you home? Jesus, Aimee, why didn't you call?"

"I wasn't home when it happened. Nick was here when I discovered it. We called the sheriff's office and a deputy came by. I didn't want to worry you." I was near tears, which always gave me a little edge with my brother. "We thought you were going to be arrested today."

Harry sat again, making a visible effort to calm himself. "Tell me everything that happened last night.

Better yet, tell me everything you've been keeping from me."

"If I do, you have to promise not to yell at me."

"I'm not promising anything. Just tell me."

I relayed my suspicions about Maybelline and described the whole sordid turkey scene while he sat shaking his head.

"Where's the evidence of this break-in?" Harry looked around the spotless kitchen with a skeptical eye.

I told him about trying to bury the mess. Just talking about it made my shin throb. "Nick took pictures, and so did the sheriff's deputy."

"Then what do you need me for?"

"I think I'm close to figuring out who killed Bonnie."

"You've been sleuthing with Nick so far. Why bring me on board now?"

"Nick thinks my theory about Maybelline—my volunteer—is too far-fetched."

"What makes you think I don't?"

"You've always been able to think outside the box. You're better at it than I am. And I won't take no for an answer."

He sighed in resignation. "This could take a while, but start talking, and don't leave anything out."

I told him everything I had learned about anyone connected to Bonnie Beardsley. We agreed that Milton and Netta Palmer were long shots. Ditto for the Underhills, although there was still some doubt about Grover Underhill. Lorraine Beardsley was also an unlikely candidate; she was just too darned happy to bother killing the likes of Bonnie.

That left Dr. Beardsley and his sister as my prime

suspects, other than a couple of dark horses. One was Jared Quinn; the other was Bonnie's unidentified uncle who worked at TMC. I added my suspicions about Mercer. When I finished, Harry went to the fridge and popped the cap on another beer.

"Is that going to help you think?" I asked.

"Nope. But it'll keep me from yelling at you. I can't believe you did all this shit without telling me."

"You were busy building a mall and getting arrested. I couldn't get hold of you even when I tried."

"You've got my attention now. You said Nick took pictures of the turkey. Do you have them?"

"No, they're still in Nick's phone."

"What about the other pictures? Didn't you say he took some pictures at that facility in Marin County? Do you have those?"

"He used his digital camera for those. I just checked my email and they weren't there." I ran over and checked again. "Still not there."

"Call him."

"I already did. Just before you got here."

Harry drained half the beer and belched long and loud. He poured the rest in the sink. "Put on a pot of coffee. This looks like an all-nighter."

"Should we call Abe? Maybe he should be here, too."

"Do you know what Abe charges per hour?"

"Do I want to?"

"No. We'll do our brainstorming first. Then we'll call him. Now how about starting that coffee?"

I went to the counter and opened the coffee can. "Sorry, it's empty."

"Then why do you have it on the counter?"

"To remind me to buy more."

"What about Jack and Amah's? We can borrow."

"This was Jack and Amah's."

"Damn. Don't you ever go to the store?"

"I stopped there on the way home to get our dinner. I forgot coffee. I'll go back to Four Corners. They're open 'til ten o'clock."

"I'll go. You keep trying to reach Nick, and keep watching your email." He stepped out onto the deck. "Lock your door. I'll be right back."

He bounded down the steps, drove down the lane, and peeled out onto the street.

I wrapped the leftover chicken in foil and shoved it into the fridge. I put the scraps in Fanny's bowl. She caught a whiff and dug in.

Nick's cell was busy, so I left another message. I hoped he was talking to Abe, getting to the bottom of the Verna Beardsley/Maybelline Black mystery.

FORTY-FOUR

EVERY TIME I tried Nick's cell, it was busy. My inbox was still empty. Ten minutes passed. Fifteen. I paced the small studio, peering out the kitchen window to watch for Harry's headlights coming down the lane.

My phone rang after twenty minutes. *Harry*.

"Aimee, did you reach Nick?"

"I'm trying. His phone's busy. I left a message. Where are you?"

"I'm still at the Four Corners Market."

"Why?"

"Flat tire."

"You're kidding."

"I wish. This isn't good, Aimee. Someone cut my tire."

"But how? You've only been there a few minutes."

"I think your intruder followed me. He must've been watching the ranch."

"But why follow you?"

"To put me out of business so he could come after you."

"Damn. How fast can you get back here?"

"Soon. He only got to one tire. I must have come out of the market before he could do the others."

"Are you sure you're safe? He might still be lurking around there."

"Not likely. It's you he wants. Keep calling Nick.

Get him out here. And barricade yourself inside. Did you buy the bear spray?"

"Yes. I picked it up a couple of days ago."

"Good. I'll be there in ten minutes." He hung up.

Stillness settled in my chest, followed by dizziness. I had forgotten to breathe. I gulped air, forcing my lungs back to life while I checked the deadbolt on my door and the locks on the windows. From my kitchen window I scanned the lane leading from the street to the llama barn. Manzanita and scrub oak cast murky shadows in the feeble light of a thumbnail moon, but the lane was deserted. If an intruder was out there on foot, the llamas surely would warn me. I located my flashlight and tested it, aiming at the floor; the beam was anemic. It needed batteries, which I didn't have. I looked out my peephole. The llamas were settled and quiet.

I went to the kitchen counter for the bear spray. It wasn't there. It had been there the night Quinn brought me home. I looked on the floor and in all my cupboards. It was gone. Had it been on the counter the night before, when I'd discovered the dead turkey? I couldn't remember seeing it. The intruder must have taken it.

I tried Nick's cellphone again. No luck.

I glanced at my computer. The message from Nick had arrived. *Maybelline Black's drugs are lithium and aripiprazole. Even if they match, Abe says it's not enough for a judge.*

Now I needed the photos from Verna Beardsley's medical chart. Nick's second message appeared, with the photos attached. I scanned them and found what I was looking for. Verna Beardsley's prescriptions. There they were. *Lithium. Aripiprazole.*

The medications matched. Good, but not good enough for a judge. What else matched? There was nothing in the chart about treating Verna for hyperthyroidism. I scanned the rest of the pages. In her discharge orders I found a brief note: *Monitoring of thyroid function recommended.*

I went online to the National Institutes of Health and used PubMed Central to start a search using the keywords *hyperthyroidism* and *bipolar mania*. There I found a case report that fit Maybelline like a surgical glove. A patient with a long history of bipolar disorder presented with comorbid hyperthyroidism and bipolar mania after recent discontinuation of lithium treatment.

Maybelline's manic behavior and exophthalmos had grown more extreme in just the two weeks I'd known her. She was inappropriately chatty from the beginning, and then there was the incident with the irate patient who doused her with water. I suspected that she had brought it on herself somehow. She had reacted strangely when I spoke to her about having dinner with Vane Beardsley and even more strangely when I brought up the issue of Orrie Mercer using the library restroom. And her unfilled prescriptions were more than three months old. If failure to take her meds was the explanation for her worsening condition, she was a walking time bomb.

No matter what Abe said, there was no doubt in my mind. Maybelline was Verna Beardsley. Her print on the acrylic toenail proved she was mixed up in her sister-in-law's death—something she couldn't have managed without an accomplice. Was it her brother, or was it some hired thug?

Maybelline had told Lola where I lived. But how did she know? I'd wondered about that earlier without thinking it through. Now I knew why it bothered me. I had seen Orrie Mercer at Four Corners Pizza just days ago. Maybe he had noticed me there, assumed I lived in Coyote Creek and mentioned it to Maybelline. But why? Was it a comment in passing, or was it because Mercer was involved somehow in what happened to Bonnie? I still couldn't quite believe Orrie Mercer would participate in the murder of his own niece. I had to know if he really was Bonnie's uncle, and Lorraine Beardsley would have the answer.

I checked the clock again. Five minutes had passed. No sign of Harry, but everything was quiet. I called Lorraine on my landline to keep my cellphone free. She answered on the second ring. I forged ahead with my apologies for bothering her and said I had confirmed that Verna Beardsley and Maybelline were the same person.

"I see," she said. "Then what is it you need from me now?"

"Do you happen to know a man named Orrie Mercer? A friend of Maybelline's?"

"Of course. He's the man Vane shot in the foot."

"He is Bonnie's uncle?"

"Yes. Ora Mercer. Dora Belcher's twin brother. He leached off Bonnie's folks for years. Mediocre intellect, drug problems off and on. He never amounted to much. They eventually cut him off financially, too."

"You said Dr. Beardsley helped him get a job at TMC?"

"Yes, but I don't remember—"

"A security guard?"

"Yes. That's it. Vane put in a good word with the security company. Vane felt he owed it to the man. I think I mentioned Mr. Mercer lost a toe in the shooting accident."

"Thank you so much."

I hung up, rivulets of sweat rolling down my ribs. Where the hell was Harry? Was it Mercer who cut his tire? Was he out there somewhere in the dark doing Dr. Beardsley's dirty work? If Mercer had killed his own niece, he wouldn't hesitate to silence me. He had been curt and seemed wary of me from the moment we met, but why? I had assumed it was racism, but there was a more likely, more unnerving reason. I remembered that first day when I asked him if we should report the putrid-smelling Dumpster. How had he responded? *It's not our Dumpster. Belongs to the Happy Ox.* That had to be the reason. He knew what was causing the stench, because he had dumped Bonnie's body in there, hoping she'd end up in a landfill and never be found. But she had been found, and he must have worried that I would remember his reluctance to follow up about the Dumpster. That would explain his transfer to duty outside the building that housed the library and his frequent use of the library's private restroom. It wasn't Maybelline he was staying close to.

It was me.

I grabbed my phone and called TMC's switchboard operator. When she picked up, I asked her to transfer me to the security office. I had to know if Orrie Mercer was on duty. After several rings, someone finally picked up.

"Hello," I said. "Who's speaking?"

"This is Jared Quinn."

"What? Why are you answering calls to Security? Why are you even there at this time of night?"

"Aimee? Is that you?"

"Yes, it's me. What's going on?"

"We have a VIP patient en route to the ER. I'm arranging—never mind, why are you calling?"

"I have a situation, too. I need to know if Orrie Mercer is on duty."

"No. He didn't show up for work. Why?"

"I think he's the one who cut my tires. He's been vandalizing my grandparents' property and threatening me. I'm afraid of what he'll do next."

"Is Mercer on the premises?"

"No. Not yet. But I suspect he's coming."

"Jesus. Are you alone out at that freaking zoo?"

"At the moment, but Harry should be here any minute."

"You need to call 911. Say you're worried about a prowler."

"Okay. I'll do it."

Quinn cleared his throat. "This VIP thing is almost under control. I can head out there in a few minutes."

"What's the VIP thing?"

"A woman tripped over her Chihuahua out by her swimming pool. She fractured an arm and a leg and opened a vein on a piece of broken glass. Lost a lot of blood. Her husband's out of town, so her bodyguard called for a Life Support Unit. It's headed out now."

"Bodyguard?"

"Pool boy. Babysitter. Hell, I don't know what the guy is, but he's the one who found her pumping blood

all over her patio." I heard the hollow echo of an overhead page in the background. "I have to go," Quinn
said.

"Wait, do you know if Dr. Beardsley is on call tonight?"

"He is, and it's a damn good thing. He's walking toward me as we speak. He's going to repair Mrs. VIP's
sliced arm as soon as we can get her into an operating room."

"Jared."

"What?"

"Bring your gun."

"Damn, Aimee, call 911. And be careful." His words
came out thin, as if he'd lost the breath behind them.

I hung up and looked out my kitchen window, hoping to see Harry's headlights. The lane was dark. His
warning after our workout at the dojo two weeks earlier came back to me. He had accused me of treating
jujitsu like a game or a sport, casually passing tests
and winning tournaments. He worried that I'd choke
if it came to a real fight. *You'd damn well better decide what you will and won't do.* Could I really gouge
Mercer's eyes out if that's what it took to stop him? A
wave of nausea washed over me at the thought, followed by a surge of doubt. What if Harry was right?

FORTY-FIVE

I TOLD THE 911 dispatcher that I thought there was a prowler on my property, that someone had broken into my home a few days earlier. I said a deputy had responded to that incident. She found the report and promised to send someone as soon as possible, but it might take a while. All the deputies were working emergency calls at the moment.

In a way, I wanted Orrie Mercer to come after me. I was certain he was the man whose crime was about to settle on my brother's shoulders, and that was intolerable. Why Mercer would kill his niece, even for money, was a mystery, but I didn't care. If I could prove it, and survive, I could clear Harry's name.

As if on cue, a distant pack of coyotes erupted into a howling Greek chorus, scoring the eerie night. The small studio closed around me like a rabbit hole while I played the role of hunted prey cowering inside.

I concentrated on the evidence and sat down to make a list of what I knew. An acrylic toenail with Verna Beardsley's fingerprint. That wasn't evidence against Mercer. I tried to think like Harry. Something tangible, something tied to Mercer. Then it came to me. The bloody deer bag. Dr. Beardsley told his ex they had used a deer bag to staunch the blood from Mercer's foot after Beardsley accidentally shot him. Hannah had said the blood on the deer bag did not match

Bonnie's. But some of it was human, from an unknown source. Had Mercer kept that deer bag? Had he used it as Bonnie's shroud?

I called Lorraine Beardsley again and rushed to the point before she could hang up on me.

"Mrs. Beardsley, please let me ask one more question."

"Miss Machado? Good heavens, you again?"

"I'm afraid so."

Her sigh told me this had better be my last call. "What is it this time?"

"The deer bag. The one Dr. Beardsley used to wrap Mr. Mercer's foot after the accident. Do you know what happened to it?"

"Vane gave all of his hunting gear to Bonnie's uncle. A deer rifle, the camo clothing, and the deer bag, I suppose, unless it was discarded at the clinic in the mountains. He said he wanted nothing to remind him of the incident."

"Did the police ever ask you about any of this?"

"No. Once they learned I was in Tahiti with Troy when Bonnie went missing, I never heard from them again."

I thanked her and ended the call. I was cut off and alone again, terrified that something had happened to Harry. It had been half an hour since he promised to be back in ten minutes.

I pondered Maybelline's connection to Mercer. She had been friendly with him, even dating him until her recent change of heart. Why had she called him a dirty liar? Why had she told me that first day at lunch that Bonnie had probably run away with some man? To cover up the crime? To protect her brother? To protect Mercer? But why hadn't Dr. Beardsley simply filed for a divorce instead of doing away with Bonnie? Why had a divorce been out of the question? Was he really that worried about a scandal?

I recalled the double date with the Underhills. We learned that night that Bonnie was into drugs and kinky sex and had gone home to her husband, wasted after her evening with the Underhills. No, we had learned more than that. Willow hadn't exactly been devastated by Bonnie's death, but she had mourned the loss of Bonnie as a conduit to a reliable drug source. A source close to Bonnie. What if Bonnie had been getting drugs from Orrie Mercer? Did Mercer have an inside source at TMC?

My train of thought was shattered by a high-pitched, ear-piercing cry of alarm. It was the unmistakable sound of a llama calling out a warning to the rest of the herd. Nothing short of a predator on the grounds would provoke that hair-raising sound. Fanny sprang into action, answering the llama with her own spine-chilling yowls while she pawed the door.

I ran to the kitchen window, but saw no vehicle in the lane, no one on foot. The pasture lay to the north of the bunkhouse, on the side of my apartment where there were no windows. The peephole on my door yielded only a glimpse of movement in the dark night. Llama or an intruder? I couldn't tell.

Fanny chose that moment to erupt in a bloodcur-dling feline screech that nearly lifted the enamel off my teeth. Nothing would shut her up. She leapt on the kitchen counter and pawed at the window, emitting guttural growls.

In the midst of this, I tried to reach Nick on his cellphone, and it went direct to voicemail. I left him a message asking him to come as soon as he could.

The braying cries of the herd started up again. I forced Fanny into her carrier and stuffed her in the closet so I could concentrate on the sounds from outside. I picked up the phone, ready to call 911 again, but hesitated, trying to determine whether the intruder was human or just a coyote on the prowl.

The anxious sounds of the animals rattled my nerves. If coyotes found the herd, the little cria would be the first victim. Any other time, I'd have run outside to scare the predator away. But this was different. By stepping outside, I'd play into the intruder's hands. If it came to a fight, I wanted every advantage.

I waited, and had just put down the phone when I heard a familiar voice snarl, "Get away, you sonofabitch." *Mercer.* What followed was a loud thud and the unmistakable "oof" of air exploding from a set of human lungs. A charging llama can drop a grown man like a sack of cement. If Mercer wasn't down for the count, he was at least on the ropes. That was my cue to act. A vision of the turkey hanging from my ceiling clinched it. The man had gotten into my apartment before; he could do it again. If he did, my only option would be a fight to the finish. Outside, I had two choices: fight or flight.

He was twice my size and most likely carried a gun. With the right leverage, I could use his weight against him, but it would be tricky to disarm him in the dark, especially if he saw me coming. Considering his age and the size of his beer gut, I preferred flight. I had no time to dither or attempt another phone call. I had to get out and run like hell before he caught his breath.

FORTY-SIX

I COULDN'T LEAVE the bunkhouse through my door. It faced the field where Mercer had tangled with the llamas. If he was conscious, he'd see me make my getaway. My only hope was to climb out my bathroom window onto the west-facing deck, where I had less chance of being spotted. Fanny had gone quiet in the closet. With a stab of guilt about leaving her, I raised the window, stuck out a leg, then remembered my cellphone on the dinette table. I crawled back inside, grabbed the phone and stuffed it in the pocket of my jeans.

Again, I crept out the window. Back pressed against the outside wall, I let my eyes adjust to the feeble moonlight while I listened for tell-tale sounds. I heard nothing but the bark of distant coyotes working up to an encore. I considered dropping from the deck to the ground below, but decided not to risk it. I already had an injured shin. If I twisted an ankle, I couldn't run. Climbing down was slower but safer. I hoisted myself over the rail and grabbed the corner support post, testing for splinters. The post was smooth from several coats of paint, making my sliding descent quick and quiet.

I crept around the south side of the barn until I reached the front corner, where I hesitated, looking longingly at my car there in the stable yard. I had the keys, but there was no way I could get in, back it around and drive down the lane without drawing fire. I had to run for it. But where was Mercer? I picked up a rock and threw it as hard as I could toward the back of the barn, counting on him to reveal himself when he heard it land. If he went west, I'd go east and head for brushy cover. I crouched and waited for him to react.

"You must think I'm a real dummy."

Fear licked the back of my neck. Before I could react, Mercer shoved me from behind, crashing me into the stairs leading up to the apartment. My forehead hit the second step, opening a gash that blinded me with a curtain of my own blood.

"Get up them steps." He grabbed the back of my neck and gave me another shove. This time both my shins slammed into the stairs, and the one I'd injured earlier shot a fireball of pain through my body, nearly making me black out.

I crawled to the top of the steps and got to my feet. Mercer stood just out of reach, pointing an ugly black handgun at my heart. "Open that door," he said.

"I don't have my keys." I did, but I wasn't about to admit it. My odds were still better outside.

He pulled a key ring from his pocket and handed it to me.

"Use mine," he said, "and don't bother looking for your bear spray." His nasty laugh turned to a growl. "Get the hell inside. Now."

Jesus, the man had keys to my home. How had he done that? Okay, he was a thug, a big, nasty goon, but maybe not so stupid after all. He'd outsmarted me, let himself into my home who knew how many times, and now I was at his mercy. Almost blinded by a face drenched in blood and crippled by a wounded leg, I was trapped with a man whose survival depended on silencing me.

While I unlocked my door, my training began to take hold. In classes and competitions I had mastered every possible configuration for disarming an attacker with a handgun. If Mercer let me live for a few minutes longer, I'd find my chance to do it for real.

"Get your ass inside."

I played sissy and obeyed with a whimper.

Inside, Mercer shoved me onto the daybed. His bulk crowded the small space, and his sour body odor assaulted my nostrils. In the light of the room, I realized he was decked out in camo from cap to boots. *Camo Man.* He waved his gun at me.

"You been warned. You shoulda kept out of it."

The fact that he was talking instead of shooting gave me some hope. I went with that.

"I don't know what you're talking about."

"Liar. You been buttin' in since day one. Like you knew something."

Day one. The day I'd asked him about the smelly Dumpster. So I was right. He thought I suspected him all along.

"That morning. My first day. Is that when—"

"Had to get her out of my garage before the neighbors complained about the smell."

"So you…?" The image of Orrie burying his niece in a trash bin left me speechless.

"Then you showed up yapping about the stinkin' Dumpster and I told you to let it go. Soon as she got found, I knew you'd be wondering why I didn't want that smell reported."

"You were wrong. I never suspected you."

"Sure you did. But I didn't do it. I didn't kill that ditzy coke-head. She was family."

Even better news. If Mercer really hadn't killed Bonnie, there was a chance he wouldn't kill me. Still, he had a gun pointed at my face, and he wasn't stupid enough to get within striking distance. I had to keep him talking until an opportunity came.

"If you didn't kill her, why not tell the police what really happened?"

"I got other problems with the law." Right, I thought. Like stealing drugs from the hospital pharmacy.

"Then tell me what really happened. If the truth will clear my brother, I swear I'll keep you out of it."

Confusion twisted Mercer's fleshy features. He blinked rapidly several times. "Who's your brother?"

Incredibly, he didn't know. "Harry Machado. The police are trying to pin the crime on him."

"That's why you're nosin' around? To protect your brother?"

"Of course. The police aren't looking for the real killer. If you didn't do it, we can help each other."

"How?"

"If you know Dr. Beardsley did it, if you were a witness, you need to tell me what happened."

I shifted position until I was sitting upright on the daybed, both feet on the floor. If Mercer came a little closer, I might have a chance. I calculated the distance between us, but it was too great. My leg was too weak to risk a jump or a kick. I had to get close enough to use my hands.

While I assessed my chances, a snarled command came out of nowhere.

"Hit the floor, asshole!"

Mercer didn't drop to the floor, but he froze, eyes wide. Seizing the opportunity, I lunged at him, twisting out of his line of fire and simultaneously grabbing the gun. I pulled it down and away, out of his grasp, and opened some distance between us. My injured shin screamed with pain, but I managed to stay on my feet.

Mercer glanced behind his back, looking for the source of the voice. When he saw no one, he looked back at me.

"How'd you do that?"

I pointed at the floor, where the source of the menacing voice marched on little bird feet across the kitchen linoleum. Jack's puny cockatiel, a scant four inches from topknot to tail feathers, had come out of hiding.

Bosco cocked his head at Mercer. *"Go ahead, make my day,"* he said. Pure Eastwood.

"Ah, hell," Mercer said. But his eyes took on a new light. From resignation back to hope. It was still boy against girl, and he expected to win.

"Don't even think about it, Mercer. I'll have real backup any minute." I hoped I was right. Harry, Nick, Quinn—they were all taking their sweet time about it. I kept the gun trained on Mercer with one hand while I used the other to pry my cellphone from my pocket. I got it open and punched 911 with my thumb.

Bosco chose that moment to take flight, landing on my shoulder and pecking fiercely at my earlobe. Startled, I managed to hold the gun, but I dropped the phone. It bounced toward Mercer, who picked it up and ended my 911 call. He punched in another number and waited with the phone to his ear.

"Put it down," I said.

He made a rude gesture. "Go ahead, shoot me," he sneered. Into the phone he said, "Get up here, now."

Now what? Who had he called? Bosco was still perched on my shoulder, and I couldn't afford any more distractions. With my eyes and gun trained on Mercer, I side-stepped over to the birdcage, and leaned my shoulder toward the open door. Bosco hopped in and started munching on birdseed. I locked the cage door and gripped the gun with both hands.

Mercer slipped the phone into his pocket. "You got backup? I got backup. Wonder who'll get here first?" He folded his arms across his beer belly, pleased with himself in spite of having his own gun pointed at his chest.

Where was Harry? He could have walked back from Four Corners by now. A glance at my clock confirmed what seemed impossible. Nine-thirty. Only ten minutes had passed since I crawled out of my window to make a getaway. It seemed like hours.

The longer I stood aiming the gun at Mercer's chest, the heavier it grew.

"Weighty, ain't it?" Mercer said.

"That's okay, when I get tired, I'll just shoot you." I'd have to shoot him. Somewhere. Not in the crotch, and not to kill, but I'd put a bullet someplace in his anatomy that would disable him. If I had the guts to pull the trigger. Harry's warning came to me once more. *You have to know what you will and won't do.*

At last I heard footfalls on the steps outside. In moments, Harry would appear and this siege would end. Mercer's eyes never left the gun in my hand.

A familiar voice from out on the deck called through the open bunkhouse door.

"Orrie? Are you in there?"

"It's about time, you dumb bitch. Where've you been?"

Verna Beardsley, alias Maybelline Black, peeked in the door, saw the gun in my hand, and said, "He's not my boyfriend."

FORTY-SEVEN

"SHUT UP AND get in here," Mercer snarled.

Maybelline tiptoed into the room, her bulging eyes fixed on the gun I held trained on Mercer. In camo garb many sizes too large, pant legs and sleeves rolled up, she was a bizarre sight—a popeyed, woodsy harridan from some hunter's Freudian nightmare.

Mercer reached out and grabbed her, pulling her body in front of him as a shield.

"Oh, hell, dearie," Maybelline said. "You should have shot the lying bastard while you had the chance."

Mercer locked his beefy arm around Maybelline's throat. "You want to save your brother's butt or not?"

"Of course," I said. But Maybelline said it, too, and I realized Mercer wasn't talking to me, he was talking to her.

"Then you better remember whose side you're on."

"Vane didn't kill that floozy. You did." Maybelline struggled feebly, but there was no way she could break loose from Mercer's grip.

"Did not," he said.

"Did too," she said. Their kindergarten dialogue was beyond annoying, and the gun was getting heavier.

"Maybelline... Verna, I know who you are. We can help each other," I pleaded. "Bonnie Beardsley was with the Underhills the night she disappeared. If you know what happened to her after she left them, you have to tell me."

"No she don't." Mercer tightened his grip, and she croaked a little *awk* sound.

"Let her go, dammit." I fired at the ceiling over Mercer's head. A chunk of plaster dropped, grazing his left ear.

He ducked and yelled, "Sonofabitch!"

Maybelline spun away from him and headed for the door.

"Stop right there," I shouted. "Take one more step and I'll shoot you in the ass."

She turned in the doorway, regarding me with disgust. "That's why you'll never get a man, Miss Machado. You're just not ladylike."

Orrie Mercer chose that moment to rush me, going for the gun. His forward momentum made it almost too easy. I blocked his outstretched arms and clipped the back of his skull with the gun butt. He slid across the floor on his belly and smacked into the wall head first.

Maybelline gaped at his limp bulk. "Is he dead?"

"I doubt it."

She looked disappointed. "Let's talk before he wakes up. And don't call me Verna. I hate that name."

"Okay, Maybelline. I'm listening."

I grabbed a nearly empty roll of duct tape from a drawer in the kitchenette. It was stiff with age and there wasn't much of it, but I managed to secure Mercer's hands behind his back while she began talking.

"First, he's not my boyfriend. Not anymore."

"When was he your boyfriend?"

"It started a few months ago. Orrie said he was crazy in love with me." Her eyelids fluttered for a moment, and a blush tinted her cheeks. "We were going to get married."

Her ex-beau stirred, moaned, and went still.

Maybelline said, "Can you whack him over the head again?"

"Not while he's out. Where's your car?"

"I don't drive. I came with him. He parked out by the street."

"Do you have his keys?"

"No. He took them."

So his keys were most likely in his pocket. That was a problem if he came to and got the upper hand. I didn't want him to have keys to his getaway car, but I didn't want to get close enough to fish for them, either.

"We don't have a lot of time, Maybelline. Tell me what you know."

She shot a wary glance in Mercer's direction. "Vane Beardsley is my baby brother. The night Bonnie went missing, Vane called me to come over to his house because she was out so late. He knew she'd be high when she got home, and sometimes it takes two of us to settle her down."

"Do you live near your brother?"

"Yes, he bought a nice little house for me just a few blocks from his home." She sniffled. "Vane is my life-line, you know. Without him, I'd probably die."

I refused to think about that.

"Tell me what happened next."

"He sent a taxi for me, and by the time I got there Bonnie was home. High on something, as usual. It was late, almost three in the morning. Vane asked where she'd been. She flew at him in a screaming rage. It wasn't the first time, either. When he reached out to stop her, his hand closed around her neck. He pushed her away, but she threatened him. Said she was going to call the police and charge him with spousal abuse. She vowed to ruin him."

That explained the bruise on her neck.

"Maybelline, isn't Dr. Beardsley right-handed?"

"Yes, but what's that got to do with anything?"

"Do you remember which hand he used when he grabbed her neck?"

"He grabbed her hands first, with his right, but she tried to butt him with her head and that's when he pushed her away with his left. He didn't mean to choke her. He was defending himself."

"Of course," I said. "Did she follow through with her threat to call the police?"

"She tried, but she was too high to dial the phone, so she swore at him and went to her bedroom."

"They had separate bedrooms?"

"Oh, yes. Bonnie insisted."

"What did Dr. Beardsley do?"

"He checked on her later, after she fell asleep. He said he was sure she'd be all right once she slept it off."

"Was he worried about her calling the police? About the abuse charge?"

"Vane didn't believe she'd do it when she sobered up. He never let himself believe the worst about her. He just went to bed, like every other time, and I went into the guest room. That's when I called Orrie."

"I understand your fear. If Bonnie ruined your brother, you'd lose your lifeline. But why would Orrie Mercer help you?"

At the mention of his name, Mercer stirred again

and gave a little snort. We waited. He started snoring peacefully, and Maybelline went on.

"Orrie said he still wanted to marry me, but I know the truth now. Orrie didn't really want me; he wanted a free ride on Vane's money."

"And the free ride would never happen if Vane's reputation was ruined. If he lost his practice."

"That's right. Orrie said he could take care of Bonnie, scare her into leaving Vane, leaving town. He said he knew things about her. Things even Vane couldn't ignore."

"Did she die that night? In your brother's house?"

Maybelline gasped. "Oh, heavens no. While Vane was asleep, Orrie came over and I helped him load Bonnie into his pickup. She was out cold on her bed— limp as a dead flounder—but still dressed, except for her shoes." Hence Maybelline's fingerprint on Bonnie's toenail. She went on. "We had to roll her up in a blanket just to carry her outside. Orrie said he'd take her to his place and have a talk with her in the morning—when she sobered up."

"So you don't know what happened after Orrie took her away?"

"No. I never saw her again. I didn't even know she had died until her body was found."

"Are you saying Mercer didn't tell you Bonnie was dead?"

"That's what I've been trying to tell you. He's a dirty liar. He swore he'd run her off. That's what I told you that first day we met at the hospital. I thought she'd hooked up with some man she knew and took off for good."

"Do you think Mercer killed her?"

"I didn't then. Now I don't know what to think. Orrie says she just up and died during the night. He couldn't bring her body back to Vane's place. It was too late for that when he found her dead in the morning. He said Vane would be the prime suspect because they always suspect the husband. That we had to cover for him."

"And you both told Dr. Beardsley you didn't know how Bonnie had disappeared during the night?"

"We had to. There was no other way. We let him think she'd run off. She had done it before. That's why he didn't report her missing right away." She squared her shoulders and raised her chin. "That's why I'm here tonight. Orrie said if we scared you away, we could still save Vane."

"Was Orrie still your boyfriend when you were together at the ballet?"

"No. I broke up with him before that." She shot him a contemptuous glance. "He doesn't know how to treat a lady."

"Then why were you together that night?"

"I got the free tickets, but I don't drive, so I let him escort me."

I thought about Mercer's pickup parked near my car at the Civic Center. Then I remembered the pickup that had pulled up next to my disabled car and how the driver had been waved on by Tango Bueller. Of course, it had been Mercer who punctured my tire.

"Did he know I would be at the ballet that night?"

"Now that you mention it, I did tell him about that when I asked him to escort me."

"But how did you know?"

"Lola Rampley mentioned it to another volunteer, who told me." *The auxiliary grapevine.*

"Mercer tampered with my tire the night of the ballet, didn't he?"

"I don't know about that," Maybelline said. "All I know is Vane is innocent."

"Maybelline, you don't have to save Vane. If Bonnie died after Mercer took her away, your brother won't be implicated. It's Orrie Mercer who'll be charged in her death."

While I waited for Maybelline to digest that, I heard the muffled sound of my phone coming from the direction of Orrie Mercer's torso. Someone was calling me, but to answer, I'd have to roll Mercer over on his back and dig the phone out of his pocket.

The ringing persisted while I calculated the risk of going for the phone. When Mercer began to squirm, I glared at Maybelline. "Roll him over," I said.

"Me?" she squeaked.

I waved the gun at her. "Do it."

She glanced around the room. "Can I hit him with something first?"

"No."

She tiptoed over to Mercer's prone form. With a strength that was surprising considering her gaunt frame, she grabbed his shoulder with both hands and tugged him over onto his back. His wrists were still bound behind him.

"What the—" Mercer's eyes opened. Maybelline shrieked and jumped back.

"Get the phone out of his pocket, Maybelline."

"No, I can't. He's mean. Why don't you just shoot

him?" She backed into the wall and slid down in a crumpled heap on the floor.

Mercer's head was clearing, and he did, indeed, look mean. It occurred to me too late that I should have stripped off his boots and socks while he was unconscious.

"Mercer, I want that phone."

"Come and get it."

"You're going to cooperate, Mercer, or you'll lose another toe. Maybe several."

"Go ahead and take it," Mercer said. "Put your dainty little hand in my pants."

"You're disgusting," I said, "but I'm going to hold this gun against your temple, Mr. Mercer, and my dainty little hand is pretty shaky. Any sudden movement and I won't be responsible for what happens." His eyes closed as the muzzle pressed against his temple. He stayed perfectly still while I reached in his pocket and retrieved the phone, which had finally stopped ringing. *No one there.*

I started to dial 911 again.

"Wait," Mercer said. "I didn't kill Bonnie." He cocked his head toward Maybelline. "I don't care what that bug-eyed freak says. I'll tell you what happened."

I stuffed the phone back in my pocket. If getting the truth out of this brute would clear Harry, it was worth the risk.

"Did Bonnie wake up after you took her away from Beardsley's house?"

He shook his head. "I left her passed out in the truck in my garage. In the morning, she was dead."

"Can you prove that?"

"Hell, no. Even if I could, I wouldn't go to the cops. I've got other problems with the law."

"So you said. Why did you bury her in the Dumpster?"

"Hey, I didn't enjoy it. I had no choice. I had to get rid of her."

My cellphone rang again. It was Harry.

"Aimee? What's going on? Are you okay?"

"Just great. Where in blazes are you?"

"Almost there. I caught a ride with a friend of Jack's."

"What happened to your car?"

"I got the first tire fixed, but another one went flat. Are you okay? I was afraid the slasher was after you."

"He was. He's here in my apartment, but I've got it under control."

"Have you called 911?"

"Yes, but that was earlier, and no one's shown up yet."

"Then hang up. I'll call them again."

"Hurry." I pocketed the phone.

Maybelline had picked herself up off the floor. "Do you still want Orrie's keys?"

"Definitely. Your turn." I held the gun on Mercer while she sidled toward him.

His hand shot out from under his back and grabbed her ankle. A scrap of duct tape dangled from his wrist.

"Help," she screeched.

He got to his knees and pulled her in front of him as a shield.

She hit him in the nose with her elbow, and when he let go, she ran across the room. Mercer charged me, ramming his head into my belly, knocking the wind out of me and sending the gun flying. I landed on my butt and he stumbled past me into the dining nook. He catapulted into the table, caught his foot in a chair, and crashed to the floor, howling, his leg tangled in the chair and cocked at a crazy angle. I felt a blackout coming on and looked away. The gun had landed on the floor halfway between Maybelline and me. I crawled toward it on my belly.

Mercer shouted at her. "Get the gun, dammit."

Maybelline grabbed the gun and pointed it at both of us. Her eyes darted back and forth at a dizzying rate.

"Shoot her," Mercer said, "then get me outta here. It's the only way to save your brother."

"No," I said. "My brother will be here any second. We can help each other. We can save both our brothers."

Maybelline looked at Mercer, who was groaning in pain, then looked at me lying on the floor, breathless. She shook her head.

"I'm sorry, dearie."

FORTY-EIGHT

WITH MY EYES squeezed tight, I waited for the bullet, heartbroken that I had failed my brother so completely.

"Aimee?" I heard Harry's voice, and he sounded puzzled. Was I in heaven already? Why was Harry there? I opened my eyes. He stood in the doorway holding Maybelline by the scruff of her camo-covered neck. Mercer's gun was in his other hand.

"Ah, crap," Mercer groaned.

"Harry?" I looked up from my prone position on the floor.

"Jesus, Aimee, your face is covered in blood."

I got to my feet, putting my weight on my good leg. "It's nothing. I cut my forehead."

"You sure?"

"Yes, I'm fine." I resisted the impulse to cry with relief and smother him in hugs. "Now that you're here, you can help me sort out this mess."

"Right. I assume the howler under the table is your villain, but who's this?"

"That's Maybelline. How did you catch her?"

"She was coming down the stairs when I got here. What were you doing on the floor?"

"Waiting to die. She was going to shoot me."

Maybelline squared her shoulders and raised her chin. "That's not true, Miss Machado. I was doing nothing of the sort."

I took a couple of test steps toward her and Harry. Despite Mercer's head butt and the throbbing pain in my shin, I could still walk. "Then why did you say you were sorry?"

"Because I was running away. Leaving you to work things out with Orrie by yourself."

"What shall I do with her?" Harry asked.

Maybelline must have read my mind. "Please don't kill me," she shrieked. "It was all his fault." She pointed a shaky finger at Orrie Mercer, who writhed in pain under the dinette table. "He's not just a killer, he's a drug dealer, too. I can tell you things."

"Shut up," Mercer roared. "You'll be sorry, old woman." He jerked his leg free of the chair with a yowl of pain and reached toward his boot, the torn duct tape still dangling from his wrist.

In a blur of movement, Harry shoved Maybelline and me toward the door. I grabbed her around the waist and held her tight, spinning away from the open door to stand with my back braced against the outside wall. Mercer's buck knife sailed out the door and *thwocked* into a post on the deck railing. After a brief scuffle, a bloodcurdling yell issued from inside the bunkhouse, then silence.

"Harry?" I called.

"Someone's dead," Maybelline whispered. "I hope it's the gigolo."

"Shhhh," I said. "Harry? Answer me, dammit."

Harry stepped out onto the deck.

Maybelline clapped her hands like a three-year-old. "Oh, goodie. Is he dead?"

"No," Harry said, "but he's not going to make any

more trouble tonight." He looked me over. "Are you sure you're all right?"

"Yes."

He used damp paper towels to clean most of the blood off my face.

"That's better," he said. "Now I need to make some calls."

The three of us stayed outside on the deck while Harry made his calls. He followed up with the sheriff's office first, then called Abe.

He was still on the phone when a set of headlights approached down the lane. A second set of lights followed. I was expecting patrol cars, but soon recognized that the vehicles belonged to Nick and to Jared Quinn. They bounded up the stairs wearing twin expressions of relief and curiosity.

"Aimee, thank God," Nick said, his eyes glistening.

"Bloody freaking hell," Quinn said, staring at Maybelline. "What's she doing here?"

Two sheriff's cruisers arrived next, followed by an ambulance. The flashing lights on the emergency vehicles and the squawking of two-way radios brought the llamas to their feet and the turkeys down from their roosts.

Harry and I recounted Orrie Mercer's criminal acts to the officers on the scene. Quinn stood by, paying particular attention to Maybelline's hysterical ramblings, but in the end, the woman's true role in the evening was unclear. Hostage or accessory? With her mental history, I figured that would take some time to sort out.

From my deck, Quinn and I watched the ambulance with Mercer inside drive away, followed by the patrol cars, one of them carrying Maybelline. Harry had joined Nick in the pasture, where they were busy calming the llamas and turkeys.

Quinn turned to me. "Are you staying here tonight?"

"Where else?"

"Anywhere. You've had a pretty traumatic time of it."

"It's over. I'll be fine."

Quinn took my elbow and walked me inside the bunkhouse. "I feel like shit. I nearly got you killed."

"How do you figure?"

"I asked you to spy on Beardsley. Mercer must have picked up on that and figured you were a threat. He's put you through hell these past two weeks."

"Don't blame yourself. Everything I did, I would have done in any case."

"You're limping," he said.

"I hurt my leg, it's nothing."

"Sit, let me take a look."

I wanted to defy his order, but my leg hurt too much. I sat in the nearest chair. He rolled my pant leg up, revealing the ugly bruise.

"Christ, Aimee. You need medical attention. You should have shown this to the EMTs."

"I didn't think of it. It's just a bruise."

"What about your head?" He held my hair up and saw the cut near my hairline. "That needs stitches. I'm taking you to the ER." He reached for my arm, wrapped it around his shoulder.

At that moment, Nick and Harry came through the door.

"What's going on?" Nick asked.

Harry kept quiet, but I could read his mind. He expected Nick to reclaim his woman.

"I'm taking her to the hospital," Quinn said. We stood there facing Nick, my arm around Quinn's neck, his arm around my waist.

Nick looked into my eyes. "I'll take her, Mr. Quinn."

Quinn hesitated, looked to me for a decision. I felt lightheaded and realized I had stopped breathing again.

"Sis," Harry said, "make up your mind."

I reached out to Nick.

FORTY-NINE

NICK DROVE ME to the hospital, and Harry stayed behind at the bunkhouse. I knew he would want to patch the hole I'd made in the ceiling with my gunshot and repair any other signs of my showdown with Mercer. The less we had to explain to Amah and Jack, the better. On the way to the hospital, Nick told me why he hadn't come sooner and why he had not answered his phone.

"I was dealing with Delta Sawyer, Buck's wife. She fell down out by the pool."

His story sounded familiar. "Was she Quinn's VIP emergency?"

"That's right. When you called I was using a tourniquet, trying to keep her from bleeding out before the ambulance arrived. She had been swimming in a bikini. She kept saying she wanted to get dressed, but it was impossible. I did manage to get a robe on her."

"Where's Buck?"

"Rella's flying him home from Atlanta."

Rella, of course. Superwoman had to be involved.

At TMC we discovered that Quinn had called ahead to the ER and arranged priority treatment for me. I was whisked into a trauma room where medical history, blood samples, and x-rays were taken. Nothing had been broken, and in record time the cut on my forehead was cleaned and stitched. My shin was slathered with some mysterious ointment that looked and smelled like

Bag Balm. I got the inevitable tetanus shot and a little envelope of free sample pain pills to tide me over until I could get my prescription filled.

When I emerged, Nick and Quinn were conferring in the ER waiting room. They looked over and saw me standing there.

"How's Delta?" I asked.

"She'll recover," Quinn said. "She lost a lot of blood, but your friend here did everything right. He saved her life."

"That's why you couldn't come. Both of you. You were trying to save Delta Sawyer."

"And nearly lost you," Nick said. "Jesus, Aimee, if only I'd known what that thug was up to."

"How could you know? I wasn't sure he was going to show up, and by the time he did, it was too late." Just then the pain pills kicked in. I murmured a weak, "Oooh" and felt myself start to crumple. Nick lifted me in his arms.

"You'd better take her home," Quinn said.

I WOKE THE next day in Jack and Amah's spare room with Fanny's warm body curled against my hip. I squinted at the clock. Two in the afternoon. Friday. I panicked for a moment, then remembered Quinn had ordered me to stay home from work. But Amah and Jack could arrive anytime. I sat up and discovered I had been sleeping in my blood-stained jeans and T-shirt.

I hobbled barefoot through the house and out the back door. Nick and Harry were on the veranda, munching chips and swigging beer. Bosco was there with them, snoozing in his cage.

"Look who's here," Nick said. "Want a beer?"

"Ugh," I said.

"How about coffee?" Harry said. "Nick just made a fresh pot."

"Okay."

Nick went inside to fetch it.

"Harry, how much of last night's mayhem is going to make the papers?"

"The Sawyer County Sheriff's Department and DA Keefer will get all the publicity, and the news media will make it clear I was exonerated. Abe's taking care of all that. Right now, we need to get our stories straight before Amah and Jack get here. They're going to know that Orrie Mercer was caught on the property, but we can soft-pedal the details."

"Right." I squeezed my eyes shut, trying to clear my head. "You start."

"They don't have to know how serious your stand-off was. Your injuries won't be obvious if you can walk without limping. We'll explain the upgrades to your little apartment by saying Nick wanted to spruce it up for you since you can't afford your own place right now."

"And why would Nick want to do that?"

Nick appeared with my coffee. "Because I'm trying to win you back." Nick handed me the cup. "Or we could tell them we're already back together. That would keep them distracted."

I took the coffee. It was delicious. Just the way Nick used to brew it when we really *were* together.

Harry cleared his throat. "Come on, Sis, let's go have a look at your digs."

With each of them taking one of my arms, they escorted me down the lane where my little dwelling gleamed with fresh white paint. The ceiling was patched, textured and painted, and the hole in the roof repaired seamlessly.

"Wow, how did you do all this so fast?"

"I had my crew drop by this morning while you were sleeping off the pain meds," Harry said.

"They did this in one morning?"

"Less than four hours. My guys are the best."

Inside my apartment I saw that my answering machine had been busy. Three messages. All from Jared Quinn asking me to call him as soon as possible. I dialed his office. After I assured him I was almost as good as new, I asked about Maybelline Black. Quinn told me that with Dr. Beardsley's blessings, his sister was headed back to Marin County for an undetermined length of stay at Green Pastures. As a parting gift, she had informed the police about Orrie Mercer's drug theft operation involving the TMC pharmacy. Turned out he'd been the source for several local coke addicts, including Bonnie Beardsley.

Quinn went on to say that Lola Rampley had volunteered to cover for Maybelline on Monday and Wednesday. *Amazing Lola.* If only I could grant her wish to meet Marty Stockwell.

"Look, they're here." Nick pointed out my kitchen window, where we saw Amah and Jack pulling into their driveway.

"I'll go," Harry said. "You'd better get cleaned up fast, Aimee. You look like hell. See if you can hide that cut on your forehead."

"I'll stay with her," Nick said. "She'll need some help."

"No, I won't." I grabbed underwear, clean jeans and a tank top and limped toward my tiny shower enclosure.

"How are you going to hide those stitches?"

"I don't know."

Nick pawed around in my kitchen drawer and pulled out a pair of scissors.

"Sit," he said. "And hold still."

I sat at my kitchen table. "What are you going to do?"

"I've always liked girls with bangs. Bangs are sexy. Especially when they swoop down kind of low." He separated a few strands and began to clip.

"Do you know what you're doing?"

"Trust me."

"I used to."

Nick picked out a few more long strands and guided the scissors with precision. "How can I convince you I'm not interested in Rella?"

"You might have mentioned your past with her before she dropped that on me at Buck's company barbecue. It pretty much spoiled the picnic."

"I would have, but she beat me to it. She said she wanted you to know that she and I weren't—"

"Still hot for each other? That's how she put it. And she calls you *Nicky*. That's annoying as hell. Every time I hear it, I picture the two of you having sex."

Nick clipped some more. "Aimee, I've never asked about the men in your past. Is there something I should know? Did someone betray you?"

"Just the usual. Guys who let me assume we were exclusive while they played the field. Most of them eventually settled on women like Rella—at least in the looks department."

"But you're so beautiful. That doesn't make sense."

"It does if a man looks at my eyes and cheekbones

and thinks *concubine*, then looks at a blue-eyed blonde and thinks *wife*."

"Most guys these days don't know what a concubine is."

"Okay, then, *mistress*, but you get the idea. Did you know Harry's girlfriend dropped him because he's half Chinese? She loved him, but in the end, her parents talked her out of marrying him."

"And you think I'd pull that on you? Don't you know me better that that?"

"I thought I did."

Nick reached for my hand, and I let him hold it. "I didn't sleep with Rella in Paris. Why can't you believe that?"

"You called me every day at noon. Except for the last night you were there. I waited until three o'clock— that's midnight in Paris. I was worried, so I called you. Rella answered and said she didn't want to wake you. What was I supposed to think?"

"I know how it sounds, but when we arrived in Paris the hotel had only reserved two rooms for us. I told Rella she could have my room and I would bunk with Buck."

"Did you?"

"Except for that last night. When I got to the room, Buck had an all-night poker game going. I had to fly in the morning, so I needed sleep. The room I'd given Rella had two beds, and I figured she'd already be asleep. Unfortunately, she was entertaining a Frenchman she'd met in the bar. Clearly, three was a crowd, so I went downstairs and hung out in the bar drinking ginger ale for a couple of hours."

"But you had to fly the next morning," I was furious with Rella for bouncing Nick out of his own room.

"Exactly," he agreed. "I had to get some sleep somewhere, so I went back up around eleven thirty and found Rella sound asleep and the Frenchman gone. I slept in the other bed. Alone, of course. End of story."

"You know, your story is so bizarre, I almost believe it's true. I need some time to think about it."

Nick gave me a long look. "Well, for my part, I wasn't particularly happy when Harry told me you'd moved out of our apartment and didn't want to see me. He said you were living with your grandparents, but he didn't mention the barn. By then, I was pretty pissed off at you for not letting me explain, and I decided to give both of us time to cool off and rethink things."

I looked up at him, feeling my anger dissolve faster than I'd imagined possible. Could I have been wrong about him? Harry had always teased me about being stubborn—a trait I recognized in myself far too often. Was my stubbornness going to cause me to lose the only man I'd ever really loved?

Nick took a deep breath. "I've done my thinking, Aimee, and I'm ready to try again. Now the ball's in your court."

"But you'll still be working with Rella." I felt my guard going up again.

"Do I have to quit my job to make this work?"

"Of course not." I was amazed that he'd even consider such a drastic action. "You love your job."

"Good. Because if I quit mine, you'd have to quit yours."

"What? Why?"

"Because your boss, Quinn, has a thing for you. Or hadn't you noticed?"

"Come on!" I shot back, but I had to admit I was pleased he brought it up. "That's not the same at all. You and Rella have a history together."

"And that's all it is. History. Everyone has one."

I let the truth of that sink in. Nick couldn't change his history. Dealing with it was up to me. I had missed him terribly, and here we were again, dancing around the possibility of a future together. Someone had to stop the dance, and this time it would have to be me.

"I guess we could take it slow, see if we can make a fresh start."

"Like a first date?" He grinned, relief showing in his face.

"Something like that."

"How about a first date with options?"

"That might work. But let's not get ahead of ourselves about the options," I replied, although I'd already been thinking about several of them.

He touched my arm, and we leaned toward each other. Just then Harry phoned, telling me to hustle. The folks were asking for me; it was time to make an appearance.

I took the scissors away from Nick. "We'll have to talk later, Harry wants us. Are you finished with my bangs?"

He held up a hand mirror. "Have a look. What do you think?"

"Pretty good. I don't think they'll notice anything, do you?"

"Only that you're more beautiful than ever," he said.

"You can skip the flattery," I said. "I've already agreed to that first date."

"Okay, then you'd better get that shower. Your grandparents are waiting."

"Right." I turned too quickly and the room spun around me. Nick caught me before I could fall, and I found myself braced in his arms, his strength and gentleness enveloping me. When his kiss came, it was sweet, deep, and achingly familiar.

"Looks like you might need help with that shower," he said.

Vanza's words came back to me. *Nick's the real deal*. Vanza was probably right, but there was only one way to find out.

"Looks like I might," I said.

FIFTY

THE SHOWER COULD have been complicated, but we were in a hurry, and I was still in pain, so we made quick work of it. With more pain pills on board, I practiced walking without a limp. It hurt, but I preferred the pain to the worry it would cause Amah if she knew I'd been injured.

The reunion went off better than we could have hoped. The folks were full of news about their trip, and eager to tell us about their hike in Washington and their new llamas.

Amah asked me to help her in the kitchen, but I knew it was a ploy to get me alone.

"So Nick is back." Her hazel eyes glowed with pleasure.

"We're not sure how it's going to work out."

"But he's back," she said. "That's a start."

Over dinner, Harry, Nick, and I told our creative version of the Bonnie Beardsley story, leaving out almost everything except how Maybelline had implicated Mercer. The courts would decide whether he was charged with murder or with unlawful disposal of a corpse. Either way, he'd go to jail for drug trafficking.

Jack's phone rang in the middle of dinner, so he let it go through to his answering machine. We all heard the caller's message. "Jack, this is Marty Stockwell. I gave your grandson a lift last night. Handsome young fellow. Doesn't look like you, does he? Just checking to see if everything's okay."

Jack fixed an inquiring stare at Harry.

"Flat tire," Harry said. "The car's been towed. Everything's taken care of." He rubbed a sudden sheen off his forehead. "Hot in here, isn't it?"

"Jack," I said, "just how well *do* you know Marty Stockwell?"

"Well enough, I suppose. Why?"

* * * * *

ABOUT THE AUTHOR

Photo courtesy of Lowell Martinson

Sharon St. George had the good fortune to spend an idyllic childhood in a small northern California town, riding horseback and camping with her family in the nearby mountains. One of her favorite pastimes was reading fiction, and a trip to the library was always an occasion of great joy. She's traded horses for llamas, but she still treks to the high mountain lakes near her home—always with a mystery novel in her backpack.

Sharon's writing credits include three plays, several years writing advertising copy, a book on NASA's space food project, and feature stories too numerous to count. She holds dual degrees in English and Theatre Arts, and occasionally acts in, or directs, one of her local community theater productions.

Sharon is a member of Sisters in Crime and Mystery Writers of America, and she serves as program director for Writers Forum, a nonprofit organization for writers in northern California.

For more information, go to:
www.sharonstgeorge.com

READERSERVICE.COM

Manage your account online!

- Review your order history
- Manage your payments
- Update your address

We've designed the
Reader Service website
just for you.

Enjoy all the features!

- Discover new series available to you, and read excerpts from any series.
- Respond to mailings and special monthly offers.
- Browse the Bonus Bucks catalog and online-only exculsives.
- Share your feedback.

Visit us at:

ReaderService.com